Understanding American Politics Through Fiction

Understanding American Politics Through Fiction

Second Edition

Myles L. Clowers
San Diego City College

Lorin Letendre
Cabrillo College Evening Instructor

McGraw-Hill Book Company

New York   St. Louis   San Francisco   Auckland   Bogotá
Düsseldorf   Johannesburg   London   Madrid   Mexico
Montreal   New Delhi   Panama   Paris   São Paulo
Singapore   Sydney   Tokyo   Toronto

This book was set in Times Roman by National ShareGraphics, Inc.
The editors were Lyle Linder and Phyllis T. Dulan;
the cover was designed by J. E. O'Connor;
the cover illustration was done by Thomas Lulebitch;
the production supervisor was Charles Hess.
R. R. Donnelley & Sons Company was printer and binder.

Understanding American Politics Through Fiction

1 2 3 4 5 6 7 8 9 D O D O 7 8 3 2 1 0 9 8 7 6

Library of Congress Cataloging in Publication Data

Clowers, Myles L   comp.
    Understanding American politics through fiction.

    1. American fiction—20th century. 2. Political fiction,
American. I. Letendre, Lorin. II. Title.
PZ1.C59Un5 [PS648.P6]   813'.5'0803   76-18872
ISBN 0-07-011450-1

To Sandy, Dana, and Jason.
L.L.

To the personification of the word "lady,"
Eleanore A. Barton.
M.L.C.

CONTENTS

Part Two.   The Constitutional Context

Part Three.   People and Politics—The Inputs

Part Four.   Institutions—The Conversion Process

Part Five.   Policy—The Outputs

PREFACE

Several years ago when the idea behind this book was first conceived, we had high hopes that our colleagues would accept the unique idea of using fiction to teach American government. With the publication of this second edition, we are both pleased and amazed: pleased that our fellow political science instructors agree with us and amazed that the idea has been so widely adopted. Success, then, for us is a second edition.

In *Understanding American Politics Through Fiction* our main focus is on the role of political fiction as a chronicle or record of public events and behavior. The authors of our selections are political scientists, columnists, novelists, politicians, and critics who have closely observed and accurately described the operation of the American political system. Realism is their objective, but fiction is their medium.

The use of fiction can be a refreshing addition to the current political science teaching material. Students will immediately realize the benefits as the writer of fiction engages them in a personal relationship with exciting and believable characters. Almost all college students read fiction avidly; few have been equally stimulated by textbooks. Fiction is thus a familiar and well-received medium in which to communicate political ideas and information. Reading political fiction can also serve as a transition into the less familiar factual and theoretical material written by political scientists.

Our purpose is not to replace the conventional American government and politics textbook, but to complement it with a different and exciting point of view. Political fiction is not necessarily better than nonfiction in achieving an understanding of politics, but it can motivate students to engage in political analysis where traditional texts have all too often discouraged such efforts. Higher education always needs more personal relevance in its curriculum and fiction allows students to relate their own experiences to the drama of political life as depicted in our selections. For these reasons political fiction can be a powerfully effective supplement to nonfictional texts.

The criteria for selecting articles follow from these considerations. After sorting through hundreds of novels and short stories with political content, we gave the highest priority to readings that were descriptively accurate, thought-provoking, and relevant to our topics. We searched for excerpts that would stimulate inquiry by raising crucial political issues, yet were of high literary quality as well. In this effort we were greatly assisted by suggestions from several reviewers of the first edition. We attempted to suppress our own biases by selecting authors ranging across the political spectrum, from Ayn Rand on the right to Pierre Salinger on the left. Political values are, of course, an inescapable part of such fiction: what we tried to achieve was a balance of viewpoints.

The most important feature of this book is its flexibility in terms of approach. The book's outline allows for easy adaptation to both the topical (institutional) and systems approaches to studying politics. The selections are organized into "Political Culture," "The Constitutional Context," "People and Politics—The Inputs," "Institutions—The Conversion Process," and "Policy—The Outputs."

In addition to the flexibility of approach, each selection has a short introduction to move the reader easily into the plot and to highlight the key political concepts that are involved, and each part has a general, more theoretical overview introducing it. We have also included at the end of each article questions that reinforce the main thrust of the article and that stimulate student thought.

Several new changes have been made in the second edition. Political culture is present in a more general way, and this part contains for the first time a poem, "Politically Perfect." The section on the Constitution is now a separate part since it did not fit in either the conversion process part or the institutions part. "People and Politics" contains several new articles, and more emphasis has been placed on political elections and campaigning. The part on institutions has a few new articles on the judiciary and presidency. Finally, a new part on policy or outputs has been added to cover this vital and yet sometimes overlooked subject. These revisions fill some of the gaps in our first edition.

This book is not the product of just two people. Many others have contributed in terms of both inspiration and encouragement. Words are not sufficient to repay the debts we owe them. However, it is to our families that we extend our greatest thanks for their patience and support.

Myles L. Clowers
Lorin Letendre

Understanding American Politics Through Fiction

Part One

Political Culture

Politics in any nation operates within a cultural context, and this context profoundly affects the kind and quality of politics practiced in a nation. Political scientists have come to realize how important the cultural context of politics is and have begun to study it in a systematic fashion. The rise of nazism in Germany gave a great impetus to this trend, for political scientists realized that simply studying the formal governmental institutions of Germany (as had been the practice) could never fully explain how and why the horrors of nazism originated in that Western European nation.

Political culture is the term that political scientists now use to describe the cultural context of politics. Political culture consists of the attitudes and orientations that people have toward politics. For instance, some Americans view politics as an effective avenue through which they can achieve certain goals, and so they participate actively in politics. Other Americans view politics as a closed club that serves only the interests of the elite, and so they become apathetic and uninvolved in the political process.

The nature and distribution of attitudes toward politics, then, have a great impact on how politics operates in each nation. In the United States,

1

for example, no politician could get away with using Hitler's techniques since they would be abhorrent to virtually every American. Such a politician would be rapidly recalled from office or would be rejected at the next election. A nation's political culture, then, defines the limits beyond which its politicians dare not go.

The attitudes and orientations that constitute the political culture are passed on from generation to generation through the process known as political socialization. For example, when a newborn child enters the world, he or she has no preconceived ideas about politics—these ideas must be learned through the socialization process. In America, the main source from which people learn their political attitudes is the family, for it is the family that is in virtually total control of a person for the first few years of life and remains in strong control for many years after that. Other agents in the political learning process are a person's peer group, religion, education, and the mass media; all can alter the political orientations learned from the family experience.

The American political culture has been termed a "civic culture," with a balance between active and passive orientations toward politics. In the civic culture, political activity, involvement, and rationality exist but are balanced by a large measure of passivity and tradition. Americans believe that they have an obligation to participate in politics and will in fact get involved if their political representatives step out of line. We are, then, a potentially active citizenry.

The passive orientation toward politics is illustrated in James Michener's *The Drifters* and James T. Farrell's "Getting Out the Vote for the Working Class." The characters in these selections are highly apathetic and alienated from politics and manage to remain uninvolved.

A special case of alienation and noninvolvement in American politics is vividly portrayed in James Baldwin's *The Fire Next Time,* a story of blacks' existence in the ghetto. Blacks have been prevented from actively participating in politics because of white racism, which remains a significant attitude in our political culture. Blacks have fought throughout American history for their political rights, but it is only in the last several decades that they have had much success.

The active political orientation is shown in Edwin O'Connor's *The Last Hurrah,* a novel about the Irish-Americans in politics. After their arrival in America, Irish immigrants became heavily involved in local politics, for they viewed it as an avenue for social and economic advancement. This idea of climbing the socioeconomic ladder has been a dominant part of the American political culture, and, although Ayn Rand emphasizes individual advancement and opportunity over group advancement, the selection from her novel *Anthem* underscores the competitive, individualistic trait in our culture.

These various attitudes and orientations toward politics are influenced by external events as much as by the early socialization process of the family. The selections from *The Ninth Wave* and "Politically Perfect" reinforce this point by showing how external concerns and popular philosophies can affect people's political behavior.

Reading 1
The Drifters
James Michener

Apathy or the lack of involvement in politics is shown to be a dominant
attitude among Americans in James Michener's indictment of affluent
American youth. Today's youths are alienated or estranged from the
conventional political, social, and economic patterns of American life,
partly because of the constant threat of nuclear destruction hanging
over their heads.

Despite their unconventional social behavior, affluent young people
appear to share a strong conservatism with the members of the older
generation. Their conservative attitudes toward politics are inherited
from their affluent parents, who strongly influence their children's political and economic attitudes, though not their social habits.

George Fairbanks, the narrator of the story, and Henry Holt, a technical representative for a large overseas company, come to realize that
their values are quite similar to those of the young Americans they meet.
The difference is that Fairbanks and Holt have "copped out" in a socially
acceptable manner, while the youths have expressed their disillu-
sionment in a socially unacceptable fashion. Perhaps, then, all Americans are "drifters," characterized by apathy and alienation, and controlled more by the course of events than by their own intentions and
actions.

Often as I walked back to my hotel at night I reflected on the discussions I
had heard in Inger's and I was amazed at how vocal the young people were
in stating their opinions and how little they read to support them. This was
a generation without books. Of course, everyone has handled volumes by
Herbert Marcuse and Frantz Fanon, but I found no one who had actually
read the more easily understood works like *Essay on Liberation* or *Toward
the African Revolution* or *The Wretched of the Earth*. It was also true that
most of the travelers had read newspaper reports of Marshall McLuhan's
theories, and hardly a day passed but someone would proclaim, "After all,
the medium is the massage," but I met no one who had read the book of
which this taut summary was the title or who knew what it meant.

There was always a dog-eared copy of the *I-Ching* somewhere in the
hotel, and many had dipped into it, but no one had read it, not even Claire
from Sacramento. The strong books of the age were unknown to this group,
and I often wondered how they had got as far along in college as they had.

On the other hand, their verbal knowledge was considerable and they could expatiate on almost any topic. Six pronouncements I noted one night were typical of the conclusions reached every night.

"We have entered what Walter Lippmann terms the New Dark Age."

"Before 1976 an armed showdown between races will be inevitable in American cities."

"The military-industrial complex rules our nation and dictates a continuance of the Vietnam war."

"A permanent unemployment cadre of seven million must be anticipated."

"By the year 2000 we will have seven billion people on earth."

"Universities are prisoners of the Establishment."

But in spite of these statements, I found that most Americans overseas were hard-line conservatives; of the many in Marrakech, the majority had supported the Republican party in 1968 and would do so again in 1972. I took the trouble to check the six young people I had seen unconscious on the floor of the Casino Royale; Claire took me back one morning, and I found that four were solid Republicans, one was a neo-Nazi, and Moorman, the honor student from Michigan who sang ballads with Gretchen, said, "I don't know what I am."

I found more than a few supporters of George Wallace, and Constitutionalists, and crypto-fascists, and backers of other ill-defined movements. The basic ideas of the John Birch Society were often voiced, but I met no one who admitted membership.

Most older people who visited Marrakech were surprised to find that among the young Americans, there were practically no oldstyle American liberals. This was true for obvious reasons. To get as far as Marrakech required real money, so that those who made it had to come from well-to-do families of a conservative bent, and throughout the world children tend to follow the political attitudes of their fathers. A boy of nineteen might rebel against Harvard University, country-club weekends and the dress of his father, and run away to Marrakech to prove it, but his fundamental political and social attitudes would continue to be those his father had taught him at age eleven. In my work I constantly met conservative adult Americans who, when they saw the young people with long hair and beards, expected them to be revolutionaries; they were pleasantly gratified to find that the young people were as reactionary as they were.

Harvey Holt exemplified this response. When he first met the gang at Pamplona he was positive they must be revolutionaries, but after several long discussions involving politics, he told me "You know, apart from Vietnam and this nonsense about brotherhood between the races, these kids are pretty solid." Later he said, "You could be misled if you listened to their songs. You'd think they were going out to burn down New York. But when you talk to them about economics and voting, you find they're just as conservative as you or me . . . but they do it in their own way." I asked him how he thought I voted, and he said, "Oh, you sympathize a lot with the young people, but I'm sure that in a pinch you can be trusted."

"To vote Republican?"

"How else can a sensible man vote?" he asked.

I was constantly appalled by the poverty of language exhibited by many of the young people, and these from our better colleges. Claire, as I have said, sometimes talked for a whole hour saying little but "you know" and "like wow," but this had a certain cute illiteracy. More intolerable was the girl from Ohio who said at least once every paragraph, "You better believe it." Whenever one of the boys from the south agreed with one of my opinions, he said, "You ain't just whistlin' 'Dixie,' bub." A college girl from Missouri introduced every statement with: "I just want you to know," while a young man from Brooklyn related everything to André Gide—he seemed quite incapable of any other comparison.

Two aspects of the intellectual life of these young Americans surprised me. The first was politics. Not one person I knew ever mentioned the name Richard Nixon; they rejected Lyndon Johnson and ridiculed Hubert Humphrey, charging these men with having betrayed youth, but Nixon they dismissed. They would have voted for him, had they bothered to vote, and would vote for him in 1972, if they happened to be registered, but he played no role in their lives. A whole segment of American history was simply expunged by these people; they had opted out with a vengeance.

I say that they would vote Republican in 1972, if they voted, and by this I mean that of all the young Americans I met over the age of twenty-one, not one had ever bothered to vote, and it seemed unlikely to me that any would do so much before the age of thirty-two or thirty-three. To hear them talk, you would think they were battering down the barricades of the Establishment, and some few I suppose would have been willing to try, but they were not willing to vote; in fact, I met none who were even registered.

In spite of this seeming indifference, there were those few I reflected upon that morning when I stood in the Casino Royale amid the stenches and the fallen forms, the few who were painfully carving out an understanding of their world, and their place in it. Because they came from families with income and advantage, they tended to he Republican, and when they settled down, they were going to be good Republicans. Some, like Gretchen, had worked for Senator Eugene McCarthy, but not because he was a Democrat; they would quickly return to creative Republicanism and the nation would profit from the forging process they had gone through.

But when I have said this about politics, I have still not touched upon the mighty chasm that separated them from me: they honestly believed that their generation lived under the threat of the hydrogen bomb and that consequently their lives would be different from what mine had been. They were convinced that no man my age could comprehend what the bomb meant to them, and even when I pointed out that a man of sixty-one like me had been forced to spend nearly half his adult life under the shadow of nuclear bombs and had adjusted to it, they cried, "Ah, there it is! You'd enjoyed about half your life before the bomb fell. We haven't." It seemed there could be no bridge of understanding on this point, and after several futile attempts to build one, I concluded that on this topic we could not talk together meaningfully.

QUESTIONS

1 Are most Americans "drifters" characterized by apathy and alienation, and, if so, why do we stress the democratic ideal of the active citizenry?
2 What is the cause of "drifting" or alienation in America?
3 Is there a difference between the alienation of young and older Americans, and, if so, why?
4 What did Fairbanks mean when he called the young people "a generation without books"?

Reading 2
Getting Out the Vote for the Working Class
James T. Farrell

In "Getting Out the Vote for the Working Class," by James T. Farrell, some typical attitudes and orientations that Americans hold toward politics are exhibited by Al Michaelson, the main character. Al strongly believes in the power of the vote and the importance of being involved in the political process. Yet as the voting progresses, his avoidance of voting increases, typifying the priorities of Americans. By engaging in social activities with Garfield, Annabelle, Tom, George, and Mort, Al is diverted from his duty to vote. Still, he, like most Americans, pays lip service to the solemnity of the occasion while increasing his alcoholic consumption, which further reduces his will to vote.

"Getting Out the Vote for the Working Class" also illustrates the failure of revolutionary movements in America. Al, a self-styled revolutionary, blames all his own as well as his country's problems on "the system," a perennial scapegoat for Americans. To protest against "the system," Al is going to vote for the Communist party, a rather mild means of protest in 1932. But by his drinking, Al demonstrates the apathy and noninvolvement that undermine most potential revolts, even among the least affluent workers.

Al Michaelson awoke at eleven o'clock. He yawned, blinked his sleepy eyes, drowsed in bed. He slowly awakened, and then he sat up in bed in the studio. A state of suppressed excitement developed in him because it was election day. Never before had an election caused him to feel like this. Election today was something new. He didn't care whether or not Roosevelt or Hoover were to be elected President. Well, he did, but he couldn't admit it, not even to himself. He wanted to see Roosevelt elected, just as he had wanted to see Smith elected in 1928. But no, he couldn't think that way.

He wasn't going to vote for Roosevelt. He was going to vote for the party of the future, for the working class. He was going to do something today. What he would do would be great, a great gesture. No, it wouldn't be a gesture. It would be a political act. Funny that he should find himself thinking this way.

He got out of bed and put on a dirty bathrobe. He stuck his feet into his slippers. He wished that Lydia was in town. But she was away. She got in only week ends now.

Al lived with Lydia. He was twenty-eight, and Lydia was forty-five. He had met her during the summer of 1928 after he had been flunked out of the University. He had gone around with Pete, the Greek, and that summer Pete had run a little theater in the art colony. He had been living with Pete in a basement until he had met Lydia. There were lots of girls around in those days but he had never had any luck with any of them. And then one night, well, there was Lydia at a party, and she took him home with her, and since then he had lived with her, a kept man.

It wasn't his fault that he was a kept man. It was the system. He had not fully realized it in those days. Now he did. Everyone around the colony, except those few social-fascists who had joined the Socialist Party instead of sympathizing with the Communist Party, now at last realized that what was behind everything was the system.

But now he wasn't going to bother about that. He wanted breakfast. If Lydia were here, she would make breakfast for him and then, when it was all ready, he would get up, and there it would be for him on the table. But she was out selling. He had to make his own breakfast.

He yawned again. Yes, today he was going to cast a vote against the whole rotten system.

II

The kitchen in Lydia's studio was partitioned off in the rear. Al set breakfast on the table and sat down. He felt like having a drink, but hell, it was too early. After voting, he would have a drink to celebrate. He pitched into his ham and eggs, ate large slices of buttered bread, and drank coffee.

It was funny—the very idea of Al Michaelson going to vote. Damned funny. Why, until the last year and a half, he had never even given a thought to politics. When he had come from Muncie, Indiana, a freshman at the University, he had dreamed of being a writer, a new Sherwood Anderson. Just think, he was hanging out now around the place where Sherwood Anderson and so many other writers had once lived, written, and attended parties.

He went on eating. He had not even tried to write in over four years. Well, the system had ruined him. Now, that he was a sympathizer of the Communist Party, he would be a new man, and he would write. If it weren't for his literary aspirations, he would even join the Party. But he could serve best with the weapon of the word. In order to do this, he first had to get experience, experience with the working class. All of his past experience was petit bourgeois, and he couldn't write about that. Not such defeatist stuff.

He poured himself a second cup of coffee, lit a cigarette, and sat thinking idly.

III

He heard the knocker on the front door. Answering it, he saw Garfield, a man of about forty.

"Come on in and have a cup of coffee," he said.

"All right. How are you?" Garfield answered in a slow drawl.

Garfield entered. Al slouched back to the rear of the studio, and Garfield followed him. Al took a dirty cup from the iron sink, washed it out, and poured Garfield a cup of coffee. He poured himself another cup. They lit cigarettes and sat facing each other.

"Voted yet?" Garfield suddenly asked.

"Can't you see I'm not even dressed?"

Garfield looked at Al.

"Yeh, that's right."

"You voted?" Al asked.

"Not yet."

"After we have this coffee, I'll shave and dress and we'll go out and vote."

"There's lots of time."

"Yeh, it isn't twelve o'clock yet. We still got all day."

They sat, both of them seemingly lost in reverie.

"You got up early today," Garfield said.

"Yes, a little early, Eleven o'clock."

"I got up early, too."

"Well, it's a big day."

"It's a big day. If the whole city was like the Fifty-seventh Street art colony, it would be a big day," Garfield said.

"What do you mean?"

"The colony is going to vote Communist."

"Uh huh! But here, pour yourself another cup of coffee."

"I guess I will," Garfield said, going to the stove.

They dawdled over their coffee in silence.

IV

"Say, I just remembered," Al said suddenly.

"What?"

"I got a little hooch left."

"Al, that would hit the spot."

Al went upstairs to the bedroom; it was partitioned off from the rest of the studio. He got out a bottle of moonshine; it was almost half-filled. He carried it down to the kitchen.

He poured out jiggers of whisky, and they got glasses of water.

"Here's to the revolution," Garfield said.

They raised glasses.

"To the revolution," Al said.

They drank.

"I've drunk worse stuff," Garfield said.

"It's better than nothing. But listen, you, I don't want to get drunk before I vote. This is something solemn, voting for the Party. We got to do it with dignity."

Garfield nodded in agreement.

"We should have done this four years ago when they elected Hoover," Garfield said.

"Here, have another," Al said, pouring out more drinks.

"Oh, thanks."

They drank.

"As I said, we should have voted this way in 1928 when Smith and Hoover ran against each other. Well, it's too bad there wasn't a Communist Party then," Garfield said.

"Sure there was," Al said.

"There was? Running a campaign, too, in the election?" Garfield asked.

"Yeh."

"Well, why didn't we hear about it?" asked Garfield.

"We weren't politicalized," Al said.

"I remember the election four years ago just as clear as I remember yesterday or last week," Garfield said.

Al poured out another drink, emptying the bottle.

"Oh, thanks," Garfield said.

They drank.

"Funny, I didn't know a thing about the Party in 1928," Garfield said.

"It took the crisis to politicalize us," Al said.

"Well, that's past. Water run under the bridge. Gin poured from the skillet," Garfield said.

They sat studying their empty glasses. Al lit a cigarette.

"What time is it?" Garfield asked.

"We got plenty of time," Al said.

"Of course. I know it."

"Hell, the polls are open all day." Garfield nodded.

"Give me one of your cigarettes, Al."

"Here, take one."

Garfield reached across and took one of Al's cigarettes.

"Got enough to go in on a bottle with me?" asked Garfield.

"Yeh, but we'll get it after we vote. We'll celebrate."

"That's a good idea."

Al got up and started putting his breakfast dishes in the sink.

V

"Let's stop in and see Annabelle," Garfield said.

"O.K." Al answered, locking the studio door.

To their left and above the viaduct an Illinois Central electric-suburban train rolled into the Fifty-seventh Street station.

They crossed the street.

"I wonder if Annabelle is up yet?" Garfield asked.

"You and she have a night of it last night?"

"We had some fun," Garfield said.

"Doesn't Tom mind?"

"What good does it do him?"

"I don't know. Ask me another."

Annabelle came to the door. She was a husky red-headed girl of about thirty.

"Oh, come on in, boys. Have a cup of coffee with us," she said.

The studio was decorated with velvet drapes, and there were odd-looking amateurish modernistic pictures on the walls. She led them to the rear, where there was a kitchen behind a partition. Tom, her husband, was eating breakfast. He was a plump, ruddy man of about thirty-five.

"Hello," he said nervously; he went on eating.

"Here, boys, sit down and have some coffee," Annabelle said.

They sat down. Annabelle brought coffee to everyone, and they sat around the table.

"Vote yet?" Al asked.

Tom went on eating.

"Tom, can't you hear?" Annabelle asked sharply.

"What, dear?"

"Al asked you, did you vote yet?"

"Oh, no. I just got up a little while ago."

"There's plenty of time to vote," Garfield said.

"Well, things sure are changed a lot around the colony," Al said.

"From when?" Tom asked.

"From two or three years ago," Al said.

"I don't see much change. A couple of young girls from the University are hanging around. Not much else," Tom said.

"I mean politically speaking," Al said.

"Yes, that way," Tom said.

"And, of course, if there have been political changes, that means that we've all changed, and that means that the colony has changed," Garfield said.

"That's right."

No one talked for a while. Tom was nervous.

"Say, got a drink?" Al asked.

"Have we, Tom?" Annabelle asked.

"I don't know."

Annabelle went to the front of the studio.

"Well, we're all comrades now, ain't we?" Tom said, looking nervously at Garfield.

"Yes, sure. We're all voting today for the Party, too. We'll scare the hell out of the petit bourgeois shopkeepers when they see the number of Communist Party votes rolled up in this district. And most of the Party votes in the whole ward will come from the colony," Garfield said.

Annabelle returned with a bottle of moonshine.

"I found this, boys. It must be left from the last party we had," she said.

"We ought to have something to mix it in," Al said.

"Tom, you go get some soda at the drugstore."

"I haven't got my shoes on, Annabelle."

"Well, you can put them on."

He got up, sulky, and went out.

"Tom, get two bottles," she called after him.

They heard the front door close.

"I would have gone, Annabelle," Garfield said.

"That's all right, Tom can do it. He's not working today."

"I would have gone, too," Al said.

"Tom's doing it."

"Well, dear, how is everything?" Garfield said.

"Tom's in bad humor this morning. He knows about last night, of course."

"Did you tell him?" asked Garfield.

"I didn't have to. He guessed. When I'm out until after three, he knows where I am. He was up waiting and was so all-in this morning, he laid off work. He's getting awful nervous these days," Annabelle said.

"Well, what'll we do about it?" Garfield asked.

"Nothing," Annabelle answered.

They heard Tom entering in front, and soon he came in with two bottles of soda. He and Annabelle mixed the drinks.

VI

"Come on, let's vote," Al said.

"There's plenty of time," Garfield said.

"You fellows go and vote now. Annabelle and I will vote later," Tom said.

"We can all vote together," Annabelle said.

"Yeh, solidarity," Al said.

"Let's have another drink," Garfield said.

"You're not crippled. Mix it," Tom said.

"I'll do that, comrade," Garfield said.

He mixed a drink for himself.

"Gimme a drink," Al said.

"Here it is. Fix it yourself, comrade," Garfield said.

"Thanks, comrade. Solidarity," Al said, going to the bottle.

He fixed himself a drink and gulped it down.

Annabelle went over to Garfield and sat on his lap. She glared at Tom. Tom didn't say a word.

"Come on, let's vote," Al said.

"Go ahead and vote, Al. I'll vote later," Garfield said.

"Al, you and Tom go and vote, and we'll be along later and vote ourselves."

"I'll wait until you're ready, Annabelle," Tom said.

"You don't have to. I said go ahead and vote with Al," Annabelle said.

Al had another drink.

VII

"Where the hell are the polls now? I forget. Is it this way?" Al asked, pointing toward Stony Island and Jackson Park. "Or is it that way?" he said, pointing toward Harper, which was beyond the Illinois Central viaduct.

"I'm going to stop in here a minute," Tom said, going to the studio next door to his own; it was an art school conducted by his neighbor.

"They can't stomach me," Al said.

"Well, you go and vote. I'll see you later."

"Oh, we got time for that," Al said.

Tom went inside his neighbor's studio, and Al was left standing alone. His legs were rubbery. He floundered across the street to his own studio and let himself in. His head seemed to be going around. He wanted a drink. He told himself that he was getting drunk and warned himself that he had to vote, so he couldn't let himself get too drunk. He had to remember to stay sober enough to vote. But, hell, he could stand another drink. One more wouldn't knock him out. He had drunk plenty more than he'd put away today without going under the table and passing out. Yes, plenty more. He rummaged about the bedroom and found another partially filled bottle of moonshine.

VIII

"George, I got to vote," Al said, sitting at the counter of the ice cream store at the corner of Fifty-seventh and Stony Island.

"Yeh."

"Yeh, I got to vote."

Al looked into his coffee.

"Today, we're all equal. All equal, all got a vote. I'm going to cast my vote. George, are you going to vote?"

"I'm a Greek."

"Well, when we win, George, it won't matter what you are," Al said.

George didn't pay attention to Al. He was clearing out the store and he went on sweeping. Al sat before his coffee for a long time. Then he drank it. He almost fell off the stool.

"Put it on the bill, George," he said, and left the store.

He staggered past the row of studios and found Tom in front of his own studio, banging on the door.

"Let me in," Tom yelled.

Al watched Tom.

"Open the door!" Tom yelled.

He pounded on the studio door again.

"Hey, Tom!" Al called.

Tom suddenly turned around and saw Al.

"What's the matter?" Al asked.

"She and Garfield are in there together," Tom said.

"Well, come on and vote, and then when we come back maybe they won't be," said Al.

"I'm a goddamn cuckold. My wife makes me into a cuckold," Tom said.

"Come on and vote against the capitalists. It's the system, that's the trouble," Al said.

"Let me in! Open the door!" Tom yelled.

Annabelle opened the door. She was wearing a kimono.

"Tom, go away. Go and . . . vote. You can't come in yet. Go away," she said.

"It's my own house."

"Tom, go away, or I go," she said.

"But . . ."

Annabelle noticed Al.

"Have you voted yet?" she asked him.

"No. I'm going now."

"Take Tom with you."

Annabelle closed the door. Tom looked at the closed door, disconsolate. He turned to Al.

"I'm a cuckold," he said.

"It's the system that's responsible. Come on and we'll both vote against the system," Al said.

IX

"Where can we bum a drink before we go to vote?" Al said.

"I don't know."

"We have plenty of time. It's only about three-thirty now, and we have until eight o'clock to vote. I think I need another drink before I go around the corner to the damned polls," Al said.

"Well?"

They stood under the Illinois Central viaduct, and they heard a suburban train rolling overhead.

"Let's go see Mort," Al said.

Al staggered down the steep curb and ran drunkenly across the street. He got up on the other side and hurried toward Stony Island, Tom following him. Mort's studio was the last one of a row facing Jackson Park, just south of Fifty-seventh Street on Stony Island Avenue.

"Hello, fellow," Mort said, letting them in.

Mort was medium-sized and in his late thirties. His studio was crowded with old furniture, miscellaneous odds and ends, and it needed to be swept and dusted.

Tom and Al slumped onto a couch on one side of the large front part of the studio.

"Mort, got a drink?"

"Gee, I haven't. I'm sorry, but I'm all out."

"Now, ain't that tough," Al said.

"You look as if you had enough already, Al," Mort said.

"Oh, no, I haven't. I need one more. I need one two more before I go vote," Al said.

"What the hell you want to vote for?" Mort asked.

"I'm gonna vote for the Party," Al said.

"What Party?"

"The Party. Mort, look at me," Al said.

"I am. You're not the most wholesome sight in the world, Al, but I'm looking at you."

"Well, look at me," Al said.

"He's looking," Tom said.

"All right, know what you see! Know what you see! You see sitting before you a revolutionist."

Mort and Tom doubled over with laughter.

"Why don't you join the Party and do some work for it?" Mort asked.

"I would. But I'm not good enough to be a Party member. I'm still only a petit bourgeois intellectual," Al said.

Mort laughed again.

"That's all right, laugh at me. Go ahead, laugh at me. But that doesn't change the situation one little iota. No, sir, it doesn't change the situation even one little iota," Al said with drunken seriousness.

"Say, I'll go buy a bottle of liquor. I need a drink. I'll be right back," Tom said, getting up.

"That's what I say, more drinks. I need one drink, I need one two drinks before I go and cast my vote," Al said.

X

"What did you say you were going to do?" Mort asked, the three of them sitting close together with glasses in their hands.

"I'm going to vote."

"What for?"

"The Party. The Future. The Workers. Humanity."

Mort laughed. He took a drink.

"Mort, don't laugh," Al said.

"Why?"

"Because I mean it. Don't laugh at my dearest and most tender sentiments."

"Dearest and most tender sentiments," Tom said, looking glumly into his glass.

"Say, what the hell is eating the ass of you fellows? Tom there is like a corpse, he's so joyful, and, Al, you're saving the human race," Mort said.

"Let's have another drink," Tom said.

"That's what I need before I go and vote."

XI

Tom lay on the couch, snoring.

"He can't take his drinks," Mort said, his voice thick.

"It's his wife," Al said, wavering badly from side to side.

"What's the matter?"

"She's with Garfield now. She threw him out of the studio to lay up all afternoon with Garfield. If I had a wife like that, know what I'd do to her?" Al said.

"What?"

"I wouldn't vote for her."

"You and your goddamn votes," Mort said.

"What time is it?" asked Al.

"Five-thirty," Mort said.

"Give me another drink," Al said.

"There isn't any more," Mort answered. Mort pointed at Tom, "Well, he won't think of his wife giving it away now."

Al put on his coat.

"What's the hurry?" Mort asked.

"I got to vote," Al said.

"Well, vote for my ass, will you," Mort said, still looking at Tom, who lay there, snoring.

"I can't. I got to vote for the Party," Al said, leaving.

It was dark outside. Al staggered to Fifty-seventh Street. He could hear the wind in the trees in Jackson Park on the other side of Stony Island Avenue.

He stood rubbery-legged on the corner of Fifty-seventh and Stony Island for a moment. He lunged forward and fumbled for the key to his own studio. He let himself in and tumbled onto a couch.

XII

Al woke up still drunk. He didn't know what time it was. He yawned. He heard a ticking noise. It was the clock. He looked at it, squinting his eyes. Ten minutes to eight. He still had time to vote. He got to his feet, put on his coat, left the studio, staggered across the street, and rapped on Annabelle's studio door. She let him in. Her hair was askew, and her opened kimono exposed one of her breasts. He saw Garfield sleeping on a couch.

He roused Garfield, who looked at him with dull eyes.

"Come on and vote," Al urged.

"Huh?"

"Come on, we all got to vote for the Party," Al said.

"Here," Garfield said, holding out his hand. "Here take my vote, vote it for me."

"We got to vote," Al said, turning at Annabelle.

"We did everything else today but vote," she said giggling.

"Gimme a drink," Al said.

Annabelle pointed to a bottle on the table.

Al poured himself a drink, gulped it down, and rushed out of the studio, almost falling on his face. He lunged on to Harper Avenue. The polls were right down the street. He had to vote. He had time. Had to vote. He staggered on. He could see election officials and policemen inside the store which served as the voting place in the precinct. He tried to open the door. A cop motioned for him to go away. Telling himself he had to vote, he rapped on the door.

A cop opened the door.

"Get the hell out of here before I run yuh in."

"I got . . . got . . . gotta vote."

"You're too late. The polls is closed."

"But I got . . . got . . . got . . ."

"Get the hell out of here!" the cop said, shoving Al away.

Al spilled on his face. He patiently fought his way to his feet and wandered off, telling himself that he had to vote for the Party.

QUESTIONS

1 How do you account for the typical American's lack of political involvement— is "the system" at fault, or are Americans simply lazy and apathetic?
2 Is there a difference between apathy and alienation, and, if so, what is the difference?
3 What does Al Michaelson mean when he says, "It's the system that's responsible"?
4 Are Al Michaelson's attitudes toward voting typical or atypical of most Americans and why?

Reading 3

The Fire Next Time

James Baldwin

James Baldwin condemns the immoral relationship between religion and racism in America in this fiercely eloquent passage from his essay entitled "Down at the Cross: Letter from a Region in My Mind." Religion, especially Christianity, is a central social characteristic of Americans that often overlaps into the political sector. Unfortunately, religious beliefs have not prevented white Americans from enslaving, persecuting, and denying political power to black Americans, including James Baldwin.

The bleak future facing young blacks is compassionately outlined by Baldwin in his opening paragraphs. Blacks today suffer a disproportionate amount of poverty and unemployment, and the wide income gap between blacks and whites has not narrowed appreciably. Young blacks search for a "gimmick" or a way to escape the reality of their oppressive situation; it does not matter to them whether the course they choose is legal or illegal as long as it serves as a weapon against "whitey."

If these conditions are ever to change, Baldwin notes, whites will have to restructure their lives and personal relationships. Unfortunately, tensions within white society still contribute directly to the discriminatory treatment of blacks. Written in 1962, *The Fire Next Time* was an ominous warning that went unheeded until our cities burned.

And I began to feel in the boys a curious, wary, bewildered despair, as though they were now settling in for the long, hard winter of life. I did not know then what it was that I was reacting to; I put to myself that they were letting themselves go. In the same way that the girls were destined to gain as much weight as their mothers, the boys, it was clear, would rise no higher than their fathers. School began to reveal itself, therefore, as a child's game that one could not win, and boys dropped out of school and went to work. My father wanted me to do the same. I refused, even though I no longer had any illusions about what an education could do for me; I had already encountered too many college-graduate handymen. My friends were now "downtown," busy, as they put it, "fighting the man." They began to care less about the way they looked, the way they dressed, the things they did; presently, one found them in twos and threes and fours, in a hallway, sharing a jug of wine or a bottle of whiskey, talking, cursing, fighting, sometimes weeping: lost, and unable to say what it was that oppressed them, except that they knew it was "the man"—the white man. And there seemed to be no way whatever to remove this cloud that stood between them and the sun, between them and love and life and power, between them and whatever it was that they wanted. One did not have to be very bright to realize how little one could do to change one's situation; one did not have to be abnormally sensitive to be worn down to a cutting edge by the incessant and gratuitous humiliation and danger one encountered every working day, all day long. The humiliation did not apply merely to working days, or workers; I was thirteen and was crossing Fifth Avenue on my way to the Forty-second Street library, and the cop in the middle of the street muttered as I passed him, "Why don't you niggers stay uptown where you belong?"

When I was ten, and didn't look, certainly, any older, two policemen amused themselves with me by frisking me, making comic (and terrifying) speculations concerning my ancestry and probable sexual prowess, and for good measure, leaving me flat on my back in one of Harlem's empty lots. Just before and then during the Second World War, many of my friends fled into the service, all to be changed there, and rarely for the better, many to be ruined, and many to die. Others fled to other states and cities—that is, to other ghettos. Some went on wine or whiskey or the needle, and are still on it. And others, like me, fled into the church.

For the wages of sin were visible everywhere, in every wine-stained and urine-splashed hallway, in every clanging ambulance bell, in every scar on the faces of the pimps and their whores, in every helpless, newborn baby being brought into this danger, in every knife and pistol fight on the Avenue, and in every disastrous bulletin: a cousin, mother of six, suddenly gone mad, the children parcelled out here and there; an indestructible aunt rewarded for years of hard labor by a slow, agonizing death in a terrible small room; someone's bright son blown into eternity by his own hand; another turned robber and carried off to jail. It was a summer of dreadful speculations and discoveries, of which these were not the worst. Crime became real, for example—for the first time—not as *a* possibility but as *the* possibility. One would never defeat one's circumstances by working and saving one's pennies; one would never, by working, acquire that many pennies, and, besides, the social treatment accorded even the most successful Negroes proved that one needed, in order to be free, something more than a bank account. One needed a handle, a lever, a means of inspiring fear. It was absolutely clear that the police would whip you and take you in as long as they could get away with it, and that everyone else—housewives, taxi-drivers, elevator boys, dishwashers, bartenders, lawyers, judges, doctors, and grocers—would never, by the operation of any generous human feeling, cease to use you as an outlet for his frustrations and hostilities. Neither civilized reason nor Christian love would cause any of those people to treat you as they presumably wanted to be treated; only the fear of your power to retaliate would cause them to do that, or to seem to do it, which was (and is) good enough. There appears to be a vast amount of confusion on this point, but I do not know many Negroes who are eager to be "accepted" by white people, still less to be loved by them; they, the blacks, simply don't wish to be beaten over the head by the whites every instant of our brief passage on this planet. White people in this country will have quite enough to do in learning how to accept and love themselves and each other, and when they have achieved this—which will not be tomorrow and may very well be never—the Negro problem will no longer exist, for it will no longer be needed.

People more advantageously placed than we in Harlem were, and are, will no doubt find the psychology and the view of human nature sketched above dismal and shocking in the extreme. But the Negro's experience of the white world cannot possibly create in him any respect for the standards by which the white world claims to live. His own condition is overwhelming proof that white people do not live by these standards. Negro servants have been smuggling odds and ends out of white homes for generations, and white people have been delighted to have them do it, because it has assuaged a dim guilt and testified to the intrinsic superiority of white people. Even the most doltish and servile Negro could scarcely fail to be impressed by the disparity between his situation and that of the people for whom he worked; Negroes who were neither doltish nor servile did not feel that they were doing anything wrong when they robbed white people. In spite of the Puritan-Yankee equation of virtue with well-being, Negroes had excellent reasons for doubting that money was made or kept by any very striking adherence to the Christian virtues; it certainly did not work that way for black Christians. In any case, white people, who had robbed black people of their liberty and who profited by this theft every hour that they lived, had no moral ground on which to stand. They had the judges, the juries, the shotguns, the law—in a word, power. But it was a criminal power, to be feared but not respected, and to be outwitted in any way whatever. And those virtues preached but not practiced by the white world were merely another means of holding Negroes in subjection.

QUESTIONS

1 Is racism still a significant attitude of Americans, and, if so, what impact is this attitude having on American politics?
2 Why does Baldwin believe that the solution to the "black problem" is for whites to learn to love one another?
3 What are some of the examples that Baldwin gives of individual and institutional racism?
4 Why and for what reasons must blacks develop their own standards of conduct?

Reading 4
The Last Hurrah
Edwin O'Connor

Most Americans believe in the melting-pot thesis, or the idea that identities of various racial, religious, and national groups that settled in America have melted away in the American "pot" or society, producing a homogeneous social system. Many of these groups, however, have not lost their cultural identity and go to great lengths to preserve their social traits and customs. These groups have adopted different attitudes and orientations toward politics; for example, some have been very active in politics while others have almost completely withdrawn from politics.

Irish-Americans, the ethnic group operating in Edwin O'Connor's *The Last Hurrah,* have traditionally been very active in politics, especially at the local level. The practice of ethnic bloc voting enabled the Irish to gain political control of many Eastern cities during the nineteenth and twentieth centuries, and so their impact on politics has been significant. One of the last of the Irish machine politicians, Frank Skeffington (a mayor and former governor), is the subject of this selection. Mayor Skeffington is discussing the interrelationships between politics and social customs with his nephew Adam, a newspaper cartoonist.

"Actually, they were both right: Knocko's wake was and it wasn't a political rally. Given the circumstances, and," he added, with a faintly deprecatory wave of the cigar, "given myself, it could hardly have been anything else. You see, what you're up against here is the special local situation. To understand what happened tonight, you have to understand a little bit about that situation, and just a little bit more about my own rather peculiar position in it."

He leaned back, relaxing against the cushions; simply, detachedly, without boast or embellishment, he began to talk about himself. It was an extraordinary procedure; just how extraordinary, Adam did not realize. For while Skeffington had long studied his city and his own relation to it, the results of these studies he had been careful to keep to himself. From the beginning of his career, he had sharply divided the private from the public side of his life. Of the many friends he had made in politics over the years, none—not Gorman, even—had been admitted to the isolated preserve of the private thought, the personal concern. His wife had been his single, ideal confidant; with her death had come a void. Because Skeffington was, literally, a family man, he had tried one day, somewhat against his better judgment, to fill this void with his son. He had talked of himself, his work, his problems and his plans, and as he talked he had gradually become aware of the look upon his son's face: that characteristic, pleasant, glazed half-smile which indicated that somewhere beneath the surface inattention struggled with incomprehension. There had been more than the look; there had been the dancing feet: they had begun an abstracted, rather complicated tapping on the floor of the study, doubtless in anticipation of their evening's work ahead. *I should have been Vernon Castle,* Skeffington had thought bitterly. He had left the room abruptly and the experiment had never been repeated.

And now, as he had one afternoon three weeks before, he talked to his nephew.

"You see," he said, "my position is slightly complicated because I'm not just an elected official of the city; I'm a tribal chieftain as well. It's a necessary kind of dual officeholding, you might say; without the second, I wouldn't be the first."

"The tribe," said Adam, "being the Irish?"

"Exactly. I have heard them called by less winning names: minority pressure group (even though they've been the majority for half a century), immigrant voting bloc (even though many of the said immigrants have been over here for three generations). Still, I don't suppose it makes much difference what you call them; the net result's the same. I won't insult your intelligence by explaining that they're the people who put me in the mayor's chair and keep me there; I think you realize that the body of my support doesn't come from the American Indian. But as a member—at least by birth—of the tribe, you might give a thought to some of the tribal customs. They don't chew betel nut, and as far as I know the women don't beautify themselves by placing saucers in their lower lips. Although now that I come to think of it," he said, "that might not be a bad idea. It might reduce the potential for conversation. However, they do other things, and among them they go to wakes. And so do I."

"Which are and are not political rallies?" Adam asked. "Or was Knocko's case a special one?"

"Not at all special, except that the guest of honor was somewhat less popular than many of his predecessors. But of course when you speak about wakes as being political rallies, that's a little strong. You have to remember something about the history of the wake around here. When I was a boy in this city, a wake was a big occasion, and by no means a sad one. Unless, of course, it was a member of your own family that had died. Otherwise it was a social event. Some of my most vivid memories are of wakes. I remember my poor mother taking me to old Nappy Coughlin's wake. We went into the tenement, and there was Nappy, all laid out in a little coffin which was kept on ice. Embalming was a rather uncertain science in those days. It was a hot day in July and there were no screens on the parlor windows; there were flies in the room. I can still hear the ice dripping in to the pans underneath the coffin, and I can still see Nappy. He had one of the old-fashioned shrouds on, and he lay stretched out stiff as a ramrod. And on his head he wore a greasy black cap, which his good wife had lovingly adjusted so that the peak was pulled down over one eye. It gave him a rather challenging look; you had the feeling that at any moment he might spring out of the coffin and offer to go four fast rounds with you. My mother was horrified at the sight, and I remember that she went directly over to the widow and told her she ought to be ashamed of herself, putting her husband in the coffin with his hat on. Whereupon the widow simply said that he'd never had it off; he'd worn it for thirty years, day and night, in bed and out. So naturally she left it on, not wanting to say good-by to a stranger. However, when Father Conroy came in, the hat was whisked off fast enough. I can remember—it was my first wake, by the way—going into the kitchen, where somebody gave me a glass of milk and a piece of cake. And while my mother was in the parlor talking with the other women, I was out there with the men, just sitting around, eating cake, and listening to them talk. I hadn't the faintest notion of what they were talking about, but it didn't matter much. I was in seventh heaven. Everybody seemed to be enjoying themselves, and I knew I was. When my mother came to get me and take me home, I left with the greatest regret; I decided I'd never had a better time. Well," he said, "so much for memories of happy days. I wouldn't imagine it would sound like very much to anyone who'd been brought up today."

Adam smiled. "It sounded like a little boy having a wonderful time for himself. Although I must say that it didn't sound very much like death. Or even a political rally, for that matter."

"Matter of fact, it was the first political rally I'd ever been to," Skeffington said. "I was just too young to know it. You see, that's what all the men were talking about: politics. There was even a moment, just before I left, when Charlie McCooey himself came in: a fat man with a red face and handlebar mustache. He was the ward boss. I didn't know what that was, at the time, but because it was one more opportunity to keep the ball rolling. It's almost impossible for an old campaigner to avoid the occasions of sin. But whether I'd been there or not, they would have talked politics anyway. It's what interests them most. It ought to: it gave most of them everything they have. I mentioned to you the other day that the main reason I went into politics was because it was the quickest way out of the cellar and up the ladder. A good many others felt the same way. A lot of the younger men wanted a nice new dark serge suit that didn't necessarily come equipped with a chauffeur's cap. And the only way out was through politics; it was only when we gained a measure of political control that our people were able to come up for a little fresh air. They know that; they think of it as the big salvation for them; that's why they talk about it when they all get together. It's a very serious part of the business of living. And when I'm around, naturally I'm expected to talk it with them. And I do. I may add," he said, "that I don't find it a hardship."

Adam thought of one more question. "And the family?" he said. "The family of the deceased, I mean. Like Mrs. Minihan tonight. How do they feel while all this is going on? Don't they sometimes mind, Uncle Frank?"

"I know what you mean," Skeffington said, "but I think you're a bit wrong there. I don't think they mind a bit. There is a contrary opinion, however. Every once in a while I see where some advanced young public servant, who still had the ring of the pot on his seat while all this was going on, publicly applauds the passing of 'that cruel and barbarous custom, the wake.' Whenever I see that I take down my little book and chalk up a new name in the boob section. The man who said it obviously hasn't the faintest notion of what he's talking about. He hasn't the remotest understanding of the times, the circumstances, of our people, the way they feel and the way they regard death. I've seen a good many people die around here and I'll probably see a good many more. Unless, of course," he added, in another of those detached and faintly chilling parentheses which never failed to jolt Adam, "I beat them to it; there's always that possibility. But I've never seen the family that thought the wake was cruel and barbarous. They expected it. They wanted it. More than that, it was good for them: it was a useful distraction, it kept them occupied, and it gave them the feeling that they weren't alone, that they had a few neighbors who cared enough to come in and see them through a bad time. And you could say, too, it was a mark of respect for the deceased: rest assured that *he* wanted his wake. I remember what happened when the Honorable Hugh Archer died. The Honorable Hugh was considerably before your time; I don't imagine you'd have heard much about him."

"No, nothing."

"He was a prominent Republican attorney who once refused ten thousand dollars offered to him if he'd defend a notorious criminal. The noble gesture was unprecedented in Republican circles, and immediately he became known as the Honorable. It wasn't until much later that it was discovered he had asked for twenty thousand. Well, eventually he died. He was a huge man: six foot four and weighing nearly three hundred pounds. At that time, cremation was just coming into fashion following closely upon Mahjongg, and they whipped the Honorable Hugh out to the incinerator on the very day he died. Old Martin Canady went to the ceremony, out of a curiosity to see how the other half died, and when he came running back to me he was literally popeyed with shock. 'By God, Frank!' he said. 'They took the big elephant before he stopped breathin' almost and what the hell d'ye think they did with him? They put him in the oven and burned him up with the Sunday papers! When the poor man finished cookin' ye could have buried him in an ash tray! By God, Frank, I wouldn't want nothin' like that to happen to me! When I go I'm damned sure I mean to stay around the house a few days and nights so's some of the old pals can come in and have a drink and the last look! What the hell's wrong with that, now?' And," Skeffington said, "to save my soul, I couldn't think of a blessed thing wrong with it. It's the way I want to go myself. . . . Well, here I am talking away, it's late at night, and you're probably eager to get back in your house."

For the first time Adam noticed that the car had stopped and that they were in front of his house; they had been there, in fact, for some minutes. He said, "Uncle Frank, thanks loads for the evening. I've had a fine time, really." Then, because he felt that somewhere along the line his comments, however courteously they had been received by the older man, had been fairly presumptuous, he added, "And forgive the side-line observations on wakes. I guess the trouble was that I really didn't understand very much about them."

"Nothing wrong with your observations at all," Skeffington said. "To tell you the truth, I was glad you were interested enough to make them. From one point of view, they were perfectly correct. All I was concerned with doing was to show you another point of view. And I'm glad you enjoyed yourself; I was hoping you would and I thought you might. Knocko's wake is the kind of thing you might not have come across in the ordinary run of events, yet in a way I think it's far more valuable to you in understanding the whys and wherefores of the campaign and the city than attendance at any number of rallies would be. I may add that it's been pleasant for me, too: it was good to have you along. When something else comes up that I think you should take a look at, I'll give you a ring. That is, of course," he said courteously, "if you'd like me to."

"Please do, Uncle Frank. And again, thanks for tonight."

"A pleasure," Skeffington said. "Good night, my boy. Remember me to your wife."

The car sped off and Adam, going up the walk, realized with a start that, until Skeffington's final words, he had not once thought of Maeve during the evening. There was nothing unforgivable in the negligence itself; yet all the same, this evening, when he was in the company of her enemy and surrounded by activities of which she would have so disapproved, she had somehow eluded his thoughts. It was odd. He looked up at the house; with the exception of the single front hall light, it was in darkness. He knew that Maeve, as was sometimes her custom when he remained late at the paper, had already gone to bed.

He thought again of the evening behind him. It was as he had told his uncle: he had had a good time, and more, a singularly interesting one. He thought again of Charlie Hennessey and Ditto Boland and Delia Boylan, and even the wretched Johnnie Degnan; he thought of the outrageously inapposite behavior of one and all in the house where Aram Minihan lay in wake. Except that now, he thought, he was by no means so sure of its inappositeness, for Skeffington's words had not been without their effect, and on the theme of the wake, Adam's previous judgments had been drained of much of their certainty.

Maeve returned to his thoughts, disturbingly. He opened the door, and entered the house; as he did so he reflected that, finally, she would have to be told. It was ridiculous to postpone it any longer; as he mounted the stairs to their room, he determined to tell her the following morning.

Skeffington went home and directly upstairs; he was satisfied with the evening's work. On his way past his son's room he saw, with some surprise, that a thin crack of light shone under the closed door. He pushed the door open; his son was lying on the bed reading a picture magazine; by his side, a phonograph played Latin-American melodies.

"Well well," Skeffington said. "Doing your homework?"

Francis Jr. looked up and said pleasantly, "Hello, Dad. What's new?"

"I'm thinking of running for mayor," said Skeffington.

An expression of mild bewilderment touched the smiling depthless face. "Sure," he said. "I know that. I've been talking you up all over the place. Like crazy."

"Like crazy," Skeffington said. "Fine. Splendid. You're home early, aren't you?"

"A funny thing happened. Well, not funny, exactly, but peculiar, you know? We were at the Club, and I was with this girl and we were doing the mambo and all of a sudden she turned her ankle for no reason at all. The thing is, she's a very good dancer, almost a professional. So I took her home, and then I came home myself."

"Lost the use of her ankle," Skeffington said. "I suppose it means more to a girl like that than to most people. Your ankles are perfectly sound, I trust?"

"Oh sure. In great shape. The best." He flexed them in demonstration.

"Fine. Well, good night."

"Good night, Dad. Sleep tight."

"Yes. By the way, you don't happen to be acquainted with Norman Cass Jr., do you?"

"No, I don't think so. Why?"

"No particular reason. Only it occurred to me that you and he have something in common. Just as his father and I have. As I say, the resemblance hadn't occurred to me until now."

He left the room and went to his own room where he undressed, washed, knelt by his bed for a moment, and then got in. It was not until he was stretched out in bed that he realized how tired he was. It was something to think about, but he was asleep before he had time to think.

QUESTIONS

1 Are distinct racial, religious, or national identities still important in American politics, and, if so, in what ways are they significant?
2 What impact do ethnic groups have on American politics?
3 What implications does ethnic diversity have on a political system?
4 Is ethnic identification increasing or decreasing? Why?

Reading 5
Anthem
Ayn Rand

Individualism has always been a central value in the American political culture, and Ayn Rand more than any other novelist has been associated with proclaiming its merits. In her novel *Anthem,* a story about past and future life, she discusses how human beings have lost their way and how they can regain their direction.

This selection concludes the novel and is wrought with political and philosophical implications. The narrator describes how people mistakenly sacrificed individual freedom on the altar of collectivism, an act that ruined civilization. The spirit of the human race, however, never perished and will be the guiding light to a new life for all humanity. It is on this optimistic note that this passage begins and ends.

I shall call to me all the men and the women whose spirit has not been killed within them and who suffer under the yoke of their brothers. They will follow me and I shall lead them to my fortress. And here, in this uncharted wilderness, I and they, my chosen friends, my fellow-builders, shall write the first chapter in the new history of man.

These are the things before me. And as I stand here at the door of glory, I look behind me for the last time. I look upon the history of men, which I have learned from the books, and I wonder. It was a long story, and the spirit which moved it was the spirit of man's freedom. But what is freedom? Freedom from what? There is nothing to take a man's freedom away from him, save other men. To be free, a man must be free of his brothers. That is freedom. That and nothing else.

At first, man was enslaved by the gods. But he broke their chains. Then he was enslaved by the kings. But he broke their chains. He was enslaved by his birth, by his kin, by his race. But he broke their chains. He declared to all his brothers that a man has rights, which neither god nor king nor other men can take away from him, no matter what their number, for his is the right of man, and there is no right on earth above this right. And he stood on the threshold of the freedom for which the blood of the centuries behind him had been spilled.

But then he gave up all he had won, and fell lower than his savage beginning.

What brought it to pass? What disaster took their reason away from men? What whip lashed them to their knees in shame and submission? The worship of the word "We."

When men accepted that worship, the structure of centuries collapsed about them, the structure whose every beam had come from the thought of some one man, each in his day down the ages, from the depth of some one spirit, such spirit as existed but for its own sake. Those men who survived— those eager to obey, eager to live for one another, since they had nothing else to vindicate them—those men could neither carry on, nor preserve what they had received. Thus did all thought, all science, all wisdom perish on earth. Thus did men—men with nothing to offer save their great num- ber—lose the steel towers, the flying ships, the power wires, all the things they had not created and could never keep. Perhaps, later, some men had been born with the mind and the courage to recover these things which were lost; perhaps these men came before the Councils of Scholars. They were answered as I have been answered—and for the same reasons.

But I still wonder how it was possible, in those graceless years of transi- tion, long ago, that men did not see whither they were going, and went on, in blindness and cowardice, to their fate. I wonder, for it is hard for me to conceive how men who knew the word "I," could give it up and not know what they lost. But such has been the story, for I have lived in the City of the Damned, and I know what horror men permitted to be brought upon them.

Perhaps, in those days, there were a few among men, a few of clear sight and clean soul, who refused to surrender that word. What agony must have been theirs before that which they saw coming and could not stop! Perhaps they cried out in protest and in warning. But men paid no heed to their warning. And they, these few, fought a hopeless battle, and they perished with their banners smeared by their own blood. And they chose to perish, for they knew. To them, I send my salute across the centuries, and my pity.

Theirs is the banner in my hand. And I wish I had the power to tell them that the despair of their hearts was not to be final, and their night was not without hope. For the battle they lost can never be lost. For that which they died to save can never perish. Through all the darkness, through all the shame of which men are capable, the spirit of man will remain alive on this earth. It may sleep, but it will awaken. It may wear chains, but it will break through. And man will go on. Man, not men.

Here, on this mountain, I and my sons and my chosen friends shall build our new land and our fort. And it will become as the heart of the earth, lost and hidden at first, but beating, beating louder each day. And word of it will reach every corner of the earth. And the roads of the world will become as veins which will carry the best of the world's blood to my threshold. And all my brothers, and the Councils of my brothers, will hear of it, but they will be impotent against me. And the day will come when I shall break all the chains of the earth, and raze the cities of the enslaved, and my home will become the capital of a world where each man will be free to exist for his own sake.

For the coming of that day shall I fight, I and my sons and my chosen friends. For the freedom of Man. For his rights. For his life. For his honor.

And here, over the portals of my fort, I shall cut in the stone the word which is to be my beacon and my banner. The word which will not die, should we all perish in battle. The word which can never die on this earth, for it is the heart of it and the meaning and the glory.

The sacred word:

EGO

QUESTIONS

1 Is America becoming more individualistic or collective, and in what ways?
2 What is Ayn Rand's concept of freedom and does it agree with yours?
3 What implications does individualism have on a political system?
4 Is America moving toward a more group-oriented society and why?

Reading 6
The Ninth Wave
Eugene Burdick

Political attitudes are influenced by external events and agents as well as by the early socialization or learning process imposed by the family, as Eugene Burdick demonstrates in his novel *The Ninth Wave.* The central attitude he describes here is worry, which is categorized into economic, personal, national, and international worries. If politicians can determine how many people have what kinds of worries or anxieties, they can manipulate the voting public and thereby improve their chances for election to public offices.

In this selection, Mike Freesmith, a political activist, is explaining to Georgia his analysis of voter attitudes, based on electronic data processing of survey results. As she listens to Mike, Georgia observes a dentist and his patient in a neighboring office, and her reaction serves to reinforce the points that Mike is making.

"A funny thing happens after the primary . . . after the Republican and Democratic candidates have been chosen," Mike said. His voice was only a shade tense. "Just put 'Republican' after a man's name and he'll get forty-five per cent of the votes. I don't know why, but it happens." Mike lifted out a little less than half of the cards and placed them on the window sill. "And the same with the Democrat. He'll get forty-five per cent of the votes just because he's the Democrat. It doesn't matter if they're crooks, cuckolds, veterans, young, old or a damned thing. Just put the label on and each of them will get forty-five per cent of the vote."

Mike took out almost all of the remaining cards. There was only a thin stack of cards left. The rest were on the sill.

"Why does it happen that way, Mike?" Georgia said.

The dentist stepped away from the woman and a burr in his hand glistened with bright red blood.

"I don't know," Mike said. "I really don't. But they do. It's like an instinct; something that tells them to split up; to divide evenly. Jesus, it's uncanny. The Great Beast splits up into two beasts; almost exactly the same size. It always happens."

Georgia looked away from the dentist's window, down at the cards in the box.

"So these cards, the ten per cent left over, they're the ones that really decide the election," Georgia said. "That's it, isn't it, Mike? You just forget about the rest . . . the ninety per cent who are going to vote Democrat or Republican and you concentrate on the ten per cent. That's right, isn't it? They're the ones you try to attract to your candidate?"

"Not attract," Mike said. He grinned. "That's not the way it works. The ten per cent that's undecided is scared. So you scare them into voting for your man. See, that's what nobody knew before. They didn't know why the undecided voter was undecided. But I found out. He's undecided because he's scared."

"And that's what the Second and Third Questions are about?" Georgia asked. "That's it, isn't it?"

"That's right. That's absolutely right," Mike said.

He went back to the table and picked up some papers that Henri had just finished.

"Here's the Second Question," Mike said. He threw the paper on the sill. "Usually the polls just ask who's going to win. But I asked a couple of extra questions."

"What's the Second Question?"

"The Second Question is: 'In general, what sort of things do you worry about?' That's all."

"What did people say?" Georgia asked.

Georgia hesitated. She felt a nag of irritation. She looked out the window again. The woman was sitting up. She opened her mouth and a spill of red liquid gushed from her lips. She smiled wanly at the dentist. His left hand was again reassuring. The right hand fumbled with a new burr; a bright sharp piece of steel.

"I don't know. Communism or the atom bomb or war . . . something like that," she said. "Maybe they're not worried about anything."

"Everybody worries about something," Mike said. "And if they're approached by a neatly dressed interviewer who says their answer will be confidential they blurt it out. Like you. Tell me what you worry about most." He pointed his finger at her. "Go ahead. Don't think. Just say it."

Georgia looked at his finger, at the neat white crescent of his fingernail, the strong bony undulations. She looked over at the machine. It rested quietly.

"I won't tell you."

"All right," Mike said and laughed. "But you had an answer. That's the important thing. Everybody does. And their answers fall into four classes. The first class is what I call 'Economic Worries.' That's for guys who are worrying about payments on the television set or unemployment or the cost of living. The second class is 'International Worries'; like fear of a war, a catastrophe with Russia, reciprocal trade, Red China . . . that sort of thing. The third is 'National Worries.' That's for people worrying about the national debt, Communists in government, politics, that kind of answer.

The fourth is 'Personal Worries.' " He grinned and shook his head. "That's for the guy who is worrying about being impotent or his kid getting polio or if the boss likes him or if his clothes look like a hick's. That's the kind of thing you were worrying about. Right?"

"Yes," she said. She did not even feel curiosity. "It was a personal worry."

The dentist took the drill from the woman's mouth and already it was a bright dab of blood.

Georgia looked down at the paper.

Economic Worries	43%
Personal Worries	49%
National Worries	5%
International Worries	3%

"I don't believe it," Georgia said. She stared at the paper. "Only eight per cent of them worry most about war and depression and the atom bomb. The rest are worried about their jobs and themselves. I don't believe it." Mike laughed and she knew he did not believe her. "What can you do with this information?"

"Wait till you look at the Third Question," he said. He put the paper on the sill. "The Third Question was 'What group, in general, do you think is most dangerous to the American way of life?' Any guesses about the results?"

"No," Georgia said. "Not anymore."

"The answers always fall into five categories," Mike said. "Just like clockwork. First, the people who say Big Business or Wall Street or the Bankers or Rockefellers or General Motors. I call that the 'Big Business' category. Second is the 'Trade Union' category. That's obvious . . . anyone who says trade unions or Walter Reuther or John L. Lewis. Third is the 'Communist Conspiracy' category. Fourth is a category you won't like much. It's the 'Jewish Conspiracy' category. That's where you put the people who say the Jews or International Jewry or Bernard Baruch. The fifth group is the 'Religious Conspiracy' . . . people that say the Pope or the Catholics or 'those snotty Episcopalians' or 'those Mormons and all their wives . . . that sort of thing."

Big Business	32%
Trade Unions	22%
Communist Conspiracy	11%
Jewish Conspiracy	21%
Religious Conspiracy	14%

"What does it mean, Mike?" she whispered. "How do you make politics out of it?"

"That's the end of the scientific part of it," Mike said. "To make politics out of it you use your common sense, your intuition."

"Sure. But what do you do? How do you use the answers?"

The dentist bent forward and his back tensed. The woman's legs suddenly went rigid, lifted off the footrest. Her hands tightened on the armrests. Then she relaxed. The dentist stood back with a bloody tooth held in heavy forceps. The woman sat up and spit into the bowl. She was very pale. Georgia felt some plug of anxiety pull loose in her mind, she felt almost gay. She was ready for Mike's answer.

"I tell them what to be scared of," Mike said. "It's as simple as that."

He picked up the ten per cent of the cards left in the box. He held them in his hand like a small club and slapped them hard on the window sill. They made a loud cracking sound. Georgia twitched as if she had been hit on the spine.

"Scared?" she asked.

"Sure . . . scared. That's what the rest of them are afraid to do; the politicians, the professors, the clubwomen, the bureaucrats, all of them. They're afraid to ask the questions I asked and if they did they'd be afraid to use the answers. But I'm not. And it's so simple. Most of the voters don't care about politics. They're bored. It's faraway, distant, meaningless. They vote out of habit, because they've been told to vote. And they always vote Democrat or Republican. Everybody knows this, but the more obvious it becomes the more everyone feels that they have to tell the voter that he's smart and has a lot of power . . . that he's important. But the really important ones are the eight or ten per cent that're scared. They're the real independents, the people whose vote can be changed."

"Can you change their vote?" she asked.

"Yes, I can."

She looked at Mike. Then she looked out the window. The dentist's chair was empty. A neat nurse was laying out fresh aseptic linen, shining new tools.

"I want to see you do it, Mike," she said.

He took her arm to lead her out of the room and through the thick soft material of the coat he could feel a slight shivering.

QUESTIONS

1 Is there a real danger, as Freesmith implies, that America's nonpolitical worries or concerns can be manipulated by opportunistic politicians for their political advantages?
2 How pervasive and effective is fear as a political weapon?
3 What is Mike Freesmith's "Great Beast" and how accurate is that analogy?
4 Is Mike Freesmith's analysis of the American people accurate, and, if so, why?

Reading 7
Politically Perfect
Judith Viorst

In this poem Judith Viorst relates the experiences of a couple who adopted the popular New Left or liberal-oriented attitudes and ideals of the
1960s and involved themselves in all the "right" causes. These attitudes
were strongly reinforced by the tumultuous events of the late 1960s and
early 1970s, and Sally's and Stu's behavior reflected these attitudes.

Gradually, however, the liberal activism decreased in the nation,
and Sally and Stu experienced things that began to contradict their New
Left beliefs. As the poem develops, the impact of these changing experiences on the couple's attitudes and behavior becomes evident.

Sally and Stu
Were married by a militant minister
(He was bitten by a Birmingham police dog),
Moved to an integrated neighborhood
(Thirty-four percent were Black or Other),
Turned down a low-cost trip to Greece
(For obvious reasons),
And have always strived to be
Politically perfect
By displaying aggressive bumper stickers,
Boycotting non-returnable bottles,
And including, at every cocktail party,
One American Indian, one Draft Resister, and Ralph Nader.

Sally and Stu
Were admitted to the nicest New Left circles
(Published writers, sometimes even Mailer),
Solicited for all the finest causes
(Panthers, Moratoriums, Defense Funds),
Advocated the dismantling of the war machine and the smashing of the
        major corporations and the total restructuring of society
(Without, of course, condoning undue violence),
And have always strived to be

Politically perfect
By giving generously,
Picketing profusely,
And including, at every Christmas party,
One unwed mother, one well-intentioned bomber, and the maid.
They have always strived to be
Politically perfect—but
Recently they met a sweet policeman
And a rotten revolutionary,
And started feeling hostile to all muggers
Regardless of color or creed,
And then he discovered he couldn't say "pig" or "right on"
Without sounding insincere,
And then she discovered that she couldn't say "male sexist oppressor"
Without sounding insincere,
And when he asked her
Was she capable of taking off her clothes and painting an antiwar symbol
      on her stomach and floating across the Potomac in the interests of
      world peace,
And her answer was no,
And when she asked him
Was he capable of annihilating his racist parents and his racist brother
      Arnold and that racist little blonde he used to go with in the
      interests of world brotherhood,
And his answer was no,
They knew
They'd never be
Politically perfect.

QUESTIONS

1 What is your personal ideal of political behavior? From what sources did you
   acquire this ideal, and does your behavior match your ideal?
2 What does Viorst mean by the phrase "politically perfect"?
3 Why can't Sally and Stu ever be politically perfect?
4 Is the behavior of Sally and Stu typical of most American liberals, and, if so,
   why?

Part Two

The Constitutional Context

In every political system that has ever existed there has been a means by which its government has been given authority or the recognized right to rule. The means can be an ideology like Marxism-Leninism for the Soviet Union and the People's Republic of China or a symbol like the monarchy in Great Britain. In the United States authority to rule comes from a document, the Constitution.

Besides being the source of authority for the American government, the Constitution provides an important context within which the political system must operate. The Constitution established the political institutions in which the key functions of interest representation, rule making, rule application, and rule interpretation operate. In so doing, it provided the legal context in which democratic politics could flourish.

The heart of the Constitution is its emphasis on limited government. The men who attended the Constitutional Convention in Philadelphia in 1788 had experienced what they believed to be too much central government power under the King of England and too little power under the system instituted by the Articles of Confederation. Thus, they wanted to create a system that would avoid these two extremes, and it was in this spirit that they wrote the Constitution. The Founding Fathers produced a form of government that could prevent oppression while reserving to itself sufficient power to run the nation.

Their approach to achieving the goal of limited government was borrowed from an eighteenth-century Frenchman, Baron Montesquieu. It was Montesquieu's belief that a just government could exist only when the three major branches of government—legislative, executive, and judicial—were separate and distinct from each other. The Founding Fathers adopted this idea but added their own principle of checks and balances. They reasoned that if the three powers of government were to remain separate from each other, there must be some method by which this separation could maintain itself. In establishing the Constitution the authors of that document divided the powers of government among three branches and gave each the means by which it could prevent the others from usurping its powers. The selection from *The Supreme Court,* by Andrew Tully, examines these principles of separation of powers and checks and balances.

The writers of the Constitution, however, believed that the principle of limited government should also be applied to the area of civil liberties or rights. By adding to the Constitution the first ten amendments (the Bill of Rights), they made sure that citizens of the United States were guaranteed certain freedoms, including freedom of speech, press, religion, and other civil rights such as privacy of person and papers. In Irving Wallace's *The Seven Minutes* the point is made that freedom of speech is an essential right of Americans, but within limitations. The concept of civil rights is viewed in the selection from Joseph Wambaugh's *The New Centurions,* in which the police, the enforcers of the laws, express their viewpoint on civil liberties and rights.

Reading 8
The Supreme Court
Andrew Tully

The following selection, from Andrew Tully's novei *The Supreme Court,*
underlines several principles crucial to the dynamics of the judicial process. Francis Dalton, Associate Justice of the United States Supreme
Court, has ordered a stay of execution for the convicted Soviet spy,
Gleason, in order to make a more thorough review of the case with the
help of his assistant, Jake Moriarty. In the meantime, Chet McAdams, the
Senate majority leader, has collapsed and died after strenuously leading
the fight to expand the number of Justices on the Supreme Court to
make it more conducive to the President's wishes. The situation is extremely tense, and the future of the country is at stake.

Despite these conditions and the risk of intense public outrage, Justice Dalton orders the stay of execution so that he can meticulously
reexamine the arguments of the defense attorney, Hoff, and thereby remove all doubt over the guilt of the defendant. Every accused has the
right to a fair and speedy trial in America; Dalton's delaying action ensures that the case would be fair as well as speedy.

In his subsequent discussion with President Hughes, Justice Dalton
calls attention to other important constitutional principles. By resisting
the court-packing bill, Dalton emphasizes that the Court's function is not
to appease the President, Congress, or public opinion; it must instead
safeguard the rule of law and separation of powers so essential to our
constitutional system. At the end of the selection, Dalton's surprise offer
to the President shows how important it is that members of the Court
keep their behavior above question and the Court's reputation intact.

For a man who had snatched only an hour's nap on his office couch,
Francis Dalton took considerable pride in the fact that physically he felt
very well. He didn't believe he could say the same for Jake Moriarty. Before
he left the office, he had had literally to lead Jake to the couch and lower
him onto it. "Sleep until tomorrow, Jake," he'd told him. "I've called Miss
Swanson and told her nobody is to come to the office today." Jake Moriarty could not have lasted long enough to be taken home; he was as comfortable as he could be with the blanket over him and Francis' old cashmere
topcoat rolled up as a pillow. They had worked on the Hoff material all
night—until five o'clock this morning. Then Francis had taken his brief nap
while Jake put the papers in order, and when Jake woke him up, Francis
was ready instantly for his final check of the papers; he had emerged from

his deep sleep completely alert. He had called the White House as soon as it was decent to do so, and John Alden Hughes had said, "Yes, of course, Francis. Come over as soon as you can." So after a long shower and a quick shave, Francis was doing just that. He settled down comfortably on the seat of the cab. There was in him a vague, elusive sadness, yet he was content; he had done his job—as it was prescribed in the rule book, and in his brain and his heart.

He was not even disturbed by the national hubbub it had caused. He glanced down at the Washington *Post* and *The New York Times* on the seat beside him, but he did not pick them up. DALTON HALTS GLEASON EXECUTION—FULL COURT TO ACT, said the *Post*. And the *Times:* DALTON STAYS EXECUTION OF SOVIET SPY—MOSCOW HAILS ELEVENTH HOUR ACT—CHIEF JUSTICE SUMMONS COURT.

The other headlines were still on Page One, too, at least in the *Post:* BEATRICE HART SILENT ON JUSTICE TROTH AND PUBLISHER DEPLORES FUROR OVER ADAMS BOOK. Francis smiled; he didn't have time for bitterness. There was a publisher with a good press department—"deploring" the furor was as good a way as any to keep the furor in the headlines. Well, all that would have to wait until other things had been taken care of. There was the fact that Mr. Justice Dalton was not exactly a national hero this morning. First the Freddie Adams scandal, and now his stay of execution for Gleason. The President was probably waiting for him with a shotgun. And the Chief Justice would not be pinning any medals on him.

Yet Bacon had sounded surprisingly mild when he phoned at one o'clock in the morning from Tucson. The Chief Justice had even apologized for calling at "this unearthly hour." And then, "Of course, Mr. Justice, this has startled me. I am having the full Court summoned back to Washington immediately. We shall take up the case tomorrow morning."

Francis said, "Of course, Chief. I expected that."

"Yes." Bacon's tone gave the impression of uneasiness. "Mr. Justice, I hardly think you can expect your action to be upheld. The stay almost surely will be vacated."

It had been still too early for Francis to know, so he had said merely, "I did what I believed right, under the circumstances. Of course, I have complete trust in the Court."

But now he knew. He had done his homework—he and Jake Moriarty. He had given Gleason the whole night; he had checked and cross-checked every page of material on file in the case. He had *studied* Hoff's appeal. And his decision had come, clear-cut and unequivocal, the kind of decision about which he could say no other conclusion was possible.

Hoff's material *had* been bogus. It had been put together cleverly and it had been convincing, up to a point. But it had failed on every one of the major tests Francis had put it to. Not only was Gleason guilty, which was not the point, anyway—what mattered was that his trial had been conducted with the utmost fairness—but the FBI had *not* erred, even in the business of the wire-tapping, and Burch's testimony was unassailable. It had taken all night to satisfy himself, but he was satisfied. The extraordinary sitting of the Court would be a brief formality; Francis would vote with the majority to vacate the stay.

Now he could reproach himself for his ugly shortness with Hoff when Hoff had found him with a midnight phone call. "God bless you, Mr. Justice," Hoff had said, and Francis had replied, "Don't blaspheme, Hoff"—and hung up. But Francis had wanted no blessing from anyone, least of all Hoff, for doing his duty. And he had been weary and irritable.

Francis glanced out the window of the cab, and found what he was looking for. The flags on the two Senate Office Buildings at half-staff for Chet McAdam. He looked back and to his left for the assurance that the Capitol's flag was also at half-staff. Curiously, it gave him comfort to see this last tribute to his friend. Poor Chet. The human sacrifice. The first sacrifice to John Alden Hughes's Court-packing plan.

The President's statement in the newspapers was a warm one, and Francis knew it was sincere. "Chester W. McAdam died in the performance of his duty. He died as a soldier, just as truly as men died on the Normandy beaches and at Valley Forge." That was true. And it was also true that, like some of those men on the Normandy beaches and at Valley Forge, Chet McAdam perhaps did not have to die. Francis had to say perhaps, because he did not know the answer to the question that had gnawed at him ever since Tom Morgan's voice told him of the collapse in the cloakroom. Chet McAdam had to fight, but did he have to die? Would he have died if the President had given him his reward on time? Francis did not know. Nobody really knew. Francis could grieve for his friend, but he could not indulge in a maudlin snap judgment condemning the President.

He picked up the *Post* with its headline McADAM FALLS DEAD IN SENATE CLOAKROOM. Frank Hoar had said it for that bitter little body of men: "My friend Chet McAdam was murdered. He was struck down by the sword of another man's ambition, another man's greed for power." It was sad that Frank Hoar should have said such an ugly thing. And yet it was one way of putting it for those who could believe that Chet McAdam would be alive this morning if it had not been for the Court bill. Francis could not agree with Frank Hoar, but now he knew one thing. He knew that he, Mr. Justice Francis Dalton, had been wrong in the past. He would not accuse John Alden Hughes of murdering Chet McAdams, but he would forever—like a Monday morning quarterback—blame the President for not finding another way to get his job done when the question came up of what to do about Chet McAdam and his lifelong ambition. He would blame himself, too, for not seeing at the time that another way should have been found, because he realized, now, that he had been too careless in his consideration of the importance of the individual. The state, in the person of the President, had had a job to do, but in battling to do that job it had dealt with the lives of individuals. Chet McAdam was something far more important than the Majority Leader of the Senate; he was an individual, with an unalienable right to life, liberty and the pursuit of happiness. That right had been abridged by the President, with the condonation of Francis Dalton, among others. He would not judge John Alden Hughes, but from now on, on that point, he would disagree with him.

He owed Gleason thanks for helping him to see things as they had to be, as they were meant to be by the men who had sat in the humidity of that Philadelphia summer and written the rules in simple, easy-to-understand language. He owed Gleason thanks for making him see that there *were* absolutes in the Bill of Rights and that they could not be tampered with lest men die unjustly, or too soon, or without proper regard for the legal necessities. In the end, the decision had to be against Gleason, but that was unimportant. What was important was that Gleason's rights—the rights of the individual—had been protected. What was important, too, to Francis Dalton personally was that he had been made to see that Chet McAdam's rights, and the rights of other individuals, had been abridged.

He felt an exultation intrude upon his sadness. He found himself exulting over a new truth within him: the truth that in a civilized republic man is responsible for his brother before he is responsible to the state. It was good and cleansing, to see the truth that the man in government, whether he was sheriff, mayor, or Supreme Court justice, was there to protect man's rights, not to make man subject to the rights or the requirements of a well-ordered state. It excited him to know for the first time that in some cases the protection of a man's rights could and *should* cause temporary damage to the state. The Russians have a great deal, Francis reflected, but they do not have that.

The cab pulled into the southwest gate of the White House and rolled up the drive to the South Portico. "Jeez, that's the President there with his kid, ain't it?" the cab driver said.

John looked in the direction of the outthrown arm, and saw the President and little Bounce. They were standing in the Rose Garden, as though at attention. Francis paid the cab driver and got out and strolled over to the father and his son.

"Hello, Francis," The President turned, with a hand still resting lightly on Bounce's towhead. "We're having a funeral. Tweet is getting a military burial."

"Come see the grave—come and see it, Mr. Justice!" Bounce was bursting with excitement.

Francis joined them on the gravel path and shook hands with Bounce, who had leaped in front of his father, before exchanging a handclasp with the President.

"Who is Tweet?" Francis asked.

"He's my bird—he *was* my bird, my canary," Bounce said. "He died. We just buried him." He kicked at a toy cannon underfoot. "See, we gave him a salute. Eight guns. That's all the shells I had."

"That was a very nice tribute, Bounce," Francis said. "I'm sorry Tweet is dead, though."

"Yes." Bounce looked down at the little grave with its wooden cross. "He was a good bird. He had a bad stomach." A tear crept down through the freckles on his cheek. Bounce kept his head down. "I've got to go now, Mr. Justice. I have to go to school. Goodbye, sir." And he ran off.

"Poor little cuss," Hughes said. "He didn't want us to see him crying." He took Francis' arm. "Francis, let's go into the office. I've got some coffee in there."

They sat down in chairs on opposite sides of a coffee table under the portrait of George Washington, and the President poured the coffee from a silver urn.

"Well, Francis." Hughes' voice was tired. "You've stirred up the animals."

"Yes, I'm afraid I have, Mr. President. All for nothing, as it turns out."

"You mean . . . ?"

"Jake Moriarty and I worked all night on the Hoff stuff. It didn't hold up. There was no new argument that was at all supported. I'll vote to vacate the stay with the rest of them tomorrow."

"Well, now." The President looked hard at Francis. "And you stayed up all night—for nothing?"

"No, not for nothing. I didn't quite mean it that way." Francis' smile was wry. "I had to stay up—to find out. You see, I wasn't sure, and the only way to make sure was to give him a stay while I checked."

The President's sigh was huge, and two little vertical lines in his cheeks saddened his face. "Francis, this is—a surprise." He put down his cup. "Damn! I don't suppose I have to tell you that I was very unhappy at the stay. It seemed—frivolous."

"I'm sorry. All I can say is that it was not frivolous. There was doubt, not very reasonable doubt, but doubt. I had to make sure."

"Yes." The President picked up his cup and sipped from it slowly. "And of course it's raised hell all over the country. It hasn't—helped." A small smile formed on his lips. "And yet, I suppose I should congratulate you, Francis. I have to admit that what you did was in the tradition."

"Thank you, Mr. President. But I'm afraid I didn't think of it in that way. It just had to be done."

"I wonder." Hughes's smile departed. "I wonder if things have to be done—if they're injurious to the commonweal." He shook his head, as if trying to clear it. "Yes, I suppose they do. I suppose I can't expect the Supreme Court to make my problems its prime concern."

Francis' voice was soft. "Our function is a different one. We have to concern ourselves with other matters, even including the rights of an enemy spy." Self-consciously, he felt rising in him an irrelevant surge of affection for poor Baker, poor Baker with his faithless wife. Baker was a part of it, too; for better or for worse, the Bakers acted according to what they believed was right.

The President took another sip of his coffee. "But you didn't want to see me just to tell me this. And you could have called me—as I'm sure you would have."

"No, I didn't come here just for that, Mr. President. John—I would like to talk to you about something else." The *John* was necessary. He wanted this to be a talk between two friends.

"Of course, Francis." The President put down his cup and smiled. There was a wistfulness about him that Francis had not seen before. "You know that we've always been able to talk—about anything. It's something we've kept, through all the years, through all this."

"John, the best thing to do is tell you outright." Francis was eager to spill it all. "I want you to know that I can't go along with you any longer on the Court bill. I don't believe in it any longer."

The President's smile was gone. "Well—this is rather a surprise, Francis. I'll admit that." His mouth turned up, but the smile wouldn't come back. "But I don't punch my friends in the nose for that sort of thing. However, may I ask why?"

"Yes, sir, of course. It's so sudden, of course you have a right to be mystified. I don't quite know whether I'll be able to put it right, but it boils down to the fact that I've discovered the individual is more important than the state. And I don't believe the individual's rights can be protected properly if the Supreme Court is changed so that it reflects one man's point of view."

Francis paused to look at Hughes, and the President said, "Go on, Francis—I'm not going to interrupt."

"It boiled up in me while I was working on the Gleason case last night," Francis said. "It suddenly occurred to me that if we had all like-minded justices on the court—justices who thought exactly as you did, or exactly as any other President did—then it might not be possible to grant a stay of execution to a man like Gleason. I knew that you had refused to grant clemency, and yet there were reasons why I felt I should grant a stay. In the kind of Supreme Court you visualize, John, that might not have been possible."

He paused, but Hughes remained silent—and grim.

"I'm afraid we—all of us—have been trying to tamper with something of vital importance to our freedoms. We have been trying to achieve conformity in an area where conformity is a peril to the country. We have militated against the left, against the Communist menace which threatens our liberties. But the fact is that if we can curb the liberties of the left today, then at some later day we can do the same thing to the extreme right, or to the center, or to any other segment of opinion which at the moment happens to be unpopular.

"Your Court plan has been the climax of your struggle to reorganize a disorganized country, to protect it against its enemies both at home and abroad, to impose a national discipline that would strengthen the country, that would give it the national competence to resist its enemies. But in so doing, you have tried to whittle down the individual's basic liberties. You have done so in a good cause—in an attempt to save the country from Communism. I trust you implicitly, John—but I trust the Constitution more. If you could do this, John, so could some other President, a bad President who seized power and became a dictator. All this should have been plain to me from the beginning, but it wasn't. Perhaps it was the atmosphere in which I grew up, when everything was such a mess and I believed the American people were in need of some good old-fashioned Cromwellian discipline. Perhaps it was my early association with your conservative movement, when I discovered that all the decent people—or those I believed were decent—were on your side, while the other side had only the malcontents and the wild-eyed pinks. Perhaps it was just something chemical in me. At any rate I realized last night that all along I had been rationalizing our right to tamper with the Constitution because *we* were all right, *we* were decent, *we* could be trusted."

Francis picked up his spoon from the saucer, then laid it down on the table. He had to say the rest.

"I was so wrong—and I believe you are wrong. What I believe now, what should always have been plain to me, is that no man can be trusted—*no man can be trusted to be a law unto himself,* even if his intentions are good. *No* man can be trusted. That is why we have the Constitution."

The President stood up and walked over to the French doors and looked out into the Rose Garden, then walked back to his chair and sat down. He took a cigarette from the box on the table and put it between his lips for a moment, but instead of lighting it, he put it down.

"A bad President," he said. "I see your point, Francis, but in one respect, at least, you're wrong. There's no such thing as a bad President, Francis. There couldn't be. The country wouldn't let any man be a bad President. Once he moves into this house, the country won't let him be the kind of man who could be a bad President. You couldn't know, because you've never been President, but that's the way it is. Thank God for it, too."

He picked up the silver table lighter and lit his cigarette. "But, of course, that's not really the point. The point is that you can't go along any longer, and you have come to me and told me so, honestly—and immediately. I do appreciate that."

Francis looked the President in the eye. "I had to tell you at once."

"Yes, you did. *You* did, because you are that kind of man. I'm not sure another man would have found it necessary."

"I'm sure any man would do the same thing."

"I'm not. Because, you see—you didn't have to. It wasn't necessary."

"Wasn't necessary? But why not, John?"

"Because, Francis, it doesn't matter any more."

The President stood up and walked over to his desk and leaned against it in the way Francis had seen him do so many times.

"The Court bill is dead."

"Dead! Dead? But the debate has just started."

"And it has just ended, Francis. It ended yesterday afternoon when Chet McAdam dropped dead in the cloakroom. When Chet McAdam died, the Court bill died with him."

"But—why? You've got the votes. McAdam totted them up for me. He was sure."

The President's voice was low, but its tone could not cloak the bitterness. "We *had* the votes, Francis. We—I—don't have them any longer. The boys have walked out on me."

Sympathy flooded up in Francis, inundating all the other feelings that had surged selfishly within him. "But this is pretty sudden, isn't it? Are you sure?"

The smile on the President's face was contrived and small. "Yes, I'm sure. I'm damned sure. It's all over now. I don't blame you, Francis. You've had your doubts all along; I saw that. I saw you struggling with them from the beginning, and I suppose I was pretty brutal about it. I wouldn't let you out from under—because I needed you. But those gentlemen on the Hill— I'm not sure I'll ever be able to understand them. They would have gone along, unwillingly, against their instincts, for the sake of their personal friendship with Chet McAdam. They were going along. We did have the votes. And now . . ." The little smile vanished and the hurt lines were creasing his forehead again. "It seems to me to be a hell of a way to legislate—with your glands."

Francis said slowly, "And now? How do you know for sure?"

"It's all there in the papers. I'm sure you saw Frank Hoar's statement."

"Oh—Hoar. That was too bad; I'm sure Frank will regret saying that. But . . ."

"Oh, Hoar doesn't matter, particularly. And the others aren't quite so ugly in their reactions. But they have reacted, Francis. The Speaker of the House called me last night, and so did Fred Pilney and Alpheus Ward and the Vice-President. They're cashing in their chips, Francis. They are not going along now with the Court bill. I didn't ask them why; I didn't have to. They are walking out because Chet McAdam is dead, and if they do not charge me with his murder, they at least hold me partly responsible. Anyway, the bill is dead."

"I'm sorry. I'm truly sorry."

"Thank you. I know you are. *You* are my friend, thank God. I don't have to apologize to anyone for what I have done in trying to put that Court bill across, and I know *you* wouldn't want me to apologize. I did what I believed had to be done. That is all a President can do. It's his responsibility, and he has to accept it. He can't do things the way somebody else wants them done, because that somebody else does not carry the responsiblity."

He walked back to the chair and sat down. "But, Francis, what I wanted to explain to you—if you haven't already seen it—is how unnecessary it was for you to come here and tell me you could no longer support the bill. You didn't have to. You could have kept quiet and let me believe you were prepared to go along with me to the last—after all, it wasn't your fault the Senate decided to walk out on it."

Francis' reply was short. "I couldn't have done that."

Hughes looked at him and reached over and put his hand on Francis' arm.

"No, you couldn't have. Thank you for being that kind of man."

"John—thank you for saying that. I do appreciate it, more than you can know. But I don't want the atmosphere in this country to be such that you, the President of the United States, feel you should thank anyone for being honest, for doing what he believes is the right thing. And I can't help thinking that if such an atmosphere exists, people like me may be partially responsible."

"We all are, Francis. That's the tragedy of man's imperfection. Because certain things have to be done—or we believe, sincerely, that they have to be done—and because of *how* things sometimes have to be done in a system whose goodness does not always prohibit obstructionism—because of the state of the world—all of us find ourselves cutting corners here and there. And, unfortunately, reaching the point where we rationalize this corner-cutting, even argue in its favor. Since man is not yet among the angels, there doesn't seem to be any other way, Francis. Often, from where I sit, I'm convinced there is no other way. It may sound strange, but I have to do things those ways, or be unworthy of the responsibility given to me. I have to do my best for the majority, Francis, while regretting the broken bones among those in the minority."

Francis waited, to be sure the President had finished. "And there is where our basic disagreement has come. Of course you must act for the majority. Every President must, in his public worthiness. But don't you see—just as your function is to promote the welfare of the people as a whole, our function—the function of the courts—is to guard the welfare of the individual, of the minorities. Our function is to decide that any interference with the basic rights of the citizenry, as set forth by the Bill of Rights, is wrong. It is wrong. Period.

"The Atkinson case and the Gleason case have taught me something. Or rather, they have reminded me of some truths, some realities, some facts of life, I had carelessly overlooked. William Allen Hume is right—it is our duty to keep the Bill of Rights abreast of the times, to use the Bill of Rights to thwart every modern, streamlined effort that comes along with the intent of abridging man's rights. It's been a long time since Thomas Jefferson and Madison, and over those years man has come up with some clever ruses to deprive his fellows of their liberties. This man is refused his rights because he is a Communist, this man because he is a Nazi, this man because he is always calling strikes. The courts must use the Bill of Rights to confound the oppressors, by whatever political names they call themselves, no matter what the temporary damage to the republic.

"There has been much talk, especially here in the White House, that the Supreme Court is forever sticking its nose into matters that do not concern it. I now disagree. I believe it is time the Court acted to expand the area in which it exerts judicial influence. In the past, the Court has been too unwilling to intervene in so-called 'political questions.' Well, political questions so-called, involve people, and where people are involved the Court also should involve itself. I go even further. It is now my conviction that the Court should watch over people who are likely to get into trouble for political reasons, and should stand between them and that impending trouble. A citizen should be protected from getting into trouble; by the time he is *in* trouble it often is too late to help him."

Francis leaned back in his chair and waved an arm self-deprecatingly. "I'm talking too much, John. I shouldn't have to make a speech."

The President's smile was a valid one, and his voice was soft. "Yes, I'm afraid you did have to make a speech, Francis. A man has to make a speech when he arrives at a new place in the road as you have. And I know how to listen."

Francis looked at his friend and was warmed by what he saw. Now was the time to pay the price. There were some debts he could not pay this good friend, but there was one decent thing he could do to help this man to whom he owed so much.

"John, there isn't much more, and I'll be brief. I'm resigning from the Court—and Bea and I are going to be married."

At first the President seemed not to have heard. He was gazing straight ahead. Then in a sudden motion, he stood up and plunged both hands in his trouser pockets.

"You want to resign?" Hughes's voice was flat.

"Yes. It's what I have to do."

"What you have to do?" Francis had never heard the President's voice so low.

"Yes. It's—I owe you that." Francis hurried on now, anxious to be done with it. "I'm not resigning because of any ideological differences we may have. That would defeat the principle of the separation of powers. I'm resigning because of Bea and me."

"What are you talking about?"

"It's quite simple. You have no right to dictate my principles, my political philosophy; I'm a member of an independent branch of the government. But you do have a perfect right to stand in judgment on my private life. You're the head of the government, and you have not only the right but the duty to insist that your appointees avoid public scandal. At first I was angry when Harry Weiss talked to me about it, but then I realized I had let myself in for all this, and that you had a right to be concerned. Worse than that, I dallied with Bea; in a sense, I held her at arm's length while I was pondering the unpleasant aspects of the situation—unpleasant, that is, to my position. We should have been married long ago."

Hughes walked over to the French doors and again stood there looking out at the grayness of the Rose Garden. Still with his back to the room, he said, "Francis, you're a damned fool."

He turned then, and put up a hand as Francis started to speak. "No, Francis, you don't really have any more to say. You've said enough. I suppose it's been my fault, the way I've poked into people's affairs, but I never dreamed you'd misunderstand. What's this about Harry Weiss?"

Francis was puzzled, "Why, he called me and said you were concerned about me—about Bea and me. He said you didn't want me to get into any trouble. So I naturally assumed you were worried about a justice of the Supreme Court being mixed up in a scandal. It angered me at the time, but now I see you had a right to be concerned."

"My God!" Hughes walked back behind his desk and sat down. "This is ridiculous. Of course I was concerned about you. About *you*, Francis, not about a Supreme Court justice. I knew how damned moral you were, and I was afraid all that stuff in the gossip columns would hurt you, deeply— irreparably. My God, you did presume—you and your damned Irish-Catholic-Puritan guilty conscience. I had no intention of interfering in the relationship between you and Bea. I'd like to point out that I knew Bea before you did, and my only regret has been that she is not marrying my brother Jimmy instead of you."

Francis was standing now, emotions piling up inside, his lips dry, his mind a confusion of thoughts. "I don't understand."

"Dammit, Francis—what do you mean, you don't understand?"

Hughes's exasperation seemed to be hurting his face. "I've just made my position crystal-clear. I was concerned about you and Bea because you were—are—friends of mine. I was concerned as I am concerned when one of Harry Weiss's children has scarlet fever. But I never intended to tell you because you were a member of the Supreme Court you could not marry the woman you loved." Hughes grinned. "Francis, you idiot, I am not the Church of England and you are not a poor, mixed-up young king. In this country, that sort of situation doesn't exist; it can't exist. I'm only the President of the United States, not the legally appointed guardian of my friends' private lives."

Through the warm excitement, the excited affection, that surged in him, Francis was trying to understand. "But I've always been led to believe . . ."

"Francis, you've always been led to believe certain things—by yourself. It was your own peculiarly rigid—and irrelevant—moral standards that led you to believe certain things." Hughes's smile widened. "Don't include me in on your Puritanism, young fellow."

Francis looked at the President, still trying to settle his thoughts, to winnow out the self-doubts. He wanted to cling to the good feeling Hughes's words had given him, but confusion was sowing suspicion in his mind: Dared he surrender himself to this good feeling, so suddenly?

"But, John—are you doing the right thing?" Francis had to be sure. He could not let his friend indulge himself in official carelessness for friendship's sake. "Are you doing the right thing? For the country? I came here to resign, because I felt I should. I still can't help believing it is the only way. It is all such a mess."

"Hell, yes, it's a mess, Francis." Hughes's voice was firm and his mouth was solemn again. "But that's your private affair. I expect you to sweat it out, like a man—and get married as soon as you can. You'll need Bea at your side to help you sweat it out. And as far as the country is concerned—well, I think the country can take care of itself in matters such as this. I believe the country, give or take a few sanctimonious old maids, eventually will conclude it's none of its business whom you marry, so long as the woman of your choice is not a convicted Soviet spy. I think you should have discovered long ago that the country as a whole consists of pretty decent citizens who are instinctively disinclined to stand in moral judgment of their fellow men. There is an inherent fairness in this land of ours that has enabled it to retain its national conscience while becoming the most powerful nation in the world. Because of that fairness, our people have not been corrupted by the power they wield."

"But, John, the people expect certain things in a Supreme Court justice." Exulting in his inner glow, Francis thought: but I must be fair, too.

"You are still confused. The country's stake in the matter is whether or not you are an honest judge, a man of principle. The country expects you to

be that, and that's all. And if I'd ever had any doubts about that, Francis—
which I haven't—you have made that clear to me today."

"Thank you, John." Now Francis could permit himself the smile he
had been denying. So this *was* the way it was coming out. Now he could
believe it, exulting in the belief. It was turning out all right, despite his fears.
And yet, a new and separate good feeling rose in him. It was good that it
was turning out this way, but it wouldn't have mattered if it hadn't, because
he had known where he had to go.

He said, "Thank you again, John," and his grin grew wider and a little
self-conscious. "I'm—rather embarrassed to say it, but I was sure you
would demand my resignation, under the circumstances."

"Under the circumstances!" John Alden Hughes threw his head back,
and there was nothing wrong with the famous Hughes laugh that filled the
room. "Under the circumstances, indeed. Francis, the circumstances
haven't changed a bit. You're the same man I appointed to the Supreme
Court. Perhaps you're even a better man, even if I don't—and never will—
agree with the premises you've just submitted to me. I appointed an honest
man named Francis Dalton to the Supreme Court and I still have an honest
man named Francis Dalton on that Court. You've insisted upon retaining
your honesty, even despite my honestly unwitting attempts to tamper with
it."

A grin spread over the President's face. "As a matter of fact, I do have
a proposition to make to you, Mr. Justice. Even though I have a new respect for you, I've still got *my* job to think about, and I'm damned if I like
the idea of having still another justice I can't depend upon on that cantan-
kerous Court. While you've been talking, Francis, I've been thinking some
Machiavellian thoughts. You have to think those kind of thoughts in this
office; it may not be pretty, but whenever something like this happens the
President has to consider how it can be turned to his advantage, how it can
be used to further the program *he* feels is necessary to the country's general
welfare."

Hughes put up a hand to intercept the words he saw forming on Francis' lips. "No, let me finish. I *have* come up with something, Francis—a
gimmick, if you will, that would permit me to turn this situation to some
small advantage. It would help me if you did resign, Francis—not now, but
in a few months' time—and then accept an appointment as head of the new
Defense Mobilization Board. That way, I could appoint a man I could
count on to the Court, and I'd still have the benefit of your services in an
important job in which I am sure you would perform superbly. I have to
offer this suggestion, Francis, because what I am trying to do here is more
important than anything else."

Francis was surprised at the swiftness of his reply; his instincts were in
full control now.

"John, I couldn't do that. I couldn't consider it. My answer has to be a flat no. I'll resign if you wish, but if I do the break will have to be clean. I would not . . . cooperate to deceive anyone."

The President sighed. "All right. I suppose I knew that would be your answer. But I had to try, because the President of the United States can't be a blasted Rover Boy. He has to look at things as I just did, in order to try to get the men he wants in the jobs where he wants them, to do the work he feels has to be done. But, perhaps, unfortunately for the country, you're not the kind of man who'll play in my ball park, Francis. I regret it; at the same time I honor you for your integrity. I may be uneasy, from a political viewpoint, at having you remain on the Court, but I'm glad I can count you among my friends. Very well, Francis, you'll stay in the Court and I'll make do somehow because I'm not giving up. I can't give up. But . . . you're quite a man, sir."

Francis sensed a new calm coming over him. He could relax. He had done what he believed was right. And it had been right—in every way. "John, you've made me feel very good," he said. His voice was low in his new serenity.

"Thank God I have, Francis. That's the way you should feel." Hughes's nose wrinkled and his smile became wry. "Now I think we're both running out of words. It's been hard on both of us—all this sentiment."

Francis smiled. "Yes." Then, irrelevantly, "I suppose I'd better go home and get some sleep." After I make that phone call, he told himself.

"You certainly should." Hughes stuck out his hand and Francis took it, and the handclasp had its old firmness and warmth. "Thank you again. Go home and get some sleep and then later . . . Francis, would you do me a favor? Come over for dinner tomorrow night—you and Bea. There'll be just Liz and me."

"Yes, of course. Thanks, John—we'd like to."

"Good." The President of the United States put an arm around the justice of the Supreme Court and they walked together toward the door. "Let's say seven-thirty or so, Francis. It'll be—at last—like old times."

Francis Dalton walked out and down the wide corridor and through the West Wing foyer, and when the scattering of early-bird reporters clustered around him, he smiled at them and kept saying, "No comment, gentlemen." He liked reporters; it was too bad he couldn't tell them something. He decided he would walk down Pennsylvania Avenue to the drugstore at the corner of Seventeenth Street to make the call. He looked at his watch. It was only nine-thirty. Well, he would have to take a chance on waking her up.

QUESTIONS

1 From a constitutional perspective, why was it so important that Justice Dalton resist the President's bill to expand the size of the Supreme Court?

2 What should the relationship be between the executive and judicial branches of government?

3 What does the author mean by "no man can be trusted to be a law unto himself"?

4 What problems arise from the separation of powers and the checks and balances systems?

Reading 9
The Seven Minutes
Irving Wallace

Freedom of the press has had a long history in America and had become an integral part of colonial American politics. When members of the constitutional ratifying conventions noticed that freedom of the press was not specifically protected in the new Constitution, they demanded its prompt inclusion. Thus, when the first Congress met, freedom of the press, along with freedom of speech, religion, and assembly, was added in the very first amendment to the Constitution.

However, freedom of the press has never been an absolute right; there have always been limitations on what can be printed. The extent of these limitations has been hotly debated throughout American history, and perhaps the most controversial area of debate has been that of obscenity. Obscenity is exceedingly difficult to define, and the Supreme Court has yet to determine a clear-cut definition of it. The judicial system has therefore had to contend with obscenity on an individual case basis that has confused the issue even more.

In *The Seven Minutes* Irving Wallace writes about the subject of obscenity, or whether the book entitled *The Seven Minutes,* sold by bookseller Ben Fremont, is or is not obscene. This is the question that the jury must answer, and Ben Fremont's attorney, Mike Barrett, outlines the basis of his defense in an opening statement.

All right. Opening statement. No argument.

"Ladies and gentlemen of the jury," Mike Barrett began, "my colleague seated beside me at the nearest table, Mr. Abraham Zelkin, and I represent the defense in this complex censorship case. Since Mr. Duncan, counsel for the State, has so ably presented the California Penal Code law on criminal obscenity, as well as the law's definitions of the words 'obscene' and 'prurient,' I see no reason to burden you by repeating what he has said.

"However, in defining this law, in understanding it, in measuring it to learn whether it fits the defendant, Mr. Ben Fremont, or Mr. Jadway, the author of the book on trial, or the book itself, we come up against a problem. Mr. Duncan has made it clear that he seeks only the truth in this case. I believe him. I am sure you believe him. I can promise you that my colleague and I, too, seek only the truth in this case. I am certain Mr. Duncan believes me, and I trust that you will believe me. In short, both sides seek the truth, and both sides believe that they have found the truth. But, oddly enough, these truths are different truths. They are two truths, and yet you and I have been raised to believe there is only one truth. To evaluate the two truths, not decide which is real and which the impostor, for both truths are real, that is the problem, your problem—to find out which is the truth that is more applicable to this case involving Mr. Fremont's sale of copies of J J Jadway's *The Seven Minutes.*

"I sympathize with your problem. After all, that most American of American essayists and philosophers, Ralph Waldo Emerson, warned us early in the last century that truth is such a fly-away, such a sly-boots, truth is so untransportable and unbarrelable a commodity that it is as difficult to catch as light itself. Yet, in laying before you the plan and certain particulars of our case for the defense, let me try to catch light and shed some of it on our own image of what is the final truth in this affair.

"You have heard the law of the state as it concerns obscenity. You have heard Mr. Duncan claim that it supports his truth and the prosecution's case. Now permit me to define our truth on behalf of the defense.

"The paramount point that the defense will make, throughout this trial, is that the word 'obscene' and the word 'sex' are not synonymous, are not one and the same."

Barret heard the scraping of a chair on the other side of the courtroom, and he turned as Elmo Duncan came to his feet.

"I must object, Your Honor," said Duncan. "Counsel for the defense is certainly being argumentative."

Barrett looked toward the bench. Judge Upshaw had knitted his brow. "I don't believe he is arguing, Mr. Duncan. He is defining. A definition can make its way from a negative premise. I am going to overrule the objection, and allow defense counsel to develop his definition. . . . Mr. Barrett. you may continue along this line, but with prudence. Take care not to exceed the limitations of an opening statement."

For a moment, Barrett's hopes had been suspended, threatened, had begun to slip out of reach. Now he almost sagged with relief, grasped hope once again, and turned optimistically to the jury.

"Ladies and gentlemen," he said with quiet insistence, "during the course of this trial the defense will try to prove that because the book *The Seven Minutes* unfolds its human drama within the framework of the sex act, that does not automatically make it a work of obscenity. A student of censorship, Robert W. Haney, has written: 'Law, as conceived in the Declaration of Independence, is not a social device to advance the cause of virtue. It is a protective device to insure the freedom and the opportunities that men need for their happiness and their development. Freedom is not the right to be virtuous; it is the right to do as one pleases, limited only when one person's exercise of it endangers freedom of others, or when it results in overt actions that society deems destructive of its own purposes.'

"Ladies and gentlemen of the jury, I cannot emphasize this interpretation of our law too strongly. Neither federal nor California state law was established to promote virtue, but, rather, to protect the citizenry against unscrupulous distortion and misrepresentation of pure and healthy sexual acts.

"The procedure of the defense in this case will be guided by the wisdom of some of the most eminent legal minds in our time. It was Judge Jerome Frank who once included the following in a decision: 'I think that no sane man thinks socially dangerous the arousing of normal sex desires. Consequently, if reading obscene books has merely that consequence, Congress, it would seem, can constitutionally no more suppress books than it can prevent the mailing of many other objects, such as perfumes, for example, which notoriously produce that result.'

"Yes, indeed, if a book is to be censored for arousing desire, when shall we bring Arpège to trial?"

Even as many of the jurors smiled, and a few of them laughed, Barrett could hear the District Attorney's stentorian objection behind him.

Barrett turned around in time to hear Judge Upshaw concur with Duncan. "Objection sustained . . . Mr. Barrett, you have gone too far. I must warn you—you are exceeding the limits of the opening statement."

Barrett bowed his head slightly. "Forgive me, Your Honor." He remembered Duncan's earlier words and repeated them. "I hope you will pardon my overenthusiasm."

He could see Duncan's scowl, then Zelkin's grin, and he confronted the jury once more. His opponent had opened the door to argument. He had taken advantage of this opening to enter into the minds of the jury. At last, he could see, they had accepted him on equal terms with the prosecutor. Fair enough.

"Ladies and gentlemen of the jury," said Barrett. "The counsel for the People has told us that in a censorship case, centering upon the social merit or lack of that merit in a work of literature, the testimony cannot consist entirely of facts, but must of necessity also include the opinion of experts. With this we concur. Whenever we can, we shall present to you facts in defense of *The Seven Minutes* and of Mr. Fremont's right to sell it. More often, since the social importance of the book—since the story of the book and the sex in the book—since the value of the book—depend upon human judgment of it, we shall present as evidence of its worth representative experts who will offer testimony about the motivations of the author and the meaning of his creative work, and we shall also present the so-called average person in whose contemporary society the book is being sold.

"The first precedent for allowing expert opinion in a trial occurred as far back as 1917, during a censorship trial in New York which concerned the French classic *Mademoiselle de Maupin,* by Gautier. In that trial the judges accepted, in support of the classic, literary testimony quoted from Henry James and other knowledgeable literary figures. Then, in 1938, when *Life* magazine was brought into court for publishing a picture story entitled 'The Birth of a Baby,' which a religious organization condemned and which the New York servants of the law charged with being obscene, lewd, filthy, disgusting—the birth of a baby filthy and disgusting—then and only then was the opinion of expert witnesses who appeared on the stand in person a decisive factor in deciding a criminal obscenity trial. Said the court when rendering its verdict of acquittal, the defense had 'produced as witnesses responsible public health authorities, welfare workers and educators who testified to the sincerity, honesty and educational value of the picture story complained of.' While the prosecution objected to the testimony of such witnesses, and while the court agreed that the prosecution was correct in its protest, the court added, 'Such evidence is, however, rationally helpful and in recent years Courts have considered the opinions of qualified persons.'

"And so the defense shall lean heavily on the opinions of qualified persons. Through these persons we shall prove that *The Seven Minutes* was created with artistic integrity, was accepted in many quarters as a literary masterpiece, and has survived to become a milestone of enlightenment in our understanding of the relationship between the sexes and of sex itself. Through these qualified persons we shall prove that contemporary community standards are not static, are not today what they were a decade or a half century or a century ago, and that J J Jadway was a prophet when he produced a work more than three decades ago that is in keeping with the shift and progress of contemporary standards as they have come to be today. And we shall prove that even if some of the book is still in advance of our times, it nevertheless deserves to be heard."

He was sorely tempted to elaborate.

Seeking time to determine whether he dared risk going beyond the restrictions of his opening statement, Barrett stepped back from the jury box and took a long sip of water from the glass on the defense table.

He considered trying to enter a quotation from Justice Douglas: "Government should be concerned with anti-social conduct, not with utterances. Thus, if the First Amendment guarantee of freedom of speech and press is to mean anything in this field, it must allow protests even against the moral code that the standard of the day sets for the community. In other words, literature should not be suppressed merely because it offends the moral code of the censor."

This was improper evidence, of course, but he might slip it through before an objection stopped him, even as Duncan had succeeded in doing in his own exhortation.

He weighed what might possibly follow this. He might then say, "It will be our argument also, supported by the testimony of witnesses, that *The Seven Minutes* must be judged by the author's utterances alone. Any evidence alleging that anti-social conduct has been provided by a reading of this book, we shall contend, is legally inadmissible, and if it should be found admissible we shall prove that it has no basis in fact. According to a definition in the California Penal Code, based on Roth versus the United States, 1957, 'Punishment for obscenity is not dependent upon showing that obscene material creates clear and present danger of anti-social conduct or probability that it will induce its recipients to such conduct.' We shall contend, until directed to do otherwise, that conduct resulting from reading a book has no legal bearing on this censorship trial. If we are advised from the bench that it does have bearing, then we shall prove, through the introduction of expert authority, that—in the words of a Supreme Court Justice—written matter is not a significant factor, as balanced against other factors, in influencing an individual's deviation from community standards."

Should this statement stand up, Barrett felt that he might try to clarify it further: "If called upon to do so, we shall prove that the reading of erotica does not beget violence. Dr. Wendell B. Pomeroy, when associated with the Kinsey Institute for Sex Research, participated in team interviews involving more than eighteen thousand subjects. He found that pornographic writings were insignificant sexual stimuli. In this trial, we are prepared to substantiate this finding with the testimony of our own witnesses. And where pornographic writings do produce, in the reader, sexual fantasies, we are prepared to prove not only that this is harmless but that often it has a salutary effect. According to Dr. Sol Gordon, of New York, 'In thirteen years of practice as a clinical psychologist, I have not encountered a single adolescent who was harmed in any way by reading pornography. My own conviction, based on experience, is that the people who organize crusades against pornography are, by and large, the same persons who oppose sex education and who spread the neurosis-breeding notion that it is possible for a thought to be evil. If such people could only realize that thoughts, daydreams, fantasies and desires are not in themselves reprehensible, a large victory would be scored for mental health.' Indeed, years ago, it was Havelock Ellis who suggested that just as youngsters find relief in an escape into fairy tales, adults find similar relief in perusing sex fiction. More recently, two eminent psychoanalysts, Drs. Phyllis and Eberhard Kronhausen, have concluded that the reading of both erotic realism and obscenity is a desirable practice because it provides a safety valve for antisocial feelings by diverting them into acts of mere fantasy."

To elaborate or not to elaborate, this at the moment was Barrett's inner dilemma. What might be attempted had passed through his mind in a matter of seconds. Now his mind tried to resolve the dilemma. Judge Upshaw had suffered Duncan's endeavor, and his own, to encompass closing arguments into opening statements, and at this point the jurist would probably endure no more. A severe or caustic reprimand from the bench would negate all Barrett had achieved for the defense. It was no use. He must abide by the rules.

Barrett's gaze dropped to Zelkin, and it seemed his partner had read his mind, for Zelkin gave him an almost imperceptible nod. Reassured, Barrett set down his glass and turned back to the jury box.

"The counsel for the People," said Barrett, "sees this case as involving itself with three issues. As counsel for the defense, I see this case as involving only one issue—not three, not two, but one single issue. The State's first issue, whether Ben Fremont did or did not distribute a book called *The Seven Minutes,* will not be an issue for the defense. We concede that Mr. Fremont displayed and sold the book. He is in the business of selling books. He is not an arbiter of literature. He is the proprietor of a bookstore in the community of Oakwood, and his activity and livelihood are the selling of books the year around. He is a member of that noble profession which Thomas Jefferson defended in 1814 when he wrote to a persecuted Philadelphia bookseller: 'I am really mortified to be told that in the United States of America . . . a question about a book can be carried before the civil magistrate.'

"As to the State's second issue, that Mr. Fremont knowingly sold an obscene book, we feel that this so-called issue is not an issue in itself but only a part of the larger issue that we recognize as central to this trial. Because, for the defense, the sole issue that remains is whether *The Seven Minutes,* by J J Jadway, is legally obscene. The entire case, as we see it, centers on what is obscene and what is not."

Once again Barrett was tempted to tread on quicksand, in an effort to underline his point.

He ached to relate what might be an effective anecdote. He wanted to say, "Can anyone dictate tastes, when tastes and taboos differ so? They differ from state to state of this Union, and in every country of this world. One is reminded of Sir Richard Burton's story about a group of Englishmen who went to visit a Moslem sultan in the desert. As the party of Englishmen watched, the Moslem's wife tumbled off her camel. In doing so, her dress slipped up and her private parts were revealed to all. Was the Sultan embarrassed? On the contrary, he was pleased—because his wife had kept her face covered during her accident."

Barrett felt certain that the jurors would enjoy this, and his point would be made. Yet he knew that he would never get the wife off the camel. Duncan's objection would stay her before her fall. There was no point in wasting the Sultan's wife now. He would save her for his summation on some future day.

With an inward sigh, Barrett decided on taking the straight and narrow forensic path.

"Ladies and gentlemen of the jury, if we can prove, as we shall attempt to do, that this book was written honestly, that its contents do not go beyond the limits of candor, when judged by contemporary community standards, that the tale it tells is artistic and of vast social importance, then we shall have proved that this work has not violated Section 311.2 of the California Penal Code. And thus, if it is not obscene, it falls naturally into place that Mr. Fremont cannot be charged with knowingly having distributed an obscene work. To state this another way, if we can prove to your satisfaction, ladies and gentlemen of the jury, that *The Seven Minutes* is not obscene, then it holds that we will have proved Ben Fremont innocent of any crime."

Mike Barrett hesitated. Earlier he had planned to conclude on another note. With a flourish, really. In fact, he had rehearsed it before coming to court this morning:

"Once, from the highest bench in the land, Justice Felix Frankfurter laid down the following dictum in voting against an appeal urging censorship. 'The State,' said Justice Frankfurter, 'insists that, by thus quarantining the general reading public against books not too rugged for grown men and women in order to shield juvenile innocence, it is exercising its power to promote general welfare. Surely, this is to burn the house to roast the pig.'

"Ladies and gentlemen of the jury, in this homily the defense has found the legend to place on the banner it will carry aloft throughout this trial, and it is our banner that shall lead us where we must go.

"We refuse to burn down our house—our house and yours—merely to roast a pig."

Beautiful. Effective. And, now, in this growingly nonpermissive atmosphere, totally inadmissible.

Damn.

What had he just said to the jury? Yes. If we can prove *The Seven Minutes* is not obscene, we will have proved Ben Fremont not guilty of any crime.

Better to leave on that pure note than on the discordance of an objection from Duncan.

Barrett fixed his gaze on the jurors.

"You have heard our promise," he said. "Soon you will hear our evidence." He paused. "Ladies and gentlemen of the jury, thank you very much."

QUESTIONS

1 What is the Supreme Court's current definition of obscenity, and does it agree with your personal conception of what is obscene?
2 Does the present court definition of obscenity agree with your concept of what is obscene?
3 What are the larger implications of the problem of obscenity?

Reading 10
The New Centurions
Joseph Wambaugh

No segment of American society is more vitally concerned with or has a more direct impact on civil rights or liberties than the police. They need to know at all times what constitutes a legal infringement on a citizen's liberty, since civil rights are so highly revered by Americans. These rights are so precious that several of the original thirteen colonies refused to sign the Constitution until essential civil rights were added.

The following chapter from *The New Centurions* concerns a police science class that all Los Angeles police cadets must take prior to becoming officers. In this session cadets Roy Fehler and Sam Isenberg debate an issue concerning search and seizure raised by their instructor, Sergeant Harris. In their comments on this particular aspect of civil liberties the cadets express certain attitudes toward the courts, popular among police, that have stressful implications.

Roy Fehler had to admit it pleased him when he overheard two of his classmates mention his name in a whispered conversation during a smoking break after class. He heard the cadet mutter "intellectual," reverently, he thought, just after he recorded the highest score in the report writing class conducted by Officer Willis. He found the academic portion of recruit training unchallenging and if it weren't for some difficulties on the pistol range and his lack of endurance on the P.T. field, he would probably be the top cadet in his class and win the Smith & Wesson always awarded to the top cadet at graduation. It would be a tragedy, he thought, if someone like Plebesly won the revolver merely because he could run faster or shoot better than Roy.

He was anxious for Sergeant Harris to come in the classroom for their three hours of criminal law. It was the most stimulating part of recruit training even though Harris was only an adequate teacher. Roy had bought a copy of Fricke's *California Criminal Law,* and had read it twice in the past two weeks. He had challenged Harris on several points of law and believed that Harris had become more alert of late for fear of being embarassed by a knowledgeable recruit. The classroom quieted abruptly.

Sergeant Harris strode to the front of the class, spread his notes on the lectern and lit the first of the several cigarettes he would smoke during his lecture. He had a face like porous concrete, but Roy thought he wore his uniform well. The tailored blue wool seemed particularly attractive on tall slim men, and Roy wondered how he would look when he had the blue uniform and black Sam Browne.

"We're going to continue with search and seizure of evidence," said Harris, scratching the bald spot at the crown of his rust-colored hair.

"By the way, Fehler," said Sergeant Harris, "you were right yesterday about the uncorroborated testimony of an accomplice being sufficient to prove the corpus delicti. But it isn't enough to convict."

"No, of course not," said Roy, nodding his thanks to Harris for the acknowledgement. He wasn't sure whether Harris appreciated the significance of a few well-placed brain-teasing questions. It was the student who brought a class to life. He had learned this from Professor Raymond who had encouraged him to specialize in criminology when he was drifting aimlessly in the social sciences unable to find a specialty which really interested him. And it was Professor Raymond who begged him not to drop out of college, because he had added so much to the three classes he had taken from the kindly round little man with the burning brown eyes. But he was tired of college; even the independent study with Professor Raymond had begun to bore him. It had come to him suddenly one sleepless night when the presence of Dorothy and her pregnancy was oppressing him that he ought to leave college and join the police department for a year, two years, until he learned something of crime and criminals that might not be available to the criminologist.

The next day he applied at City Hall wondering if he should phone his father or wait until he was actually sworn in, as he would be in about three months, if he passed all the tests and survived the character investigation which he knew would pose no problem. His father was terribly disappointed and his older brother Carl had reminded him that his education had already cost the family business in excess of nine thousand dollars, especially since he could not wait until he finished college to marry, and that in any event, a criminologist would be of little use to a restaurant supply business. Roy had told Carl that he would pay back every cent, and he certainly intended to, but it was difficult living on the policeman's beginning salary which was not the advertised four hundred and eighty-nine dollars a month—not when they deducted for your pension, Police Relief, the Police Protective League, the Police Credit Union which loaned the money for the uniforms, income tax, and the medical plan. But he vowed he'd pay Carl and his father every cent. And he'd finish college and be a criminologist eventually, never making the money his brother Carl would make, but being infinitely happier.

"Yesterday we talked about the famous cases like Cahan, Rochin, and others," said Sergeant Harris. "And we talked about Mapp versus Ohio which any rookie would know was illegal search and seizure, and I mentioned how it sometimes seems to policemen that the court is lying in wait for bad cases like Mapp versus Ohio so they can restrict police power a little more. Now that you're policemen, or almost policemen, you're going to become very interested in the decisions handed down by the courts in the area of search and seizure. You're going to be upset, confused, and generally pissed off most of the time, and you're going to hear locker room bitching about the fact that most landmark decisions are five to four, and how can a working cop be expected to make a sudden decision in the heat of combat and then be second-guessed by the Vestal Virgins of the Potomac, and all that other crap. But in my opinion, that kind of talk is self-defeating. We're only concerned with the U.S. and California supreme courts and a couple of appellate courts. So don't worry about some of these freakish decisions that an individual judge hands down. Even if it's your case and it's one you wanted to win. Chances are the defendant will be busted again before long and we'll get another crack at him. And the judge's decision ends right there on the bench. It's not going to have a goddamn thing to do with the next case you try.

"Now I know I got you guys pretty confused yesterday with the problems of search incident to a lawful arrest. We know we can search when?" Sergeant Harris waved a burning cigarette vaguely toward the rear of the room.

Roy didn't bother to turn toward the voice which answered, "When you have a search warrant, or when you have consent, or incident to a lawful arrest." The voice Roy knew belonged to Samuel Isenberg, the only other cadet whom Roy felt might challenge him scholastically.

"Right," said Sergeant Harris, blowing a cloud of smoke through his nose. "Half you people will never get a search warrant in your entire careers. Most of the two hundred thousand arrests we make in a year are made on the basis of reasonable cause to believe a felony has been committed, or because a crime has been committed in the officer's presence. You're going to stumble onto crimes and criminals and bang! You've got to move, not take six hours to get a search warrant. It's for that reason that we're not going to talk about this kind of search. I've saved the other kind of search until today because to me it's the most challenging—that's search incident to a lawful arrest. If the court ever takes this kind of search away from us we'll be nearly out of business."

Isenberg raised his hand, and Sergeant Harris nodded while taking an incredible puff on the cigarette. What was a fairly good-sized butt was now scorching his fingers. He snuffed it out as Isenberg said, "Would you repeat, sir, about the search of the premises ninety-five feet from the defendent's house?"

"I was afraid of that." Harris smiled, shrugged, and lit another cigarette. "I shouldn't bring up those cases. I did what I criticize other officers for doing, bitching about controversial cases and prophesying doom. Okay, I just said that it hasn't yet been defined what *under the defendant's control* means in terms of search of the premises incident to the arrest. The court has deemed in its infinite wisdom that an arrest ninety-five feet away from the house did not give officers the right to go into the house and search under the theory of the defendant having control of the premises. Also, I mentioned that in another case a person sixty feet away was deemed to have control of a car in question. And then I mentioned a third case in which officers arrested some bookmakers in their car a half block away and the court held the search of the car and premises was reasonable.

"But don't worry about that kind of crap. I shouldn't have mentioned it anyway because I'm basically an optimist. I always see the glass half full not half empty. Some policemen predict that the courts will eventually strip us of all our right to search incident to arrest, but that would cripple us. I don't think it will happen. I feel that one of these days the Chief Sorcerer in Washington and his eight little apprentices will get themselves together and all this will be straightened out."

The class tittered and Roy felt himself becoming irked. Harris just couldn't resist criticizing the Supreme Court, thought Roy. He hadn't heard any instructor discuss the law without taking a few shots at the Court. Harris seemed reasonable but he probably felt obligated to do it too. So far, all of the cases Roy had read, that were so bitterly opposed by the instructors, seemed to him just and intelligent. They were based on libertarian principles and it seemed to him unfair to say such thoughtful decisions were unrealistic.

"Okay you guys, quit leading me off on tangents. We're supposed to be talking about searches incident to a lawful arrest. How about this one: Two officers observe a cab double-parked in front of a hotel. The fare, a man, gets out of the front seat. A woman comes out of the hotel and gets in the rear seat. Another man not with the woman walks up and gets in the back seat with the woman. Two policemen observe the action and decide to investigate. They approach and order the occupants out of the cab. They observe the man remove his hand from the juncture of the seat and back cushion. The officers remove the rear cushion and find three marijuana cigarettes. The man was convicted. Was the decision affirmed or denied by the appellant court? Anyone want to make a guess?"

"Denied," said Guminski, a thin, wiry-haired man of about thirty, whom Roy guessed to be the oldest cadet in the class.

"See. You guys are already thinking like cops," Harris chuckled. "You're ready to believe the courts are screwing us every time. Well you're wrong. The conviction was affirmed. But there was something I failed to mention that contributed to the decision. What do you think it might be?"

Roy raised his hand and when Harris nodded, Roy asked. "What time of day was it?"

"Good," said Sergeant Harris. "You might've guessed, it was an unusual hour. About 3:00 A.M. Now on what grounds could they search the cab?"

"Incident to a lawful arrest," said Roy, without raising his hand or waiting for Harris to nod.

"Who were they arresting?" asked Harris.

Roy was sorry he had responded so quickly. He realized he was being trapped. "Not the defendant or the woman," he said slowly, while his mind worked furiously. "The cabdriver!"

The class burst out laughing but was silenced by a wave of Harris' nicotine-stained left hand. Harris bared his large brownish teeth in a grin and said, "Go ahead, Fehler, what's your reasoning?"

"They could arrest the cabbie for double-parking," said Roy. "That's a violation, and then search incident to the lawful arrest."

"Not bad," said Harris. "I like to see you people thinking even when you're wrong."

Hugh Franklin, the broad-shouldered recruit who sat next to Roy at the alphabetically arranged tables, chuckled louder than Roy felt was necessary. Franklin did not like him, Roy was certain. Franklin was an all-American jock strapper. A high school letterman according to the conversations they had the first few days in the academy. Then three years in the navy, where he played baseball and toured the Orient, thoroughly enjoying himself, and now to the police department, when he couldn't make it in Class D professional baseball.

"Why is Fehler wrong?" Harris asked the class, and Roy became annoyed that the entire class should be asked to attack his answer. Why didn't Harris just give the reason instead of asking everyone to comment? Could it be that Harris was trying to embarrass him? Perhaps he didn't like having a recruit in the class who took the trouble to do independent study in criminal law and not just blindly accept the legal interpretations which evolve from the police point of view.

"Yes, Isenberg," said Harris, and this time Roy turned around so that he would not miss Isenberg's annoying manner of answering questions.

"I doubt that the search of the cab could be justified incident to the arrest of the driver for double-parking," said Isenberg carefully, his dark-lidded black eyes moving from Harris to Roy and back to the instructor. "It's true the driver committed a traffic violation and could be cited, and a traffic ticket is technically an arrest, but how could you search the cab for contraband? That has nothing to do with a traffic violation, does it?"

"Are you asking me?" said Harris.

"No sir, that's my answer." Isenberg smiled shyly, and Roy felt disgust for Isenberg's pretense of humility. He felt the same toward Plebesly and the diffidence he showed when someone expressed admiration for his athletic prowess. He believed them both to be conceited men. Isenberg was another one, he knew, who was just discharged from the army. He wondered how many men joined the Department because they were simply looking for a job and how many like himself had more serious motives.

"Was the search incident to the arrest of anyone?" asked Harris.

"No, I don't think so," said Isenberg, clearing his throat nervously. "I don't think anyone was under arrest at the time the officer found the contraband. The officer could detain and interrogate people under unusual circumstances at night according to Giske versus Sanders, and I don't think there was anything unreasonable in ordering them out of the cab. The officers had a justifiable suspicion that something unusual was going on. When the defendant reached behind the seat I think that might be construed as a furtive action." Isenberg's voice trailed off and several recruits including Roy raised their hands.

Harris looked at no one but Roy. "Go ahead, Fehler," he said.

"I don't think the officers had the right to order them out of the cab. And when were they arrested, after they found the narcotics? What if they would have got out of the cab and just walked away? Would the officers have the right to stop them?"

"How about that, Isenberg?" asked Harris, lighting a fresh cigarette with a battered silver lighter. "Could the officers stop them from walking away, before the contraband was found?"

"Uh, yes, I think so," said Isenberg looking at Roy, who interrupted him.

"Were they under arrest then?" asked Roy. "They must have been under arrest if the officers could stop them from walking away. And if they were under arrest what was their crime? The marijuana wasn't found for several seconds after they had them already under arrest."

Roy smiled indulgently to show Isenberg and Harris there were no hard feelings at having proved Isenberg wrong.

"The point is, they were not under arrest, Fehler," said Isenberg, addressing Roy directly for the first time. "We have the right to stop and interrogate. The person is obliged to identify himself and explain what's going on. And we can resort to any means to make him submit. Yet we haven't arrested him for any crime. If he explains what's going on and it's reasonable, we release him. I think that's what Giske versus Sanders meant. So in this case, the officers stopped, interrogated, and recovered the marijuana during their investigation. Then and only then were the suspects placed under arrest."

Roy knew from Harris' pleased expression that Isenberg was correct.

"How could you prove someone else hadn't dumped the marijuana behind the seat?" asked Roy, unable to dull the sharp edge on his voice.

"I should've mentioned that the cabbie testified to cleaning out the back of the cab earlier in the evening because of a sick passenger who threw up back there," said Harris. "And no one had been in the back seat until the woman and the defendant got in."

"That certainly makes a difference," said Roy, appealing to Harris for some concession to his interpretation.

"Well, that wasn't the issue I was concerned with," said Harris. "It was the question of searching prior to an actual arrest that I wanted someone to bring out of this case, and Isenberg did it beautifully. You all understand, don't you?"

"Yes sir," said Roy, "but the case would certainly have been reversed if the cabbie hadn't testified to cleaning out the back that same evening. That was certainly an important point, sir."

"Yes, Fehler," Sergeant Harris sighed. "You were partly right. I should've mentioned that, Fehler."

QUESTIONS

1 If judges are supposed to be the interpreters of the law and the police are supposed to ensure that citizens uphold the judicial interpretations of laws, what is the danger in the attitudes expressed by the Los Angeles police cadets to our constitutional system?
2 What should constitute a "legal search and seizure?"
3 Should criminal procedures like the search warrant be more precisely defined and why?
4 Do the views of the police toward civil rights differ significantly from the general public, and, if so, why?

Part Three

People and Politics—
The Inputs

In Part One, "Political Culture," we viewed the political impact or consequences of attitudes and orientations toward politics. In Part Two, we
looked at the constitutional framework or context of American politics. We
now turn to the impact that people have on American politics through the
expression of public opinion, voting, political party activities, and interest
group activities. These are all ways in which Americans can gain access to
their government and ensure that politicians serve the people as well as
themselves.

Public opinion and voting (the formal expression of public opinion) are
two vital links between Americans and their representatives in government.
Politicians measure the public pulse by reading public opinion polls, listening to constituents, and exposing themselves to a wide array of mass media
information. There are many factors that influence political decision making other than what the public thinks, but the astute politician keeps a
constant eye on shifts in public preferences. Politicians who ignore their
constituents' opinions may find themselves voted out of office in the next
election.

The section on public opinion and voting behavior focuses on the ways in which the public's opinions influence and are influenced by politics. In *All in the Family* a contrast is drawn between the old ways and the new ways of appealing to voters. *The 480* demonstrates that scientific analysis of politics can not only ascertain the current political attitudes but also determine the means by which those attitudes can be manipulated. This point is further developed in *Dark Horse,* which shows the importance of polling and pollsters in modern elections.

While public opinion and voting behavior are means by which Americans can express their individual interests, the process of aggregating or combining those interests into more general demands is accomplished through political parties and interest groups. Parties, while not mentioned in the Constitution, are an important mediator between Americans and their government. Most Americans express a preference for one of the two major parties, and as a result, our two-party system has been quite stable.

American political parties are huge, decentralized organizations whose main tasks are to take stands on the issues of the day, help organize governmental institutions, and, most importantly, help recruit and elect officials to staff our government. This last function is seen in *The Politician* or opening selection in Political Parties and Elections, in which the process of recruiting or selecting candidates is shown.

After the candidate is selected, the next step is the party convention. Fletcher Knebel and Charles Bailey's aptly titled book *Convention* shows all the complexity, confusion, hoopla, and human drama that characterize a presidential nominating convention. The candidate's ensuing problem of trying to appeal to the electorate during the campaign that follows the convention is examined in Edwin O'Connor's *All in the Family.*

Interest groups, the other means by which Americans can organize to express their demands, is the last topic in "People and Politics." Political parties are usually too large and unwieldy for the average person to have much effect on them, and so interest groups have arisen as an alternative way of pursuing political interests. Interest groups accomplish this by pooling many people's resources and aiming at a few specific and therefore attainable goals. Citizens whose interests have been too often ignored, such as blacks, women, Chicanos, Indians, the elderly, and consumers, are finding that pressure groups are a much more effective way of getting their voices heard than trying to use the regular channels of government.

Many political scientists thus see groups as the heart of the political process and the two selections in the Interest Groups section lend credence to this view. In *The Ninth Wave* an interest group is trying to get its stands adopted by choosing the "right" candidate to support, perhaps the most effective technique that such groups employ. In *Power* a labor union delegation uses another typical interest group method when it attempts to persuade an officeholder, the President, that its cause is just.

Public Opinion
and Voting Behavior

Reading 11
All in the Family
Edwin O'Connor

The heart of local politics in America used to be the ward heeler. This
was a person who was responsible to a political boss for a small geo-
graphic area or ward. He had to make sure that those people were given
jobs, food, clothing, shelter, and any other essentials that they needed.
In turn, the ward members would vote for the "right" candidate on election day. This system came to be known as the political machine, since
the ward could be counted on to automatically elect the boss's chosen
candidate as long as its material needs were being met.

   This system of political bosses and machines was known as the
"old politics"; however, with the election of Franklin Roosevelt as President in 1932, this system began to crumble. Americans became more
and more concerned with what was happening in Washington than in
city hall, and power began to shift away from local bosses to the federal
government.

   Another change brought more trouble for the local bosses; in place
of the old machine-trained politicians came the college-trained and
idealistic candidates who owed no political debts to anyone. Furthermore, they disregarded the party machine and emphasized radio, television, and other mass media, and large volunteer campaign organizations. These new campaign methods became the heart of what is now
called the "new politics."

   Certain aspects of the old politics still persist, however, and conflict
at times with the new politics. It is precisely this point that Jack and
Charles Kinsella are discussing in the selection from *All in the Family*.
Jack is a former newspaperman who worked for Frank Skeffington, once
a powerful political boss who served as mayor and governor. Charles is
Jack's cousin and present Governor of the state and the epitome of the
"new politician."

By the way, how did you make out with the Commander? Did you have a
pleasant chat?"

   "Fascinating. Thanks a lot."

   "I thought it might be useful for an old-timer like you to see that even
in the new politics some things haven't changed."

   "Including techniques," I said, and I told him now what I had suspected at the time: that in diverting the Commander to me he had deliberately
been using an old Skeffington ploy.

   "Oh," he said, "I'm not above borrowing techniques. Especially if they
work. Incidentally, I don't share Pa's feeling about your old boss. I don't

buy the legend, either, but he was better than Pa thinks. He knew how to get elected most of the time, and he knew how to maneuver all of the time. I'd say a man who could do that was a pretty fair politician."

I said, "That isn't exactly the same thing as saying that he was a pretty fair governor, is it? Or mayor?"

"I guess it isn't," he said pleasantly, "but then, I guess he wasn't." He looked at me again with the same slightly amused expression and said, "Do you really think he was, Jack?"

I said, "That's the old argument, isn't it? I've heard it ever since the first day I met him. I don't know how good he was. I do know that he's the only one who ever did anything. And I know that if I just look around this city today, about every major improvement I can see—buildings, tunnels, roads, playgrounds—was started or finished or helped along by one man. So I guess that's a kind of answer, isn't it?"

For someone who quit politics in disgust," he said, "you're surprisingly loyal to old politicians. Or at least to one old politician. Although I wouldn't mind betting that hasn't much to do with politics." He added shrewdly, "It's probably all personal. Anyway, I know those major improvements. Or those of them you can see: half of them have fallen down. Your old friend's contractor pals didn't always use the best materials. By the way, you never happened to look at the city's books for the years all this improving was going on, did you?"

I said defensively, "Crooked books, I imagine?"

"No," he said, "not crooked. You're behind the times, Jack: you believe in the legend. I don't want to strip this picturesque old figure of even a shred of his glamour, but he wasn't the great quixotic crook people still think he was. The awful fact is he wasn't a crook at all. Or not much of a one. By the standards of his time, that is: remember that those were the days of 'honest graft.' But the books weren't crooked. They were worse: they were incredible."

"I'm not too surprised. I don't think bookkeeping was his strongest point."

"I'd agree with that," he said dryly. "You know, when I first went to City Hall I thought I'd better have a look at the records, just to see what had been going on. Well, to begin with, I had to find them. It wasn't easy, as you can imagine, but they finally turned up in some side room as dark as a closet, full of old newspapers and sneakers and underwear and, naturally, the official records of the city. All this was presided over by a little old Irishman who'd been there forever and who—again naturally—couldn't read. I got the books out, I had the city's accountants go over them, and then I put Pa's people to work. It all added up to one thing: Skeffington had no financial sense at all. None. He couldn't have known the first thing about money. Except that you took it in and you paid it out, from anyone and to anyone, and of course it became a matter of policy to pay out more than you took in. That was the way he ran the city, and that was the way he ran the state. And it never hurt him for a minute. Not many people knew about it, and most of those who knew didn't care. That's the way things were then. He was very popular, and that's what elections were around here in those days: popularity contests."

I thought of his own enormous margin of victory; I said, "And you don't think they are today?"

"Sure they are, but there's a difference, isn't there?" he said. "It's not that simple any more. Look at it this way: yesterday I got eighty-five thousand votes more than Skeffington did on his best run. Of course we have more voters now, but there are a few things left you can't blame on the population explosion. My percentage of the total vote was still way ahead of his. And why? Because I'm more popular now than he was then?" He smiled again and said, "Nobody is. We both know that. Nobody's got that kind of popularity any more. It was a personal thing that depended on tribal loyalties, immigrants on the way up, racial spokesmen, Communion Breakfasts—there's some of that still around, of course, but in Skeffington's campaigns it was the big thing. You could do very well for yourself if you could get up and tell a few funny stories, quote Robert Emmet, and shout 'Ireland must be free!' for a finish. Today it's slightly more complicated."

"You need a whole new set of quotations," I said.

"That's right. Among other things."

"Which ones? Who are you quoting these days, Charles?"

"Roosevelt, George Washington Carver, Ben-Gurion," he said imperturbably. "And, just occasionally, Robert Emmet. So as not to slight a minority group. And then on another level, and because I have an extremely well-read staff—you've heard about my support from the intellectuals—Eliot, Unamuno, Aquinas, and Alexander Pope. We try to box the compass, you see." He gave me the look he had given me twice before, and said, "Quotation-wise."

It was to me a curious and a fascinating conversation—curious because although the room was still full of family, Charles and I were talking in unbroken privacy: none of the others had even come our way. And yet I had no feeling that we were deliberately being "let alone"; it was rather as if the general family atmosphere had relaxed with the finish of my Uncle Jimmy's centralizing performance, and the party had split up into little groups, each one returning for a moment to its own habitual concerns. Phil and Flossie had gone over by the fireplace where Phil was talking in a low voice, and Flossie was listening and slowly pulling on her gloves. Directly above their heads on the rear wall hung a large painting which I had noticed earlier, but which I looked at more carefully now. I knew that I had seen it somewhere before, that it had some special significance for me, but just for the moment I couldn't place it, pin it down. Then, suddenly, I remembered: it was the painting of my Uncle Jimmy in his Knight of Malta costume that I had last seen so many years ago in his Irish castle—had it now been permanently transferred to Charles's house? My Uncle Jimmy himself had moved from the center of the room and had joined my Aunt Gert who, having been silent for most of the evening, was now talking emphatically to him; I gathered that this might be business, for she did not at this time seem to be on the point of any merriment. What she was telling him must have been of some importance, for he was listening without his customary impatience, but even so, every once in a while I saw him shift his head just slightly and flick a fast inquisitive look in our direction. It was not his habit to be left out of anything, not even for a moment, and while it was now clear that whatever my Aunt Gert was saying was significant enough to keep him with her, I knew that he ached to be over here with us, listening to his son.

He might have been surprised by what he heard—although, come to think of it, perhaps not. I was. Not by anything Charles had said—for by now I didn't really care whether Skeffington had been a great governor or a good mayor or even a financial responsible; it was all in the past, and whatever he had been couldn't modify my affection for someone who had been unfailingly kind to me, and with whom it had been such great fun and so exciting for a young man to be, day after day—but by the authority, the easy confidence with which he said it. The same man who, twenty years ago, had known nothing about politics and who could hardly bear to sit through my stories about Skeffington and City Hall and local politicians, was now calmly setting me straight on the facts of my old scene and of political life in general. It was a queer reversal, more than a little incongruous, and yet as I listened to him talk, so easily, so surely, so peculiarly impressively, I didn't think of this at all. What I did think of was that Charles seemed to have changed far more than I had suspected, and I think it was only now, in these few moments of talk, that I began to realize what I suppose I should have realized long before: that Charles was *in fact* the Governor, and that as Governor, and as the man who had worked to become Governor, he was a different and indeed a far more formidable figure than the Charles I had always known.

But all this came from a manner, an attitude, a presence, for there was certainly nothing formidable in anything he said. He talked on casually, apparently in no hurry at all—although of course he knew very well that everyone downstairs was waiting for his reappearance. Just as, of course, he knew very well that they would continue to wait: in this gathering no one was likely to go home imprudently. He said to me, "It's all changed, in every way. It's a matter of style as much as anything else. Frank Dooley is a good example. Do you remember him?"

"Vaguely. I remember the family, of course." The Dooleys had been a conspicuous political family: Frank Dooley's grandfather had been a ward boss, his father had run the state senate, his uncle had been a Superior Court judge for decades. But Frank himself . . . I said, "He hasn't done well, has he? Wasn't he supposed to be a comer? It seems to me they used to talk about him that way."

"He's old hat," Charles said. "He's actually younger than we are, but people think of him as an old-fashioned pol, and that's the kiss of death these days. He had all sorts of possibilities. He's not bad-looking, he dresses well, he's a good talker, and his father sensed which way the wind was blowing in time to send him to a non-Catholic college. The first Ivy Leaguer in his family. The New Breed. But it didn't work. He got to the City Council and that's as far as he'll ever get. He wants to be attorney general and he wouldn't be a bad one. He's reasonably bright, he's not bad on civil liberties—that's the big thing today, by the way—and he doesn't steal. But the minute he leaves the ward he's done. As soon as he gets in a campaign he starts talking like his father. He starts out on the rights of the Negro to equal employment opportunity and then, before he can stop himself, a bit of a brogue creeps in, a 'God love you!' slips out, and that kills him. He just reminds people of yesterday. Thirty years ago he would have been a shoo-in. Today he's a born loser. In a way it's a pity, because he could be useful to someone."

"But not to you, I gather."

He shook his head. "No, not to me. There's too much going against him. Too many drawbacks. Including the fact that in the primary he nearly killed himself trying to stop me from getting the nomination. I guess I think of that as a drawback."

"No magnanimity, Charles?"

"I know the word," he said. "It's sometimes pronounced 'folly.'" He smiled again and said, "It's too bad you can't talk to your old friend. He could tell you all about that."

"How about Skeffington?" I said. "How does he fit the changing-style theory? You don't think he'd do well if he ran today?"

"You used to be a vaudeville buff," he said. "Remember a thing called *Change Your Act or Go Back to the Woods?* Well, I think he'd have had to change his act. And I don't think he would have, and I don't think he could have. So I think he'd probably have had a very hard time. That's the diplomatic answer. If you want to know what I really think, I think that today he wouldn't last five minutes."

I felt one more surge of old loyalty; I said, "Work it the other way. I mean, let's suppose you'd been running in his day: how long would you have lasted?"

"Oh," he said, "that's a different story. In my case . . . say three minutes." He looked at me and laughed and said, "So it's lucky for both of us

we came along when we did, isn't it?" And now for the first time he looked
at his watch; the conversation was over. He said, "Feeding time. I've got to
see a lot of people. Marie probably told you we're going to Rome for a
couple of weeks?"

"Yes. Rest period . . ."

His eyebrows went up just a little. "Is that what Marie said?" he said.
"She must have thought you were a spy. Did you ever try to rest in Rome?
And at Pony Brady's? That's wild and woolly country, Jack."

I remembered that years ago, in his more hectic days, Charles had not
been unknown in that wild and woolly country; I said, "You think you can
handle yourself?"

"I'll try," he said dryly. "In fact I can hardly wait to try. I've spent
most of the past couple of months in the western part of the state: La Dolce
Vita out there is a bean supper at the Epworth League. Have you ever been
to a bean supper, Jack? I've been to lots of them lately. I don't know of a
better reason for going to Rome. Anyway, we'll be back before long, and
when we do let's get together."

"Good, fine." And then, not really meaning anything by it, but just
making casual small talk in a half-joking way, I added, "Socially? Or professionally?"

And for some reason this seemed to catch him by surprise, and I saw
just a momentary change of expression before he answered. "Any way you
want to play it," he said. "Socially by all means. I'll even guarantee to keep
Marie out of those domestic affairs. Professionally—well, that's up to you,
isn't it? You call it. I'm agreeable. I've told you that before and it still goes.
You can come along any time you want to. The trouble is that you don't
really want to, do you?"

By now I was embarrassed at my own clumsiness in having brought it
up; it was something we had talked about now and then over the years, and
never to anyone's satisfaction. I said, "No, I guess I don't. Apart from
everything else. I like what I do now, and I couldn't do both. Besides, I
don't see where anything like that would be very useful—to use a word of
yours—for either of us. Especially for you. I'd always have the out that
everything's grist to the mill, new material and so on, but I don't see what
you'd have to gain at all."

"Oh," he said, "I'd think you could almost leave that to me. I've been
known to think of myself occasionally." And then, although his face didn't
change, remaining as quietly pleasant as ever, his voice became more sober,
more reflective. "It's a funny job," he said. "No complaints, you know,
because I wanted it, and I worked like a dog for it. We talked about popularity. All comparisons aside, I had at least a measure of that in my favor,
and I had a lot of other things going for me too. If your name is Kinsella
around here, that's not a bad head start in itself. We've both always known

that, and Pa still packs enormous weight. And then there's Marie and all the peculiar snobberies of the whole family situation: all those little Irish secretaries daydreaming away. A kind of glamour, I suppose. I got the Catholic vote because everybody knows I am one. I got the non-Catholic vote because the others don't think I'm a very good one. Or, as they'd put it, I'm not 'typical.' "

"That matters still, doesn't it? I keep hearing that it doesn't, that block voting is all gone, or mostly gone. I've never believed it."

"James sometimes talks like that," he said. "He's very bright and he knows a lot, but he makes one mistake: he thinks ecumenicism has reached Ward Five. No, it still matters. There's a surface civility, and it's not as obvious as that old magic scream, 'He's one of our own!' but it's there, all right. And it's respected: just look at the careful assortment of trash at the head table of the average interfaith dinner. Jack got to be President, but by a hair: he was almost licked by it. Oddly enough, in this situation, it benefited me. And then of course I was lucky in my opponent. He could have won, but first he got clumsy and then he panicked. And finally, I had another advantage. I know I won't shock you when I tell you that to win cost money. Fortunately I had it. And I used it."

I had heard, from the time I had come back to the city, that this had been the most expensive campaign in the history of the state, and now I couldn't resist going to authority. I said, "How much money, Charles?"

"A lot," he said. "I won't tell you more than that because I really don't want to shock you." Again there was the slight smile and he said, "I want you to preserve your illusions. Anyway, I won—and I know why I won. And having won, I think the idea is that I'm supposed to run the state. I can do that all right, but it won't be easy. I told you earlier tonight that being Governor was a little like being mayor, only more so. It's the 'more so' that counts. I used to deal with the City Council; now I'm going to have to deal with the legislature—which is bigger, tougher, smarter, more complicated, and impossible as it may seem, more corrupt. So it's no cinch. But I have a certain amount of experience, and I'm not exactly unarmed. Although I could use a few helping hands."

"I thought you had plenty of those," I said. "What everyone seems to be talking about is your organization, and how strong it is."

"They're very good," he said. "They're all competent. Some of them are more than that. And a few of them I can even trust. You can't reasonably ask for more than that. What I wouldn't mind having around is someone closer, someone I can not only trust, but whom I've known—and who's known me—for a long time. I have a feeling there are times when that's important. Even indispensable."

QUESTIONS

1 What are the main characteristics of the "old politics" and the "new politics"?
2 What elements of the "old politics" were part of Kinsella's campaign?
3 What elements of the "new politics" were part of Kinsella's campaign?
4 What impact has the "new politics" had on the political process?

Reading 12

The 480

Eugene Burdick

Eugene Burdick, a political scientist who specialized in American voting behavior, focused on a particular aspect of that behavior in his novel *The 480*. Of the many pieces of political propaganda to which voters are subject, one of the most important is the public opinion poll. Everyone checks to see if her or his candidate is leading or trailing, by what percentage, and what the trends are in the polls. Although the public expresses great interest in these polls, it remains in the dark as to the mechanics and logic of polling.

In this selection young Madison Curver is introduced by his law partner, Bookbinder, to a political professional, Levi. They discuss the nature of public opinion polling, the role of public opinion in elections, and the predictive value of polls. Levi's reactions to the information given to him by Madison are enlightening and very illustrative of the general public's typical reactions to polling.

The door to Bookbinder's study opened and Madison Curver came in. He was tall, almost too thin, and he walked with a slight stoop. He is fit, Levi thought. He looked like the squash or handball type. His narrow face was as intellectual as Levi had expected, but it also had a quality of curiosity which showed when he swung his head around the room.

"You must be Mr. Levi," Curver said. He walked over and shook hands. "Book has told me about you. Classmates at Harvard."

Levi had never seen such self-assurance in so young a man. It was the very opposite of glibness. It was a certitude, and easy way of walking, an absolute absence of shyness. As Curver bent over him, Levi could see that the young man dressed well . . . he was wearing a handmade tweed suit which was not new but was beautifully put together. His shoes were old, creased by hundreds of wrinkles, but the leather had a deep fine glow. Levi smiled. Even after forty years in finance he could not escape the old days, when he had worked in the garment district.

"Good of you to join us, Mad," Bookbinder said. His voice grated.

"Sorry, Book," Curver said. "Long-distance call. Urgent." He shrugged gracefully, slid into a chair. He lit a small green Filipino cigar.

"Well, Mad, if you're comfortable enough and it's no strain and your cigar is well lit, then I might just ask you a few questions," Bookbinder said.

"But of course, Book. Feel free," Curver said, exaggeratedly tapping ashes into a crystal ashtray.

"Oh, Christ, Levi, I should have fired him a year ago," Bookbinder said. "No respect for age and authority."

"I would have if it were my firm," Levi said. Curver shot him a glance. Levi's face was smiling but his voice was firm. Curver knew Levi was no one to joke with. He and Book were not only classmates; they were friends, widowers, self-made rich, politicians to the bone and anonymous.

Curver looked easily at Levi. He took out a pad of 3-by-5 cards and began to write on them with a pencil.

"Don't start that doodling, Mad," Bookbinder said. "It makes me nervous."

"It's not doodling, Book," Curver said. "It's my form of shorthand; you get used to it in a few minutes."

"It's what?" Levi asked. He felt a slight irritation. Curver interested him and at the same time was somehow offensive.

"It's a kind of shorthand I worked out," Curver said. He leaned forward and showed Levi a card. It was covered with unfamiliar signs with a few letters showing one word *Levi*.

"With dictating machines and tape recorders," Bookbinder said, "I think shorthand for a lawyer is a waste of time."

"Some people freeze when a tape recorder goes on," Curver said. "But they think I'm just a compulsive doodler."

"What does the card say?" Levi asked. He disliked asking the question, but he could not resist.

"It just gives today's date, the names of those present . . . your name is short so I put it down once and after this I'll just use my sign for *L*. And a proposed agenda."

Levi straightened in his chair. Book had told him about Curver before, but this was not quite what he had expected. Book had taken Curver into the firm three years ago, straight from Columbia Law School. He was old-rich, old Midwestern rich, but he never talked about it. He carried one of the heaviest work loads in the office and still had time to go off to seminars on things called "systems analysis," "statistics in the behavioral sciences," and "SES indicator use by interviewers."

Such a boy should be married and have a family, Levi thought. Book had mentioned Mad was interested in women, but never talked of marriage. The girls in the office were silly over him.

"You've got an agenda?" Book asked.

"Why not? It never hurts," Curver said. "Only three items on it. First, can the incumbent President be beaten? Second, Dr. Cotter's work. Third, discussion of Simulmatics Corporation."

"Let's skip the first one," Bookbinder said, "and go right to Cotter. Does Cotter know what he is talking about?"

"No."

"Then why the hell did you give me his report to read?"

"Because Cotter is the best of the pollsters, that's why," Curver said. "He has no imagination, no flair, he hates guesses, lacks intuition. That's what you want in a pollster. Also his results are usually better than those of the politicians. And the Simulmatics people are way ahead of Cotter."

Bookbinder and Levi both swung their heads. Curver laughed.

"Any time some kid Ph.D. has more political know-how than Jim Farley or Whitaker and Baxter or Joe Kennedy or Dirksen I'll pay your bar bill at the Club for a month," Bookbinder growled.

"Okay, Book, you want some evidence?" Curver asked. "Nineteen sixty is a good year to compare. The pollsters were getting a lot of problems ironed out. Out in California Teddy Kennedy was running the campaign for JFK in the eleven Western states. Every week he got reports from the pros. From the potbellied boys with the big cigars who hung around the pool halls and the courthouses and talked to precinct captains and made deals on government contracts and raised money for the Democratic Party and said they had their finger on the pulse of the people. They all predicted victory in their areas. I saw the reports. They kept talking of 'good party morale,' 'peaking the campaign,' 'tough precinct organizations.' It was all crap. A smart guy named Lou Harris was running a confidential poll for Kennedy. His reports went to Teddy too. Harris indicated that Kennedy might lose *all* the Western states, including California."

"Kennedy won only New Mexico and Nevada," Levi said drily. "For a total of seven electoral votes."

"That's right. Seven electoral votes," Curver repeated. "The point is that the pros honestly believed the Democrats were going to win big. All of them. And Lou Harris and Teddy Kennedy knew the Democrats would lose small. The simple fact is that the polls are better than the pros if you're trying to guess who's going to win an election."

"Just a minute," Bookbinder said. "What about all the polls indicating that Dewey was going to lick Truman in 1948?" His eyes lit up, recalling the event. He grinned at Levi. Levi had supported Dewey, Bookbinder had supported Truman.

"The pollsters made a mistake," Curver admitted calmly. "They were new at the game. Polls were only eighteen or twenty years old and there wasn't enough money behind them yet. They stopped polling during the last month when a lot of people switched over. Most pollsters were dinosaurs in 1948. They made mistakes, like phrasing the questions incorrectly. Also, and Book won't like this, they assumed that the undecideds would split evenly. They ignored the fact that the incumbent President has a grip on people. They hate to turn him out. So most of the undecideds voted for Truman."

"I don't see that the polls are any better now," Levi said.

"That's because you don't read them and perhaps don't understand them when you do," Curver said. There was no insolence in his voice. "Both Gallup and Roper are up out of the primeval slime and galloping around pretty fast these days. Some of the younger people are doing even better."

"Why do we need Cotter?" Bookbinder asked.

"For just one purpose," Curver said. "To tell us *what* the voters are thinking about. He's already suggested something, Book, that has you in a spin. His results indicate no one can beat Kennedy next year. Read the rest of the polling literature and the thing becomes even clearer: we're electing a President for eight years these days."

"I don't believe that for a minute," Bookbinder said quickly. "And if we are, it's unconstitutional." He hesitated. "I don't really mean that, but it's unhealthy."

"Can Cotter tell us *why* the power of the incumbent President is so great?" Levi asked softly.

"He doesn't have a clue and if he did he wouldn't dare breathe it," Curver said. "This man believes he is as precise as a physicist and physicists don't go around predicting how experiments will work out. But there is a way to find out why voters vote the way they do."

"I don't want to hear it again," Bookbinder said. "But go ahead; let Levi know what is happening to politics."

"You get the services of an outfit called Simulmatics—which also thinks it is very scientific—and then you combine that with the reports from some shrewd psychiatrists and you have just about as much as we are going to know about the *why* of anything going on inside one hundred and eighty million different heads."

"Go on," Levi said.

Curver hesitated. It was so difficult. He knew Levi and Bookbinder would oppose whatever he said. They would disbelieve it, would think he advocated it, would distort it. And the whole damned thing was so fugitive, so hard to catch, so difficult to say easily . . . and so incredibly important.

"It's not easy, but I'll try," Curver said. "Take a group identified as Southern, wealthy, urban, professional, third-generation." Curver paused. "How would they vote?"

"Oh, Christ, Mad, that's easy," Bookbinder said. "They're either Democrats who vote like Republicans or recent converts to the GOP because they hated Roosevelt so much."

"The *why* is not so difficult, Curver," Levi said. "I think Book caught it pretty well. They'll vote for the Republicans or a states' rights party just because of the Democratic position on civil rights. Or Bobby Kennedy. Or high income tax."

Curver smiled. He inhaled the cigar, watched it shrivel a quarter of an inch.

"You didn't give me time to add the last adjective," Curver said. "It was *Negro*."

There was silence in the room. When Bookbinder spoke it was a soft wondering voice.

"Southern, wealthy, urban, professional third-generation Negroes," he said. He reached in his desk, took out a box of cigars and offered it to Levi. Levi took one and the two men began the small diverting ritual of rolling, tipping, smoothing, snipping, and lighting their cigars.

"Mad, are there enough such people to influence a Presidential campaign?" Bookbinder said. "I doubt it."

"And you would be wrong, Book," Curver said.

"Which would not be a new thing," Bookbinder said.

"First, because winning the undecideds is what the campaign is all about. The party regulars turn out in just about the same numbers, but the undecideds may or may not come out on Election Day. So you pick up a tenth of one per cent here and half a per cent there and pretty soon it amounts to something. So those wealthy Negro professionals in Southern cities are important. First, because they vote. Second, because they get out the Negro vote wherever the Negro can vote. They influence others."

"How do you know how these people are going to vote?" Levi asked.

"You go out and ask a few of them and you take their behavior on past issues and you run this through a computing machine and you come up with an analysis of where they stand on various issues," Curver said. Levi started to interrupt and Curver lifted his hand. "That is what the Simulmatics group does. But we can take their information and give it to the psychologists and psychiatrists who have really studied Negroes in the group and finally you tease out *why* they think the way they do."

"Curver, how many of those Negroes have gone to a psychiatrist?" Levi asked.

"Maybe damned few. If they haven't we send the psychiatrist to them," Curver said and slumped lower in his chair.

"How many groups do these Simulmatics people have?" Bookbinder asked.

"For analyzing a national election they have four hundred and eighty groups, Book. People don't even know they're in a group so don't act like your precious democracy is being raped on the street. They went through every poll worth looking at and after a lot of work came up with four hundred and eighty groups which seem to react and vote the same way. And now they know a lot about each of those groups, so much, in fact, that they can simulate how the group will act before the group has even heard of an issue."

"That's what I object to," Bookbinder snapped. "Even if the groups exist it's wrong that people don't know they belong to such a group and, shut up a minute, Mad, if you know that much about a group you're going to start to manipulate it."

"Book, I don't think Curver is suggesting that," Levi said. He had a softly persuasive voice. "These people have just developed a new tool. Now maybe they can use the tool in an immoral way, but we have to wait and see."

Levi paused and then went on slowly. "I'm always interested in individuals. Now, as they change jobs and locations and income their vote is going to change, isn't that true?"

"That's correct," Curver said. He had sunk down so far in the chair that his knees were higher than his head. He chewed on one pencil and with the other he wrote on his cards.

"Take a Jew in 1920 and tell me how he would vote," Levi said, and Curver knew he was dealing with a shrewd man used to cutting to essentials. And also someone who did not especially like him.

"Tell me his age in 1920, where he lived, how much he made a year, and his occupation," Curver said.

"But you don't understand about Jews," Levi said. "There are Russian Jews, German Jews, the old aristocratic Sephardic Jews, Polish Jews. They were, and still are, all split up, don't communicate much with one another. You don't know a thing about that."

"The fact is I do, sir. But it's also a fact that I don't need to," Curver said. "Can you answer the questions I asked?" He glanced down at his cards. "Would you like me to repeat them?"

"My memory is good," Levi said. "This Jew was twenty-five years old in 1924, he lived on the East Side; he made, let us say, four hundred and fifty dollars a year, and he worked as a coat presser."

"Anything else?" Curver said. He was not taking notes now.

"Maybe he is a college student. Maybe planning on law school," Levi said.

Bookbinder realized Levi was describing his own background. They had met at Harvard Law School and had been among the oldest students in their class. Levi had never practiced law because courtroom appearances made him nervous. Instead he had gone into finance and was now in a web of operations which he ran easily, anonymously, and at enormous profit. His second life was politics.

"And in 1928?" Curver asked. "His income and occupation."

"Let's say around five thousand and he is associated with a brokerage firm," Levi said.

"Let's skip to 1936. What's his income then and his job?"

"Maybe thirty thousand and he's in general finance. That close enough?" Levi asked.

Bookbinder leaned back in his chair, grinning. It was Levi's career and probably Mad knew it, but that wouldn't help him much. Mad had worked himself into a box.

"You told me once that it was silly to make guesses about how individuals would vote," Bookbinder said. "You're only interested in groups. Now here you go trying to guess how one single Jew voted in four different elections."

From the depths of the chair an arm waved. Curver took the sharp pencil from his mouth, tossed the dull one on the rug.

"In 1920 our subject voted for Eugene Debs, the Socialist," Curver said. "In 1924 he voted for Robert La Follette, Progressive and Socialist candidate. In 1928 he voted for Alfred E. Smith, Democrat. In 1936 he voted for Landon. Since then he voted for every Republican candidate except in 1952 he voted for Stevenson. That should be right with the possible exception of the Stevenson vote."

Levi looked at the cards in Curver's long fingers. They were somewhat dirty. The man must work with soft-lead pencils a lot. Bookbinder was looking at Levi, a grin on his face.

"That is correct," Levi said. Bookbinder's grin faded. "Even to the 1952 vote for Stevenson. That's quite impressive, Curver."

"Not really, Mr. Levi. The most important determinant of voting behavior is income, then occupation, then where one lives. Jews, whether they are Sephardic or Polish, tend to vote Democratic when their income is low and then switch to Republican as it gets above ten thousand dollars a year. If the voter's social-economic position remains the same, so does his vote."

Bookbinder moved his big bulk in his chair. He forced himself not to chomp on the cigar.

"Anybody ever use this Simulmatics outfit in an election?" Levi asked.

"Kennedy did in 1960. Then the group was in its infancy, but Kennedy gave them some problems to work on. He was interested to see how much of Ike's popularity would rub off on Nixon. All the pros were saying 'Don't worry about the Negro vote. It will come back to the Democratic Party once Eisenhower is off the scene.' The Simulmatics people got out their tapes and fed them into the computer. They found that the Negroes had shifted not just to Eisenhower, but many had transferred their allegiance to the Republicans."

"Why?" Bookbinder asked.

"I told you that the Simulmatics people don't know why, but they can make some damned good guesses," Curver said. "Earl Warren, a prominent Republican and an Ike appointee, had written the first big desegregation judgment. The white Democrats in the South were keeping Negroes from registering and maybe the dissatisfaction with those Democrats started to drift up North. Maybe they started to distrust people like Fulbright who was a good pious liberal Democrat on everything under the sun, but the moment the civil rights thing came up he was strangely silent."

"What did Kennedy do with the information?" Levi asked quietly.

"First of all he believed it," Curver said. "Oh, he kept patting the pros on the head and telling them they were doing great, but he had learned long ago the pro with the longest experience is likely to be the most out of touch. Second, he started, with what seemed a great burst of spontaneous enthusiasm, to be very, very strong on the civil rights question. Remember that phone call Kennedy made to Martin Luther King's wife when King was thrown in the Southern jail? Remember the speeches in which he kept hitting for civil rights?"

"Anything else?" Bookbinder asked.

"Sure. Take the fact that Kennedy was a Catholic," Curver said. "Everybody had a different answer. Most of the pros, the old experienced hands, remembering Al Smith, told Kennedy to play it down. Others said it had already been ventilated enough . . . forget it. What would you have recommended, Book?"

"I'd have told him to forget it," Bookbinder said. His voice was truculent. "Don't heat up an unpopular subject."

"Remember it was August of 1960," Curver said. "The Gallup Poll had Nixon leading with fifty per cent of the votes, Kennedy trailing with forty-four per cent, and six per cent undecided. The Simulmatics people 'simulated' how their four hundred and eighty groups would react if the Catholic issue was raised."

"Deliberately raised?" Levi asked softly.

"Use your own words. We agree on the *raised,* anyway."

"Who would do it deliberately?" Bookbinder asked.

"Kennedy," Curver answered. "Nixon had laid off the subject and the tons of crackpot fundamentalist literature going around only circulated among people who were already so anti-Catholic they wouldn't vote for Kennedy. So the only person who could use the issue effectively was Kennedy."

"That would be very close to cold-bloodedly fomenting intolerance," Levi said.

"Or it might be putting a reverse twist on intolerance," Curver said. Levi wished suddenly that the young man would sit up straight. His head was almost invisible. It was disturbing to have sharp words come from a mouth one could not see.

"The Simulmatics report ran something like this, leaving out all the technical stuff.

1 JFK was trailing Nixon.
2 JFK had already lost as much as he probably would on the Catholic issue, although if it got hotter he might lose a few more Protestants in the Bible Belt and Southern California.
3 But if the anti-Catholic issue got any more bitter—and here listen carefully, Mr. Levi—there would start to be a reaction. A lot of Protestants would feel that the anti-Catholic thing had gone too far. They would drift back toward Kennedy because although they might be suspicious of a Catholic in the White House they feared religious intolerance even more.
4 Any more embitterment of anti-Catholicism and the Jews would be solid behind Kennedy.
5 If the Catholic issue kept coming up it would consolidate the Catholic vote behind Kennedy."

There was a long silence. Bookbinder got up and went to his small bar, swung it open, and mixed them each a Scotch and soda.

"This could become a nightmare, Levi," Bookbinder said. "That's why I wanted you to hear it. Let a madman or just some very ambitious power-seeker start to use stuff like this and the whole game is changed. He would be getting at people in a way they are not even aware of."

"That's possible," Curver said. "But let's take a look at politics before the computer came along with its big stack of tapes. It was pretty damned irresponsible then. Pretty much of a nightmare. Remember the cute stories they used to pass around about FDR? He had paresis, colored mistresses, was given half of Bermuda as a gift in exchange for giving Britain the fifty destroyers. And the sweet things they said about Eleanor. That was decency in politics? And then McCarthy with his handful of lists and ranting accusations against whoever crossed his path. Nice and clean, eh? Ever read about the ditties they made up about 'Cleveland's little bastard'? Look, a big part of politics has always been an underground of wild rumor, fantasies, filthy jokes, stories about corruption and boozing in the White House and dipping into the public trough."

"Those old politicos were playing on prejudice and irrationality," Book said, "but they did it haphazardly, just making wild stabs and hoping they'd hit the public nerve."

Levi stood up and walked toward the bar. He glanced at Curver as he passed. The boy had not moved since he had sat down. He seemed nerveless, like an Indian or Asian who could squat endlessly in one position.

"If you could use this kind of approach to learn how to 'embitter' an issue, you could also use it to take the bitterness out of an issue," Levi said.

"Book, maybe the way to reduce anti-Semitism is to bring it into the open and have it discussed. Maybe we could also find out why people become anti-Semitic."

Bookbinder stared down at his glass. His whole posture rejected what Levi said. Finally, he shook his head.

"Levi, part of our protection in politics is that fact that no one really knows how it works. If one man can refine it to a science he or the next guy won't be able to resist temptation. And if he was the wrong man, that would be the end."

"But if everyone knows what is going on, then they all have the same advantage," Curver said.

Bookbinder ignored the comment.

"Did the Simulmatics people tell Kennedy how to act during the TV debates in 1960?" he asked.

"They did," Curver said. "Keep in mind that all they really do is make a kind of 'symbolic imitation' in advance of how these four hundred and eighty groups might react. Kennedy would have been silly not to try and find out before the debates how the groups looked at both him and Nixon."

"What did he find out?" Bookbinder asked.

"First that Nixon was regarded as being 'super-cool.' Kennedy was regarded as more 'friendly.' More people thought Kennedy was 'trustworthy.' Among Jews only four per cent thought Nixon was the 'most trustworthy.' On almost anything that affected personality, Kennedy came off better than Nixon. Only on 'competence' did the voters give Nixon the nod," Curver said. "So the Simulmatics groups told Kennedy to stay away from Nixon's super-cool position. They said that Kennedy could make use of his more personal traits—including a range of emotions such as fervor, humor, friendship, and spirituality—and thus cause Nixon to 'lose' the debates."

Levi sensed, with a slight shock, that Curver was quoting the last sentence from memory from a report.

"Maybe that's why the debates were such a farce," Bookbinder said. "Lot of damned foolishness and no one learned a thing. That's not politics. Politics is knowing what you believe and going out and trying to persuade the people to go along with you. But this damned pollster approach means taking the pulse of the people and if they get a fever you stand up and say 'Fever is great.' I'm for fever and motherhood and against men who sweat on TV screens."

"Book, listen to me a minute," Mad said. Bookbinder's voice faded. "Listen, because I think it means something. How did we get into this? Because I told you that not in our lifetime would an incumbent President be licked for a second term if he wanted to run. Right? You said I was crazy. But Hoover was the last incumbent to lose and it won't happen again. If the incumbent acts, he gains support . . . even if he makes a whopping mistake."

"What about someone who comes in with a reputation as big as the President's?" Bookbinder asked. "Someone like this Thatch fellow in India? He's been on every TV program, in every magazine and newspaper for the last month."

"Book, it's possible," Curver said. "But do you know what this challenger would have to be? For example, he'd have to be 'sincere.' Meaning that people believe he is above avarice, ambition, and pride. Book, the most sincere person in America in recent times has been Kate Smith. Ike beat Stevenson on sincerity, among other things. Ike looked more sincere. Ike wasn't as sincere as Kate, but more than Adlai. Second, your man has to be a hero. A shrewd old observer named Frazer who wrote *The Golden Bough* once said that people want their leaders to 'belong to a higher order of humanity than themselves.' It's possible to find someone like that, but usually he is the incumbent President."

Levi waited a good long minute.

"I think that's right, Mad," Levi said. "But I'm old. I remember listening to Debs. That's how old I am." He pulled his long thin body to its feet, walked over and stood beside Curver at the window. "My father was sick but I got him out. We went down to Central Park and my father stood there with a handkerchief to his mouth drenched with some patent medicine that was supposed to cure TB. I remember we were in the middle of a group of Italians who stank of garlic and red wine. They chanted agreement with Debs as he spoke and I don't think they really understood a word he said. My father listened, sniffling at the handkerchief and eyeing this wild stranger. At the end of the speech he put his hand up and Debs looked down at him like a hawk about to pounce. 'Do you believe that a forty-hour week is desirable and possible?' my father asked. Debs slowed down, smiled, spread out his hands and said, 'It is possible, desirable and, comrade, inevitable.' The crowd went wild. My father sniffed at his handerchief."

"And your father voted for Debs," Bookbinder said.

"He never spoke to me about Debs as a personality," Levi said, "but he voted for him. My father was for a forty-hour week because it was humane, not because he loved Debs."

Curver looked at the two men. They were not weak; they had principles. But now they seemed to sag. Maybe, Curver thought, it was an accident of light, the passing of a cloud's shadow over the window, a sudden need for blood sugar, a protective gesture. He had seen the posture before. Not nice. It came when a man got the word he was going to be punished . . . and no one had told him why.

Levi recovered first. When he spoke his voice had its usual soft and precise quality.

"Book, let's don't fool ourselves," he said. "The young man has just described a technique, a tool, an instrument. We're here because we believe some things are more important than techniques. One such thing is that the

President should not just automatically be re-elected. So we are going to back the best men running against him and if there aren't any good ones we'll find one." He smiled. "Or we'll try like hell. Could we talk a minute, Book?"

Instantly Curver uncoiled himself from the chair. The excellent cloth of his suit was wrinkled, but that was the only indication he had been through a long conference. He shook hands languidly and left the study.

"Book, if this Thatch person you've mentioned measures up and we've got any chance of getting him interested, we'll have to try the new ideas Curver described to ever get him to the Convention," Levi said.

"I'm opposed to it," Bookbinder said.

"I gathered that," Levi said. "But you've been around long enough to know this thing will take a lot of doing. So let Curver go ahead and try. We can watch him closely and we'll still have control over the campaign. I'll get five people to put up ten thousand each just to see."

"I didn't think you would," Bookbinder said.

They walked to the door. Just before Bookbinder opened it, Levi said, "Did I ever tell you that one of the last things my mother did before she died in 1952 was to vote for Eisenhower. She was ninety and she loved Ike. Also she insisted he must be Jewish."

Bookbinder had heard Levi's story before but he liked hearing it again.

"You watch that Curver boy, Book. Smart kid. Probably Jewish."

Bookbinder shut the door and leaned against it, laughing. Levi always left him feeling better.

QUESTIONS

1 How accurate is public opinion polling according to Curver, and how could scientific analysis of public opinion be used to manipulate voters during elections?
2 What role should public opinion polling play in a campaign?
3 In what ways could polling and voting analysis be used to manipulate voters?

Reading 13
Dark Horse
Fletcher Knebel

Since its inception in the 1930s, modern public opinion polling has developed into a highly accurate and exact science. The application of
behavioral science techniques and the advent of the computer have enabled polling to make major advances in a surprisingly short period of
time. Polling's precise nature has made it highly attractive and useful to
candidates and incumbents, and most politicians today employ pollsters
to a high degree. The uncanny ability of pollsters to determine in advance what the American voter will do and why assures them a highly
important position in politics.

In *Dark Horse* Fletcher Knebel offers a glimpse into the inner workings of public opinion polling. The main character, Arnold Swensson, is
the "priest of priests" in the temple of public opinion, and the narrative
reveals just how important he is and why.

Arnold Swensson strode into his Manhattan office, 565 Fifth Avenue, on
the stroke of 7 o'clock the next morning. The nation's most skillful, se-
cretive and expensive conductor of political polls switched on the lights,
hung his coat on a hall tree and pushed a button on the electric coffeemak-
er. Unlike many early morning toilers in New York that morning, Swensson
was eager to begin work.

He was a large, solid man, built as though to provide a model anchor
for less stable humans, and his bald head glowed above a fringe of neatly
trimmed graying hair. Swensson smiled but rarely, finding life a serious
transit which, as far as he knew, afforded but one crossing per person and
therefore was not to be taken lightly or frittered away on emotional yo-yos
and frisbees. What fascinated him and made his life a monolith of purpose
was his belief in the utter predictability of human behavior, including his
own.

Swensson had risen an hour earlier with a sense of expectation that
quickened as he clicked through his morning routine, tooth brushing and
gum massage, mouth wash, shower, shave, dressing, breakfast, page one of
the New York *Times*, elimination and the vigorous nine-block walk to the
office. His mind dwelled on those two lines, transmuted from neat rows of
numbers, that ran toward each with steady, unbending insistence. He found
great beauty in those lines, a mirroring of truth as precise as Ralston
Crawford's painting of a long highway bridge in which the railings, con-
verging in perspective, became at last a remote pinpoint.

Swensson had remained flexible and open-minded for a week, but last night he had glimpsed the shape of things to come and he looked forward to the morning with such eagerness that he gladly would have forgone his sleep if that would have speeded events. As it was, he slept soundly and dreamed of a series of geometric designs in gorgeous colors that slid into one another in endless progression approaching the infinite.

Arnold Swensson ran the most sophisticated poll in the world and this October it was at the exclusive service of Governor Hugh Pinholster under high security precautions at a cost of $28,000 a day. This broke down to $14 per interview, for each twenty-four hours. Swensson's organization questioned two thousand people across the nation. All polling was done by telephone, although the results were carefully weighted by a complex formula to account for those voters who had no home phone. One hundred forty interviewers, operating in two shifts of seventy each, manned the phones in little compartments spread along tables in a Lexington Avenue office building in Manhattan. The dialing crews consisted largely of graduate students of the social sciences at New York universities, supplemented by a few housewives and unemployed professional people. They were paid $50 for an eight-hour shift, but most of them were as interested in public-opinion sampling techniques as in the money.

Calls fanned out over the Bell system's WATS (wide area telephone service) lines, affording unlimited long-distance calls at a fixed monthly rental. Every call resulted from a random selection of a phone number by a computer that performed highly complicated calculations, including the allotment of a higher percentage of calls in those area codes located in states with the largest electoral votes. The computer juggled area codes, exchanges and the final four-digit numbers with lightning speed, serving up long lists of random numbers for each operator. Interviewers also followed a booklet of questions designed to reflect the voting population's profile in such items as correct proportion of males and females, heads of households, first-time voters, elderly citizens and, of top importance, those most likely to vote.

The calling began every morning at 10 o'clock and continued until 2 the next morning. While no call entered a home after 11 P.M. local time, the New York dialers worked until 2 A.M. because of the three-hour time spread to the West Coast. Operators sprinkled calls to time-distant Hawaii and Alaska through the day. Operators wasted two of every three calls because the computer-selected random numbers included phone booths, churches, schools and business establishments. With few exceptions, those reached at home co-operated willingly. They liked being called long-distance, appreciated the thoroughness of the questioning and, above all, relished the thought that their single vote was significant enough to attract the interest of a professional poller.

Dialers filled out coded forms after each interview and supervisors transferred the data to punch cards. Twice a day figures from mechanical tabulators were fed into a computer console. Instantly rows of figures clattered onto a long sheet that leaped convulsively from the electronic typewriter. A bonded security officer folded the sheet, placed it in a thick manila envelope, put the envelope in his inner breast pocket and walked rapidly the five blocks to Swensson's Fifth Avenue office, arriving each morning and evening at 7:15.

This morning Swensson glanced repeatedly at his watch as he awaited the arrival of the messenger. He drank coffee, filled his pipe, relighting it several times, and looked out the window without seeing anything. At last, two minutes late at 7:17, the young messenger came into the office and waited until Swensson signed for the delivery. Opening the envelope and unfolding the sheet, which was eighteen inches wide and perhaps six feet in length, Swensson became conscious of his tension. His stomach, that emotional refuse dump, groaned as a new load of cans, bottles, cartons and other sensory discards tumbled about. If he was certain of what he would find, he thought, why so discombobulated?

He scanned the rows of figures with rising excitement, noting a number here and another there as his vision hopped around the sheet. Then, suddenly, a glow suffused his body and the tension drained away. He was right. The figures confirmed his hunch as accurately as if they had been hatched in his own brain. But first, the precaution of a double-check.

He telephoned Fred, his morning supervisor in the Lexington Avenue bucket shop of polling.

"Did you eyeball those key numbers on the dupe, Fred?"

"Yep, they're okay, Arnold. They check out with the input. No problem with the nine-oh-four this morning. All nice and tidy."

"Fine. I'll be over around ten."

Swensson took a large sheet of graph paper from his desk drawer and glanced at the two lines, one red and one blue, that ran across the graph. Consulting numbers on the computer print-out, he used a blue pencil to extend the blue line about half an inch, then duplicated the process with a red pencil and the red line. Finally, using an ordinary lead pencil and ruler, he extended both lines by a series of light dots and wrote down two letters and a number in a corner of the graph: "T N 2."

"Perfect." Swensson breathed the word with awe. He might have been Christopher Columbus, sighting the low, tropical shoreline of Watling Island in the Bahamas, or Hiram Bingham beholding the long-hidden glories of the lost Inca fortress, Machu Picchu, in the Andes of Peru. For all three men, Chris, Hi and Arnie, there was that supreme vault of the human spirit, that vindication of lonely prescience. By God, they had been right!

Swensson glanced at his watch: 7:28. He could call Hugh Pinholster in two minutes and he would use those two minutes planning just how to break the news.

Swensson's relationship with his most recent client had been sealed when he began polling in the Pinholster-Hudson race in late September. A man with Swensson's record and prestige could set his own terms. In the last quarter of a century, he had polled in more than four hundred political contests, including every presidential race and a host of battles for governor, senator and mayor. He had picked wrong only once, missing a run for governor of Missouri largely because the client refused to pay for what Swensson considered to be an adequate sample. His highest error had been 4.7 per cent, his average error 1.2 per cent, but in presidential elections his last pre-voting figures averaged slightly less than 0.4 per cent off the mark. Swensson had polled for such notables as Eisenhower, Kennedy, Johnson and Rockefeller. Although his price was steep, expenses were also lofty and Swensson netted only about three hundred dollars a day profit for himself during the short-lived political-polling season. He made his living from market surveys. In politics, he was a man who worshiped numbers and their meaning for election day.

Swensson insisted on certain rules. He would communicate only with the candidate himself. With Pinholster, he had an arrangement that he would call the governor at 7:30 A.M. each day wherever Pinholster happened to be. The client pledged not to reveal figures except to a few, close, trusted advisers. Under no conditions were poll results to be leaked to the press. Thus, when the Los Angeles *Times* printed Swensson data Wednesday, Swensson had threatened to end his service unless Pinholster tightened his security. The candidate vowed that henceforth he would hold the daily results as inviolate as his campaign promises, a somewhat ambiguous pledge, Swensson thought. Actually, Swensson traced the leak to his own shop and fired the offending assistant supervisor.

Arnold Swensson could so dictate to future Presidents because of all the new high priests in modern America—the diet druids, the sensitivity gurus, Zen Buddhist mystics, Satan cultists, ecology zealots and the chieftains of the youth tribes—none had quite the impact on the course of the republic as the political pollers. And in the temple of public opinion, Swensson was the priest of priests.

After consulting Pinholster's itinerary, Swensson placed his call to the candidate at the Sheraton-Blackstone in Chicago at 7:31. Pinholster's light, breezy voice, fraught with empathy and yet withal, Swensson felt, a trifle untrustworthy, came on the line promptly. They traded their usual, brief amenities.

"Okay, Arnold, shoot. I've got my form here." No one called Swensson "Arnie," although Pinholster had tried it their first day.

"All right, Governor. Going across, make it 1050 under A, 772 under B, 178 under C, 52.5 under D, 38.6 under E, 8.9 under F and plus 1.1 under G."

For Pinholster the figures translated swiftly as follows: Of the 2000 most-likely-to-vote people polled across the nation in the last twenty-four hours, 1050 said they would vote for Pinholster, 772 for Quinn and 178 did not know. Expressed in percentages, Pinholster had 52.5, Quinn 38.6 and 8.9 were undecided. Column G, Quinn's gain or loss over the previous day's polling, showed a gain of 1.1 per cent.

"Oof." Pinholster emitted a half-whistling sound. "I don't like that one point one gain, Arnold."

"It's not pretty," conceded Swensson. Actually, he thought the number a thing of beauty. No offense to Pinholster, just a question of aesthetics. One day 1.2, another 1.1, another an even 1. The Column G figure had not varied more than 0.2 percent since the Pinholster-Quinn matching began eight days ago.

"You said you might make a projection today, Arnold." Pinholster's tone struck a tentative note.

"I did. . . . Governor, I regret to tell you this." But within him, Swensson could feel the fires of elation. "The lines cross at T N 2 on your graph."

Except for a faint, extraneous symphony of far voices, silence overtook the line.

"Tuesday, November 2?" asked Pinholster.

"Yes."

"That's election day."

"Yes, I know."

After a long pause, Pinholster said: "Let me get this straight, Arnold. Are you telling me that if things keep rolling as they are, we've got trouble on election day?"

"That's about the size of it." And, thought Swensson, he'd known it last night, deep in his brain and his gut, thus beating the poll by twelve hours. Instead of commiserating with the client, he felt like dashing off a happy paper for the American Statistical Association. "We have to face the fact that we have a trend."

The trend, that ominous and implacable abstraction, had moved as smoothly as a ship on compass heading in calm seas. Starting with thirty per cent of the vote the night of his nomination, Quinn's blue line rose day by day with an average lift of 1.1 per cent every twenty-four hours.

"You actually put the election in doubt then?" It was as though Pinholster had asked which day the world would end.

"Well, of course, we have the variables. You crank in my average error of 0.4 per cent, you look at places like Chicago where the organization can influence your tally on the upside. . . ." Swensson never used such words as "steal" or "fix" with clients. "Then you consider Quinn himself. A man given to the, well, bizarre in campaigning might say something deeply offensive to a statistically important bloc, or get into a brawl or perhaps give the impression of mental instability. . . . Let's put it this way. The numbers say doubtful, but with the variables, you look in better shape than Quinn does."

"Any recommendations from the depths?" Pinholster was braving it now, the cool, imperturbable image.

The depth interviews embraced a series of questions asked every fourth person polled. They were intended to probe the voter's psychic caverns for substrata of prejudice, longing and trust.

"Sure," said Swensson. "As I told you earlier in the week, foreign policy is your trump suit. Let's look at Question Six in the depth interviews. 'Suppose another war breaks out in the Middle East, threatening world peace. Which candidate would you rather have in the White House handling the crisis?' Yesterday 56.7 per cent said Pinholster, only 32.1 per cent said Quinn and 11.2 were uncertain. Quinn gains only slightly on this question day by day. You retain a big lead there. So the message is loud and clear."

"I can't understand how I can be so far ahead on the foreign business and still keep dropping over-all."

"It's the old story, Governor. Bread and butter dominate elections and Quinn has the kitchen image."

But it was more than that, Swensson felt. He preferred to stick close to the numbers with clients, but he had his own theories, privately nursed. From the start of the September polling, he had sensed a lack of basic trust in Pinholster. The governor's image was one of deftness, agility, suppleness. Voters liked him, but they did not trust him deep down as they had Eisenhower, for example. Pinholster led the polls because the voters trusted Hudson even less. But with the sudden appearance of Eddie Quinn, the ball game changed radically in the seventh inning. The initial depth interviews indicated that Quinn's two appearances on television projected a picture of independence and integrity of person. People might dispute or even abhor what Eddie said, but they sensed that he was his own man, a solid fellow who would not flutter about in every breeze. In short, people trusted Eddie to be himself. Swensson surmised the second day that Eddie would gain in the poll as people overcame their aversion to the novelty and the shock of what he said. If Swensson were explaining the phenomenon to Charlie Herron, who had financed some of Swensson's polls in the past, he would put it in banker's terms. Eddie was the rough, blunt construction foreman, without funds, credit standing or social acceptance, who comes into the bank unannounced and solicits a large loan to start his own building company. He is turned down, but he returns again and again until the banker, persuaded at last of the applicant's ability and stubborn commitment, extends him a character loan and even urges his own wife to invest money in the new enterprise.

Eddie began his nineteen-day campaign by projecting an image of a good, warm, reliable man of the people, and Swensson believed that a man whose initial impression was appealing only rarely failed to gain as the days went by. So the daily tallies, showing Eddie on a gradual but steady rise, did not surprise Swensson. In fact, he already had wagered two thousand dollars of his own money at attractive long-shot odds. But that was all hunch and theory, and with the client, Swensson stayed glued to the numbers.

"The depths show your clear superiority on foreign issues," said Swensson. "If I were in your shoes, Governor, I'd hit that hard in every speech. Without saying so, I'd make the voters visualize Eddie Quinn at a summit conference with Ryabchikov or conferring with Pompidou or Willy Brandt. Voters will feel uneasy, I think, about pictures like that."

"I agree, Arnold. I sense my strength in that area. I'm going to exploit yesterday's break, the Russians knocking off the talks on the Berlin Wall. Anything else?"

"Yes. I think from now on we ought to get a computer print-out every four hours. It won't cost that much more, let's say seven hundred dollars a day, and then we can get a running check on the trend."

"Okay, do it. And Arnold, call me any time if you spot a change. Flo will put you through wherever I am. . . . Oof, this is hard to take at this hour in the morning."

"Anything can change, Governor. The numbers aren't ordained in heaven." But once they started to flow in a steady current, thought Swensson, only an act of God could guarantee a reversal.

"Oh, one thing, Arnold. Quinn had a bad day yesterday, rain, hippies, a squabble over pot, a crack about a Department of Offense. Do your breakdown figures show any change after, say, nine P.M.?"

"That'll take a minute." Swensson skimmed rows of figures, looking for key numbers. "Let's see. Most of the late numbers are from the West. . . . Well, I can't be definite without more work, but if Quinn hurt himself, it doesn't seem to show up yet. We'll know more later on."

"Okay, then, until seven-thirty tomorrow, unless you have some news."

Swensson labored for two hours over his master charts, then prepared to walk to the Lexington Avenue quarters to watch the beginning of the telephone calls at 10 A.M. He loved the clutter of voices amid the rasp of dialing and the busy beat of the tabulating machines, for he knew that beneath the noise, as though in a subterranean channel, the numbers flowed quietly and steadily at a predictable speed toward a foreseen destination. But first Swensson called his friend, Don Pugh, his betting blind for wagers with the Philadelphia bookie.

"Is Quinn still five to one, Don?"

"Yeah. No change."

"Put another thousand on Quinn then."

"Will do. See you, Arnold." Pugh seldom questioned his friend. In their arrangement, by which Pugh picked up a tenth of the winnings and shared none of the losses, words were superfluous.

After hanging up, Hugh Pinholster sat for several minutes staring at the numbers on his coded form sheet. It is axiomatic that political candidates distrust polls which show them lagging and place great faith in those that depict them running ahead. Yet Pinholster found himself in the tormenting position of reading results of a poll that showed him in front by landslide proportions, but pondering a pollster's projection which had him winning or losing by a whisker eleven days hence.

True, Swensson had an enviable record for accuracy and Pinholster knew that he never made a projection for a client until satisfied that a trend was under way. But how could this be? How could Swensson predict with any certainty that the voters would continue to swing to Eddie Quinn in a fixed percentage day after day? Pinholster found it incredible that the American people actually would come close to electing a man who scattered outrageous remarks around the countryside, who had no qualifications for high office and who offered thin, naïve, simplistic remedies for the most complex of social ailments.

Still, those numbers. Quinn, 38.6 per cent, up 1.1 per cent from yesterday, 2.2 points from Wednesday, 3.2 from Tuesday, 4.4 from Monday, 5.4 from Sunday, 6.6 from Saturday, 7.6 from Friday and 8.6 from Thursday night after Quinn's nomination. The numbers rang through Pinholster's memory. There was something immutable and changeless, and therefore evil, about the progression. If Eddie suddenly proposed today that the State Department be shut down and all foreign policy abolished—and who could guarantee that he would not?—would he still gain 1.1 per cent tomorrow in Swensson's poll?

Not a man given to self-pity, Pinholster nevertheless began to feel sorry for himself now. They were unfair, those ever-growing numbers, a naked, deformed parade, marching straight ahead, oblivious of anything Pinholster might do or say. He walked about the Blackstone living room, gazed down on Michigan Avenue and tried to think out broad strategy for the eleven remaining days before those goddamn red and blue lines met at their unholy rendezvous.

QUESTIONS

1 Are the Arnold Swenssons "high priests" or "devils" in the democratic election process?
2 In what ways can pollsters "slant" their analyses?
3 Should pollsters be subject to rigid controls by the federal government?

Political Parties
and Elections

Reading 14
The Politician
Stephen and Ethel Longstreet

A successful political party must offer suitable candidates to the electorate. Consequently, party leaders are constantly trying to recruit new and talented people who will not only run for office but will carry the party to victory. In return, of course, the party expects some loyalty in the form of support for the party's other candidates and postelection appointments for the party faithful. A party and its leadership remain in power by nominating and supporting the "right" candidates.

"Big Ed" Higgins in *The Politician* is an old-line party leader who needs a suitable candidate for a state senate seat. As he and his colleagues evaluate the prospective field, they come up with some interesting criteria for the candidate. When they finally do reach a decision on a possible candidate, they encounter a person who views the party in a different light.

Edward Emmett O'Clerigh (Big Ed) Higgins lived in a huge ugly pile of red fieldstone and yellow brick, put up in the '70's of the last century by a now-forgotten beer brewer. The grounds followed an old post road and were beautiful and well cared for. Big Ed liked his monster of a house, his large, oversized family, the feeling, as he said (too often), that "a low Mick like me who began as a short-order cook now has sons who go to Holy Cross and Notre Dame, and my daughter is the wife of a professor at Fordham; was married in St. Pat's in New York, with the Cardinal himself performing the services. So don't ever forget it's getting out the votes that makes this a great country."

Big Ed was six feet three and looked taller and wider, and his red handsome face had a purple tinge to it. His slate-colored eyes had the sharpness of a hunting hawk whose hood had just been taken off. He was a wise, alert, and active man who acted the part of a rough diamond. He was the biggest, most important political boss of the Party and was not interested in public office for himself. He liked to run things skillfully. He was an honest man in the sense that he never directly stole a dollar from the public till, bribed a jury, or had a murder committed. The man existed as a vital force, perhaps a needed force.

Big Ed was a replica of the old time city boss that we are told is no longer with us, but has been and always will be where there is a two-party system of democratic procedure, with spoils, interests, and lobbies. And where voters must be organized into blocs on issues, prejudices, and dreams.

On a sunny day before the fall nominations for state office, Big Ed sat in his high-ceilinged parlor—he never permitted it to be called living-room—under a bank of pink and green oil paintings of children with dogs, cows, and ponies. Settled around Big Ed were the large fish of the Party, and some smaller fry like myself. We were digesting the rich lunch, inhaling from large cigars, and holding, most of us, a fist around a shot glass of a yellow Bourbon whisky from our host's own charred oak kegs.

Big Ed said in his high small voice (a surprise in so large a man), "Now we haven't won a national election in a long time. We can take state governor's seats in sixteen states if we get out the local votes on some popular candidates. The Opposition is getting greedy and careless and taking graft with both hands in the barrel."

"We'll come back," said Judge Orley.

Close-The-Door Dooley took a swallow of his whisky and nodded. "I've no worries locally as to mayor and the county jobs. And we're behind the governor with fifty thousand extra votes. But you don't expect us to have anybody good for state senator here. Why, our party hasn't won that one since the Civil War put some chowder-head in against a carpetbagger."

Judge Orley snorted and killed his cigar. "Damnedest thing to divide the state as we did then. Now my grandpappy said . . ."

Big Ed smiled, holding up his hand to show that, much as he loved Judge Orley, he didn't want ancient history. He stood up and walked to a picture of a little girl in a white fluffy dress putting a blue ribbon around a lamb's neck. "It's important we get the governor back in. We're going to take a national election sometime in the next few tries and we need this state; it's the key state for a whole block of electoral votes. Why the devil, Stove Lid, haven't we elected a state senator from here?"

Stove Lid Novak ("Why, he's *so* honest nobody ever saw him steal a red hot stove lid"), the Hunky political boss, was sitting in the back. He swallowed cigar smoke and coughed. "I tell you, Edward, because we never had nobody to put up that could stand out real good against the Opposition candidate, that's why. The Bixelbys, Fitzgeralds, the Lees, and Wimmsons are very fancy old-time plantation folk, that's why."

Big Ed turned to me, scowling. "Jake, why don't you run?"

"Why waste my time, Mr. Higgins? I can't see the fancy tide water families voting for a Polack night-school lawyer."

Someone in the back of the room coughed and said smugly, "We need a pigeon."

Big Ed inspected his large carefully groomed hands. "We need an upstanding candidate and don't call him names—not yet. Let the Opposition call him the names."

Stove Lid said, "Edward, I keep thinking."

Close-The-Door Dooley stood up with a bounce. "Ed, what about this young Barraclough, the Yale character with the yacht."

I said, "His family have been members of the Opposition since it was named. Why, his great-grandfather helped found it."

Big Ed waved a hand at me to hold back and looked at Close-The-Door Dooley. "No man rejects public office if he wants it, eh, Dool? What's about this promising young fellow?"

"Paul Barraclough," said Close-The-Door Dooley, "has everything. Family, background, looks, a standing in a good law firm, a pretty wife, two cute kids."

Stove Lid Novak said, "And he's got the money, Edward, to finance his own campaign, that's why."

I stood up and made futile, embarrassed gestures with my hands. "This is a pipe dream. What makes you think Paul Barraclough would accept an unelectable nomination of office from our party?"

Big Ed came over to me and put his arm around my shoulders with a friendly warm pressure. "Jake, you're so right. Why don't you go right over and ask him?"

Judge Orley smiled. "Take the shoat by the teat to find out if there's milk."

I didn't feel very happy as I looked around the neat parlor. These meaty men were the leaders of the Party in the East, mixed here with the local bosses. I had attended many smaller meetings on lower levels. This was the first time I had been invited to a top level gathering of the policy makers, the actual brain and muscles of a vital, strong political system. I sensed a sudden terror in myself: had I been invited for just this thing? I felt miserably beyond my depth. "Why should Paul Barraclough listen to me?"

Big Ed slapped my shoulder twice. "A fool now would offer you the state chairmanship of some committee, Jake—or a seat on the platform at the next national convention. But I know you only want the best man running for the senate, and that's Barraclough. Whatever rewards are due you, you'll get in time. You're young yet."

I was acutely aware—that moment—as I had never been before that a political party was a gathering of faces, of minds and manners, dedicated or ambitious, honest or dishonest, but all geared to a kind of mystic ritual. When the ritual worked, it seemed like a kind of magic that out of nothing but voices and cigar smoke seemed to produce public offices, ideas, speeches, hopes and a kind of cynical yet parental feeling for the welfare and the devotion of the faceless collection called "the people." I felt it all bitterly now as I sweated and accepted my mission. I left the overheated parlor and went out into the crisp shiny day to drive to Paul's house. . . .

Now I was on my way to ask Paul Barraclough a question. I couldn't decide whether Big Ed Higgins had favored me or exposed me to ridicule with this errand to talk to Paul. I drove up to the white front door and the white marble steps. The door had been repainted again. There were two small birch trees on the lawn, held up by guy wires.

I rang the bell. A thin maid with a very pink face and a sniffling nose said, "The family is in the garden."

"That's all right," I said, and I walked through the house and out into the small garden. Janet sat under the vine arbor of still-green Concord grapes and watched casually from habit the two babies laid on blankets in the grass. Paul, in a boating cap, was smoking a highly polished pipe and driving wooden stakes into the ground with the back of a small ax. He had a powerful drive, and I saw he enjoyed banging the stakes down.

He stood up, smiled and held out his hand. "Well, surprise. I'm just getting some stakes down to anchor a playpen for the girls."

Janet stood up. "You haven't seen them, have you, Jake?"

I inspected the babies with that solemn awkwardness of all people who are afraid of children. I said, "Healthy, aren't they?"

Paul nodded. "Here I am again, as usual, Jake, captive in a house of women."

There was a solid bench built of unpainted pine planks. I sat down. "Paul, I'm here, or rather I was sent. Sent by Ed Higgins. I'll say it fast. He wants to know if you'd run for state senator this fall on the Party ticket."

Paul took the pipe out of his mouth and exhaled smoke slowly. He looked at Janet, whose face was the flushed pink of surprise. "Run for political office?" Paul asked, as if I were joking, but not being very amusing.

"That's right."

Paul began to laugh, head back, waving his pipe. "I see it. You need a pigeon."

I nodded.

He said, "A pigeon you think can pay for his own campaign."

Janet said, "Paul, you're being rude."

"No, that's about it," I said, getting up. "I'll go back and say you wouldn't think of it."

Janet, just the tip of her tongue showing between her teeth, stopped me by holding firmly onto my arm. "Paul hasn't refused yet."

I said, "The Barracloughs wouldn't change parties."

Paul was watching Janet. The pipe held in his mouth didn't wriggle.

Janet said, almost fiercely, "Paul hasn't said he wouldn't run."

We both looked at Paul. He had turned away and was tapping the blade of the ax lightly into a fence post. When he looked up at us, he said softly, "Janet, what do you think?"

She said, "You could ask for time to decide."

I said, "Why don't you come back with me to the meeting, Paul? Tell them yourself. You ought to meet them anyway."

"I was going down to check 'Adventure IV.'" He looked at Janet. She had picked up one of the babies and was wiping its mouth gently with a small square of linen. Janet had retired into herself after her first strong reactions. Paul looked at me and chopped the axhead deeply into the post and left it there. He rubbed his hands together.

"All right if I go like this? I still want to check the keel seams. But perhaps we'll find out instead what is the secret, the true manna of political success."

As we got into my car and drove around the corner past Hannah's town house, Paul turned away and looked instead toward a row of poplars whose leaves were shimmering silver in the wind.

The men were still in Big Ed Higgins' parlor. There was more order. They had broken up into a higher and a lower group. Stove Lid Novak was checking off names on a list, and old Judge Orley, who owned a fine collection of Renoir's and Degas's, was examining an inane picture of a large dog pulling a little girl in a two-wheeled wicker cart.

Paul followed me in, hands in the pockets of his blue yachting jacket, dominating the room with his easy smile. Big Ed, who couldn't be touched, and Judge Orley, a man of genteel breeding, remained at ease. The rest felt crude and ill-dressed suddenly. I could see that. Paul's poise of blood and manners was a handicap to him. It made him stand out in any gathering. He was to turn this to an advantage later in his career, but at his first meeting with the party bosses his striking differences from the usual candidate didn't help him.

I made the introductions. Close-The-Door Dooley winked and slapped Paul on the back. "Care for another cruise on the 'Seahoss,' Paulie, and a swim in the Potomac?"

"No, thank you." Paul turned to Big Ed. "Mr. Higgins, Jake tells me you are looking for a patsy to run for the state senate from this district."

Paul, when he wanted to, could use slang with the ease of a man who liked it or was amused by it, but Hannah's training, I was sure, hinted to him that it was not strictly in the best of taste.

"We're thinking of it, Barraclough. We haven't made any commitments yet. Just looking over the prospects."

"Of course," said Paul, sitting down. "I couldn't make up my own mind right away either."

Judge Orley said, "We'd give you a hell of a good ride, Mr. Barraclough."

"I'm sure you would, Judge. And it's tempting. If I do decide to, it would be only on certain conditions."

Big Ed rocked himself back and forth on the soles of his fifty dollar shoes. "*We* usually make the conditions."

Paul nodded and smiled. "We'll have to exchange conditions then."

Judge Orley said, "You wouldn't mind becoming a Party regular?" He motioned Paul to sit down.

"If I ran, of course not. But I'd still retain my right of private choice of candidates and issues."

Stove Lid Novak nodded. "Loyalty is what we want in a candidate. If we run you, Mr. Barraclough, there can't be any question of . . ."

Big Ed cut in crisply as he sat down facing Paul. "Barraclough, you know me by reputation. I never double-crossed a man, or asked him to do a dirty thing. I play square and I play hard. And I don't play like a gentleman. Politics isn't a game with me. I believe in the Party, and I believe we give the people the best we can find." Big Ed relaxed and permitted himself a little smile. "Right now you're the best we can find for this office."

Paul said, "I don't honestly know if I want to go into politics. I'll let you know one way or the other by the end of next week."

"Have a drink," said Big Ed. "Stay for dinner."

"No, I have to get out to my boat. Thank you, gentlemen. I shan't decide anything till next week."

The word "shan't" brought a double-take from Stove Lid Novak.

It was an interesting contrast as Big Ed and Paul went to a corner of the room to say personal good-bys to each other. Big Ed Higgins was a cold and logical man, and he did not treat a candidate with any special kindness. He had contempt for most of the political personalities ("meat heads," "slobs," "fartsacks") he usually found and controlled. But Paul had at once refused to be pushed into any category familiar to Big Ed. Paul would meet the political boss only as an equal, and he would admit to no blind loyalty to any private or party codes that were in conflict with his own ideas.

QUESTIONS

1   Why is the recruiting of candidates for office so essential to a party's success?
2   In what ways do political parties recruit possible candidates?
3   What criteria should be used by political parties in recruiting possible candidates?
4   How democratic is the process of candidate recruitment in America?

Reading 15
Convention
Fletcher Knebel and Charles W. Bailey, II

Convention, a novel by Fletcher Knebel and Charles W. Bailey, gives the reader a glimpse into the atmosphere of a political party's presidential nominating convention. National American political parties are very curious political entities; the only time that they are really organized is every four years when they hold their presidential conventions. In addition to nominating the party's candidate for the nation's highest office, the convention also defines the party's stands on the burning issues of the day and ratifies the presidential candidate's choice for the number 2 spot on the ticket. Following all this, the campaign begins, after which the organized party returns to hibernation for four more years.

Besides the hoopla, balloons, and pretty girls that have become associated with the party conventions, Knebel and Bailey stress the serious business of choosing the party's standard-bearer. Governor Bryan Roberts and Secretary of the Treasury Charles Manchester are waging a tremendous struggle for the top spot. The scrutiny to which these presidential candidates are subjected and their constant vulnerability give insight into the functions of political party conventions.

Archie DuPage opened the door, but a blast of trumpets rang down the corridor and drove him back inside the hotel room.

California, here we come!

Around the corner and down the hall trooped one of the amateur bands already plaguing the convention like trilling locusts. First came an enormous poppy, state flower of California, held high by a youth in gilt pants and jacket. Next pranced a drum majorette, attired in a strapless golden costume that began at mid-breast and ended at mid-thigh. Behind her, in single file, marched a dozen young musicians of both sexes, all shimmering in golden garments, all playing instruments of high decibel potential. The racket caromed off the walls and burst through the open doorway of suite 2306.

Archie winced and closed the door, but the noise pursued him through the cracks and over the transom.

California, here we come!

Bryan Roberts, he's the one!

Six female voices set the tempo, then the trumpets and trombones joined in, and by the time the marchers reached the Royal Skyway suite, the sound was deafening. Most of the group passed the door without recognition, but the last noisemaker, a lad belaboring a bass drum, paused long enough to shout:

"Don't worry in there. Roberts will take you for vice-president!"

The clamor dwindled gradually as the band turned the next corner, but it left some casualties. As Archie peered out again, a door down the hall was jerked open and a man wearing only pajama pants shuffled sleepily into the corridor. He rubbed a patch of graying hair on his chest and looked at his wrist watch. The man, who was a minor functionary in the headquarters, saw Archie's protruding head, then shook his own.

"Not even ten o'clock yet, for Chrissake," he grumbled in Archie's direction, "and already the nuts are at it. Thank God for our side. At least Charlie Manchester don't have so many lunatic bands."

The complainant retreated into his sanctuary and Archie went back to the sitting room of suite 2306 to see what was detaining the others. As usual, it was the telephone.

The candidate was speaking into the white phone, one of three on the desk. Secretary of the Treasury Charles B. Manchester held his tall frame erect and his blue lightweight suit showed the sharp creases of morning. Two other aides stood beside him, somewhat impatiently. The day had just begun in Manchester-for-President headquarters, but already Archie sensed the quiver of disrupted schedules.

"That's very thoughtful of you, Mr. President," Manchester was saying. He toyed with the telephone cord and his tone was one of respectful affability. "Well, I hope it doesn't blow the tube on your set. It's a little early in the day for statesmanship on television. . . . Don't worry about that. The farm issue won't be mentioned. . . . I know, I know. . . . Again, thank you, Mr. President. I certainly feel better for your call. . . . Goodby, sir."

Manchester grinned at his three assistants as he hung up. "The old fox. He pretended he wanted to wish me well before the press conference, but he was really worried about the farm thing. Afraid I'd get trapped. All right, let's go."

The four men filed out of the suite, Manchester in the lead. He did not seem to be moving fast, but the others had to hurry to keep up with his long, easy strides. Archie noted how straight the candidate held himself and involuntarily squared his own shoulders to correct his youthful slouch.

Charles Manchester's figure would have looked trim in any group and his carriage made him appear taller than six feet. He strode along with an air of casual confidence, and only a hand tugging at an ear lobe told Archie that the candidate was preoccupied. Archie guessed that Manchester was thinking ahead to the press conference and the unpredictable questions that would be coming.

Obie O'Connell was concerned with the recent past, not the future, and he was grouchy as he hurried his tubby body in a rolling gait beside his candidate. "That damn California song," he complained, "uses itself up quicker than anything since Taft and his 'Four-Leaf Clover' in '52."

"I like it," Manchester said. "It's got zing."

O'Connell massaged his puffy face. "You haven't seen enough conventions, Charlie," he said. "The first time, you love everything."

Louis Cohen edged between the candidate and the manager. Cohen, the "issues man" who taught political science at Princeton, had a face that seemed molded in a perpetual frown. His thin features appeared frail under the heavy frame of his glasses and he looked more unhappy than usual.

"Mr. Secretary," he said, "the President is right about the farm program. You really can't go into it now. It'll be a month before we have that study group paper—even if you're nominated."

"What do you mean 'if,' Louis? asked Manchester. He beamed down at his little professor as they walked along. Archie DuPage marveled that a man could look so radiantly confident so early in the day. "We'll win," said Manchester, "on the first ballot."

"The last ballot," O'Connell corrected. "You always win on the last ballot."

"The last ballot," Manchester agreed, and he grinned again.

They were approaching the elevators, but DuPage steered Manchester away with a hand on his elbow. "Let's take a service elevator," he said. "The Hilton may have fourteen elevators, but they started skipping floors yesterday. It'll be murder by Monday."

The service elevator contained a laundry cart. A white-coated employee held the cart with one hand while he worked to dislodge a piece of food from a molar with the other.

"Good morning," said Manchester, "I'm Charles Manchester."

"I know," replied the service man. He said it flatly, as though celebrated personages were a routine fixture in his world.

"And your name?" asked the candidate.

The man was startled. "Joe," he said. "Joe Greimer."

"Democrat?" asked Manchester.

The hotel employee nodded, abruptly ceasing his toothpick labors in embarrassment.

"That's a pity," said Manchester. "You really ought to give the Republican program a hearing, Mr. Greimer. If union men would only—"

"I'm getting off here," said the employee. The elevator had stopped at the fourteenth floor. Manchester, however, moved slightly and the man found his exit blocked.

The candidate's full attention was focused on the stranger. He asked the man how much he made and how many children he had. Under the questioning, the laundry worker's look of apathy was replaced by one of surprised pleasure. The others could feel the warmth of the connection being soldered between Joe Greimer and the Secretary of the Treasury. Archie whispered to O'Connell: "Wouldn't you love to have a picture of this?" O'Connell nodded. "If we could only get him two minutes with every voter in the country," he replied, "it would be a landslide." Louis Cohen looked at his watch. "He's going to be late," he protested.

Manchester finally stepped aside and the laundry man left, pushing his cart of soiled linen. Joe Greimer was smiling and he winked at Archie. "Some guy," he said with a flick of his head toward Manchester.

As the elevator descended the rest of the way to the mezzanine floor, Archie thought about his candidate. This sudden concentration on a person—any person—was no political trick. Manchester did it time and again, though frequently such a meeting would riddle his schedule. He seemed to have a compulsion for involvement with strangers. He disliked crowds, as Archie knew only too well, and so he broke them into tiny fragments. When he spoke, he spoke to the individual. In conversation, he became absorbed in the thoughts and problems of the other person. Charles Manchester, Archie had decided long ago, was a walking person-to-person program.

And how *could* Manchester lose the nomination? Big, cheerful, smart, compassionate, a leader with the magnetism that marked a winner—he was all of these. Above all, Archie thought, he looked like a winner, and what this Republican convention wanted most was a winner in November.

The victory four years ago had whetted the party's appetite. President Stuart's ill-health dampened hopes for a few months, but since he'd stepped aside and anointed Manchester as his successor, the party felt good again. Well, perhaps "anointed" wasn't quite right. Stuart merely declined to comment when Senator Floberg of Iowa, the Senate leader, said he understood that if the President were a delegate to the convention he'd cast his vote for Manchester. But that was enough. The party knew that Manchester was Stuart's choice. Privately, the evidence was even more solid. The President had called three times since their arrival in Chicago on Thursday.

As of this Saturday morning, August 12, with the convention due to open Monday, the challenge of Governor Bryan Roberts of California was somewhat less than frightening. A candidate needed 655 votes to win the nomination; count as he would, giving Roberts two thirds of the doubtfuls, Archie DuPage could reach a grand total of no more than 450 for the Californian. Manchester had almost 200 pledged votes from the primaries and another 500 hitched as securely as anything could be in politics.

Archie ran his fingers through his curly black hair and congratulated himself on his political acumen. A Yale graduate with a public relations office in his home city of Rochester, he had done some publicity chores in the Stuart campaign. He moved his one-man firm to Washington with the advent of the new Republican administration. When Manchester entered the Stuart administration as Under Secretary of the Treasury, fresh from the bank in Cincinnati, Archie persisted until he landed a public information job with this newcomer to politics. When Manchester moved up to the cabinet a year later, Archie went with him. He admired Charles Manchester's intelligence, his quick adaptability to the alien forum of politics, his humor, his easy grace, his confidence, his courage. If he were to fault his boss at all, it would be for his frankness. Sometimes the Secretary blurted out the truth when silence would have served him better. But what a guy! Manchester was made for the White House, and Archie, thirty-three, hankered for a seat of his own in that place of power.

The miscellaneous clamor of a convention—"a drunken cocktail party mated to an iron foundry," O'Connell called it—enveloped them as they stepped out of the elevator. A young girl, recognizing Manchester, shrieked and jabbed him in the stomach with an autograph book. The Secretary scrawled his high, looping signature and gave her a private smile. In a booth labeled "Have a Coke—With Manchester OR Roberts," another girl in a starched white uniform waved wildly. A crowd came from nowhere, pressing around the candidate with the flushed and aimless pleasure of unexpected proximity. O'Connell scowled and beckoned to a Chicago policeman nearby, and soon the four men from 2306 were burrowing through the gathering throng, Manchester sandwiched between the officer and O'Connell while Cohen and DuPage struggled to stay with them.

Manchester walked into the high-ceilinged Grand Ballroom, with its shimmering crystal chandeliers, at 9:58 A.M., on time despite his chats with the President and the laundryman. The buzz of conversation increased as the Secretary smiled, nodded and mouthed an inaudible "hello" to several newspapermen in the front row. Four television cameras focused on him and a shoving mob of still photographers began shouting indistinguishable and conflicting orders at him. His three aides sat down on the platform as Manchester stepped to the lectern and, precisely at 10 A.M., held up his hands for silence. The relative quiet that ensued was pierced by a shout from the rear of the room, where a few dozen gate-crashing spectators had gathered.

"The Man! The Man! The Man Who? Man-ches-ter!"

Manchester grinned and held his palms out in a muffling gesture.

"I appreciate the enthusiasm," he said, "but I'd ask the partisans to— uh—quench their ardor for the next half hour. This time belongs to the press, and it has its job to do. All right, ladies and gentlemen, I'm at your disposal. If you'd be good enough to state your name and affiliation—I'm sure your employers won't mind the publicity."

The opening laugh was friendly. The stenotypist recorded it in muted clicks on his keyboard as Manchester palmed the side of his head, where the neatly combed black hair was streaked with gray, and nodded to the first questioner.

"Corson, Associated Press. Mr. Secretary, some of your backers are talking about a first-ballot victory. Do you agree?"

Manchester moved his shoulders forward as he grasped the lectern, and a smile again softened the rather sharp lines of his lightly tanned face. "You must be telepathic. My mentor, Mr. O'Connell, informed me only five minutes ago—and I quote him—'you always win on the *last* ballot.' " A second laugh, heavier this time, rolled from the four hundred newsmen. "Obie insists that at a convention it's always done that way. Since he's my only manager, I think I'd better not fall out with him before the roll is called on Thursday."

"Why aren't Mrs. Manchester and the children with you?" The question erupted unbidden in a southern accent from a large, blonde woman in the front row.

"I'm afraid I didn't get the name, Mrs. Oliver." This time the laugh was a roar and Archie DuPage glowed. This thing was starting well. "Independent Alliance, isn't it?" Manchester added. The female journalist nodded in triumph, happy for the personal plug on all four networks.

"Well," Manchester went on, concentrating on Mrs. Oliver as though she were the only person in the room, "there's really no mystery. My wife is at our place on Lake Winnipesaukee in New Hampshire, baby-sitting for our granddaughter, Amy. If I should be nominated—with, I hope, the help of the New Hampshire delegation—Mrs. Manchester will fly here after the balloting. We just felt that the convention atmosphere was a bit too hectic for family life."

"What about the children?" Mrs. Oliver was not ready to yield the spotlight.

"Jake and Martha really aren't children, you know," replied Manchester. "Jake is rather new on his first job with a bank in San Francisco, and like most banks it takes a dim view of its young men plunging into politics in full view of the depositors. Martha's husband Ed is at sea with the Navy, so Martha's with her mother and the baby at Lake Winnipesaukee. I think that about takes care of the Manchester family. Let's just say that if you want to see my wife next week, you might ask any delegates you see to vote for me."

All right, all right, Archie thought. That's about enough humor, Mr.

Candidate. You're not running for toastmaster. Remember what happened to Adlai. As if he had heard the plea, Manchester dropped the easy smile and looked seriously at the crowd of newsmen.

"Carl Johnson, Des Moines *Register.* Mr. Secretary, the latest Iowa poll shows that only thirty per cent of the farmers in our state favor the Stuart administration farm program. Do you have something new in mind?"

Manchester nodded. He could imagine President Stuart sitting before the television set in the oval office at the White House, and he yearned fleetingly to say exactly what he thought—that the Stuart farm program was a shambles and would have to be abandoned. But he had been warned by the President and by Louis Cohen. He frowned as he spoke.

"I haven't seen that particular poll, but I would wager that even those who oppose the program would agree that the President has tried in good faith to find a sensible solution for what seems a perennial problem in this country. I might say it's one problem we're lucky to have, really. But the program does have shortcomings. The President recognizes that and I recognize it. We have a task force at work, and by Labor Day at the latest the Republican party will have a sound program ready for American agriculture. It will be fiscally reasonable and it will be calculated to do the job. Until then, I can assure you and our farm people that it's a problem uppermost in my mind."

The press conference settled down to serious, if not always significant inquiry. Roberts was claiming Nebraska. Was that justified? No. Would Manchester debate Senator Hendrickson, the Democratic nominee, on television? Of course. Was he being briefed by the CIA on intelligence matters? Not yet, but of course as a member of the National Security Council (a dig at Roberts, whose Sacramento statehouse was a continent away from such pinnacles of government) he kept abreast of all major developments.

Did he favor deficit financing? No. Pay-as-you-go was the basis of his fiscal thinking. Why had he become a candidate? Because he found he enjoyed the challenges of government and the greatest challenges were those of the Presidency—and because he thought he could make a contribution to his country. Manchester said this slowly and carefully, and he knew it rang true, because he meant it. He had thought about it many, many times.

Would he lower the social security retirement age? Take sides between Israel and the United Arab Republic? Cut foreign aid? Meet with the Canadian prime minister? Ask statehood for Puerto Rico? The questions came like a barrage and he faced the fire with only an occasional sidestep. Manchester glanced once at Archie and found him looking quite content.

An elderly man stood up in the middle of the room. His voice did not carry, and there was a pause while a hand microphone was passed to him.

"Thank you. Calvin Burroughs of the Burroughs newspapers, Mr. Secretary. There have been speculative stories out of Washington to the effect that you favor a substantial cut in defense spending. To my best recollection, you have not stated your views publicly. Could you do so now?"

"I'd be happy to, Mr. Burroughs," Manchester answered. He paused a moment, selecting his words, although he knew in general what he wanted to say. "This country has carried an enormous defense burden ever since World War II. We shall have to continue major outlays in this area. The Soviet Union has met us part way in reducing some of the tensions, it is true, but it would be foolhardy to think that the long cold war is over for good. And then of course, we have the steadily growing menace of Red China. So we have to maintain a large and alert defense establishment. But with that understood, we must recognize that a new element has entered the situation in the last few years. The United States today has enough nuclear weapons, and can deliver them, not only to eradicate Russia from the face of the earth, but literally to erase civilization itself. In short, the question now arises—do we need more? My mind is open on the question, but I must say I approach it in the negative. I would have to be shown that we needed more nuclear warheads, or delivery systems, than we now possess. Does that answer your question?"

Burroughs had stayed on his feet through the answer. Now he raised the little microphone again. Archie glanced at O'Connell. The manager's chubby face was tensed.

"In part, yes, sir," replied Burroughs. "But it leads straight off to the obvious question. As you know, there are a number of big contracts pending of the kind you mention, ones that won't go into production for some time yet."

"I'm aware of that, and I know that as a metropolitan publisher, Mr. Burroughs, you are perhaps even more familiar with them." Manchester spoke carefully. "I don't think it would be proper for me to comment on existing plans, except to say that if I am nominated and elected, I would want to re-examine each one in some detail."

A man in the second row stood up quickly. "Corson again, AP. Does that mean a hold-down on all new weapons systems?"

"No, I didn't say that." Manchester stroked the back of his head. Archie noticed it; it was a familiar sign that the Secretary was troubled. "There are weapons systems and weapons systems. For instance, the Navy is working on a hydrofoil warship that would be able to travel at upwards of sixty knots even in a heavy sea. That kind of advance we must always encourage, and with considerable funding, if necessary. I am referring to weapons systems which would do nothing more than deliver a great nuclear load a second or two faster."

Questioners were on their feet all over the room. The pack was alerted.

O'Connell now wore a frown almost as deep as that normally carried by Louis Cohen.

"McIntosh, *New York Times*. Are you implying, sir, apart from the delivery systems, that the United States already has a large enough arsenal of nuclear weapons?"

"I am," said Manchester, "within certain well-defined limits. If we discover a really new principle, or method of explosion, why, of course, I would favor its development. But merely the piling up of more existing weapons, no. I'm against that."

The buzz of conversation in the room rose to a steady hum. Chairs scraped as more reporters got to their feet. Questions now followed one another like quickening raindrops in a summer shower.

"What weapons systems now under consideration do you have in mind, Mr. Secretary?"

"I would not want to particularize. That would require expert study."

"But you mean, sir, you won't give the green light to a new delivery system of the type you mentioned?"

" 'Won't' is pretty final. I would be most cautious, put it that way."

"There is one major contract for a delivery system that's just been let, Mr. Secretary, for the Daphne missile, and we've been given a ten-billion-dollar figure on it. What about that?"

"That contract was approved by the Secretary of Defense and by the President."

"Well, as Secretary of the Treasury, Mr. Manchester, do *you* approve it?"

"I'm not here as Secretary of the Treasury. I'm here as an individual and as a candidate for the Republican nomination for President."

"Does that mean you do not approve of the Daphne contract?"

"I think my answers indicate my feeling."

"So, if you are elected, you'd re-examine the Daphne contract too?"

"Now, let's understand just what we're talking about. The Daphne contract was let several months ago. It will require a year of preliminary design work. While this is expensive by personal standards, no substantial commitment of funds will be necessary for another year yet."

"Does that mean, Mr. Secretary, that Daphne would be re-examined?"

"Well, yes. All such matters would be, as I said."

Two reporters near the door ran from the room. One caught his pocket on the doorknob as he went and the sound of ripping cloth cut through the rising medley of noise in the hall. Archie DuPage left his chair and whispered to Manchester. The candidate shook his head and turned back to the microphones.

"Let me try to put this matter in perspective," he said, "since I seem to have touched your news sensibilities. This country, according to the last official figures of the Joint Committee on Atomic Energy of the Congress, has ninety thousand nuclear warheads or bombs in stockpile. If they were detonated at one time, it's a question whether any human being would survive anywhere on the globe. All I'm saying is that enough is enough.

"The same thing applies to the long-range delivery systems. We have several dozen, from Atlas to Minuteman to Polaris. Here again, to be absolutely candid about it, enough is enough. Now, as I understand the argument for the Daphne, it would cut the delivery time from our launching pads to Moscow by about twelve seconds. When we talk about spending ten billion dollars to shave twelve seconds off the time required to bury humanity, I think it has some of the elements of sheer idiocy."

"What was that last word, sir? Idiocy?"

"Well, perhaps idiocy—that was the word, yes—is too strong but, gentlemen, I do feel strongly on this subject."

O'Connell groaned softly. Later, seeing a shot of himself at that instant on filmed television, he was shocked by his own stricken look. Professor Cohen cracked his knuckles. Archie DuPage felt uneasy, but didn't quite know why. A pang in his stomach reminded him, for the first time that day, of his ulcer.

"Mr. Secretary, Universal Forge has announced the hiring of ten thousand new employees to handle the Daphne contract. Would they be laid off?"

"I wouldn't have any comment, one way or the other, about Universal Forge's operations. I'm merely giving you my candid views on something that I think is vital to this country—and to the world."

"Sir, are you willing to make your argument that 'enough's enough' an issue between you and Governor Roberts?"

"Oh, I would think the Governor would feel much as I do. The sentiments of the opposition are something else again. We'll just have to wait and see what Senator Hendrickson and the Democrats have to say."

"Thank you, Mr. Secretary!"

These final words—shouted by a wire-service reporter as he broke for the door—turned the press conference into a tangle of heads and arms as newsmen pushed their way to the exits. The bank of partisans in the rear melted away after another explosion of joy for the candidate. A policeman again escorted the Manchester group toward the service elevator, and as they crossed the mezzanine floor, Archie thought he could sense a new excitement. Laughing women jumped to get a look at the candidate over the heads of those who pressed closer. The whole floor seemed to be a forest of curious faces, all seeking a look at Manchester. Burroughs the publisher, was shoved against the Secretary.

"Excuse me, Mr. Secretary," he said. "But I think you've made a convention out of this tea party."

"Apparently so." Manchester's brief smile suggested that he was not quite sure what Burroughs meant.

In the shelter of the service elevator, O'Connell slumped against the wall of the car and began kneading his face again.

"Honesty, honesty," he said with a heavy sigh. "It causes a hell of a lot more trouble in politics than corruption."

Manchester looked puzzled. "You think I went too far, Obie?"

"Far?" O'Connell's pale eyes darted from the candidate to DuPage to Cohen. "I don't know about the distance. All I know is that when you've got a nomination sewed up you don't usually throw out a big surprise all of a sudden."

"What do you think, Archie?" asked Manchester.

Archie took a deep breath. "As always, boss, I admire your candor and what you said was great. But the timing? I'm not sure President Stuart—"

Manchester interrupted, clenching his fists in frustration. "Dammit, I can't keep my mouth shut on every important issue. I'm willing to cover up for the President on something like the farm problem, and I can go along on a lot for the sake of keeping people happy, but I'm not Stuart's patsy. It may not be so smart, but on something as important as this I'm going to be my own man."

He stopped abruptly, as if apologizing for his outburst. Archie, rebuked by Manchester's unexpected anger, remained silent, but Cohen, his dark face brooding, offered: "It's high time it was said, but I'm not sure it had to be said today."

O'Connell looked balefully at Manchester. "The time to have popped off like that," he said, "would have been Thursday—right after the last ballot."

QUESTIONS

1 National nominating conventions in America subject party candidates to a tremendous amount of exposure and pressure; do you think conventions serve an important political function by doing this?
2 What are some alternative ways of nominating presidential candidates?
3 Are candidates subject to too much exposure and pressure from the mass media?

Reading 16
All in the Family
Edwin O'Connor

After the candidates are recruited and the convention or nominating process names the party's choice, the campaign for election begins. Campaigns have many functions; they allow issues to be aired and considered and the needs of the people to be expressed. From the party's standpoint, campaigns serve to activate the party faithful to contribute money, effort, and votes. Furthermore, campaigns must be designed in such a manner as to win over the undecided or uncommitted voters.

During the course of the campaign, interest groups begin to unite behind their chosen candidate or party, thereby forming a coalition of interests. The candidate must perform a balancing act to hold this party coalition together, offering enough rewards or deprivations to hold the groups in line.

The strategy of winning votes is a delicate one, as explained by Phil Kinsella, brother of the newly elected Governor (Charles), to his cousin Jack in this selection from *All in the Family*. Winning elections requires a blend of practical and theoretical knowledge, and some luck, as Phil indicates.

I was suddenly curious to know what he had thought of the whole campaign; I said, "Now that it's over, did you think he'd win all along?"

He nodded. "Sure."

"No doubts?"

"Doubts, yes, but only because you're foolish if you don't realize that accidents can happen. And probably will. But I knew that if we got our share of the breaks we were in, and in big. It wasn't by any means as hard as the mayoralty fight, no matter what you may have heard. And neither one of us ever thought for a minute that it would be. Surprised?"

"Yes, a little. I would have figured Consolo as much tougher than that on past performance alone."

"The trouble with past performance is that it's in the past. Everyone is over the hill sooner or later, and we thought Consolo had just about had it. He'd lost a lot of support where he'd always been strongest—with the Italians. When he first ran I don't think there was an Italian in the state who didn't vote for him: he was their boy. But everything changes, including Italians. We had polls taken, and every one of them showed that by now the Italians were getting tired. They didn't want just another Italian in there, they wanted a good Italian. Well, there just wasn't one around—at least, not one who could run for governor. So they voted for Charles—I don't suppose the 'Kinsella' hurt there, by the way. It was the old confusion all over again. Remember: 'Hey, are you Irish or Eyetalian?' "

I remembered: it was a family joke. When I was a boy in school I had often bitterly regretted having one of those names—Costello was another— which was subject to mortifying misinterpretation. In a way proud of the name because it was my father's, my mother's, I nevertheless longed for something clearcut: Sullivan, Murphy. But now, years later, ambiguity apparently had paid off. . . .

"Whatever the reason," he said, "when they ditched him he was dead. He had to be: without them he just didn't have the horses. Anyway, for my money he was always overrated. He had this reputation for almost supernal cunning: well, I had a couple of long sessions with him and I couldn't see it. What I could see was a rather stupid man who'd had almost supernal luck. And now the luck had run out and he had nothing—or very little—left. So that's why I figured it would be easy. On top of which we got a few breaks, we had the organization, we had drive, we had the money. And we had Charles."

First things last? I said, "In short, a breeze?"

"No," he said. "Not a breeze. Damned hard work all the way."

"No fun?"

"Well, you know: a funny thing happened to me on my way to the State House. Funny things are always happening around here: the whole state's a joke machine. But overall it didn't add up to much fun: as I say, it was mainly hard work. Not fighting Consolo; just keeping our own crowd in line. Which was no cinch, believe me."

"The celebrated coalition?"

"That's right. Labor for Kinsella, Small Business for Kinsella, Ministers for Kinsella, Negroes for Kinsella, Professors for Kinsella, Conservatives for Kinsella, Liberals for Kinsella. And—inevitably—Independents for Kinsella. You name it, we had it. It took a little doing to get them all in under the same tent, but we did it. We put them all together and then we found out we had to do something more: we had to keep them all together. And the one way, the *only* way, we could keep them together was to keep them apart: as far away from each other as possible. A slight paradox. You follow?"

"Yes, sure." It wasn't hard to follow: the rivalries, the potential clashes, the hurt feelings and the jealousies inherent in this reluctant combination were easily imagined. And now, again, I remembered the talk we had had on that night five years ago; I said, "But isn't that more or less what you wanted? You were out to take control away from the stumblebums by broadening your base: wasn't that the whole idea?"

"That's right. And we did. Of course we've still got the stumblebums—
you don't get rid of an army of hacks and grafters overnight, and they're
still important: look at Cogan, for one—but the point is they don't have
control any more. We have that."

"You and the coalition."

"Yes, but we run the coalition. With some difficulty, but we do. The
real trouble is that each group wants Charles all for itself. Just by the way,
nobody's any worse there than the Professors. They don't want their piece
of flesh, they want the whole body. One hundred per cent: they want him
for their very own. They want to serve him up for dinner, they want to eat
him up. And failing him, I'll do. Fortunately Charles is just about tooth-
proof and I'm not so soft myself, so we survive. But it's not easy." He
sighed and said, "They all want something different: well, okay, you expect
that. The Negroes, of course. They're catching up and they're shooting for
everything now: fine. Maybe not fine, but understandable. The poor bas-
tards haven't had a fair shake for so long that all they want to do is grab the
dice and run. But you can deal with them—at least you can deal with
whichever spokesman you're talking to at the moment. And with them it all
means something, it's exciting, it's real, and at least you feel you're in the
land of the living. Whereas with some of the others . . ."

He shrugged, and I said, "The Professors? You don't love the eggheads
any more, Phil?"

"There's a certain kind of arrogance that puts me off." he said. "I
suppose we're arrogant enough in our way, but it's not *that* way. I talked to
a couple of them here tonight: they have a rather peculiar idea of their own
contribution to the campaign. The fact is that it wasn't all that great. Do
you know Kurt Vogelschmidt, for instance? Have you met him?" Switching
to mimicry, he said, "Haff you as yet had zat disdigdt blesshure?"

"No. I know who he is, of course." This owl-faced, mountainous refu-
gee from savage European oppressions had come to America at the outbreak of World War II. Weighing close to three hundred pounds, paralyz-
ingly articulate, he had bullied a succession of Midwestern political science
faculties into helplessness until finally, ten years or so ago, he had wound
up here in the city for emergency abdominal surgery. He had remained to
teach and to talk. There were rumors that he had been on the point of
beginning a distinguished political career in Vienna when the war had un-
happily intervened; these rumors remained rumors, but it was a fact that he
was now one of the most vocal of academic political activists, and I remembered seeing his name heading a list of professors who had vigorously supported Charles. I said, "He's . . . what? To the campaign, I mean. The
Brain Trust? The big theory man?"

"I'll tell you just what he is," Phil said. "He's a waste of time. He's my
mistake. I got him in; I thought he packed a little weight with the others.

Well, he does. But not enough. Not enough, for example, to justify calling me every other night around one in the morning to tell me what he expects of Charles on the basis of his own keen analysis of Austria before Dollfuss. The hours I've spent listening to that chucklehead outline a strategy which would be just swell if only Consolo were Franz Josef! At first I thought he was kidding; by the time I caught on it was too late. And all the while, chirping away in the background—because she's an intellectual type too, you see—is his charming wife Elli, who weighs a cool thirty-five pounds, has bangs, wears knee socks, lives in the past, loves Bartók, hates supermarkets, and serves a special kind of iron strudel she bakes herself! It's ghastly beyond belief. It drives you right back to the stumblebums: I'd a lot rather spend my time chewing the fat with One-Eyed Danny Geegan of the Police Athletic League. At least I'm sure we got his vote. For all I know charming Elli wrote in one for Leopold Figl."

I said, "He's dead, I think."

"That's all right with me," he said. Then he smiled quickly and said, "That shows you how parochial I've become. Do you think this state is getting to me?"

"What about Charles?" I said. "How does he get along with them?"

"Better than I do. That's partly because I'm with them more. But also he's more patient and he's developed this great self-control. And that marvelous way of looking gravely attentive, as if he were really listening hard to what you were saying. That's big magic in the academic league: they're all talkers. And then they also misread Charles rather seriously. They know he's not really one of them, but they think that in a way he is, they think he values them especially, and they think that now he's the Governor they'll all do very well."

"And they won't?"

"No," he said soberly. "They can't: it's not in the cards. Oh, they'll do all right, but that's not what they want. They want a little power. They want to be right up there with Charles, running the show. They haven't got a prayer: Charles is much too smart to let that happen. He knows exactly what they've given him, and he'll make some sort of equivalent return: equivalent, but no more. Well, some of them will accept that, and others won't. But if they don't, what are they going to do about it? Support somebody else? Who? You see in a funny way they're a little like the party hacks: they may not much like what's happening to them, but where else are they going to go? And nobody knows that better than Charles."

QUESTIONS

1 Why are political parties often called coalitions of interests?

2 How are the various interests held together in a political campaign?
3 Do campaigns allow for the full public discussion of issues and needs of the people?

Interest Groups

Reading 17
The Ninth Wave
Eugene Burdick

Eugene Burdick's novel *The Ninth Wave* considers perhaps the most widely misunderstood part of the American political system—the interest group. Interest groups provide an important resource for politicians in the form of information and serve the important function of representing interests that people hold in common when other political institutions fail to represent them. The public, however, usually views interest groups as a menace to the general good. The objectives of an interest group to secure and protect political advantages for its members do not necessarily conflict with the public's interests, but this is an area about which there is a great lack of information and misunderstanding.

In the following excerpt two members of a senior citizens' interest group, Mr. Appleton and Mrs. Sweeton, meet with Mike Freesmith, the campaign manager for gubernatorial candidate Cutler. Their interest in this meeting is in finding out just where the candidate stands on their issues before pledging their support to him, an effective technique that interest groups employ. Freesmith's purpose in this meeting is either to gain the support of the senior citizens group or to reduce its importance. The outcome of the meeting is both surprising and disturbing.

They stood up and walked up the aisle. Hank looked at the rows of identical, round, prosperous faces. They were attentive and alert. They gave off an aroma of Odorono, Aqua Velva, Old Crow, good perfume and tobacco. When they stepped out of the hall at once Hank caught the old, familiar cheap odor of the hotel.

Mike walked over to the little room across the hall and knocked on the door. One of the neat clerkly looking men opened the door. Mike spoke to him. The man nodded and went into the hall.

When they got to the room Mike took off his coat.

"Call up and order some beer," Mike said. He went to his briefcase and began to haul out documents. Georgia ordered the beer and some chicken sandwiches. Almost at once there was a knock on the door. Mike went over and opened the door.

"Hello, Mr. Appleton, come right on in," Mike said.

Mr. Appleton was a small thin man. He had a long thin neck with red skin, folded like turkey's skin into tough slanting rolls. He looked as if he had once been much fatter and his bones and cartilage had simply shrunk inside the bag of his skin. He had bright glittering eyes, hard with suspicion. His shoes were very shiny and when he sat down he carefully pulled up his pants legs to save the press. His shoes were high. He wore a white shirt, but the points of the collar were tiny and yellow; the kind of yellow that comes from home washing and long careful storage and putting mothballs in linen drawers.

Mr. Appleton was followed by a woman whom he introduced as Mrs. Sweeton. She was formless in a black crepe dress. She wore a long string of coral beads around her neck and they hung to her waist. The beads were large and yellow, like the aged teeth of some large animal. Her fingers never left them alone.

"It's your meeting, Mr. Freesmith," Mr. Appleton said. "You asked for it. So tell us what's on your mind. Mrs. Sweeton and I will talk to any politician that wants to talk to us. We represent the Senior Citizens Clubs of Long Beach, Gardena, Seal Beach, and San Pedro. So what's on your mind?"

"I'm not a politician," Mike said. "I'm just a lawyer."

"That's right, you're just a lawyer," Mr. Appleton said and laughed a dry thin acid laugh. "But maybe you represent a politician. So get on with it."

Mr. Appleton sat with a simple proper arrogance, his back not touching the chair, his feet squarely on the floor. There was something mathematical, precise, clean and unattractive about him.

"How do your people feel about Cutler?" Mike asked.

"Don't know yet. Haven't seen his pension planks yet. Next question?"

"What would you like to see in a platform, Mr. Appleton?" Mike asked.

"You know that. A pension that senior citizens can live on, an act by the legislature that will make pension funds the first obligation on state funds, the administrator of the pension fund to be a friendly person. It's all on the record. We've said it before. We'll say it again. It's all on the record. Next question?"

Mr. Appleton sat calmly in the chair, rigid with confidence.

There was a knock on the door and it swung open. A waiter walked in with a tray on his shoulder.

"Six Pabsts, chicken sandwiches. That right?" the waiter said. He swung the tray down onto a table. Mike pitched him a half dollar.

"Like a bottle of beer or a sandwich, Mr. Appleton?" Mike asked.

"Don't drink," Mr. Appleton replied crisply. "Go right ahead, though. Go right ahead."

"Mrs. Sweeton, excuse me," Mike said. "Would you like a glass of beer or a sandwich?"

Mrs. Sweeton's brown round eyes moved for the first time since she entered the room. She had been sitting quietly, her fat smooth hands manipulating the jagged coral beads. Since the tray came in the room, however, she had been staring out the window. Now her eyes focused on the sandwiches, examined the soft white bread, the green lettuce, the rich mound of potato salad on each plate, the brown heap of potato chips.

As if she were remarking on something novel and unique and quite unrelated, she said, "It's been so long since breakfast," and after a quick look at Mr. Appleton she stared out the window again.

Georgia picked up a plate and passed it to Mrs. Sweeton. Staring out the window, quite obliviously, Mrs. Sweeton took the plate and her soft sure fingers quickly grasped the sandwich and put it to her lips. She turned her head away so that they could not see her take the first bite.

"Would you like me to send out for some tea or milk, Mrs. Sweeton?" Georgia asked.

The gray hair moved quickly and she looked up at Georgia.

"Oh, don't send out for anything. I'll just drink whatever you have here," Mrs. Sweeton said.

She did not look at the glass of beer as Georgia pressed it into her hand. She took a deep drink of the beer and then put a wisp of a handkerchief to her lips to wipe away the foam.

"Go on, Mr. Appleton," Mike said. "You were saying that your aims were all on the record. Do you think Cutler is in agreement with those aims?"

"Can't tell, I said," and his voice was as cool and thin as shredded ice. "If we ever get him on record we'll know what he stands for."

"Your people would not approve him though on what you know now?"

Mr. Appleton brought the tips of his fingers together in what was clearly a gesture of pleasure. "No," he said. "No. We wouldn't approve him or any other pie-in-the-sky, big-bellied lying politician. Not until we saw their platform in black and white. If his pension plank is right we'd support him. But we wouldn't really believe him until we saw the right laws roll out of Sacramento." Mr. Appleton paused a moment. He glanced coolly at Mrs. Sweeton, at the big attractive tray of beer and sandwiches, at the big suite of rooms. "We're not as stupid as we were ten years ago, Mr. Freesmith. And we're a hell of a lot better organized. We don't buy very easily now. We've got a program and we're going to get it. Franklin Roosevelt framed us, Upton Sinclair framed us. But we ain't fools anymore. We're organized."

He stopped abruptly. Like a man who has already said too much. He stopped tapping his fingertips together and twisted his hands together into a mass of thin fingers and white knuckles.

Mrs. Sweeton was frightened and she put the glass of beer down on the table. She continued to nibble at the sandwich. Her teeth worked deftly and minutely at it, wearing it down with nervous small bites so that she chewed incessantly.

"Mr. Appleton, what did you do before you retired?" Mike asked.

"I was a carpenter. Journeyman carpenter. Iowa first and then California. Good one too. Laid three thousand feet of oak flooring in . . ." he stopped slowly and glanced at Mike. "I was a carpenter."

Mike poured a glass full of beer. He did it slowly. He poured the beer down the side of the glass and watched the thin collar of foam climb slowly up the side. He turned the glass upright just as it was perfectly full. He took a bite of a sandwich and then pushed a handful of potato chips in his mouth. The sound of the chips being crushed was the loudest noise in the room. Mike wiped his hand across his mouth and smiled at Mr. Appleton.

"Mr. Appleton, have you got a minute to spare so I can tell you a little story?" Mike asked. "It's a very short story. Very short."

Mr. Appleton's bright birdlike eyes swept over Mike with a look of hard pity. His hands uncurled and he tapped his fingertips together; the five fingers of one hand gently bouncing off the five fingers of the other hand.

"A minute, Mr. Freesmith? I've got lots of minutes," he said and cackled shrilly; a harsh arrogant sound; chickenlike and hard; utterly confident. "Sure. I've got a minute."

"You see, Mr. Appleton, we know a little bit about how our elder citizens, our senior citizens, were treated in other societies," Mike said in a soft voice. He looked relaxed and powerless. Sweat marked his armpits and blotched the front of his shirt. His eyes were half closed against the heat and the glare of the sun that came in the venetian blinds. "We know, Mr. Appleton, from anthropology and sociology that every society tends to protect its most productive members . . . the men and women who can work the hardest, reproduce, fight wars, invent things, expend energy. In tough times the entire society will instinctively protect its strongest members. An old Eskimo will make up his mind one day and wander off into a storm and die if the food supply gets low enough. He does that because he knows that if he doesn't the younger people might force him out into the storm. And so he goes by himself."

"Mr. Freesmith, my people are waiting for me back in the Convention Hall," Mr. Appleton said and his upper lip was drawn thin. "They want to know what Cromwell stands for. They don't want to hear horror stories."

"Sure, sure. Just a minute," Mike said. He took another drink of beer. He put more potato chips in his mouth, crunched them loudly. "Just hear me out. Let me tell you about one society and the way it took care of its older people. This was a society that was hard pressed by its enemies . . . pretty much the way the United States is today. They began to worry, wonder if they could stand the pressure, argue about how they'd do in a war. They worried about whether they were strong enough and what they ought to do to keep strong. What they finally did was have all the citizens take off their clothes once a year . . . all at the same time. Then they would all gather naked in the public square and march in front of a committee of wise men. It was pretty clever really. All the young bucks would see girls they were interested in and it would become obvious that they were interested and, even more important, that they were capable of doing something about it."

Mike paused and looked at Mr. Appleton. Mr. Appleton was looking straight ahead, but his eyes were a deeper color and they had lost their hard suspicious look. His tongue licked at the corners of his dry old lips and he almost smiled.

"Round and round the public square they'd march," Mike went on. "Everyone buck-assed naked. And slowly they'd pair off. The strong young men would pick the strong young women they liked and the committee of selection would let them leave the square and wander off into a grove of trees nearby. Then what would be left would be old people who obviously couldn't do what was necessary. Thin old geezers with skin hanging around their waist and knock-kneed; fat old men with pot bellies and double chins. Old hags; no corsets or girdles to hide them. Just their white old ruined childless flesh for everyone to see. No muscles left; no energy, no nothing. Understand?"

Mr. Appleton was still sitting very straight, but his eyes were unfocused and vague. His face seemed slightly dissolved. He crossed his arms across his chest and rocked back and forth.

"Understand, Mr. Appleton?" Mike asked. "No energy, no nothing?"

Mr. Appleton's eyes roamed around the room and then fastened fiercely on Mike. He nodded savagely.

"Finally the only ones left in the square would be the old people," Mike said. "They'd walk around and around, the old naked men and the old naked women . . . with the committee giving them a cold eye. Waiting to see if the old men still had it in 'em. Or if anyone wanted the old women. The committee didn't say a thing. They didn't do anything. But after a while the old men and women would disappear. They would wander off. Not into the grove but out into the countryside and far away from the town. Out of the society altogether. Gone. Gone forever. Some of the stronger ones became slaves or shepherds, but none of them hung around." Mike paused a minute and took another sip of beer. His teeth, when he bit into the sandwich, looked very white and strong and he looked up with a grin.

Mr. Appleton twisted in his chair. Mrs. Sweeton sobbed distantly and fumbled for the beer glass with her hand. Hank handed it to her and she drank deeply and then wiped off her lips with the back of her hand. There was a smear of mayonnaise on her chin. Mr. Appleton was trying to smile, but his teeth made a thin, chalky sound as they ground together in a desperate effort to keep his chin from gaping and wagging.

"You're . . . you're . . . you're . . . a savage," Mr. Appleton said finally and snapped his mouth shut. Saliva ran from the corner of his mouth and in a bright silvery streak down his chin. He leaned far back in the chair. Suddenly he looked very frail and small; almost childlike. Some thin strong certitude had snapped and his jaw hung open and showed the false pinkness of his dentures and the real pinkness of his tongue.

"No. I'm not savage," Mike said softly. "I'm just trying to tell you the facts of life. The story is true. It happened in Sparta and the man who wrote it down was Lycurgus. Go to the public library and check it out. Read it. It really happened."

"Well, it's uncivilized," Appleton said, but his voice lacked conviction. His tongue clacked softly against his false teeth.

"You have to realize that America's in a crisis today," Mike went on. "Just like Sparta was. Russia is looking down our throat. Pretty soon there's going to be a war. And people will get scared. They'll wonder if we're strong enough to win. And they'll take a cold look at who can help in the fight and who can't. Every society does it, Mr. Appleton. Every single society that's under pressure does exactly that. When we take that cold look we might decide that our senior citizens are a liability; a handicap."

"It's not so," Mrs. Sweeton said. There were tears in her eyes, but her face was not anguished, it was frightened. "No one thinks that in America."

"Look, Mrs. Sweeton," Mike said. "Did you ever hear of euthanasia until recently? Of course not. It's a polite term for murdering people who don't have any good reason for living anymore. Right now euthanasia would only be applied to congenital idiots, incurable cancer and things like that. But let things get really tough; let the battle really begin, and that will change. Someday soon someone is going to suggest that maybe euthanasia be applied to people over a certain age . . . everyone over a certain age would get the works. It's in people's minds already; you can see it stirring around; just waiting to be said. You don't see many young people anymore, but they're talking about it; gnawing away at the idea. Worries 'em. And the word euthanasia keeps popping up."

"You shut up. You're a god damn liar," Mr. Appleton said. He was crouched in the chair, like a tiny defensive monkey. His old splayed carpenter's hands were held out in front of him. "You're lying. That's what you're doing."

"Mike, my God, don't talk like that," Georgia said. She looked at Hank, but he was staring at Mike. Her voice was thin; at the shatter point. "Even if it's true don't say it."

"But it's true," Mike said. "I have to say it. If these people are going into politics they better find out the facts." Mike reached out and shuffled through the papers on the coffee table. He picked up a sheet. "Now, look at this report. It's from UNESCO. It's a survey of what age groups suffered most in Russia and Germany during World War Two. Do you know that the old people, people over fifty-five, just about disappeared from those two countries? No one knows just how, but they did. They just vanished away. Starved, maybe, or sent off to Siberia or killed from overwork or something. But they're gone. Just as if the Germans and the Russians decided that the old people had to go first."

Mr. Appleton moved his bent, tough carpenter's hands, but no words accompanied them: only a sound like a muted sustained yelp.

"The point is, Mr. Appleton, you don't want to press a society too hard," Mike said. "Those slick young men down in Long Beach that run your organizations tell you you can get anything you want if you just push hard enough. But maybe you'll get more than you bargained for. Maybe America is saving up a surprise to hand you. Maybe you'd better protect yourself."

Mrs. Sweeton stood up as if she were going to leave the room. She stood hesitantly and then Mike looked up at her. He did not smile and for a few moments they looked at one another. Then she saw the sandwiches and the broken look left her face; she went soft with desire. She picked up a sandwich, pushed it savagely into her mouth, roughly jabbed the bits of chicken past her lips. Little bits of lettuce fell unnoticed on her neat black bosom.

"What should we do?" Appleton asked. His voice was thick and mechanical; as if the words were made only by the false teeth.

"The first thing is to forget all that stuff about calling yourselves senior citizens or the deserving elderly or any other term like that," Mike said. "Just face the facts. You're old, marginal, used-up, surplus. All right. How do you protect yourselves?"

Mike picked up a folder. He opened it and spread the paper on the table. The top item was an architect's sketch of what looked like a great sprawling army camp with Quonset huts and barracks neatly arranged in blocks.

"Now the worst problem that old people face is adequate housing," Mike said. "Cromwell is prepared to undertake a state program of old-age camps where everyone past a certain age could have an individual room, adequate food and an issue of clothing. The camps would be out in the country. They would be nicely built. It wouldn't be luxurious, but it would be safe. Now the thing the old people have to do is . . ."

When Mr. Appleton and Mrs. Sweeton looked up their eyes were bright and clear like the eyes of very trusting and loyal children. They watched Mike's lips move, but they scarcely heard his words. They nodded endlessly.

When the old people left Mike stood up. He walked to the bathroom door. He turned.

Hank spoke very slow, with careful deliberation, reaching measuredly for the words.

"Mike, you dirty, dirty, dirty bastard, you deliberately . . ."

And then he stopped. For a grin was spreading over Mike's face. It was not a hard grin or without pity. But it was certain; absolutely sure.

Mike waited, but Hank did not speak. Mike turned and went into the bathroom.

QUESTIONS

1   What important functions do interest groups perform in American politics as shown in this selection?

2   What advantages were the senior citizen's group trying to obtain from politics by meeting with Mr. Freesmith?

3   What was the outcome of the meeting between the senior citizen's interest group and the politician's agent (Freesmith), and what implications are there for the success of that interest group in politics?

Reading 18
Power
Howard Fast

Another method that interest groups employ is lobbying, that is, trying to persuade political decision makers to support the group's interests. The representation of various interests before decision-making bodies is a constitutional right under the freedom of petition clause, but most Americans regard it as unsavory. Nevertheless, lobbying remains an effective form of communication between governmental decision makers and the people (represented by interest groups).

In his novel *Power*, Howard Fast creates a situation in which an interest group, a coal miners' union, lobbies the President of the United States. Ben Holt, the union leader, and his adviser, Mr. Cutter, give their frightening assessment of the situation in the coal industry. Holt and Cutter use a lot of factual information to substantiate their claims, a highly effective lobbying technique.

"Sit down, please, gentlemen," he said, glancing meanwhile at the note Denny had handed him. Then he said to the stenographer, "We'll be off the record until I indicate otherwise. Better that way, I think," he concluded, glancing at Ben, who was watching him thoughtfully and with great interest. The stenographer was well trained, for I was to observe that a nod of the President's head was sufficient to place us on the record, a slight shake of his head enough to halt it. "I expected Mrs. Goodrich," he said to Denny, and at that moment she entered, a brisk, sharp-faced gray-haired woman who was the Secretary of Labor. She nodded at the President, and took a chair next to Denny. They sat at one side of the desk, the stenographer at the other, Ben and I facing it.

"Well, Mr. Holt," the President began, "I've heard a good deal about you. I guess that doesn't surprise you?"

"No, sir, it does not."

The President smiled and said, "We do have this in common. Between the two of us, we've been called everything under the sun. How much of it was deserved, time will tell, but I suspect that in both cases, there is exaggeration. Sometime, we'll talk about that. Right now, we'll talk about coal."

"That's what I am here for," Ben agreed.

"Good. I can see that Mr. Cutter brought a large brief case, so you are probably armed with every fact on coal that one could conceivably require. But let's leave the statistics alone for the moment. If I were to ask you, Mr. Holt, to tell me in very few words what is wrong with the coal industry, how would you reply?"

"The industry is sick," Ben said shortly.

"But isn't that true of almost every industry in America right now?"

"It is, Mr. President, but for other industries, it's a recent sickness. Ours is chronic. The coal industry has been sick for a hundred years"—the President nodded slightly and the stenographer began to put down Ben's words—"and this depression only sharpens the pains."

"Why is coal different?" the President demanded.

"Because, sir, mining is different. The very nature of mining makes it singular, and it's always been that way. The miner digs a hole in the earth and crawls into it, and since the first mines were dug five thousand years ago, it's been a dirty, rotten, and different job."

"That's not to the point," the President said, with a slight show of irritation. "I want to know why you feel that coal mining today is basically different. You were talking about sickness. What is coal's particular sickness?"

"Slave labor," Ben said flatly.

"Just what do you mean by that? I don't want slogans, Mr. Holt. Suppose we talk directly to the point."

"That suits me, sir. The point is this. One of the richest deposits of bituminous coal in the United States, if not in the whole world, lies here in the East. Its northern extremities are the northern borders of western Pennsylvania and eastern Ohio, and from there it runs southward, through Pennsylvania and Ohio, encompassing most of the state of West Virginia, the whole of eastern Kentucky, a small wedge of Virginia, a thick slice of central Tennessee, and more or less the northern half of the state of Alabama. Now you can divide this vast area of bituminous fields by drawing a line parallel with the southern border of Pennsylvania. North of this line, with varying degrees of success, depending upon the time and the circumstances, we have been able to organize the miners into the union. Thereby, we have been able to maintain a certain level of wages, not very high, not very uniform, but enough for miners to live like human beings when they worked.

"South of this line. with a few exceptions, our union does not exist. The last time we made a large-scale effort to organize miners in this vast area, which stretches from Pennsylvania to Alabama, was in 1920. I went into West Virginia then, with a staff of union organizers, and we were met by armed thugs, whole armies of company police, and every imaginable type of violence. Thousands of coal miners were driven out of their homes, terror was resorted to, and finally an army of miners faced an army of company police, the two sides drawn up in what threatened to be an actual war—"

"Are those the facts?" the President said to Mrs. Goodrich.

"More or less. There was provocation on both sides, and finally army units were sent in to prevent an outbreak of what could have been localized warfare."

"And since then, Mr. Holt?" the President asked.

"Since then, Mr. President, we have failed in every attempt to organize in the South. The result is that the southern miner is little better than a slave. The fact that he has been reduced to almost indescribable poverty, that he lives more like an animal than a human being, that he never handles cash but spends his existence in debt to the company store, and that he is the constant victim of undernourishment, pellagra, and beriberi—these facts are in the nature of a personal description and condition. They can be put aside. As far as the industry is concerned—"

"They can't be put aside, Mr. Holt," the President interrupted.

"Sir?"

"I am not used to putting the personal condition of the citizens of this country aside, Mr. Holt."

They were watching each other and measuring each other. In one way at least, in their manner of imperious command and self-assuredness, they were remarkably alike, but in every other way, they were as apart as the two poles, the President precise, restrained, controlled, his speech meticulous and clean as the bare, shining surface of his desk, his emotions as alert and as calculated as his voice, his interest in Holt dulled by a seed of distaste for the big, vital, fleshy man who faced him—and Ben Holt loose, relaxed, and wary at once, bristling inwardly at the closeness of an aristocrat, sensitive, seeking for an insult, a rejection or an innuendo where none was meant, defensive but unafraid, pulling over himself, bit by bit, now and through the time to come, that fierce, frightening cloak of pride that marked the digger from all others.

"Nor am I," Ben answered slowly, his voice deepening, his eyes narrowing. "You asked me for the condition of an industry and an explanation of its sickness. What these miners in the South suffer is a badge of shame this whole nation wears; but the same treatment that turns their lives into hell is destroying the American coal industry. In 1928, when we were able to negotiate a contract under union terms, the miner got seven and a half dollars a day—nothing to write home about for the hardest work man has been able to cook up, but enough to keep body and soul together. Today, there isn't a mine in the country where we can negotiate such a contract. Today, it's a great victory to get four dollars a day, and the last operator who signed a four-dollar-a-day contract with me said, 'Well, Ben, I might as well give you that extra dollar as give it to my creditors. I'll be bankrupt in sixty days anyway.' And he was, Mr. President—bankrupt before the sixty days were up. And why? I will tell you why, sir—because the coal operators in West Virginia and Kentucky and Tennessee and Alabama are paying their miners one dollar and fifty cents a day. Yes, sir, one dollar and fifty cents a day for ten hours of tunnel work. Fifteen cents an hour. There's no colliery in the North that can meet such competition, and within another two years there won't be a southern mine operator who doesn't face bankruptcy."

There was no immediate reaction to this. The President sat there staring at Ben, and Ben met his look. The silence stretched before the President turned to Mrs. Goodrich and asked,

"Does your information bear this out?"

She riffled a folder on her lap, and said that to the best of her knowledge, southern wages ranged from two-fifty to three dollars a day.

"Can you back up your statement?" the President asked Ben.

Ben glanced at me, and I dug into the brief case. I handed a file to the President, explaining, "Here, sir, are a list of southern collieries employing, roughly, some sixty-seven thousand miners. That is, at peak production. At any given moment, employment figures may be less than one quarter of the total, but the operating personnel can be considered in terms of some sixty-seven thousand available miners. For the past twenty-four months, wages at these collieries have averaged from one dollar and twenty cents a day to one dollar and sixty cents a day—for a workday from eight to eleven hours. As far as the individual worker is concerned, monthly wages average in a spread from twelve dollars to seventeen dollars. We use the spread to compute our averages, since it gives a better picture than the single figure. You will find there the names of the collieries, the names of the owners, so far as we can determine, and the numbers of workers at minimum to full employment."

The President's face was like stone as he opened the file and began to examine it. Mrs. Goodrich rose and stood next to him, looking over his shoulder. Denny glanced at his watch, scribbled a note and passed it to the President, who brushed it aside and shook his head angrily. Denny rose and tiptoed out of the room, and as the President and Mrs. Goodrich went over my figures, the silence deepened, broken only by the metallic ticktock of a tall clock in one corner of the room and by our breathing. Ben and I dared to glance at each other, and Ben nodded. Denny returned to the room, glancing at us as if to admit defeat. The half hour had passed.

Suddenly, Mrs. Goodrich snapped at me, "Just how reliable are these figures, Mr. Cutter? I have an instinctive mistrust of statistics."

"So do I, Mrs. Goodrich," I replied. "These figures can be checked. I will leave the file here—we have other copies. I can only say that when I offer something like this to the President of the United States, I do not do so lightly. These are figures gathered by our own organizers and sympathizers, and we believe them sufficiently to stake the union's reputation on them."

"Then you still attempt to organize in the South?" the President asked, looking up from the file.

"I attempt to," Ben nodded. "I still have to live with myself, Mr. President."

"We all have to live with ourselves, Mr. Holt."

"Yes, Mr. President," Ben replied, as if swallowing his impatience and anger, "but the time element varies. I've lived my entire life with this. The men in my family did not die in bed—they died in the mines."

"Do you have the facts on accidental deaths in the South?" Mrs. Goodrich put in. "Diseases—specifically, I mean?"

As I handed her those files, I said, "And would you like the figures on starvation, Mrs. Goodrich?"

The President glanced at me sharply and said, "Just what do you mean by that, Mr. Cutter? I won't have implications. If you have something, come out with it!"

I handed her the file, adding, "It is naturally incomplete. People have a habit of dying quietly in the mountains of Kentucky and West Virginia. But here are almost eleven hundred case histories, three hundred and twenty men; the rest are women and children. Names, towns, ages, and case history wherever that is possible."

She almost tore open the folder, and she and the President stared at it dumbly. Ben threw me a single glance, but within it such a flicker of appreciation and pride that it wiped out every indignity I remembered from the past.

"You, sir!" The President lashed the words at Ben. "Do you mean to tell me that here in these four states, eleven hundred people died of starvation?"

"Only over the past three years," Ben answered calmly. "There are the names, the facts, and the figures."

"You seem very sure of these facts." Mrs. Goodrich said to me.

"I am. Those facts are my business."

"What I want to know," the President said harshly, choosing Denny for his whipping boy now, "is why these statistics are not available to the government? Or are they lies?" Denny shook his head hopelessly, and the President said to Ben, "I don't think you would dare come here and attempt to hoodwink me, Mr. Holt?"

"I would not."

"Mrs. Goodrich," the President said, his voice icy in his need for control, "I want these facts checked. I don't want them disproven. These damned statisticians of ours can prove or disprove anything. I want them checked. If evidence is left out, I want that too, and I want to know why the Department of Labor has not informed me that during the past three years, eleven hundred coal miners and their dependents died of starvation. In these United States! I want to know where shame begins and where shame ends and how much of it we have to bear. And I want an information service in your department that can bring me as much information as this man Cutter. I don't think that's asking too much. Do you?"

Mrs. Goodrich shook her head. "I can tell you, however, why we haven't informed you of this. We didn't know about it. We've only been in practical operation for a few weeks. There's a lot to learn. Do you have anything else you'd like to show me, Mr. Cutter?"

The President stared at me morosely as I took another file from my brief case. "One more thing, yes, a list of the coal operators in Pennsylvania, Ohio, Illinois, Indiana, Missouri, and Ohio who have filed bankruptcy proceedings. Over twelve hundred during the past year, mostly small operators, family mines, so to speak."

"Small businessmen," Ben nodded. "I know every one of them—either by name or sight. Decent people who believe in this country and our way of life. Their reward for such belief was ruin."

"You'll spare me the preachment, Mr. Holt," the President said thinly, staring at our latest exhibit. "All right, here you are. You've presented your case—"

"Forgive me, only a small part of it."

The President was not used to being interrupted in the middle of a sentence, and I was a little puzzled by the way Ben constantly and deliberately provoked a temper already exacerbated. Afterwards, he told me that his fear was that the President, at each particular moment, would accept our facts, lay them away wrapped in pity or sympathy, and propose a vague assuagement in a vaguer future. Ben's notion was that by provocation and irritation, he could force the President to throw the solution into his lap. Perhaps he was right, for now the President stared at him for a long moment, and then said in a voice of ice,

"A small part of it, yes. But you didn't come here for sympathy, Mr. Holt. You've spelled out the sickness. Now suppose you outline the cure."

"There is only one cure."

"Only one? Modesty appears to be one of your virtues, Mr. Holt."

"No, sir, Mr. President—neither modesty nor immodesty enters into this. Mining is my life, the only thing I've studied and the only thing I know. And I tell you that the only cure for this situation is to make the right to organize workers into a trade union as unbreakable and sacred as the right of free speech. This will equalize the North and the South as producers, save hundreds of operators from bankruptcy, firm prices immediately, establish a uniform minimum wage and minimum price—and establish over-all the trade union as the enforcer of standards of fair price and fair competition. There is no other way to give dignity and the right to a decent existence to coal miners." Ben hesitated a moment, staring directly at the President, then added, "There is no other way to save the industry either."

Now, in silence, the President studied both of us thoughtfully, two men he did not like, two arrogant, almost insufferable men who had presumed to come as teachers instead of pleaders—knowing full well that with any other president they would have been shown the door long before now. He watched Ben curiously, thoughtfully, yet distantly, as if his mind were already elsewhere. He was tiring, I felt, and I also felt that no one in that room, myself included, was inclined toward sentimentalism. Should I except Ben? Mark Golden, in moments of great anger, would define Ben Holt as a "mental slob." It was a filthy, nasty backhanded definition of a man, and you had to know Ben Holt a long time to comprehend the strange truth of it, not a validity in terms of contempt but a furious tag for something soft and gentle inside of Ben Holt, deep inside of him and well hidden. If we had laid eleven hundred corpses dead of starvation upon the desk of the President, only one person in the room truly wept for the dead—that was Ben Holt. An hour later, he would be using those same corpses cheerfully and cunningly, but now he wept for them; and when the President looked at his big, earnest face, he saw the face of an angry if unlovable prophet; and if he never understood this man, Ben Holt, that was not surprising. Few others did.

"You know what you're asking?" the President finally said.

"I imagine others have asked for it. I imagine you've thought of it."

Without any emotion now, the President said, "Have you thought about the power such a law would put in your hands?"

"The world moves with power. Mine or someone else's. Now the southern operators have the power. If you break their power, you must give the power to someone else."

"I think there are other ways," Mrs. Goodrich said.

"There are no other ways."

Denny spoke suddenly, "You can't just write such a law and pass it. There's never been a law like that. It would change every basic concept of America."

The President watched Ben and said nothing.

"It would not," Ben replied, a note of boredom in his voice now, and the thought in my mind of what a consummate actor he could have been, had his ambitions ever turned in that direction. "It changes nothing. We fought it through in the North. We have the right to organize—by common law, if you will, or by our own blood and guts. It will simply apply a civilizing influence in the South."

"And if such a law is not forthcoming?" the President wanted to know.

"All right," Ben nodded. "You leave us two choices. Give up. Let the industry die in the North. Our miners won't become slaves. The union can die, and the industry will die with it—"

"And the other choice?"

"To go into the South with guns. I tried that once. I'll never try it again, so it would have to be someone else's choice. I hate guns. That's not the way I work, and I don't believe in issues that are decided by armies. I don't like to see something like this destroyed. It's easier to pass a law."

"Is it, Mr. Holt? A law has to be enforced."

"Give us the law, and we'll enforce it."

"I don't make the laws, Mr. Holt."

"I think you do, Mr. President—your voice carries."

"Very well, we'll see."

"And that's all you leave me with?"

"Do you want a commitment, Mr. Holt?"

"I do, sir."

The President shook his head. "You know I can't give you such a commitment, Mr. Holt. Let me say this: coal is the food and lifeblood of this nation, and coal will be dug. Of that, you may be sure. And you may also be sure that so long as I have a voice and a will, the men who dig coal will not die of starvation. But I make no commitments. We will both of us do what we can—and make no foolish promises or prognostications. Do you agree?"

Then, to all effects and purposes, the meeting was over. We remained there a little longer, and then we met separately with Mrs. Goodrich, leaving her our charts, statistics, and material. Denny escorted us from the White House, to where an official car waited to take us back to the hotel.

Not until we were in the car and in motion, did Ben permit himself a grin—a grin that seemed to spread all over his face and down through his body.

QUESTIONS

1   What techniques does Ben Holt use to represent the interests of his coal miners' union, and how effective do these techniques seem to be?
2   What kinds of evidence did the coal miner's representatives use to persuade the President?
3   What benefits does lobbying provide to office holders?

Part Four

Institutions—
The Conversion
Process

In all civilizations certain structures have been created so that the rules of society could be made, applied, and interpreted. Over a considerable length of time these structures gained permanence and developed into institutions which became such integral parts of the political system that it would be difficult to conceive of the system without them. The Congress, Presidency, bureaucracy, and judiciary are America's major political institutions.

All these institutions in the political system contribute to the conversion of inputs, which we viewed in "People and Politics," into outputs, which we will consider in the final part entitled "Policy." The subtitle of this section, "The Conversion Process," refers to the crucial function these institutions perform in translating Americans' demands and interests into public policies that all citizens must abide by.

The first institution that we examine in this part is the Congress of the United States, made up of the Senate and the House of Representatives. Congress was designed to be the source of laws, the arena where public policy is decided through debate and deliberation. The daily routine of a

139

modern congressman is shown in *A Life in Order,* which calls into question the conception of the congressman as the public's dedicated and loyal representative. Drew Pearson's *The Senator* demonstrates that the heart of the legislative process is the congressional committee system, where laws are actually developed and scrutinized. The selection from *Advise and Consent* indicates that personality and philosophical differences among congressmen have an important impact on how laws are passed or decisions made.

The second institution, the Presidency, was designed to be the branch that enforces the laws of the land. As head of the executive branch, the President ensures that the laws are carried out or applied properly. The office of the Presidency has grown into the strongest of the original three branches of government, and Congress in the mid-1970s attempted to reverse or at least halt this trend toward executive supremacy. Each of the three selections on the Presidency focuses on a different aspect of this dominant institution. *On Instructions of My Government* examines the problems that the President has in trying to harmonize the dual roles of leader of his party and leader of the nation, while *Night of Camp David* gives a frightening glimpse at what can happen to the President when the responsibilities of the office become too great. *Thirty-four East* exemplifies the built-in tension between the Presidency and the Vice-Presidency.

The next institution, the federal bureaucracy, is often called the fourth branch of government. While not specifically provided for in the Constitution, the bureaucracy has grown in size, complexity, and importance to the point that it has to be considered more than just the President's servant. The executive departments, bureaus, and agencies that constitute the bureaucracy were originally designed to serve the executive by impartially administering and enforcing the laws. As the two excerpts in this section indicate, however, the bureaucracy has great discretion and independence that make it difficult for the President to control. *Vanished* demonstrates the potential danger of bureaucratic autonomy, while *On Instructions of My Government* emphasizes the hazards of dependence on the bureaucracy for information.

The final institution that is covered in this section is the judiciary or court system. The task of interpreting the laws passed by the legislature and enforced by the executive is performed by the nation's judges, who have to make decisions in extremely controversial areas. The judiciary was designed to be above politics, but it has often found it necessary to step into the "political thicket." The Supreme Court has had to decide cases involving states' rights, slaves' rights, segregation, prayers in schools, and arrest rights. No matter what the Court decided, it made enemies. Tully's *The Supreme Court* fully describes the operation of this godlike tribunal. *The Blue Knight* focuses on judges' difficulty in balancing the rights of criminal suspects with the safety of the community, and *The Seven Minutes* examines the questionable yet steadily increasing practice of plea bargaining.

Despite the principle of separation of powers, there is a great deal of overlap between the functions of these four major institutions. For instance, the Presidency is now the primary source of proposed legislation (Congress's assigned function), and the federal bureaucracy today makes and interprets many rules (Congress's and the Supreme Court's duties). The four institutions perform many functions that were not originally allotted to them by the Constitution. The danger of this trend toward multiple, over-lapping functions was made clear in the Watergate scandal of 1973–74, in which several governmental agencies were improperly, if not illegally, used by the Presidency to protect its dominant position. Watergate vividly illustrated just how important and yet how precarious the balance of power is among the major political institutions in America.

The Congress

Reading 19
A Life in Order
Arthur Hadley

This selection, from Arthur Hadley's novel *A Life in Order,* gives an inside
view of a typical congressman's day and reveals the mechanics of the
politician's mind. Although Representative Dent has just survived an air-
plane crash, he quickly resumes "business as usual" while calculating
the political mileage he can get from his narrow scrape with death.

Congressman Dent symbolizes what has changed in politics as well
as what has remained the same. The "old politics" is reflected in his
ambitious opportunism and his two-faced approach. Conscious of his
lowly position in the political hierarchy, he looks beyond his activities to
the prestigious Senate seat for which he may be a candidate two years
hence. In order to win that nomination, he follows the old maxim of "telling them what they want to hear." He expresses a dislike for such practices, yet sees them as expedient and necessary.

The "new politics" is manifested in Dent's overriding concern for
his image, a factor that can make or break today's candidate. Dent is
conscious of symbols and is systematic about everything he does. From
his quick smile to his choice of transportation, every action performs a
calculated function to create the proper image.

At 6:45 a.m. his bedroom and his wrist-watch alarm rang within ten seconds of each other. Dent struggled from his heavy cocoon of sleep and
lurched, limping slightly, to the bathroom, where he automatically turned
on his bath, relieved himself, and shaved. Then, pulling his schedule out of
his briefcase, he settled into the hot bath water for a planning session.

Here in his hot bath, back on schedule, yesterday's events seemed
nonactual. Would he ever take Dee McTurk out, he wondered? He'd send
a telegram to the Speaker of the House about the crash; try and set the
stage for a subcommittee on air safety with himself a member. He winced
inwardly at this trading off the dead; but the crash was a public relations
gift.

He picked up his schedule for today from the table beside the bath,
reading:

7:30	New York City Scoutmasters Association Breakfast. Hotel Edison
8:45	West Side Hadassah, Spring Meeting, Breakfast. Hotel Wyoming
10:00	Mrs. Joel Smitkin, 310 West 68th Street. Kaffeeklatsch
10:45	Mrs. William Farbster, 200 West 62nd Street. Kaffeeklatsch

11:30   Mrs. Frank Boyd, 115 Central Park South. Kaffeeklatsch
12:15   Mrs. Frederick Donner, 309 East 40th Street. Sherry
12:45   Advertising Executives and Copywriters Association, Hotel Waldorf,
         Green Room
 1:30   Office appointments
 5:00   Mr. and Mrs. Lyman Blitzner, cocktails, 9 East 72nd
 7:00   East Side Community Associations, dinner, Hotel Westford
 9:00   Citizens Committee for Mayor Wagner, dinner, Hotel Taft
11:00   Chelsea West Reform Democratic Club—look in, drinks with leaders
         after

He could skip his afternoon office appointments, let his assistant, Sam Kleinman, take them, and use that time to gain publicity from the air crash. He ran through several imaginary scenarios, from press releases to inspecting the wreckage, finally deciding to charter a plane and refly the course on which the crash had occurred. That was clean, noncommittal, and scientific and should produce a picture in the *News* and *Tribune* as well as TV and radio coverage.

He flipped over to his Saturday schedule and began to figure his sleep time for the weekend. He'd just had four and one-half hours. He'd get through with the Chelsea West leaders by 1:30 or 2:00. Bed by 2:30 at the latest. His first Saturday breakfast was not till eight. At least four and a half hours' sleep tonight. Sunday he had another late political rally and then a Holy Name breakfast at 7:30 Sunday. Four hours tomorrow night. Sunday night he would be back in Washington with his children. He could sleep from 10:00 till 8:30 and still see Jim and Jane before they went to school. Ten and a half hours' sleep, plenty to start the week fresh.

By the time he had bathed he was fully awake. The Dent secret of starting the day: Don't take the extra half hour of sleep, get up slowly, baby the system awake. Only if he was really beat did he sleep to deadline.

He got out clean underwear, white; a clean shirt, white; and opened his closet to choose a suit. They were all dark gray or blue, colors that showed off his blue eyes, with almost invisible pinstripes, red, blue, or white, to give them life. He'd be talking to admen and women about serious topics and be photographed worrying about air safety. He selected a conservative dark-red pinstripe.

Sarah sat up with a shake and a yawn, and he went around to her side of the bed and kissed her.

"Oh, Daddy," she stretched and kissed him gently on the forehead, "I'm so glad you're alive."

"Just luck, Sarah. This great pilot, the chief pilot of the airline, Mc-Turk, just happened to be flying us. He was good enough to save us. I went out with him afterward; a fabulous guy."

"It must have been hideous. You should have come home."

"It was like combat. It happened so fast I didn't feel much till afterward."

"You take such risks, Daddy."

"We should be from California; not have to campaign on weekends."

"I worry so about you."

Dent gave her a friendly pat. "I'll be careful."

He checked that the ends of his necktie were exactly even, tested the tension of his garters, and picked up a pair of well-shined shoes, inspecting the laces. "Why bother to shine them, if you don't like to?" his son, Jim, had asked last year. He'd used the question to explain to a five-year-old the importance and craziness of symbols. How if you'd been in a good fight you often didn't want to wash up. You wanted people to see the dirt on you and realize you'd been down before you won. Shined shoes were the same way, a symbol you were so important you didn't have to muddy your feet.

"I miss the children getting up in the morning," he said.

"I certainly miss them too. And I'm not the one who is campaigning."

"Yeah." Sarah was quick to anger before her morning coffee. "I'll meet you at the Blitzner cocktail party. I'll need you there. You lunching with your father?"

"Umm." Her lips were firm, jaw out. When Sarah began to flame it took time to bank the fires. Part of what makes her such a great campaigner, he thought.

"Ask him about Buffalo, will you. It's been two months since I've had a speaking invitation from there. And Sam hasn't heard anything. Something's up."

"All right."

"And you might ask him for ideas on how to get publicity from this crash without appearing ghoulish. See you darling." He kissed her briefly again, then headed for the kitchen and his ritual glass of orange juice. He loved fresh orange juice, the cold acid-sweet taste of it supplying the final jolt that shot him awake.

He found a small pitcher of fresh juice in the ice box—trust Sarah—and poured himself a large glass, then called Jean Aaron, his New York appointments secretary, another key person in his political life.

"Good morning, Jean."

"Oh, good morning Mr. Dent. Thank God you're alive."

"When I look at today's schedule, I'm not so sure about that thanks. How are you?"

"I'm fine, sir. Are you all right?"

"Sure. I can get through the Hadassah breakfast by myself. Can you meet me in the lobby of the Smitkins' building at ten? I may be five or ten minutes late."

"Are you sure you can handle Hadassah by yourself?"

"Certainly."

"Don't forget Pat Levy will be there."

"I'll know her. See you at the Smitkins'."

Jean Aaron was his memory. His own memory for people was a standard joke among his staff. At the start of his political career he'd even gone so far as to take a memory course that stressed mnemonic devices. After graduation he confidently called an important Harlem leader named Dodge, Mr. Pontiac all evening (medium-priced-car association). He introduced a labor leader named Plotz as Stone (slang-word-for-drunk association). And finally one of his fundraisers named Monroe he called Hayworth (sexy-actress association). Now he used Jean or Sam for names; and if they weren't there, just smiled a "hi-ya, friend."

He didn't like to call Sam this early, so he left a detailed message with his answering service for Sam to scrounge up a free plane from the Long Island charter operators whose license he'd had reinstated when their own Congressman had failed. He called weather next: clear and colder. That meant his heavy coat. He checked his pencil, notebook, watch, briefcase and wallet, put on his heavy overcoat, and set off to the Scoutmasters' Breakfast, the first dubious battle of today's political war.

He didn't have to campaign so hard so early this year just to stay in Congress. Barring acts of bizarre chance he was in good shape to win eight months from now in November. In '54 and again in '56 he'd had to go flat out every day. In '54 he had been an unknown lawyer leading a divided Democratic party against a Republican incumbent in a district that had gone Republican for eight years. The very chanciness of the district had allowed him to win a primary and run. No old pro had claimed the seat as his fief; nor had any moneyed reformer put it genteelly in his pocket. If '54 was bad, '56 looked like the end of Congressman Dent. He was a one-term Democratic Congressman in a Presidential election year, running against the vote-getting magic of Eisenhower.

Fortunately the Republicans were so convinced he was beatable they staged a Donnybrook of a primary for the privilege of wiping his ass. As so often happens the candidate that won, while strongest with registered Republicans, was weakest with Democrats and Independents. The Republicans never quite united after their bloody primary; and Dent had several secret strengths. Sam Kleinman had joined him and was weaving an uneasy but vote-productive alliance of old line and reform clubs. His war record helped with the Catholic voters and his support of liberal causes with the Jewish money. Various good-government groups and the *Times* endorsed him. For once the "Citizens for Dent," instead of fighting with his professional organization, worked to deliver votes. Sarah tallied with several key women's organizations. Exhausted, he squeaked through.

By the law of politics he could now rest in 1958.

But there was a Senate seat up in '60. Dent wanted not just to win but to win big. So the king-makers had to sit up and notice what he could do in a district that used to go Republican. Unfortunately the Senate seat, held by a genial but ineffective Republican called Chattleworth, was so obviously up for grabs that many more powerful men than he wanted it. The prize would be handed out at the Democratic State Convention two years from now. Among those who would control the convention he was at present the first choice of only a few. But he was the second choice of a good number. With a big win this time and good luck and more exposure upstate and in the suburbs, he had a definite chance.

He took a cab part way to the Scout Breakfast, then got out to walk the last twelve blocks. He turned left on Madison toward Park Avenue, striding his usual block every forty-three seconds. On the corner the foundations were being dug for a new building. He could spare three minutes to watch.

He stopped by a huge yellow air compressor the size of a small bus, the second in a line of five, standing close enough to be warmed, but upwind, so the diesel fumes did not blow over him. The metal-banded air hoses, the thickness of pythons, writhed over his head into the excavation, carried on a corridor of four by fours above the sidewalk. The diesels and compressors blanketed him with sound, pleasant and warm, like a tank park in the early morning.

Dent looked closely at the construction crew. By God it was integrated. It wouldn't have been two years ago. You had a small part of the action, he thought proudly. He looked up Park Avenue and saw that the derrick and trailer truck carrying beams for the pile driver were blocking two and a half lanes of traffic. That was both totally illegal and absolutely necessary. The police precinct would be making a good thing off this job. Well, let them, he thought, they didn't get paid enough. Graft was part of the tribute society shelled out for rapid progress.

As Dent stood in the cold spring sunshine, the roar, the jolt of rough work, the dust blowing on him, the diesel fumes in his nose, the explosion of energy all about, human, machine, and fuel, combined and burst inside him with a thrill like that felt by an evangelic congregation hearing the first chords of "Rock of Ages." "Don't fence me in," he roared at the diesels. Hell, nobody could hear him over all the racket. A giant black tending the machines looked up and smiled. Dent grinned back. That man knew. You were part of building or you weren't. You liked power or you didn't. In or out.

He turned and walked toward the hotel and the Scoutmasters' Breakfast, depression flooding in behind his elation. For this corner was probably the last place in America that needed an old building torn down and a new one thrown up. The new structure would house no one, instead hold offices, speeding the rich in their flight to tax havens in the suburbs while increasing the daytime congestion. Uptown, some fifty blocks or two miles north—beyond effective tank action but well within artillery range—building was desperately needed. But there, where the deprived of Harlem were penned ten to a room, shucked of hope, no jackhammers rang or derricks swung. How could he ever harness human greed to help the needy rather than serve itself? "Help me move the fast buck to the slums, men." With what shocked silence the voters would receive those words.

The scoutmasters fed him orange juice (frozen), scrambled eggs, bacon, milk, and coffee (hotel, weak). The ministers of the three faiths said grace, the Protestant minister being black, as were about one-third of the audience. All of them up so early, Dent thought, to feel the pleasure of belonging to something bigger than themselves. Probably they'd first asked the Senator to speak, then maybe the Governor, next the Mayor—though hizhonordamayor was not much on the breakfast circuit; and finally ended with him, Old Second-Choice, Dent.

"What are you going to talk about, Congressman?" the president of the organization asked him.

"I thought I'd say a few words, and I mean a few only, on the peculiar problems we face here in this city."

"That's getting to be a popular subject," said the secretary on Dent's left.

What do you want, thought Dent, for weak coffee and tough scrambled eggs at 7:30 in the morning from the farm team—Camus?—He crinkled his sincerest smile. Actually he was going to tell the scoutmasters how great they were and while they were glowing from that, slip in a little something humble about how great he was. The core of his speech was his fond recollection about his old scoutmaster at school who had molded his life. In truth, Dent had joined the Boy Scouts at St. Luke's because they got an extra holiday and could remember nothing about the scoutmaster except that he had gravy stains on his vest.

But Dent's office had checked with St. Luke's, his old school. St. Luke's had searched their records and come up with the man's name. Dent had prepared a story of how this man, Patrick Hood, had helped a boy to find a place in the group. This would lead him into a story about a bull who couldn't find his place in the group. Then he'd swing into brotherhood, the impossibility of brotherhood in bad environments, run through his efforts to help the city, throw in a few statistics (Dent the educated Congressman), and close with an invitation that they bring their scouts to visit his office whenever they were in Washington.

The chairman rose and rapped against his water glass for silence.

"Our speaker this morning," the scoutmaster began, "quite literally had a brush with death on his way here to address us."

Damn it, thought Dent, he'd forgotten about that. He had to have a personal attitude toward yesterday. One that avoided that old vote-loser, religion.

He would talk about McTurk and the human factor. People ate that up in this machine age. What the hell was the name of his scoutmaster at St. Luke's? He glanced hastily at his file card.

The speech went off adequately. Several of the scoutmasters introduced themselves afterward and commented that they lived in his district. He got their names and addresses in his book. They'd get a follow-up letter. Communication was his critical need—the damn New York newspapers and TV programs were so full of what was happening in Paris, Moscow, Israel, or the jet set, about the only chance an area Congressman had to get a mention was to be caught stealing.

He glanced at his watch. Five minutes to Hadassah breakfast. He'd be about ten minutes late.

He got his coat from a chair near the door, where he'd carefully left it. Another Dent rule: keep track of your own coat. You can waste fifteen minutes because the boob who says, "Help you with your coat, Congressman," loses it. He gripped the hands of the organization leaders, exchanged a few final platitudes and bolted.

Outside there were no taxis. Damn. To use a rented car and chauffeur this early in the campaign was too expensive and ostentatious. He couldn't be seen in a city car, because economy and good government were part of his image. So he was stuck with taxis. As his friend, Congressman Red Donner, proclaimed tongue-in-cheek, "Good government is my greatest challenge."

A cab pulled up ahead of him to drop its passengers in the middle of the block. Two women were standing on the corner in front of the taxi waiting and waving. Dent sprinted up from behind, opened the cab door as the driver started toward the women, and jumped in.

"Mac, I was going'—" said the driver.

Dent looked at the driver's license: McGrath. "I'm the speaker at a Holy Name breakfast on West 67th Street. The boys will kill me if I'm late."

"You're da boss."

Dent hoped the women had not recognized him.

Dent gave the cab driver an extra dollar, put on his I'm-glad-to-see-each-and-every-one-of-you smile, and entered the lobby of the Hadassah breakfast hotel. Oh joy, the efficient ladies of Hadassah all wore little name tags, he could read them without peering. He'd have an easy second breakfast. He advanced on the four ladies bearing down on him and stuck out his hand. The most important one would grab it.

Congressman Dent, sipping canned orange juice, looked out over the tables of earnest, munching faces packing away breakfast. Bang into his mind came a new angle for his canned brotherhood speech. How sisters were naturally more friendly and loving than brothers; and that one should talk not about the brotherhood of man but the sisterhood of people because women paved the way. That was the type of verbal nonsense audiences sucked up. He smiled inwardly.

He and fellow politicians might crack private jokes against organized women; but this society would die if women dropped their active part. Their men were out hustling items people often did not need, while their women tried to do something about bad housing, crippled children, poor schools, the lacks in their own lives. Their men had the same lacks, indeed the vacuum in the men led to the vacuum in the women; but the men, being busy, believed they were full. The women were conscious of loss. Part of his vote-getting success was his ability to fill this loss, tap the electricity in organized women.

He hated his ritual brotherhood speech he was about to deliver. What these ladies, what all Americans, desperately wanted to believe about brotherhood, what Dent would tell them, was summed up in the driveling sweetness of the song from *South Pacific:* "You have to be taught to hate." They found this belief: warm, gooey, cozy, and satisfying. It took the responsibility away from them and put it on society, parents, teachers, anyone who had corrupted their sweetness.

Privately Dent believed the exact opposite. He reasoned that in the jungle from which man had struggled, the stranger was feared and therefore hated. The Bible had been concerned that man should move beyond loving his family to loving his neighbor. Now survival required that men love, or at least respect, people vastly different from themselves: other countries, other races. That required teaching, time, restraint, politeness, tolerance, all the complex fabric of society.

Each generation had to relearn to expand its circle of love. People got bored with this effort and listened to any pied piper who told them they were naturally good and all that hatred inside them just came from society's corruption, was put there by the establishment. Nonsense. Men didn't have to be taught to hate, to crucify. They raced to be first to drive the nails.

His canned brotherhood speech went well. He could feel the return begin: the pulse of strength, the physical excitement, listener feeds back to speaker. That vital nourishment the politician draws from the people pool in which he swims. The women's approval caressed Dent, quickened him, aroused him, freshened his hackneyed words. "Remember, children have to be taught to hate," he told them. And they burst into loud applause; the circuits between them closed, their voltage up.

He finished, naturally, with a panegyric to Israel. This he found easy to do. He liked democracy and bravery and felt that small state had both.— Even if some kibbutzim he'd visited had reminded him of concentration camps minus gas chambers and with better chow.—

"As Churchill called England during the war against the Nazis 'an

unsinkable aircraft carrier,' so we today can call Israel 'an unsinkable carrier of democracy.' " As he ended the ladies rose and applauded him. Even
when he sat down their applause continued. Once again, he thought, the old
lies work.

Dent turned toward the president and smiled. He had not been paid
for the speech. Time to throw the lance of quid pro quo. "You know, Mrs.
Prinz, there's a request I'd like to make. As a Congressman in New York I
have a real problem. A smalltown Congressman can reach people through
local newspapers, radio, and TV stations. Find out what the voters think
that way. I can't. I have to put out my own newsletter about what's going
on. But it's hard to find informed people to send it to. I admit there's a little
politics in the letter; but mostly it's information about events in Congress;
and questions about what people want me to do. I'd certainly appreciate it
if I could send an assistant, Jean Aaron, round for a copy of your mailing
list. Believe me, no solicitation or political material would be sent out. Just
the newsletter."

The president paused. Dent kept the smile on his face and his blue eyes
on her.

"It's against the rules. But you're a firm friend. I think an exception
could be quietly arranged. Have your assistant ask for Mrs. Asher."

He stayed at the breakfast a few minutes more to be polite, and left.

QUESTIONS

1 Could Congressman Dent remain a successful politician if he ignored images,
   appearances, and clichés?
2 Is he really representing the interests of his district by being so concerned with
   these things?
3 What kinds of activities does Congressman Dent perform during the day, and
   why is each one important to his reelection?

Reading 20
The Senator
Drew Pearson

Drew Pearson, the late political columnist, aimed his incisive, critical
talents at the United States Senate in his novel *The Senator*. The real
work of this institution takes place not on the floor of the Senate cham-

From *The Senator* by Drew Pearson. Copyright © 1968 by Drew Pearson. Reprinted by
permission of Doubleday & Company, Inc.

ber, but in its committees. In committee meetings, particularly the executive sessions from which the public is barred, a bill can be passed, amended, or defeated by a whim of the committee head, the most powerful person on the committee. This is the place where the "nuts and bolts" of legislation are assembled.

Senator Benjamin Hannaford, the main character in *The Senator,* is the head of the Senate Interior and Insular Affairs Committee. The committee is meeting here in executive session to consider the New Wilderness Bill, a piece of legislation proposed by Senator Hannaford which could bring him a great deal of money. The conflict is an excellent illustration of how a Senate committee operates.

The executive session of the committee, which means it is closed to the public, was in room 3302 of the new building. My own favorite among the hearing rooms is the Senate Caucus room, 318 in the old building. This chamber with its lofty ceiling, marble pillars, and crystal chandeliers is truly impressive. Ben preferred the more compact rooms in the new building. He could control committee members better. "I like a small corral," he told me. "Keep the ponies from straying too far, and I don't have to spend so much time in the saddle."

At an executive session, the press is not in attendance. No lobbyists either, except when invited as witnesses. Only the senators and their staff participate. Needless to say such executive sessions are very important. Secrecy is demanded; but leaks to the press do occur. A good deal of the confidential business, including so basic a matter as preliminary votes, is not revealed, and is, indeed, deliberately left out of the record. Senatorial hair tends to get let down at these closed sessions.

I do not want to give the impression that these executive sessions are conspiratorial plots against the public weal. Hardly. We are still an open society. And the vast, nay the overwhelming, majority of our lawmakers are honest men. It is simply that the complex business of governing this complex country would never get underway unless a certain degree of privacy were permitted our legislators.

There were the usual friendly greetings, exchanges of jests, as the senators settled around the semicircular table. I kept the mimeographed copies of the letter to the President describing the bill inside my briefcase. Meanwhile, I tried to size up the members to see where we stood. Including Ben, there were sixteen on the committee—seven of the opposition party. But neither party would hold to the lines on a hot potato like the New Wilderness Bill. There would be trades, deals, crossing of party lines and the like.

As chairman, Senator Hannaford had an enormous advantage. I do not think the public is sufficiently aware of the power of the chairman of a

Senate Committee. He is a king. He alone decides when meetings shall be called. He decides on the agenda. He approves staff appointments, often giving members of his own staff, or those on the staffs of friendly senators, committee jobs. (I was *ex-officio* staff director for Interior and Insular Affairs in addition to being Ben's number-one aide.)

A chairman also determines the membership of subcommittees, ignoring foes if he chooses, loading them with colleagues who see eye-to-eye with him. In the case of the Interior Committee, moreover, a lot of pork is available. In fact, it is probably, with the exception of the public works committee, the super-pork operation, or, at any rate, the most venerable and custom-bound. There is an easement for this nice fellow; a river project for that good soul; an improved park for that friendly chap who votes right.

Cynical? I think not. That is the way of the world and the way of the United States Senate, and a lot more good than evil comes out of the system. It has worked amazingly well all these years; let the amateurs and idealists show me a better system.

I checked off in my mind "sure things" on the committee—senators who would go with Ben, even if the New Wilderness Bill called for the filling in of Grand Canyon with cement.

Item, there was Sidney Stapp of California, dapper "Swinging Sid," scourge of the chorus line at the Gayety Theatre. He dazzled us with his white-on-white shirt and his white-on-white tie and his actor's smile. Senator Stapp was a theatrical lawyer, representing great chunks of the entertainment industries. We may have had the best-looking stable of girls on the Hill (decent, refined ladies, I add) but "Swinging Sid" had us beat when it came to conventions. He was in our party, a comer, a man with an eye open for the main chance.

Item, there would be support from Senator Alford Kemmons of Nebraska. Poor Alf. He was on the skids, and he didn't know it. He was in debt; he drank too much; he had wicked friends who were not discreet; he was in over his head, a man who had no right to be in the United States Senate. He listened to too many voices.

All over his native state, they were throwing testimonial dinners for Alf, and the question of where the dollars were going—into Alf's personal exchequer or into his political fund—was being raised. He had a weakness for people who did favors for him—no matter how trivial. I studied Senator Kemmons' lean figure, the wobbling bald head that seemed to rotate on a set of ball bearings, the roosterish neck, and I felt pity for him. He was in our pocket.

Item, "the meanest man in the Senate," Senator Gabriel T. Tutt of Alabama. He would support the New Wilderness Bill and he would swing another vote, probably Jack Mull of Georgia. I do not believe in stereotypes. Some of the most charming men I have known have been racists.

Certain scoundrels I have known are do-gooding liberals. What a man professes and what he *is* are not always congruous. But in the case of ancient Gabe Tutt, the man himself was what he preached and believed. He was a bigot, a drunkard, a bully, an intransigent who lent aid and comfort to every violent strain in American life. He was the tiger incarnate, and a drunken tiger at that. Once at a meeting of international jurists, Gabe had started a screaming tirade against "Missus Roosevelt, Adeline Stevenson and all them damn Jew liberals!" and had to be escorted from the conference room.

But he was an old hand who by right of seniority and his protected status in the club (the club is a sort of Wildlife Refuge) was untouchable. Senator Tutt crusaded against beards, pornography, divorce, and radicals. His Puritanism, though soaked in bourbon, was sincere, and his colleagues feared and protected him.

As I studied his blunt face, his white crewcut, his severe mouth, the face of a hanging judge, a corrupt sherriff, I wondered who was the greatest menace to our institutions—Angel López Garcia of Chicago, or Gabriel T. Tutt.

These were our three allies—Senators Stapp, Kemmons, and Tutt. A cynic might remark that this trio consisted of a lecher, a weakling, and a bigot. But that would be only partially true. Senators are men, after all, and they have their failings. Each of these colleagues of Ben's had something to commend them: "Swinging Sid" was an excellent corporate lawyer and was a crackerjack on entertainment industry problems; Kemmons did well by his farm constituents; and Gabe Tutt could act swiftly and intelligently in matters concerning national defense.

"Gentlemen, the committee will come to order," said Ben cheerfully. "This is an executive meeting of the Senate Interior and Insular Affairs Committee to . . ."

I held my breath, awaiting the reaction.

". . . to consider S.671, the New Wilderness Bill, introduced June 4th on the floor of the Senate."

Even "Swinging Sid," whom I had forewarned, looked a bit surprised. Everyone understood that the bill was dead, that the President had acceded to the wishes of the conservationists, and that Ben would not dare bring it up again.

There was a murmuration around the table. Then a few nervous laughs. Then they began to read Ben's letter to the President outlining the need for bringing the bill before the committee as soon as possible.

A BILL to amend the powers of the Secretary of the Interior as outlined in the Wilderness Act of 1964 and to take account of the National Forests and National Parks as permanent heritages of the American people . . .

The flossy language was nonsense. What the bill boiled down to was a change in the procedure set up in the Wilderness Act of 1964 in which fifty-four wilderness areas in the National Forest were created. Under that act, every ten years, the Secretary of the Interior was to review every roadless area of 5000 acres or more—plus roadless islands in the wildlife refuges—and determine its suitability for preservation as a wilderness. Under our bill the Secretary could review the wilderness areas, *annually,* and could, if he deemed it *in the national interest,* and if the President and the Congress concurred, open certain areas to "multiple use." Multiple use meant a lot of things. To Ben it meant timbering, oil drilling, mining—all the things that the members of our projected Conglomerate were so good at.

"I don't understand this at all," Senator John Tyler Lord said uneasily. "I don't understand this one bit."

The Vermonter's eyes goggled. He had not addressed the Chair, as is customary, but had merely sent his voice curling up to the ceiling.

"I take it, Mr. Chairman, this is the same bill that was introduced in the Senate some weeks ago?" Alf Kemmons asked.

"It is, Senator," said Ben. "I open this meeting for consideration of the measure and to arrange to hear witnesses."

"Mr. Chairman," John Tyler Lord piped. "No one was advised that this was to be on the agenda."

Ben smiled, then waved a hand at me. "Senator, you can blame my assistant, Mr. Deever, who was supposed to notify committee members."

"I would have come better prepared had I known," Lord said.

Senator Hannaford beamed at him. "Senator Lord, I'm sure your assistant can run back to your office and bring you reams of handouts from the conservationist lobby. Why don't we proceed with discussion of the bill on its merits?"

Lord's back stiffened. He had never forgiven the way Ben had manhandled him on the debate on the oil depletion allowance. "Were I the chairman of this committee," Lord sniffed, "I would be the last man in the world to mention the word lobby—"

"Gentlemen, gentlemen," Senator Webb Urban of Wyoming said evenly. "This is pointless. The chairman has seen fit to introduce this bill again to the committee. True, he did not notify us. He acted alone in securing the President's approval to submit it. I am not happy with such a procedure. But the chairman was within his rights."

"What is the purpose of a yearly review by the Secretary?" John Tyler Lord persisted. "I asked that question three weeks ago, and I'm still not satisfied with the answer."

"The purpose?" Ben asked. "The purpose is to further protect the national wilderness from exploitation."

"Indeed?" Lord asked. "It would seem to me just the opposite. The key phrase here, the operative phrase is 'in the national interest.' Who is to decide what the national interest is? The 'national interest,' according to a Secretary of the Interior may involve the drilling of oil wells in Yellowstone Park. That may not be *my* national interest, but it may be the interest of the oil people—"

"May I inquire," asked Senator Webb Urban, "why the President changed his mind?"

Senator Hannaford nodded. "Certain aspects of the bill that he did not fully understand were made clear to him," he said. "The multiple use provision for example."

Webb Urban cleared his throat. "I take it the chairman was the one who made these points clear to him."

Ben looked at Urban. "Of course. That is one of my functions as chairman."

Inexplicably, Alf Kemmons began to laugh—that gargling, stupid laugh of his. "Yeah, you don't get invited down to Ramada City," Kemmons burbled, "without getting a little religion on the side!"

There was a shocked silence. Webb Urban's face froze. He was an elder of the Mormon Church.

"I am sure the Senator from Nebraska is joking," Urban said coldly. "I am disturbed at the precipitous way in which the Chief Executive's mind was changed, and the precipitous way in which this measure is being presented."

"So am I," said John Tyler Lord.

Senator Lester Goodchapel, sitting next to Webb Urban, shook his pumpkin-like head. His eyes were mangled behind extra-thick lenses. "Golly, I'm with Senator Urban on that one. I'm a little mixed up."

"Was it not decided, Mr. Chairman," John Tyler Lord went on, "that the case made by the Conservationist Society of America was sufficient to prove that this bill was a green light for exploitation of the National Wilderness, that it would mean opening up our forests and rivers to bulldozers and drilling machines and power saws? Was that not agreed upon?"

"Not by me, Senator," Ben said. "I have always rejected the Conservationist opposition to multiple use. I still do."

"And the President does now?" Webb Urban asked.

"He does," Ben said. "And Mr. Hackensetter will so testify in a few minutes on behalf of Administration."

"We will respect the President's wishes, of course," Urban said, "but the chairman will permit us to call witnesses of our own."

It was a bad omen, a very bad omen. Let me talk a little about Senator Webb Urban of Wyoming. He was of that breed of gray, quiet, discreet, rural men who are at the very heart of the Senate Establishment.

As I have mentioned, he was a Mormon. He was a lawyer, a man of moderate means. Most of his clients were ranchers and farmers. He did not smoke, or drink alcohol, tea, or coffee. He ret red at 9:30 every night and was up early to pray. Physically he blended into his environment, so that in the halls of the Capitol, he was almost invisible. Of medium height, medium build, clad in medium gray suits, and dark blue ties, bespectacled, gray, square-faced, thin-lipped, quiet-voiced, he reminded me somewhat of Harry Truman as Vice-President, the man I had seen in newsreels sitting silently beside Roosevelt.

I cannot ever recall hearing Senator Webb Urban say a single thing of consequence on the floor of the Senate. He never raised his voice. He steered clear of partisan arguments. Above all he was fanatically honest. Not that the vast majority of the men in the Senate are not. But honesty was part of Urban's religion. Two examples will suffice. He was sedulous about putting postage stamps, paid for out of his own pocket, on every single piece of personal mail. He refused to use the congressional franking privilege which is so often abused. Once he was known to have personally tracked down a letter to the Senate post office so that he might put a stamp on it—a new girl in his office had used a franked envelope. (It was his electric bill.)

On another occasion, a testimonial dinner for him was held in Cheyenne to raise campaign funds—although this phase of the dinner was not revealed to Urban. In his naïveté he thought all those nice people just wanted to get together for a nice evening of steak, beans, and soft drinks. When, a few days later, the dinner committee presented him with a check for $9000, he flew into one of his rare rages and gave the money to an orphanage.

And so, as the debate droned on I feared Webb Urban's polite antagonism. I sensed that Ben Hannaford was uncomfortable also—a rare situation for my boss. Let me explain. When it gets down to close votes, to issues that may swing one way or the other, one must normally have the support of the Establishment, the Club. There is very little to be feared from the zealous outsiders, the amateurs, the journalists, the patricians, the college professors—the John Tyler Lords or the Maury Eisenbergs. The men who really count are those quiet men from country constituencies, who through some heaven-made covenant, some hoary tradition, represent the mystical essence of the Senate. Webb Urban, in his Sears Roebuck suit and his two-dollar ties was the very heart of that mystical essence.

He would oppose the New Wilderness Bill and he would vote against reporting it out of committee. But we had not counted on his vote anyway. The question was—how many votes would he pull away from us?

"I was under the impression," Lord said shrilly, "and I said this weeks ago, that the act of 1964 is very clear on protecting the national forests. The order of declaring wilderness areas roadless in perpetuity is very simple—a review every ten years by the Secretary of the Interior, approval by the President, approval by Congress. The areas then become legislated wilderness areas. They can't be touched. It's worked so far. Why change it?"

"Times have changed, let me remind the junior senator from Vermont," Ben said. "We have world-wide obligations. The supplies of precious minerals, resources, timber are running short—"

"They are *not*," Lord snapped. "There is a five hundred page survey by the Conservationist Society that the chairman is quite familiar with to disprove that contention. The national forests are but a tiny fraction of our potential resource producing land. Why open them up?"

"Let me assure the members," Ben said, "that this need not be the final version of the bill. It can be modified as the committee sees fit." He paused. "To a degree."

I began to make notes on the committee line-up. We had to hold everyone in our own party. It would be rough. Lord was a lost cause. He was more adamantly against the bill than anyone in the opposition. That left Lester Goodchapel. We needed his vote. I was fairly certain that Ben could work on him and win him over. Lester was one of those eminently forgettable men, a member of the great army of "insulted and ignored." He was never asked to appear on TV panel shows, or the "Today" show. Once he had shown up at the NBC Washington studio and discovered he had been called by mistake.

"I shall oppose this bill in committee," Lord said finally. "And I shall oppose it if it gets to the floor of the Senate. And if it passes, I shall fight for its repeal."

"Afraid we're out to kill all your woodchucks and daisies, eh, Senator?" Kemmons asked brightly.

Lord ignored him.

"I'm against it also," Webb Urban said. "At least in its present form."

A few others joined in to state their opposition. Lester Goodchapel said nothing.

"I appreciate these expressions of opinion," Ben said. "I see that the Secretary of the Interior has arrived, so gentlemen, if it pleases the committee members, I'll call on Secretary Hackensetter."

There was "Giveaway Gordon," steel-rimmed glasses glinting, followed by two sour-faced young aides. Most Interior people *believe* in woodchucks and pin oaks. They were not happy with their boss Hackensetter.

The Secretary took his seat facing the Interior and Insular Affairs Committee, adjusted his spectacles and began to read.

"The President authorizes me to state that he is in accord with the principles of S.671," Hackensetter began. "And wishes me to convey . . ."

QUESTIONS

1 What are the powers of the committee head in the Senate?
2 Is the head's dominance of the legislative process justified?

3 What personality types do the Senators exhibit on this committee, and what
effects do these personalities have on the committee's discussion?

Reading 21
Advise and Consent
Allen Drury

The following selection from Allen Drury's *Advise and Consent* presents
the workings of the United States Senate, often called the world's most
exclusive club. A smoke screen of politeness and courtesy often ob-
scures the real views and important operations of this prestigious institution. Senators' differences have a considerable influence on the outcome of the legislative process.

An important function of the Senate is portrayed in this excerpt—
the constitutional duty to "advise and consent" to the President's nominees. This duty was designed by the Founding Fathers to be one of the
checks and balances by which the three branches of government could
ensure that no branch could gain undue influence over the others. By
rejecting his nominees, the Senate could make it clear to the President
that he was overstepping his bounds in some way.

The characters that this selection focuses on are the leaders of the
Senate—Majority Leader Bob Munson, Minority Leader Warren Strickland, and Vice-President Harley Hudson—and the wily Southern Senator, Seab Cooley. Senator Cooley obstinately opposes the nomination of
Robert A. Leffingwell for Secretary of State, the important business
pending before the Senate. A tense atmosphere pervades the Senate as
a result of Cooley's filibuster, an attempt to sabotage the nomination
through nonstop debate.

The minute he stepped on the floor Bob Munson could sense that major
events were under way, for as always when the Senate was about to get into
a hot debate there was an electric tension in the air. Senator Hendershot
was standing impassively at his desk, a slight scowl on his face, while the
Clerk droned again through the roll; around the chamber there was a kind
of instinctive tightening-up and battening-down-the-hatches. Members
were putting their papers aside and settling back, the pageboys were darting
about again, bringing glasses of water to those who thought they might be
impelled to speak; above in the public galleries the tourists were leaning

forward eagerly, the press gallery was rapidly filling up. There was a general eddying-about all over the chamber, and this time the Clerk was not having any trouble getting a quorum. Well over fifty Senators had come in already, Harley Hudson was back in the Chair, and the stage was set. Bob Munson just had time to reach his seat, say a hurried thank you to Senator Trummell and smile at Warren Strickland across the way when the Clerk concluded triumphantly:

"Mr. Wannamaker! Mr. Welch! Mr. Whiteside! Mr. Wilson!"

And the Vice President, after a hurried consultation with the Clerk, made it official.

"Sixty-eight Senators having answered to their names," he announced, "a quorum is present."

Senator Munson jumped up. "Mr. President!" he said, just as Paul Hendershot said the same. Paul looked distinctly annoyed, and Senator Munson hastened to reassure him.

"Mr. President," he said, "I just wanted to ask the distinguished Senator from Indiana how long he intends to speak, because for the benefit of other Senators, I desire to seek a unanimous-consent agreement on the pending Federal Reserve bill as soon as he concludes. Was the Senator planning to speak for fifteen minutes or so?"

At this there was a quick murmur of laughter and far over on the other side John Winthrop of Massachusetts snorted and remarked with audible sarcasm, "Nice try, Bobby!"

"I have no idea at all how long I intend to speak," Paul Hendershot said dryly, looking about the chamber in his peering, storklike way, "but I think I can assure the distinguished Majority Leader that it is apt to be slightly more than fifteen minutes. In fact," he added with one of his sudden bursts of indignation, "since the Senator asks, maybe it will be fifteen hours!"

"Attaboy, Paul," said Cecil Hathaway sotto voce, somewhere in the back. "You tell him, kid." Bob Munson smiled pleasantly.

"While I am sure we would all find fifteen hours of the Senator from Indiana edifying," he said, "he *is* normally so incisive, so cogent, and so expeditious that I still anticipate that fifteen minutes will be more like it. I was only asking the Senator."

"That's the trouble!" Paul Hendershot snapped, unappeased. "That's the way this whole shabby business is being handled. Rush, rush, rush, from the very first moment. I think—in fact, I am prepared to say it for a fact, that there is a deliberate, underhanded attempt to railroad this nomination through the Senate."

At this Bob Munson flushed angrily, and he was glad to see that Stanley Danta, Orrin Knox, and Lafe Smith were all on their feet, and that across the aisle Warren Strickland was rising deliberately to his.

"Now, see here!" he said with a touch of real anger in his voice. "I have not been party, nor has anyone I know, including the President, been party to any attempt to railroad through any nomination. I resent the remarks of the Senator from Indiana. Mr. President, I regard them as a deliberate, underhanded insult to me personally. I take them as a personal affront."

"That may be," Senator Hendershot said angrily, "that may be. I am sorry if the Senator takes my remarks personally. If he takes them personally, I apologize. But someone somewhere in some secret seat of power in some place in this government is trying to railroad this nomination through. It is not the distinguished Majority Leader. It is not the distinguished President of the United States. It is, perhaps, no one known to God or man. But someone is doing it, and the Senator knows it."

"Mr. President," Warren Strickland said quietly, forestalling a retort from Senator Munson, "Mr. President, it seems to me that just possibly, at this beginning of what promises to be a long and controversial episode, that Senators might refrain, at least at this stage of the game, from personal imputations and allegations. Not only is it against the rules of the Senate, but it is against the rules of common sense. We have to live with each other, and remarks such as those of the Senator from Indiana do not contribute to our living together in harmony. I regret that the distinguished Senator from Indiana has seen fit to indulge in such language so early in the debate over the nomination, and I am sure that upon reflection he will wish to modify his language in future. Courtesy and common sense would seem to make such a course advisable."

"I know what I think," Paul Hendershot said in a milder tone, "but if I have offended anyone, as I said, I apologize. Now, Mr. President," he went on, as the others resumed their seats, the tension lessened a little, and the Senate and galleries settled down again to listen, "what is behind this peculiar nomination as it comes up to us from the White House?"

Up at the Chair Senator Munson was in hurried conference with the Vice President.

"For Christ's sake," he whispered heatedly, "what did you say to Paul?"

"I didn't say anything to the old bastard," Harley whispered back with equal heat. "He started right in on me the minute I got to him. He said Seab had been talking to him about it, and he agreed with Seab, and he was going to say so. I asked him to wait until next week, and you saw how he obliged."

Bob Munson shook his head angrily.

"He's hopeless," he said. "Thanks anyway, Harley. Don't give up. There are plenty of others that need attention."

"I won't," the Vice President whispered. "You can count on me, Bob."

"Is there some sinister plot against the stability of this Republic?" Paul

Hendershot was demanding, pacing back and forth behind his desk, as Bob Munson returned to his seat. "Is this some devious design by which we will be betrayed behind our backs by high officials presumably entrusted with our safety?"

At his side Senator Munson noted that the adjoining desk had finally been claimed by its rightful occupant. Seab was sitting with his legs stretched out, his hands folded across his ample stomach among the lodge and Phi Beta Kappa keys, his head forward in a half-drowsing way. But he wasn't asleep Senator Munson saw; a little pleased smile was on his lips and he was humming "Dixie" quietly beneath his breath.

"Dum-de-dum-dum-dum-de-dum-de-dum-de-*dum-dum*," he was humming as Bob Munson leaned toward him fiercely.

"Well, I hope you're satisfied," he said in a savage whisper.

"Didn't think of Paul, did you, Bob?" Seab asked softly. "Didn't expect *him* to blow up, did you, now?"

"I'm not surprised," Senator Munson said. "I'm just surprised you're not in it. Since when did you hide behind somebody else to do your dirty work for you? One thing I thought you had, Seab, was the courage of your convictions."

"So I have, Bob," Senator Cooley said placidly. "So I have. I'll be talking in a minute."

"I hope so," Senator Munson told him, "because I want to answer."

"Are there not other patriotic men, better equipped to fill this great office, to whom we could accord confirmation more willingly?" Senator Hendershot demanded, and Senator Cooley rose slowly at his desk.

"Mr.—President," he said softly, and the room quieted down. "Will the Senator from Indiana yield for just a moment to me?"

"I am glad to yield to the distinguished and able Senator from South Carolina," Paul Hendershot said promptly.

"Can it be?" Senator Cooley asked softly and slowly. "Can—it—really—be, Senators, that this is the *only* man of all the millions in this great Republic, who is so distinguished and so able and so filled with his country's interests, that he must be named to this high post? Can it be that there is no—other—man? I find it hard to believe, Senators. I find it *mighty* hard to believe. Of course, now, I may be mistaken. It may be he is the—only—one. It may be there is no other among us who has the ability and the integrity and the patriotism and the concern for America of this man. But doesn't it seem a little strange to you, Senators, that he should be the—only—one?"

"Mr. President, will the Senator yield?" Lafe Smith asked crisply from this desk off to the side. Senator Cooley looked around slowly and a paternal smile came gently over his face.

"I am always delighted to yield," he said softly, "to our able and accomplished young colleague who always knows so much about what we all should do."

"That may be," Lafe snapped, flushing, "but if it is, it is immaterial. Does the Senator presume to think he knows more than the President does about what is needed for the office of Secretary of State at this critical juncture of our affairs? Does he think he knows better who the President can work with than does the President himself? I learned early when I came here of the omniscience of the distinguished president pro tempore of the Senate, with all his long decades of service, but I did not learn then nor have I learned since that he is infallible on all subjects under God's blue sky."

Senator Cooley smiled in his placid way.

"Now there, Senators," he said in a tone of wistful regret, "you have an example of the passions this man Leffingwell can arouse. Able young Senators, reared in the ways of their fathers, taught to be courteous at their mothers' knees, turn on their elders and rend them because of their passions over this disturbing man. It's disgraceful!" he roared suddenly, raising one hand high above his head and bringing it down in a great angry arc to strike his desk with a bone-jarring crack. "It's disgraceful that this man should upset the Senate so! Let us have done with him, Senators: Let us reject his nomination! Let us say to the President of the United States, give us a patriot! Give us a statesman! *Give us an American!* "

A spattering of applause broke from the galleries and Harley Hudson banged his gavel hastily.

"The galleries will be advised," he said sternly, "that they are here as guests of the Senate and as such they are not permitted to make demonstrations of any kind. The galleries will please observe the rules of the Senate."

"Mr. President," Bob Munson said icily, standing side by side with Seab but looking industriously at the Chair, "will the Senator from Indiana yield to me?"

"I yield," Paul Hendershot said.

"The Senator from South Carolina," Bob Munson said bitterly, turning his back on him and facing the Senate, "brings to bear all of his famous eloquence and invective on Robert Leffingwell. It is not the first time that he has opposed Robert Leffingwell, and it will not be the last; but I venture to assert that his efforts on this occasion will meet with the same success with which they have met on other occasions. Colorful language and dramatic oratory, Mr. President, are not what the Senate needs on this occasion. This occasion is too serious for that. The Senate needs a sober and careful appraisal of this nominee to determine, in its own time and in its own high wisdom, whether he is fitted to fill the great office of Secretary of State of the United States to which the President has appointed him. The Senate is not in a mood for stunts, Mr. President. The matter is worthy of better than that from us."

At this the visitors in the galleries who hadn't applauded the first time broke into a rather hasty riffle of approval of their own, and again the Vice President started to gavel them to silence. Half a dozen Senators were on their feet shouting, "Mr. President!" however, so Harley thought better of it and hastily recognized Brigham Anderson.

For a moment, in one of those mutually appraising lulls that come in a heated debate, the senior Senator from Utah looked slowly around the chamber, aware of Henry Lytle sitting nervously on the edge of his chair nearby, of Archibald Joslin across the aisle looking upset in a dignified sort of way, of Johnny DeWilton, white-topped and stubborn, of George Keating watching blearily, and Nelson Lloyd listening intently, of the scattering of clerks, administrative assistants, and members of the House who had come in to stand along the walls as they so often did during major Senate clashes, of the tourists gawping and the press gallery scribbling furiously above, and the pulsating tension in the room. Then he looked directly at the Vice President and began to speak in a calm and level voice.

"Mr. President," he said slowly, "it is obvious already what all of us have known would be the case since we first heard of this nomination this morning. It has startled, and in some cases dismayed, the Senate. It has created already intense controversy and even bitterness. It has begun to divide us even before we have had a chance to unite on the only issue that should concern us here: can this man represent the United States in the councils of the world as we in the Senate wish it to be represented? The Senator from South Carolina asks if he is the only man who can do the job. That, I submit, is not the question. He is the only man before us, nominated by the President of the United States, to do the job. It is beside the point who else might do it; he is the only man selected to do it. It is up to us now to determine whether he can or not, on his own merits and in his own right. It is this question to which our energies should, indeed must, be directed now . . . Senators will recall that I have had occasion in the past to be critical of this nominee, indeed on one occasion to oppose and vote against him. It may be that I shall have occasion to do so again before this nomination is disposed of. The point now is that this nomination is not disposed of, that it has only begun to be disposed of; and that as of now, I do not know what I shall do on this nominee. Nor, I submit, does any honest Senator who is not blinded by prejudice or personal spleen know what he will do on this nominee. That is a secret the future holds, and I submit that we would be better advised now to leave it with the future, until this nomination has gone to committee and come out upon the floor in regular order for us to debate and vote upon."

"Mr. President!" several Senators said insistently as Brigham Anderson sat down, and Harley saw fit to recognize Orrin Knox. Paul Hendershot protested at once.

"Mr. President," he said in his acerbic way, "I believe I have the floor.

I am not aware that the Senator from Illinois has asked me to yield to him, and I am not aware that I have yielded to him. I did not think I would have to instruct the Vice President in the rules of the Senate."

For once Harley looked really angry, and the Senate thought, with some delight, that for once it might see him provoked into angry retort. And for once, it was not disappointed.

"The Senator from Indiana," he said coldly, "is not equipped to instruct the Vice President in anything, let alone the rules of the Senate. The Senator from Indiana has the floor and may dispose of it as he pleases."

"Very well," Senator Hendershot said tartly, "then I yield to the Senator from Illinois."

"The Senator from Illinois," Harley said in the same cold voice, "is recognized by grace of the Senator from Indiana."

Amid a general titter, Orrin stood stolidly at his desk, absent-mindedly rearranging the papers upon it. When the titter died he looked up and far away, as though he were seeing things the Senate could not see. This trick of his always brought silence, and it did now.

"Mr. President," he said in his flat Midwestern tones, "I thank the Senator from Indiana for his courtesy, and I commend the Vice President upon his. It is not easy for the Vice President to preside over the Senate when passions are stirred as they are on this nomination. The Vice President at best does not have an easy job, and in my opinion he discharges it in a manner that should bring the commendation rather than the criticism of Senators who are privileged to work with him."

At this unexpected and startling compliment, uttered against a background of their differences at the convention, Orrin's shattered presidential hopes, his intermittent bitterness toward Harley since, and all the rest of it, there was an audible murmur which the Senator from Illinois ignored. The Vice President, looking first astounded, then greatly pleased, bowed his head slightly in acknowledgment. Senator Knox went on, in the same rather faraway manner.

"Mr. President," he said, "what is the issue here? It is not, as the senior Senator from South Carolina says, whether this man is the only man who can do the job; it is, as the senior Senator from Utah says, that he is the only man before us who has been selected to do the job. Like the Senator from Utah, I too am in doubt about this nomination; I too have opposed Mr. Leffingwell in the past, and I too may do so again in this instance. But I do not know at this minute whether I will or not, and I too submit that no Senator of integrity who really has the interests of his country at heart in this time of her deep trouble can know at this minute either. There is much involved here, Mr. President; much that has not yet even begun to be brought out. We have barely scratched the surface of this nomination and all its implications. I too," he said, his voice rising suddenly, his left arm shooting out before him with a paper still held tightly in his hand, his whole body twisting with the vigor of his utterance, "I too would like to take the easy way out, Mr. President. I too would like to demagogue. I too would like to say, "This man did something to me once, and so I will oppose him forever!" I too would like to imply that there is 'some sinister plot against the Republic.' The point is, *I do not know* and neither does anybody else. It is so much poppycock to say anybody knows. It is nonsense. It is demagoguery. I will have none of it. I will give him a fair hearing and I will make up my mind after the facts are in. Who among you"—and he turned slowly full around, searching from face to face while the Senate sat in absolute silence—"who among you is so petty, so uncharitable, and yes, so unpatriotic, that he will do otherwise in this hour of this country's need?"

After which, having proved that Seab was among his equals when it came to rafter-raising, he sat slowly down and returned to the impassive perusal of his papers while the galleries and Harley went once more through their little routine of impulsive applause and cautionary gavel banging.

"All right," Paul Hendershot said bitterly. "All right. Then I will ask the distinguished Senator from Minnesota a question. I will ask him this, if he will give me an answer: is it not true that the President of the United States called in the Senator from Minnesota this morning and asked him to rush this nomination through, perhaps by next Monday afternoon, if he could possibly do it? Is it not true that this plan was concurred in by the Senator from Minnesota and the distinguished Majority Leader? I want to know the answer to that, Mr. President, and then I yield the floor."

Tom August got up slowly in his protesting, mole-like way, and looked around the chamber as if seeking solace and support. Apparently he thought he saw neither, for he gripped his desk so hard the press gallery could see his knuckles turn white, and when he spoke it was in his usual soft voice but with an unusual edge of angry resentment.

"Mr. President," he said softly, "I do not like the tone of the senior Senator from Indiana, nor did I, earlier, like the tone of the senior Senator from South Carolina. These are not tones normally heard in the Senate, Mr. President, and it seems to me there has been a strange loss of courtesy here this afternoon. It is not becoming to the Senate, and I as one member protest it. The Senator from Indiana asks if the President of the United States did not ask me to, as he puts it, 'rush this nomination through,' when we talked this morning. I am not privileged to divulge my conversations with the President of the United States, and even if I were, I doubt if I should divulge them to the Senator, that is the senior Senator, from Indiana. However, I say this only: the President of the United States very naturally wishes this nomination expedited as much as possible. I assured him that insofar as it lay in my power I would co-operate to this end, subject always to the wishes of the Senate. This, I venture to state, is nothing sinister; it is the natural request of a President and it is the natural rejoinder of a member of his own party who happens to be chairman of the great Committee on Foreign Relations." And with an asperity very rare to him, he added as he sat down, "I would suggest to the Senator from Indiana and the Senator from South Carolina that if they think they can make anything of that, they do so."

"Mr. President," Senator Hendershot began angrily, "Mr. President—" But Senator Cooley forestalled him.

"Mr.—President," he said in his slow, deliberate, opening manner, "again I beseech Senators to contemplate for a moment the spectacle we are making of ourselves here. Who is causing this bitterness and hatred and division among us? Robert—A.—Leffingwell. Who is disrupting the friendly and cordial flow of legislative interchange, so necessary to our country's welfare? Robert—A.—Leffingwell. Who is turning this Senate into a cockpit of angry emotions? Robert—A.—No, Senator, no, Senator, I will not yield. I see my friend, the distinguished senior Senator from Michigan, the great Majority Leader of this Senate, who has sat beside me—or, rather, I should say, beside whom I have sat—for all these many years, Mr. President, in the greatest brotherhood and love and harmony—he is on his feet, Mr. President, seeking recognition, asking me to yield—still beside me, Mr. President, but oh, what a difference! Now he stands beside me in bitterness and hate, no longer my brother, no longer my companion in this great legislative body, Mr. President, his face contorted with passion, his tongue thickened with hate, and why, Mr. President?" He bent low toward the Senate, his voice sank far down, and the answer came in a gusty whisper that swept the room: *"Because of Robert A. Leffingwell!* No, Mr. President, I will not yield to my former brother, or to those other great and distinguished Senators whom I see ranged eagerly before me, the great Senator from Illinois, Mr. Knox, the great Senator from Utah, Mr. Anderson, the kindly and always patient Senators from Connecticut and Idaho, Mr. Danta and Mr. Strickland, my able and determined young friend from Iowa, Mr. Smith—no, Mr. President, I will not yield to them for they, too, turn to me faces full of hate *because of Robert A. Leffingwell.* I abominate him, Mr. President!" he shouted abruptly, striking his desk so violently that the ink pot hopped out of its slot and sprayed its contents across his midriff, while the galleries gasped. "I abominate him! He is no good, Mr. President! He is evil, Mr. President! He will destroy our beloved America, Mr. President! I beg of you, Senators"—and both arms rose high above his head in an evangelical exhortation—"I beg of you, if you love our dear country, *reject this man!*" For a long moment he held the pose and then his arms came slowly down.

"And now, Mr. President," he said softly, turning to Senator Munson with a sleepy little ironic smile, "if my brother the distinguished Majority Leader will permit me, I am an old man, and I should like to sit down."

And he did so, making no attempt to clean his clothes, but only allowing his coat to fall open a little wider so that all could see his scars of battle.

Of the many courses open to Bob Munson at that moment, he chose the one that long experience told him was best under the circumstances.

"Mr. President," he said with a calmness that cost him, but he knew he must display it, "I suggest that the Senate return to the regular order of business, the Federal Reserve bill. I ask unanimous consent that the Senate vote on the bill and all amendments thereto at 4 P.M. Monday, the time between now and then to be divided equally between the Majority and Minority Leaders."

"Without objection," Harley Hudson said rapidly—and perhaps because the transition of mood was so abrupt, there was none—"it is so ordered."

"I yield twenty minutes to the senior Senator from Washington, Mr. Welch," Senator Munson said and sat down, reaching over as he did so to pick up Seab's empty inkwell from the floor and, without looking at him, replace it carefully in its socket on the desk.

QUESTIONS

1 Why is it so important that the Senate consider, and confirm or reject, Presidential appointments?
2 What caused the Senators to become so emotional and discourteous to each other in this election?
3 What kinds of tactics did Seab Cooley use to sway the other Senators to his side?

The Presidency

Reading 22
On Instructions of My Government
Pierre Salinger

Pierre Salinger's book *On Instructions of My Government* is an intriguing
novel because of the author's special background. As press secretary to
Presidents Kennedy and Johnson he was able to observe and participate
in the inner workings of the White House. He knows a great deal about
the political roles that a President must play through firsthand experience, and this knowledge is invaluable to the student of the Presidency.

One of the most important roles that Presidents play is that of leading their political parties, particularly during election years. At such times
Presidents are concerned with both their own reelection campaigns and
the responsibilities of leading their country. In this selection Salinger
reveals some of the problems and conflicts that exist for the President in
trying to balance the roles of party leader and Chief Executive.

The President, as always, got up at six-thirty. He flung aside the heavy
drapes in the bedroom on the second floor of the White House and glanced
only briefly at the south lawn and, in the near distance, the Washington
Monument, glistening in the first rays of the sun in a cloudless sky. Then he
sat on the edge of the antique four-poster bed until the sudden brightness
brought him to full wakefulness.

On a table within reach of the bed was a complex of telephones and
intercom buttons—an electronic mistress that had driven most First Ladies
in recent history to occupy an adjoining bedroom. Even in bed an American President can never be more than seconds away from communication
with heads of other major governments or the remotest of America's military outposts.

There were three telephones on the table—all manned at the other end
twenty-four hours a day. The first, connected with the regular White House
switchboard, was for routine non-security calls. The second was an open
line to the White House Communications Agency in the basement of the
West Wing. From it, he could speak around the world on lines secure from
eavesdropping. The third was a direct two-way line to the headquarters of
both the Strategic Air Force and the nation's missile command. If he ever
had to use it, it would probably be his last word from the White House
before he and other high-ranking government officials and their families
were evacuated from Washington.

The third telephone had rung only once—during the administration of John F. Kennedy. He answered it with foreboding. "This is the President." The incredulous voice at the other end said, "I must have the wrong number. I'm trying to reach a French laundry." The mystery of how the call was able to penetrate the supersecret system was never solved, although a White House communications specialist spent more than ten years trying.

The President hit one of the intercom buttons and a minute later a waiter brought a tray of coffee and orange juice, a stack of newspapers and a hand-delivered letter that had come after the President went to bed. It was from National Party Chairman Jim Mallory, urging the President to delay the announcement that he would seek his party's nomination for a second term. The President read it angrily, threw it aside, then glanced at the front pages of the New York *Times,* the Washington *Post* and the Baltimore *Sun.* All three gave prominent play to his address the night before in Philadelphia to the convention of the National Association of Manufacturers. He had cast himself in the role of the budget-cutter—always a ritual performance before the NAM. He had told his audience that there were limitations to what he could accomplish, that seventy per cent of the federal budget was written into law and was untouchable—for example, Social Security, Medicare, veterans' benefits and debt retirement. But the remaining thirty per cent, over which he did have control, had been cut to the marrow. He had taken a long, hard look at foreign aid—particularly to those countries in Latin America and elsewhere that were unwilling to help themselves. And the new budget told such countries loud and clear that there was a limit to America's generosity and patience. That brought the biggest applause of the night.

The President turned next to the editorial pages of the three newspapers. This morning, for a change, there were no cartoons, editorials or columns attacking the administration. He was as sensitive to such criticism as an actor to bad reviews. The only aggravation this morning was the letter from Mallory. The President pressed another button on the intercom and told the White House garage to send a car to Georgetown to pick up the national chairman.

Mallory's private telephone rang a minute later, waking him from a sound sleep. He looked at the bedside clock—six forty-five. It had to be the President. No member of his staff would wake him at such an hour.

"Jim, there's a car on the way over there for you. I'll expect you here in half an hour."

"It's that important?"

"It is."

The President hung up, then buzzed the Secret Service to inform them Mallory was on his way and had clearance to come directly to his suite. The national chairman shaved with a cordless electric razor on the ten-minute ride to the White House and tried to organize his defenses against the harangue he knew was coming.

The preferential primaries across the nation were now over and the President's position was precarious. His name had been on the ballot, but against his wishes, in only two states—Oregon and Nebraska, which automatically include all probable aspirants on the ballot except those who are willing to declare in writing that they are not and will not become candidates. That, of course, the President could not do. Despite a heavy vote in his own party because of concurrent primaries for the House of Representatives and the Senate, thirty-five per cent of the voters withheld their votes from the President. There was unanimity among national commentators that Oregon and Nebraska were indicators either of indifference or of outright disaffection within his own party.

The California primary, a week later, was an even graver portent. There, a youthful faction in his party had qualified its own slate of electors, pledged to support a liberal Negro senator from New York. The President, unwilling to lose the state's electoral votes by default, had no choice but to ask the governor of California to form a favorite son delegation in opposition. It was obvious to the voters, of course, that the second delegation was a front—that the governor would withdraw after the first convention ballot and support the President.

But there was little interest in the contest. Only sixty-one per cent of the voters cast ballots for the opposing delegations, and the governor's slate won by an embarrassing ratio of only three to two.

But the President had always been lucky in politics and the long series of hard-fought primaries matching contenders in the opposite party had produced a front runner against whom he would have the best chance in November. Harlan Grant, the senior senator from Illinois, had won all of the primaries from Nevada to New York, except in those states where he chose not to oppose a native son. Grant was handsome and articulate, perfectly cast for the politics of the television era in which charisma has become a more significant qualification for the nation's highest office than intellect, commitment or capacity for leadership.

But Grant was also a demagogue, thrust into national prominence by his exhortations against the gains won by black America, against the dangers of the new détente with the Soviet Union and against the President's refusal to crush with force the new Communist regime in Bolivia. He was, contradictorily, an isolationist in domestic policy ("We are two Americas—black and white—and we must accept it") and an adventurist in foreign policy ("Our own survival demands that we destroy the nuclear capability of Communist China before it can destroy us").

Nor had Grant been above exploiting the divisions and hatreds in American life in the wake of the unsatisfactory conclusion, four years earlier, of the war in Southeast Asia.

Jim Mallory knew that primaries, for many millions of voters, are little more than an opportunity to express their prejudices and fears, their resentment of the intrusion of government in their own affairs and the compulsion for a simplistic resolution of the crises they woke up to every day with the morning newspaper.

But Mallory also knew that when it came to the ultimate choice of a President the majority of Americans reverted to a soberer judgment. Harlan Grant might win the nomination of his party. It should, in fact, go to him by virtue of his willingness to enter the primaries and by his long record of victories. But it was most unlikely that he could win in November—even against an incumbent whose early prospects were not encouraging. The President, at least, was a known quantity—and the same anxieties that drove many Americans to support Grant as a token of protest would later impel them to turn away from the unknown and violent changes he might bring.

The car swung through the southwest gate and came to a stop in front of the diplomatic entrance to the White House, where an usher was waiting to escort Mallory to the elevator and to the President's suite. Sitting outside in the corridor was a man holding a black leather valise on his lap. It was known humorously as the "golf bag," but there was nothing amusing in its contents—the code numbers the President would dictate to our nuclear defense and attack force if he ever had to use the third telephone. The man, or his relief, was never more than steps away from the President—day or night, in the White House or away from it.

The President was dressing when Mallory arrived. "Jim, I think you're playing games with me on my announcement, and I can't say that I like it."

"I'm doing what I think is right for the party."

The President, knotting his tie in front of a wall mirror, turned sharply. "The party? *I'm* the party, and don't you forget it." He gestured to Mallory to follow him across the hall to the family dining room, where coffee and rolls were set out on the table.

"A week ago, Jim, I approved the letter to the A list announcing that I'm running again. I thought it would be in the mail by now. Instead, you send me this letter saying you want to hold off on it. Why the stall?"

"It's not a stall. I just think it's unwise."

"My God, Jim, we're only a couple of months away from the convention."

Mallory took the plunge. "I'm going to level with you whether you like it or not. I just happen to think that it's best for you to be non-political for as long as possible. You took a beating in Oregon, Nebraska and California. Your rating in the polls has never been lower. Very frankly, you couldn't pick a worse time to announce."

The President flushed. "What the hell difference does it make? Everybody knows I'm going again."

"That's exactly the point. Why announce the obvious this early? One, you cut yourself off from a hell of a lot of free TV time. Two, everything you do becomes political instead of governmental. Why set yourself up as a target for Grant sooner than you have to?"

The President was unimpressed. "Christ, he's all over TV now. Maybe I'm the one who ought to be demanding equal time." He studied the national chairman warily. "You know what I think? That you don't want me to announce at all. You want me to go into an open convention."

"That's it exactly."

The President threw his napkin on the table. "That has to be the silliest goddam idea I've ever heard."

Mallory was calm. "No, you should let the party come to you. The way you're looking now, we should create at least the appearance of a choice at the convention—and there's not one chance in a thousand that you would lose it."

"I don't like the odds." The President got up from his chair. "I want that letter in the mail before the end of this week."

"You have the authority to order me to do it, but I still insist—"

The President cut him short. "I also have the authority to hire and fire national chairmen."

That same afternoon the A list—persons who had contributed in four figures or more to the President's last campaign—was fed into computers at the party's national headquarters. The list was in the form of magnetic cards and the data was voluminous: the name, address and commercial or professional association of the contributor; his birthday; the name of his wife; whether the President had ever met him personally and, if he had, if they were on a first-name basis; his history in party politics, and much more.

But the computers were programmed to extract only that information pertinent to this letter, and the computer tapes were then fed into a battery of robottype machines which simultaneously were receiving another tape of the actual draft of the letter.

First one tape and then the other would alternate in activating the robottype, whose speed was four hundred words a minute. The computer tape led off with the name, address and personal salutation. Then the letter tape, by electronic signal, took over:

"I want my closest friends to be the first to know that I have made the decision to seek my party's nomination for a second term. . . . I am determined to follow through on the great initiatives this administration has set in motion . . . I know I can count on you, as I have in the past, for guidance and assistance."

The electronic duet continued through the entire letter, switching from the basic text to a repetition of the first name of the recipient in three different paragraphs; a reference to the President's concern with the contributor's specific financial interests, and closing with the President's regards for his wife—again with the first name.

There was also a postscript in the President's hand, written by an automatic stylus, expressing the hope that "we can get together the next time I'm in . . ."

One of the letters, to a defense contractor in Omaha, arrived while he was at the office. His wife couldn't believe it was actually a personal letter from the President. She tested the typescript with an eraser, and it did erase. Then she wet a finger and ran it lightly over the President's signature. The ink did smudge.

Her husband was a more important man than she had thought.

QUESTIONS

1 What did the President mean when he said in the excerpt, "I'm the party, and don't you forget it"?
2 What difficulties was the President having with his political party?
3 What new communications technique did the President use to announce his candidacy for reelection?

Reading 23
Night of Camp David
Fletcher Knebel

Fletcher Knebel, a political reporter, focuses on the office of President in his novel *Night of Camp David.* The Presidency, one of the most responsible positions in the world, is also one of the most stressful. Knowing that the fate of 200 million Americans and the rest of the world as well could be radically changed by just a single act is an awesome responsibility for one person. It is no wonder that Harry Truman remarked upon assuming the Presidency that he felt as if the weight of the world had fallen upon his shoulders.

In *Night of Camp David* President Hollenbach has decided to drop

From pp. 78–90 in *Night of Camp David* by Fletcher Knebel. Copyright © 1965 by Fletcher Knebel. Reprinted by permission of Harper & Row, Publishers, Inc.

Vice President O'Malley from the ticket due to the Vice President's involvement in a scandal. The Chief Executive then summons a freshman
Senator, James MacVeagh, to come to Camp David to talk about the
Vice-Presidency. During the course of their discussion MacVeagh de-
tects some things which indicate that perhaps there has been too much
pressure for the President to bear.

On the drive to the Catoctin Mountains, Jim sat in the front seat with
Smith, and they talked while the agent drove. MacVeagh joked about
Hollenbach's custom of sitting in the dark at the mountain lodge, but Smith
said the agents rather liked it. Despite their security precautions, some nut
could always wriggle up the far side of the mountain with a rifle and take
aim through a telescopic sight. If the lights were on, the President would
make a fine target through the picture window. No, if a president had to
have a quirk, that was a good one to have. Hearing Rita's story of frequent
light dimming at Camp David thus confirmed, MacVeagh wondered whether her source was this handsome, dark-featured agent with the shining teeth.
He asked Smith if he was a bachelor. "Yeah, still lucky after thirty-two
years," he replied. Well, Smith could do worse than Rita, thought Mac-
Veagh, even if she had shown that she could blaze like a wildcat. He
cringed at the memory.

MacVeagh had to knock at the door of the President's lodge this time.
A muffled voice bid him enter. The room was darkened again, and Jim had
some trouble finding the President in the gloom. Hollenbach stood in a far
corner, his back to MacVeagh, and he was looking through the big window
down the stretch of parkland which served as the one-hole golf course. The
snow had melted now, save for ragged clumps near the lodge and under the
pines and hardwoods which framed the fairway. A half-moon rode high
behind a puff of cloud, and the hilltop shadows were sharply etched as
though in an engraving. In the fireplace one huge log smoked above a
bright bed of coals. The room held the tang of hickory smoke.

Hollenbach turned and walked toward MacVeagh. There was no greet-
ing and his long face was set without a smile. He wore khaki pants, mocca-
sins, and a black turtleneck sweater that made him look as though he had
stepped from a vintage photograph of a college football team in the days
before the forward pass. Hollenbach reached into his pants pocket and
handed MacVeagh a crumpled newspaper clipping.

"Just what kind of man is this Craig Spence?" he demanded. His voice
rasped.

MacVeagh tried lo read the clipping, but the print was too small for the
dim light. He looked questioningly at the President.

"Because I happened to say that seven people were under consideration for vice-president," said Hollenbach, "Spence has the gall to liken the situation to 'Snow White and the Seven Dwarfs.' Just for the purposes of a cheap quip, he's willing to hold the office of President of the United States up to ridicule. I thought he was a friend of yours."

"He is, Mr. President." MacVeagh chuckled. The President was joshing him. "Actually, it does describe the thing pretty deftly, doesn't it?"

"You think that's funny?" Hollenbach glared at him.

"Well, sure . . ." MacVeagh stopped. If Hollenbach was fooling, he was the world's best actor.

"I definitely do not." The President's voice grated like rock rubbed against rock. "It's a snide little crack designed to demean the President. Snow White! As though I were some juvenile innocent wandering around in a wicked world, ready to be fleeced."

"Oh, now, Mr. President," said MacVeagh, "you're reading too much into it. I imagine Craig was merely indicating that you're a good president faced with a choice of men who are all a considerable cut below your ability."

"Nonsense!" Hollenbach shouted the word. He clenched his fingers into fists. "It was the phrase of a crafty columnist who knows exactly what he's doing. He's trying to belittle the presidency and drag it down to his own smart-aleck level."

MacVeagh was too flabbergasted to reply. He could feel the anger flowing from the President in the shadowy room, but it seemed to have an unreal quality, like a river without a source. They stood silent for a moment. Then the President sat down heavily on the couch facing the window and motioned MacVeagh to a seat beside him.

"Something has to be done about these irresponsible newspapermen," said Hollenbach. He bit out the words. "Freedom of the press is one thing, but unbridled license to degrade and ridicule officials who devote their lives to this country is something else again. I know we can't legislate responsibility, but one thing I can do. I can cut off Craig Spence's sources at the White House."

MacVeagh frowned in the dark and looked at Hollenbach as though seeing him for the first time. What the devil . . .

"Spence is an ingrate," continued Hollenbach. "He's had the run of the White House, four or five exclusive stories. I've given him at least an hour of my valuable time to two separate interviews. And then to repay the favor with a crack like that. Talk about biting the hand that feeds you . . ."

Hollenbach halted and watched the firelight for a moment. When he spoke again, his voice was still edged. "I'm beginning to wonder, Jim, if there isn't some kind of conspiracy afoot to discredit me in the eyes of the country. First O'Malley's outrageous action and now this. And these aren't isolated cases, believe me. I could tell you of other instances . . ." His voice trailed off, and when he resumed it was just above a whisper. "Other men have tried . . . I know . . . I've had to take steps to protect myself. It's almost as if there were a net closing . . ."

Hollenbach's voice slid away. He sat brooding, his legs outstretched toward the fire, his thin face, tautly furrowed, held in dim profile to Mac-Veagh. There was a canyon of stillness between them.

"Damn it!" The President's curse exploded in the quiet room, and MacVeagh realized that this was the first time he had ever heard Hollenbach swear. "O'Malley is the worst. He was more than a vice-president. He was part of the family, privy to every decision and secret of the administration. No president ever treated his vice-president with the courtesy and solicitude I gave to Pat O'Malley. And then, like a murdering brother, he turned on me and tried to crucify me with his filthy little deals. And then he had the audacity to stand in my White House office Tuesday night and say that he was sorry. Sorry! When he plotted the whole sordid business, from start to finish, in an effort to defeat me in November. Well, it didn't work. Thank God, the American people have a conscience, which is something that can't be said for a man who was never anything but a Pittsburgh ward boss."

The President paused for breath, then he plunged on. "It proves the need for a law that would let law-enforcement agencies, such as the FBI, monitor telephone calls. With that law on the books, O'Malley never could have got away with that arena deal. When he made those calls to the chairman—and talked to Jilinsky—we'd have known something was up and could have moved in to stop it."

Tap the telephone of the Vice-President? Jim felt glazed and numb, as though he were midway in a dream where the scenes kept repeating themselves endlessly. The man beside him, speaking with measured fury, seemed an utter stranger, and he wondered what had become of the self-assured, radiant Mark Hollenbach. Whatever the object of this Saturday night session, thought MacVeagh, it was lost now. Mark needed sleep and rest.

"I think perhaps I'd better go," said Jim. "We can have our talk another time."

Hollenbach looked startled. He swung around to face MacVeagh, stared at him a moment, then burst into laughter. It was the deep, hearty, familiar laugh that MacVeagh had heard a dozen times.

"Oh, excuse me, Jim," he said, "I had no right to foist one of my moods on you. You're up here to learn about our plans. Thank goodness, you're a new breed. With Hollenbach and MacVeagh, a team of the old and the new, it will be a brand-new administration next January. The O'Malleys, the Spences, and the rest will be forgotten. We've got things to do, boy."

Hollenbach rose, took several long strides and swung around, his back to the fireplace. He stood framed in the gossamer light cast by the rosy mound of coals, and an easy, relaxed smile spread over his face. He thumped the heels of his palms together. MacVeagh felt a quick easing of tension, as though someone had slapped his back in a moment of fright. The President he knew and admired was back again.

"Jim," Hollenbach said slowly, "I want my second term to be a great one. I want intelligent men around me, men who can think long-range, as I said, and I want a vice-president who can grasp new concepts without being shackled by prejudice. Look, let me explain it—and this is the reason I wanted you up here tonight.

"Despite our prosperity, this country is in deep trouble—abroad. We all recognize that. The changes in the world are violent ones, and they're hurtling along with a speed unknown before in history. We've got to find an anchor to help ride out the storm. We've been searching since the end of World War II—foreign aid, alliances, containment, massive retaliation—but we've never found one. But, Jim, I think I've found the anchor. I can't mention it before the election. The people will have to be educated up to it. But after the second inauguration, I'll reveal it."

The President was exuberant now. The familiar flush came to his cheeks and his eyes shone like the dropping coals in the fireplace behind him. He was talking swiftly, occasionally glancing at MacVeagh, but for the most part speaking toward the great window as though addressing a multitude beyond. Jim knew the signs. The President was in the vise of one of his ideas, and the intellectual seizure became a physical emotion, a force in the room.

"I call it the grand concept, Jim," said Hollenbach, "or the concept of Aspen, if you will, since I first thought of it here one night."

The President paused. There was no sound in the room save for a sputter amid the fireplace coals. Hollenbach's eyes seemed fastened on a distant point beyond the picture window. Jim felt a tremor of anticipation. He leaned forward on the sofa.

"The idea," continued Hollenbach, "is to forge the mightiest core of power the world has ever known. Not just an alliance, but a union—a real union, political, economic, social—of the great free nations of the globe."

Hollenbach glanced at him, and Jim knew a comment was called for.

"If you can name the great nations, Mr. President, you're a genius." He kept his tone light, but he found himself caught up in Hollenbach's enthusiasm. "After the United States, I add Russia and Red China and then I run out. And I assume you're not talking about the Communists."

"No. No." Hollenbach flung an arm toward one end of the room. "Look to the north, Jim. . . . Canada! Canada!"

"A union with Canada?" MacVeagh squinted at his wrist watch in the gloom. 10:15. A little late for bizarre jokes, he thought.

"Right. A union with Canada." Hollenbach stared at McVeagh, and Jim could sense, if he could not see, an intensity in the gaze.

"Canada is the wealthiest nation on earth." Hollenbach's words raced after one another. His eyes were fixed on MacVeagh's and he tensed again as he had when speaking of Spence and O'Malley. "The mineral riches under her soil are incredible in their immensity. Even with modern demands, they are well-nigh inexhaustible. Believe me, Jim. Canada will be the seat of power in the next century and, properly exploited and conserved, her riches can go on for a thousand years."

The fervor seemed to radiate from Hollenbach now, almost as real as the circle of firelight. MacVeagh wondered why he himself never heaved with such profound emotion. Perhaps that was the difference between the leader and the led. He tried to shake the spell by breaking into the President's hurrying monologue.

"The new imperialism, huh?" he asked.

Hollenbach eyed him suspiciously for an instant, but suspicion melted quickly and the President's features were gripped anew in trembling excitement.

"An enlightened imperialism, yes, in a way," he said, "but really a union of survival for both countries. But Canada is only part of it, Jim. Canada is latent power. What this country needs almost as badly as more power is character and stability. For a perfect union, we also need Scandinavia."

"We need what?" MacVeagh experienced an odd floating sensation as he often did when witnesses before his Senate subcommittee drifted into the abstruse jargon of the space age.

"Scandinavia." The President's voice quivered, and with spread fingers he pressed hard against his hips. "Sweden, Denmark, Norway and Finland, to be specific. They will bring us the character and the discipline we so sadly lack. I know these people, Jim. I'm of German extraction, but many generations ago my people were Swedes who emigrated to Germany. . . . Your wife's of Swedish stock, isn't she?"

MacVeagh nodded a hypnotic assent.

"You know what I mean then. You see, Canada will bring us the power for the future, Scandinavia the character, the steadiness. . . . It's the grand concept for survival . . . a union of know-how, that's us, with power and character. . . ."

Hollenbach sped on like a runaway train, barely pausing for breath, leaving no gaps into which MacVeagh could move with a question. He appeared to anticipate all inquiries. Why not England? Great Britain was finished as a major power, attenuated, effete, jaded. All that the English had to contribute—and it had been tremendous in its day—America already had absorbed. England was weak, introspective, plagued by memories of faded glory. France was too flighty and defensive, inclined to bicker any decision to death unless it emanated from Paris. Italy had culture, but no power or root stability. Germany, proud of her industrial growth, was arrogant and domineering again. . . . But with the merger of know-how, power and character, the United States, Canada and Scandinavia, the new nation under one parliament and one president could keep the peace for centuries. The president of the union should be a man who dreamed the dreams of giants. This was the grand concept. To it, Mark Hollenbach would dedicate his entire second term, his life if necessary. It was the only sensible bulwark against creeping Communism in Africa, Asia and Latin America. In union, America would survive and prosper. Alone, shielded only by the paper ramparts of NATO, SEATO and the rest, America would perish.

It was after eleven o'clock when Hollenbach concluded on a swelling evangelical note. His face flamed like the firelight, his fists were clenched and sweat studded his forehead. Though the effort had been the President's, MacVeagh felt exhausted. The silence in the long, low room had a clamor of its own. A gust of wind raised a flurry of old snow beside the lodge and the snow swept high on the window like frozen lightning. Bewildered, MacVeagh felt as though his head were stuffed with wool. He searched for words.

"That's an awful lot to take in one night, Mr. President," he said lamely.

"Of course it is." The President spoke softly, sympathetically, some of the heat seeming to drain from him.

"But I can't understand why you exclude England, France and Germany from such a union," said MacVeagh. That wasn't all he didn't understand, but he felt like an ant before a confusingly mammoth cake. He had to nibble somewhere.

"I only exclude Europe at the start," said Hollenbach, and his face quickly lighted again. "Right now, Europe has nothing to give us. But once we build the fortress of Aspen—the United States. Canada and Scandinavia—I predict that the nations of Europe will pound at the door to get in. And if they don't, we'll have the power to force them into the new nation."

"Force?" MacVeagh's voice sounded distant to his own ears.

"Yes, force." Hollenbach smashed a fist into the palm of his other hand.

"You mean military force, Mr. President?"

"Only if necessary, and I doubt it ever would be. There are other kinds of pressure, trade duties and barriers, financial measures, economic sanctions if you will. But, never fear, Jim. England, France and Germany, and the Low Countries too, can be brought to heel. The union of Aspen will have the force to exert its will. We'll be the lighthouse of the world, a beacon of peace for centuries."

"Have you thought about the type of man who would lead such a union, the prime minister or the president, I think you said?"

"Yes, I have." Hollenbach turned his face upward and his eyes seemed to measure the beams above him. "He should, of course, be a man above national boundaries, a dedicated man, an idealist perhaps, yet a practical politician. The Scandinavians have produced many of that type, some of whom have served devotedly at the United Nations. I'm not sure, Jim, but if I could see the union come to life in my second term, I would, of course, do everything humanly possible to help it through the formative years. If the call came to lead, I would not shirk my responsibility."

"I see." MacVeagh saw that Hollenbach's sensitive features were rapt, as though infused by a holy vision. "As I said, Mr. President, that's an awful lot to absorb in one session."

"Sleep on it, Jim," advised Hollenbach quietly. "You're the first man I've confided in, and I've done it because I want us to be true partners of government. Naturally, the grand concept is difficult to assimilate, all in one dose. You'll need to think about it, but when you have you'll come to the same conclusions I have. Together, Jim, we can save this country and change the course of history for centuries to come."

"I certainly will think about it, Mr. President." He knew his words sounded remote and trifling, but he could think of nothing else to say. His thoughts failed to navigate properly in his head of wool.

Hollenbach waggled a warning finger at him. "That's all between us, Jim. Keep it to yourself. There are people who are out to get me, and the grand concept—if it leaks out too early without proper explanation—could be used against me. If little men, mean little men of no vision like the O'Malleys, the Spences and the others, if they got hold of it, I could be made to look the fool." He shook himself, as though to ward off the mere mention of O'Malley and Spence.

"I realize that, Mr. President," said MacVeagh.

Hollenbach put an arm around MacVeagh's shoulders and guided him toward the door. "I suppose you'll want to get home to your waiting wife," he said. "Besides, Evelyn is coming up early tomorrow. We're going to try to relax for a day. I owe her the day. She deserves it. She doesn't get many any more."

Hollenbach called for the car, and while they waited, he steered Mac-Veagh to a wall bookcase, and drew out an object from a small case on a shelf. He held it out, and in the flickers of firelight Jim saw that it was a silver fountain pen.

"I used that to sign the last nuclear treaty," said Hollenbach, "but someday I want to use it to sign the new union into life. I would dearly wish that the union could come into existence right in this room—the union and the creation of Aspen."

The President swept his arm toward the big window, and Jim could see the gaunt, leafless trees casting their intricate shadows in the moonlight. In the distance the next mountain range shouldered the gray sky under a headdress of tiny stars. Hollenbach sighed.

"I love it here," he said. "It's the only place to breathe the first life into the union. Until then, Jim, I want you to keep the fountain pen. Let it be our talisman, and let's hope it brings good luck to a president and a vice-president who've got mountains of work to do."

"Thank you, sir." Jim fondled the pen, then slid it into a pocket of his windbreaker.

The President opened the door. The car was there with Luther Smith at the wheel again. Hollenbach shook MacVeagh's hand in parting.

"Remember, Jim, together you and I can do great things for our country."

"Good night, sir."

MacVeagh climbed into the back seat of the limousine. As they passed the guardhouse and the saluting Marine, Smith attempted to open a conversation, but Jim turned it aside and sat staring out the window. He cupped his chin in one hand and sat immobile, almost transfixed, and only half saw the trunks of trees march by as the car twisted and turned down the mountain road and sped into the high valley and through the darkened town of Thurmont.

His thoughts became weird flashes which changed abruptly like a kaleidoscope. Sweden, maroon on a map, Norway in green. A vice-president with a wife of Swedish stock. . . . My God, he hadn't caught the significance. Could that be his link with the grand concept? . . . Mark Hollenbach, his crew cut bristling like a mop of spikes, striding toward Hudson Bay in a black turtleneck sweater. Walking, walking, with earphones strapped to his head and the murmurs of a thousand exotic conversations pouring in from telephone lines across the continent. O'Malley, Spence and the Chicago banker, Davidge, standing mute and stunned in the background. . . . Hollenbach on a dais in Stockholm, wearing robes of royal purple, and studying a military map of Europe with a cluster of generals in strange uniforms. . . .

Then Jim saw a medic's hut in Viet Nam, and now, for the first time, he did not resist the full memory. The picture formed. A corporal, in the early grip of fever, leaped from his cot and, arms waving crazily, cried that he was being pursued by snakes. Then he began to babble of a shapeless scheme for victory. A doctor and two nurses seized him and the man soon collapsed on his cot again in a spasm of chills, but the grotesque scene remained etched in a recess of MacVeagh's memory.

Through the night, speeding on the superhighway below Frederick, another thought formed, ugly, menacing. He could not banish it, even though it brought a knotting of his stomach muscles, the way fear always affected him. He felt shattered, undone, and he knew he needed the advice of someone he could trust. Pat O'Malley? No, not Pat, although it was ironic that he should think first of the man he was tapped to succeed. Grady Cavanagh, the Supreme Court justice with whom he'd fished and philosophized? No, not on this problem.

Maybe Paul Griscom? Yes. Griscom, the discreet old political lawyer who wore his clothes like an unmade bed. He'd been consulted by every administration since Harry Truman's and his clients stretched from Seattle to New Delhi. R. Paul Griscom. He would call him first thing in the morning. Then he realized why he had selected Griscom. The old lawyer was not only a friend of his but a close family friend of President Mark Hollenbach.

In his jacket pocket Jim felt the fountain pen—talisman of Aspen. Warm waves of air blew over him from the car's rear heater, but he found himself shivering, and he knew it was the clutch of fear. Jim MacVeagh had reached the conclusion that the President of the United States was insane.

QUESTIONS

1 Can you note any similarities between the behavior of Hollenbach and O'Malley and the behavior of a recent ex-President and ex-Vice President of the United States?
2 What impact was the pressure of the office having on President Hollenbach?
3 What was Hollenbach's "grand concept" that convinced MacVeagh that the President was mentally unbalanced?

Reading 24
Thirty-four East
Alfred Coppel

"The most insignificant job ever created" was the way that John Adams characterized his job as the nation's first Vice President. His analysis is quite accurate because the Vice President has almost no significant constitutional duties besides the formality of presiding over the Senate. The office lacks a power base since Vice Presidents owe their positions to Presidents who probably chose them for some political reason such as to appeal to powerful interests in the electorate or to balance the ticket. It is no wonder, then, that the relationships between Presidents and Vice Presidents have not been the most desirable.

Recently, however, Presidents have been assigning their Vice Presidents more important duties as diplomatic representatives, political infighters, and domestic council heads. These responsibilities have helped to augment the importance of the office.

In *Thirty-four East* Alfred Coppel illustrates the relationship between the President and his Vice President. The President is sending Talcott Bailey on a diplomatic mission that Bailey disagrees with but that will help the President's political stance. Accordingly, the atmosphere in the room is highly charged.

In Washington, a cold rain was falling. Through the high Georgian windows of the Oval Office, the President could see the wet gleam of lights on Pennsylvania Avenue, but the rain was misty and dimmed with lights beyond into a blurry twilight.

He turned from the window and sat wearily behind his desk, conscious of the fact that he was tireder than he should be and that his body ached more than was reasonable in a man not yet sixty. He rubbed unconsciously at the dull pain in his arm and marshaled his thoughts once again.

His visitor waited, primly silent in the chair across the desk. There was always about Talcott Quincy Bailey an air of moral superiority that his political enemies chose to call priggishness, and it was a fact, the President thought, that it was impossible to be around the Vice President for long without the uncomfortable feeling that one was being weighed and somehow found wanting.

Bailey was a New England aristocrat by birth, wealthy by inheritance, and a liberal intellectual by training and conviction. He would not have been the President's choice for a running mate; he had been forced on him by the extensive changes in party rules that had made the selection of a vice-presidential candidate a matter to be decided exclusively by the delegates to the national conventions.

Still, Bailey had been a running mate he could accept. He had proved his value by providing the margin of victory in a close election. He appealed to that coalition of intellectuals, pacifists, and theorists who vocally remembered the incredible disarray of American politics in the early seventies, the scandal of the Watergate affair, and even the spectacle of a Vice President ousted for corruption. These perennial protesters with the long memories were Bailey's constituents—and without them, the party would have failed at the polls. The problem was how to contain such a volatile coalition peaceably within an administration committed to moderation and reconciliation.

The warm light of the graceful room seemed to form an island of safety and comfort amid the frigid dampness falling on the city from the lowering sky.

The fact is, the President thought wryly, Talcott Bailey looks more properly at home in this gracious house than I do. The Vice President's face was narrow and ascetically handsome, lined only deeply enough to give it a touch of what the women of the news media called "a fine virility." During the campaign there had been more than one reporter who had commented on the generally held opinion that the bottom of the ticket outdid the top in "charisma." Bailey was tall, over six feet. The President was not. Bailey had a full head of ash-blond hair turning silver that curled fashionably over his collar and around his temples. The President was balding and still given to the personal style of his prairie-state homeland. The Vice President was an economist by training. He had served previous administrations in that capacity and had developed a number of rather startling programs for tax reform and welfare systems—none of which were found acceptable by the party conservatives, but which were appealing to the university and inner city voters. These were the groups, heavily represented at the national convention, who had put Talcott Quincy Bailey on the ticket.

What most troubled the President, however, was not Bailey's economic radicalism. It was his deeply held conviction that the major cause of the nation's troubles over the last twenty years was the power and adventurousness of the military. Bailey was popularly known as the "Dove," and he earned the nickname almost daily by the outspokenness of his pacifism.

The argument that had kept them here in the Oval Office until almost midnight had been precipitated by Bailey's personal and acidly stated opposition to a supplemental defense appropriation requested by the administration to support a further three years of American commitment to the Peacekeeping Force in the Sinai Peninsula created by the Cyprus Accord.

The President broke the lengthening silence, speaking with authority. It was late and he was tired and he was increasingly impatient with the Vice President's resistance to anything and everything military. "I have considered your suggestions, Talc, and I have decided against giving them weight in this situation. The Peacekeeping Force is essential to our foreign policy. We can no longer simply allow those people to behave like children playing with matches in a powder magazine—and nothing will keep them from it but armed soldiers from the big powers. Everything else has been tried, Talc, even the pragmatic reasonableness of old Henry Kissinger. You know how every settlement has eroded until they are right back at each other's throats again. No, it has to be a long-term interposition, and the United States must continue to meet its responsibility. There can be no question of a reduction in the size of our component."

"If that's your final word, Mr. President—" Bailey said.

"It is. I've talked to Fowler Beal, and there will be no difficulty in the House."

"The Speaker is a very amenable fellow," Bailey said dryly. The point was a sensitive one, because Beal was an old political lieutenant of the President's, better known for his dumb loyalty than for any legislative intelligence.

The President's eyes, red and nested in wrinkled, graying flesh, turned hard. "I wouldn't have it any other way, Talc. And to make certain there is no problem in the Senate, either, I want the bill moved up for consideration the day after tomorrow."

Bailey's quick anger was only barely suppressed. "But I will be in Sinai then, Mr. President. Or have you decided to go yourself—"

The President cut him off abruptly. "No, I have not. I most particularly want *you* to meet Rostov and sign the treaty renewal. You understand me."

Bailey composed himself with difficulty. What was wanted was the name Bailey on the Cyprus Accord, as insurance of approval of the treaty, and all it implied, by Bailey's supporters. What it implied, of course, was that the military remained a necessity to the nation. The United States, after the bitter experience of Vietnam, was still, with the Pax Americana-Russica, to play policeman to the world. "I understand you perfectly, Mr. President," he said heavily.

The President said, "Talc, I wish we could come to some agreement on this point."

"I don't think that's possible, Mr. President," Bailey answered.

The President's eyes sparked with rekindled anger. "You are such a bloody prig, Talcott. There's a world of moral arrogance in you."

"If you say so, Mr. President. Is that all for tonight?" He started to rise, but the President stopped him with a weary gesture.

"I'm sorry, Talc. I shouldn't have said a thing like that. I'm tired, I guess. My staff tells me I'm getting hard to live with. My wife and the girls are in Palm Springs. I should try to get away for a couple of days and join them. The desert air might improve my disposition. It could use some improvement, I think."

"A few days at the Palm Springs White House sound like a good idea, Mr. President." Bailey said.

The President grinned. It was his most famous expression, boyish and radiating warm charm. "I'll think about it," he said, dismissing the subject. "There's a personal matter I want you to handle for me in the Sinai."

"Of course, Mr. President."

"I mean besides not antagonizing General Tate and his soldier boys." the President said, smiling. "I will have a letter delivered to you that I want you to hand-carry to Judge Seidel. I want to see if we can get him back into the federal judiciary."

Bailey made no immediate comment. Jason Seidel had been a law-school classmate of the President's, had served four terms as a congressman and twelve years as a federal judge before taking the unprecedented step of resigning from the bench to accept a commission in the General Staff Corps and an assignment as young Tate's chief of staff in the United States Sector of the Peacekeeping Area. He belonged, as did the President, to the moderate wing of the party, and he was, Bailey suspected, the President's unofficial representative in the headquarters of the U.S. Component of the Peacekeeping Force. Now there was some talk that Justice Carmody would retire from the Supreme Court—the man was eighty and in poor health—and it was rumored that the President was thinking of appointing Seidel to the high court in Carmody's place. Bailey felt a surge of angry disapproval. To appoint a conservative like Seidel, a man with friendships in the military, in place of a grand old liberal like Carmody was an outrage.

The President said, "You are putting on your puritan face again, Talc. What is it? Seidel?"

"Are you seriously considering him for the Carmody seat?"

"It is a possibility." The President raised a cautioning hand. "Don't condemn what you don't understand, Talc. Seidel's brilliant—decent, too. It was a considerable personal sacrifice for him to go to the Sinai with Bill Tate."

"He's from the Middle West, so it would be a popular appointment in some sections of the country, I suppose," Bailey said.

"I am aware that he would not be the favorite nominee in Cambridge or New Haven." the President said. "But in some circles that might be considered an advantage."

The Vice President flushed. "Are you going to make your meaning-of-moderation speech now, Mr. President?"

"No, Talc. Not tonight. I'm too tired and you've heard it before. You and I have fundamental differences of opinion on the functions of leadership in a democratic society. You believe the people elect us to do what we know is best for them. I believe they elect us to do, insofar as we can, those things they want done. You are an oligarch, at heart, Talc. I suppose, considering your birth, education, and experience, you've come a long way. But you are not really convinced that even a free people can be trusted to govern themselves."

"That's very interesting, Mr. President."

"Don't be too offended, Talcott. I admire your obvious quality. You are a moral, decent man. It is simply that when push comes to shove, you honestly believe that the people haven't the right to control their own lives. You know better than they how they should live."

"That's a cruel indictment, Mr. President."

"I don't mean it to be, Talc. For a good many years control of the people for their own good has been the essence of political practice in this country," the President said, depressed by the intransigent self-righteousness of the man. He said abruptly, "Well, it's late. Let's wind this up."

The Vice President stood, but paused before withdrawing.

"Was there something else, Talc?"

"What about the press?"

"What about them?"

"Taggart is still in Bethesda." The vice-presidential Press Secretary had entered Bethesda Naval Hospital for a gallstone operation one week earlier. Wags on the White House staff insisted that Taggart had suffered his attack deliberately, after attending a briefing on the climate and terrain of the Sinai Peninsula.

"Take Jape Reisman. He knows the area, and I won't need him—" a slow smile broadened into the presidential grin— "in Palm Springs."

"Very well, Mr. President."

"Good night, Talc. Have a pleasant trip."

"You, too, Mr. President."

As the Vice President let himself out of the Oval Office, the President caught sight of the ever-present warrant officer sitting in the hallway, the case containing the war codes on his lap. He saw the man, or one of his colleagues, nearby many times every day, but the sight rarely failed to move him. A man very like him sat just so in the Kremlin. Like the ghosts at the feast, they never allowed one to forget how tenuous a thing was peace, and how it depended so delicately on the rational behavior of practical men.

For my country's sake, and the world's, the President thought, I hope Talcott Bailey never has to carry such burdens.

QUESTIONS

1   How can you reconcile the facts that the Vice President is "only a heartbeat away from the Presidency" and that he performs few important political duties?

2   What are the main differences between the President and Vice President shown in this excerpt, and how did these differences aid in their election?

3   What important assignment did the President give to Bailey, and why did he give the Vice President this particular assignment?

The Bureaucracy

Reading 25
Vanished
Fletcher Knebel

Key characteristics of the American federal bureaucracy in general and the Central Intelligence Agency (CIA) in particular are revealed in this selection from Fletcher Knebel's novel *Vanished*. President Roudebush summons his press secretary, Gene Culligan, to participate in a serious conference with the CIA director, Arthur Ingram. The President's aide, Stephen Greer, has recently disappeared, adding to the tenseness of the situation.

    The CIA had initiated Operation Flycatcher to use young atomic scientists as intelligence agents, but had not informed the President of the operation. This highlights the discretion bureaucrats exercise in the federal government; the President is informed only about matters that his bureaucrats define as important. As Arthur Ingram indicates, bureaucrats see things from a perspective different from that of the President, and so they are not wholly his servants.

    The CIA's perspective, in fact, is quite different from that of the President and the rest of the federal bureaucracy. The agency operates in secrecy and tends to reach its tentacles into almost every aspect of government. Ingram's suspicion of Gene Culligan reflects the CIA's distrust of the other agencies of the bureaucracy, which compels the agency into such projects as Operation Flycatcher. These clandestine, sinister characteristics of the CIA raise a crucial question as to who really controls the agency.

Arthur Ingram was already seated in the oval office when I entered. He nodded to me, curtly, I thought. The CIA director disliked people like me sitting in on conferences involving the Agency. I was half inside, because of my service to the President, and half outside because of my obligations to the press. Although I held top security clearance, I'm sure Ingram considered me a risk, emotional if not patriotic. He sat stiffly upright near a corner of the President's desk. The No. 1 intelligence man was immaculately groomed as always, his trousers sharply creased and his crossed feet shod in cordovans with a gleaming polish. Ingram held his rimless spectacles in his hands, his fingers framing them in a precise semirectangle. The narrow, tanned face wore an expression of wary confidence as though this were his command post and the President and I were calling at his request.

Ingram was an adroit, intense, aloof man, even though he might conceal the aloofness behind a shield of congeniality when he entertained legislators at the Agency. He was also suspicious of others, whether innately or by the nature of his current trade I did not know. His personality traits were the opposite of Roudebush's candor, forthrightness, and warmth. I suppose that is why I always felt on guard in Ingram's presence.

The President was leaning back in his chair, the big hands clasped on his stomach. His glasses were pushed aloft in the thatch of gray hair. He grinned at me, but it flashed off quickly. I sensed a tension in the room.

"Have a chair, Gene," he said. "I've merely told Arthur that I wanted to discuss the Agency's operations among scientists. Why don't you just sketch the affair as you did for me yesterday."

"Yes, sir," I said. "Yesterday noon I and Miguel Loomis, the son of the Educational Micro president, had luncheon in the Ring Building with Steve, and—"

"Steve?" cut in Ingram. His thin eyebrows were arched.

"Stephen Greer."

"Oh," said Ingram. He managed to impart a dismissive inflection to the word as if to imply that anything involving a man who vanished in the night was subject to discount. I was puzzled, since I assumed Ingram had inquired sympathetically about Greer before I came into the room. Thus the name should have been fresh in his mind.

I told the story as Miguel related it the day before, adding for Ingram's benefit a few words about the political importance of Miguel's father, Barney. This last bit was perhaps gratuitous, for I knew that Ingram followed the nuances of politics as closely as we did in the White House.

When I finished. Ingram's eyes left mine and went inquiringly to those of the President. Roudebush lolled informally in his chair. Ingram sat stiffly erect.

"Well, Arthur," said the President in a pleasant tone, "what about it?"

"Except for a few unimportant details," said Ingram, "the story is correct as far as it goes. We initiated the atomic scientists' project last fall and used the Spruance Foundation as a conduit for funds."

"I see," said the President. "Does this project have an Agency name?"

"Yes," said Ingram. He colored slightly. "Operation Flycatcher."

I could understand his embarrassment. Both the Agency and the Defense Department had a gift for appending lilting names to their covert undertakings. The blacker the mission, the more euphemistic the label. In this case, one could picture a crested flycatcher standing on a birch limb and pealing his song of spring while young physicists skulked about and conversed in hooded whispers.

"And why was I not informed of this?" asked the President.

"Because of our quite explicit understanding at our first session after you took office," said Ingram swiftly. "I keep a memorandum of our discussion in my desk as a constant guideline. You said you wanted to be consulted on broad policy, on major new undertakings of a sensitive nature, but that you could not and would not deal in day-to-day details of Agency operation."

"Arthur, do you consider the manipulation of young atomic scientists to be a day-to-day detail?" The President's tone was low, curious, rather than hostile.

"I would take exception to the word 'manipulation,' Mr. President." said Ingram. "We supply funds to graduate students who inevitably will swell the nation's reservoir of skilled scientists. In return, we receive—or I should say we are beginning to receive—some valuable information on nuclear developments abroad."

"I don't recall that this ever came before the National Security Council," observed Roudebush.

"No, sir. As I say, I interpreted our understanding as applying to the Council as well."

"Is Operation . . . uh . . . Flycatcher confined to young men, or have you also tried to recruit some of the older nuclear scientists?" asked the President.

"So far," said Ingram, "we have confined it to men working on masters' and doctors' degrees. We hope, of course, that many of these men will continue to serve the Agency throughout their careers. But we did not deem it wise to approach the older physicists, chemists, and engineers at this time. In most cases, their attitudes have . . . well, hardened, shall we say."

"Did you weigh the consequences in the event the Agency's hand was exposed?" asked Roudebush. "The CIA isn't exactly loved abroad as it is."

"Of course, Mr. President." Ingram seldom groped for an answer. "Very few of our recruits yet know the exact connection between Spruance and the Agency, and those who suspect it are, I must say, the kind who place the national interest ahead of personal ambition in science. Loomis is the first young man to raise a substantial question from an antagonistic viewpoint."

"Who is this Mr. Rimmel, who heads Spruance for you?" asked the President. "A Maury Rimmel is a member at Burning Tree, the one who searched for Steve last night. Is that the man?"

"Yes, sir." Ingram obviously did not intend to amplify that brief answer, but he saw the President's continuing look of inquiry. "A number of businessmen co-operate with us, as you know, some without compensation, some for a fee. Rimmel is paid a fee."

"How much?"

"I don't have the figure in my head, but I believe it is on the order of fourteen or fifteen thousand a year."

"Fifteen thousand to run a nonexistent foundation?" asked the President. "That seems more than ample, to put it mildly."

"He does have to fend off questions about the foundation," said Ingram. He looked down at his glasses as though measuring them. "That takes a certain brand of acumen."

"I see." The conversation lapsed for a moment.

It occurred to me that Ingram would find it quite handy to have a man on a CIA retainer circulating at Burning Tree among its members. The implication was Machiavellian, of course, and I wondered if I were being overly suspicious.

So the President's next comment surprised me.

"I suppose none of Rimmel's fellow members at Burning Tree are aware of his Agency connection," he said.

"I would doubt it," answered Ingram. "As you know, the basic law protects the identity of Agency personnel and, uh, consultants."

"I'm a member, you know," the President said dryly. He paused, then added: "Frankly, I thought the only mystery about Maury Rimmel was whether he really earned his pay as a steel lobbyist."

There was silence again, rather heavy this time. An ordinary American voter, I thought, would never credit this scene: The President of the United States informing his intelligence chief that he was unaware of the CIA connection of a fellow member in a private club. Ingram toyed with his glasses, betraying for the first time a dent in his self-assurance. But he made no comment. The President clasped his hands behind his head and stared up at the ceiling.

"Arthur," he said, "we have more than a question of Intelligence economics here—the value of information obtained per dollar spent, as it were. We have a moral question."

"Just what do you mean, Mr. President?"

"I mean you're in the covert business of twisting young American scientists into something they don't purport to be to their fellows. Science prides itself on open access to all knowledge, from whatever source. Scientists must share, seek, and exchange information in an atmosphere of mutual trust. Now you come along and turn these young men into secret agents whose real mission is to spy on their colleagues, both American and foreign. I'd say that raises a prime ethical issue."

"I disagree with you, Mr. President. The project differs but little from a dozen other highly successful operations of the Agency."

"I wonder." Roudebush studied Ingram for a moment, then he turned to me. "How did Mike Loomis put it yesterday, Gene?"

"He said American physics was being 'tainted and corrupted' by the CIA connection," I said. "He contended his friends were being bribed to inform on their colleagues."

Ingram flicked a hostile glance at me. I was the unbidden visitor. "I would say that's a highly emotional verb," he said. "Not very many young men, except perhaps the New Left radicals, would confuse service to their country with bribery. . . . And, of course, in this case, since the boy is half Mexican, I'd say we'd have to consider a latent antipathy for the United States."

"Oh, come now, Arthur." The President smiled briefly. "I don't know the young man, but I do know his father. Miguel Loomis was born and reared here. He's an American who happens to be bilingual because his mother is from Mexico."

"I merely point a possibility," said Ingram coldly. "I may be doing him an injustice."

"Isn't that beside the point anyway, Arthur?" asked Roudebush. "If there had never been a Miguel Loomis, and I learned of this . . . this venture of yours . . . I'd have very grave reservations."

"I'm sorry we differ, Mr. President." said Ingram.

The President sighed, and I sensed that this abyss between viewpoints was an old one for these men.

"Arthur," said Roudebush, "I can't understand why I wasn't briefed on this operation along with other major Agency undertakings."

"I suppose, Mr. President, I didn't weigh it on the same scales you do." A note of apology slid into Ingram's voice. "In a total budget of a half a billion dollars, some three or four hundred thousand over-all doesn't bulk very large. I assure you, sir, there was no intent to withhold information from you. Perhaps it would be better all around if my future briefings went more thoroughly into minor Agency operations." Ingram stressed the word "minor."

"Yes, I think so," said the President. There was silence again, definitely strained this time. Roudebush arose, pushed his hands into his coat pockets and walked to the French doors. He stood for a moment, gazing at the back of a Secret Service man on duty on the outside walkway.

"Arthur," he said when he turned to us again, "why isn't it possible to obtain the same information you get from the young scientists via normal embassy and Agency channels?"

"I just don't believe we'd get the same kind of result," said Ingram. "Mr. President, until last fall we had to rely on a rather limited structure for our information on foreign nuclear weapons. We do, of course, have a few—a precious few—agents in nuclear installations abroad. And a number of reputable scientists—again the number is deplorably small—have volunteered information to us after their travels abroad or attendance at international conferences."

Ingram's tone had become confidently professional. He was in his element now. "I am building for the future in Operation Flycatcher."

While I managed to retain a straight face, I wanted to laugh each time

I heard that phrase. The thought was a droll one—flycatchers impressed into the muffled legions of espionage—and I wondered what brain at the Agency packaged these dark missions in such festive wrappings.

"I envision the day," Ingram continued, "when vital information will roll into the Agency from several hundred trained scientific agents who have reached top levels of their professions. You must remember, Mr. President, that many eminent American scientists today have a higher loyalty than to the United States. They regard the world of science as a kind of frontier-free society in which information should flow as easily as would commerce around a globe without tariff barriers. We have evidence of imprudent contacts between American and Communist scientists which appear to breach our own security regulations. Frankly, many of these men do not trust any government, including their own. And hundreds of them are still laboring under a guilt complex for having worked on the atomic bomb. I can appreciate this kind of emotional trap, but I can't sympathize with it."

Ingram paused and squared his shoulders. "In sum, Mr. President, I'm trying to indoctrinate a new breed of scientist, with first loyalty to the United States of America. Operation Flycatcher is our vehicle. I think it's an excellent investment of time, money, and energy."

The President had stood by the French doors as he listened. Now he returned to his desk.

"To use your words, Arthur," he said, "I can appreciate your viewpoint here, even if I cannot sympathize with it. Perhaps, from a cold intelligence appraisal, your Flycatcher project makes sense. But I have to look at this from a higher vantage point, one that takes in the whole scope of our relations with the rest of the world. And what I see, I do not like." He looked directly at Ingram. "To be blunt, Arthur, the CIA wouldn't be exactly crippled if we ended this operation?"

"Crippled, no." Ingram flushed under his tan. "Handicapped, yes."

"This thought has been running through my mind," said Roudebush. "Suppose I had a son, and suppose he, as a young physicist, had been approached by your people. What would my son say to me when he found out that the CIA was infiltrating the ranks of his colleagues? And, further, wouldn't he find it incredible when I denied knowledge of the operation? . . . Arthur, there is a corrupting aspect of this that I don't like at all. Not at all. These young men of science are exploring the wide world of knowledge, seeking the essence of matter, the precise nature of the universe. They must be free to test, probe, and weigh. If they are merely to be the subsidized front for old men and old ideas—and by that I mean you and me and our whole generation—then their careers become a sham." The President tilted back in his chair. "I think if I were in Miguel Loomis's shoes, I'd be just as disturbed as he is."

"I take it you want Operation Flycatcher dismantled," said Ingram quietly.

"I do." Roudebush smiled. "Actually, of course, Miguel Loomis has left us no alternative. If CIA support is not withdrawn, he plans to expose the connection publicly."

"He could be handled," said Ingram, leaving the clear implication that President Roudebush could not. "I respect your wishes, sir, and although I do not agree with you, the Spruance support of Flycatcher will be terminated and the project closed down."

Ingram sat perfectly straight in his chair, still framing his spectacles in that neat little half rectangle of fingers.

"Good," said the President. "I appreciate your co-operation, Arthur." The compartment door was closed.

Ingram, sensing it, arose from his chair and folded his unused glasses into the leather case at his breast pocket.

"I'm sorry about Stephen Greer," said Ingram. "I know it must be a shock to you, Mr. President."

I'm the one who felt the shock. It seemed inconceivable to me that Ingram would not have mentioned Greer the moment he entered the President's office.

"Sue Greer is the one I'm worried about," said Roudebush. "So far she's holding up. The whole business is extraordinary. The police don't have a solid clue."

"If the Agency can help in any way, please call me at once," said Ingram.

"Thank you, Arthur. For the moment, I think we should let the police handle the case."

As Roudebush walked Ingram to the door, he indicated by a nod that I was to remain. He returned to sit on the corner of his desk, his favorite informal roost beside the golden donkey pen set. His first remark was unexpected.

"Gene," he said, "I suppose you're going to write your version of this administration someday?"

"I had thought of it, Mr. President. No definite plans, but . . ."

He waved a hand. "I hope you do. You might be the best man. Your position, half fish of the media, half fowl of this office, ought to give you a fairly objective viewpoint. Personally, I can't stand these fawning memoirs that follow the late king like so many paid mourners. Jack Kennedy once said there was no such thing as history. I agree with what I think he meant. But you might come close."

I grinned in relief. "I'm not much for the establishment line anyway."

"Good, I hope you've been keeping notes. On this intelligence matter, you definitely should. I think we're in for quite a time. Who, for instance, would think the CIA director would keep secrets from his boss? . . . Or plant a shifty agent in his locker room?"

We eyed each other. Roudebush grinned, then we both broke into laughter. This man *is* different, I thought. I could imagine the irate explosion of a Dwight Eisenhower or a Lyndon Johnson at a similar revelation. But Roudebush, God bless him, also saw the irony. After our laughter quieted, he became serious again.

"Gene, can you give me one good reason why Ingram should be using graduate students in physics as servants of the Agency?"

"Ingram thinks it's sound," I replied. "But I sure don't. Frankly, Mr. President, in my book that Spruance Flycatcher operation is a crude, cynical business."

He nodded. "I agree completely with young Loomis. This Flycatcher thing is repellent to me. It's the kind of operation that erodes faith in our own institutions. It is corrupting, and it's nasty, and the man who conceived the idea can't have much appreciation for the values of a free society." He shrugged. "But that's Arthur Ingram. . . . Damn it, just recalling what he said makes my blood pressure go up all over again."

"You didn't show it."

He shook his head. "No, anger is lost on Ingram. We've been over this ground before. He can't see that if we adopt Communist methods in our zeal to contain them, we wind up defeating ourselves, war or no war. What is left of our open society if every man has to fear a secret government agent at his elbow? Who can respect us or believe us when some of our best young scientists go abroad as the instruments of a hidden agency?"

He left the corner of the desk and walked back toward his chair, his head lowered as he scuffed at the carpet.

"The whole CIA has gotten out of hand." he continued. "Subsidizing intellectuals and labor leaders, buying up university research brains, fomenting revolutions, clandestine paramilitary operations—a whole ball of wax that was never contemplated when the Agency was set up to gather vital information abroad. That's its job, and that's all it should be doing. . . . Of course, it's partially my fault. I should have cracked down long ago. But at this desk, there is always some other crisis, crying to be handled at once."

QUESTIONS

1 The prime functions of the American national bureaucracy are to carry out or administer the laws of the land and to serve the executive branch. What danger do you see in the recent expansion of the bureaucracy to the extent that the President can no longer keep track of its routine affairs?

2 What justification did Ingram offer for not informing the President of Operation Flycatcher?

3 What danger do bureaucrats like Ingram pose to the President's success in office?

Reading 26

On Instructions of My Government

Pierre Salinger

Perhaps one of the bureaucracy's most important functions is to provide the President with accurate, complete, and timely information. The bureaucracy's information gathering, evaluation, and transmission process is particularly critical in the area of foreign affairs, where information sources are quite diverse. It was because of this that the Central Intelligence Agency (CIA) was created—to act as a clearinghouse for information on foreign nations. It was expected that the agency would increase the efficiency and speed of information compilation and transmission.

While accomplishing this goal, the CIA created other problems. The President has only one major source of information in this area, which could make him dependent and vulnerable. Perhaps Pierre Salinger, who was President Kennedy's press secretary, was recalling the Bay of Pigs incident (1961) and the Cuban missile crisis (1962) when he described a similar situation involving the fictional Latin American state of Santa Clara in his novel *On Instructions of My Government.*

Since the President's crisis announcement two months earlier that China was on the verge of mass-producing an intercontinental range ballistic missile, joint American-Soviet surveillance of the nuclear test center at Lop Nor had come up with a discovery of major significance.

The Chinese were moving the vast complex from Sinkiang Province, adjoining the Soviet Union, to a new location in the Himalayan state of Tibet, near the border of India. The transfer came as no surprise. Lop Nor was much too vulnerable both to Soviet missiles and to attack by the forty divisions of Red Army infantry and armor along the Sinkiang boundary.

In his report to the President, the director of the Central Intelligence Agency was optimistic on two points. The move from Lop Nor should delay flight-testing of the ICBM until at least the first of the year, and the proximity of the nuclear center to the Indian border would worsen the already tenuous relations between Peking and New Delhi.

Aerial observation of the Tibetan site, however, would almost certainly involve violations of India's air space, for which the CIA would have to have presidential approval. It was given promptly by the Chief Executive and without consultation with the neutralist government of India.

In the intelligence reports from Bolivia and Santa Clara, the President also found grounds for believing that a nuclear confrontation with China was far from imminent.

CIA agents in La Paz and their horde of informants could unearth no information to suggest that the Communist government was preparing to site the missiles of their Chinese ally. Nor did orbital satellites and over-flights by the Blackbird—the SR-71 spy plant—produce photographic evidence of launch site construction.

It was the same story in Santa Clara—except for the alarms of Ambassador Hood.

In its surveillance of enemy nations such as China and Bolivia, which had a formidable defense of surface-to-air missiles, the Blackbird flew at evasive altitudes up to seventy thousand feet. Even at that extreme range, however, and at speeds up to two thousand miles an hour, its sensitive cameras could produce images of amazing clarity.

The Arroyo Seco had no defense against overflights and high-altitude photo reconnaissance of it was known among the CIA pilots as the milk run. But General Gi You-gin, even if he had had the appropriate weapons, would not have tried to drive them off. He knew that their cameras were recording ground activity that would give the CIA absolutely no basis for suspicion and would, to the contrary, persuade the photo analysts that the arroyo was a conventional artillery defensive position and nothing more.

There were, of course, daily changes in the topography of the arroyo. The artillery emplacements, dug hastily by bulldozers within hours of the original assault, were now being reinforced with steel and concrete. There were also new excavations for subsurface storage of fuel and ammunition and for billeting of the guerrilla force.

On the steep slope facing south toward Ariella, where most of the federal casualties had fallen the first day of battle, a zigzag road was being cut to link the heights with the highway and rail line in the narrow gorge.

Day after day the eight telescopic cameras in the Blackbird's belly turrets examined every square yard of the rebel position. After exposure, the film was fed into automatic developing equipment aboard the plane and the reels were parachuted to a drop zone in the Canal Zone where a supersonic courier plane was waiting to fly them to Washington. Within hours of the overflight the footage was in the hands of specialists at the National Photographic Interpretation Center. They first examined the general terrain of the arroyo to determine if the new construction was assuming the pattern of all known launching sites—depots for storage of the missiles and their transporters, bombproof shelters for storage of nuclear warheads, computer fire control centers and trackage for delivery of the weapons to the launching pads. But they found nothing suspicious, even on the infra-red footage which could penetrate camouflage.

The photo interpreters next examined the film from the SR-71's extreme telephoto cameras, whose resolving power was such that enlargements could clearly define the faces of rebels working in the arroyo. From this footage they were able to calibrate the diameter of electric wires criss-crossing the position and declare flatly that there were no cables—above ground, at least—that could carry the voltage to operate the computer fire controls for even a short-range missile. The analysts gave special attention to the gun emplacements, which could be convertible into launching pads. But it was their opinion, after stereoscopic examination of the concrete foundations, that they were too shallow to support the thunderous recoil of an ICBM firing.

And thus, routinely, the report of the Interpretation Center to the Committee on Overhead Reconnaissance, the Defense Intelligence Agency and the President's military adviser, was always the same. There was no evidence of missile base construction at the Arroyo Seco.

The President had other intelligence reports that were equally reassuring. It would be impossible to move ICBMs to Chinese seaports from either Lop Nor or the new complex in Tibet without detection by Soviet, Japanese or Nationalist Chinese agents within China. And, just as significant, there had been no movement of Chinese missile technicians from the test centers. In 1962 the Russians had sent hundreds of specialists to Cuba to man Castro's IRBMs and their defensive ring of surface-to-air missiles. China was sending none and Paco Jiminez could not fire even the simplest of rockets without their expertise.

The only prominent Chinese nuclear artillerist who had not been seen publicly in recent weeks was General Gi You-gin, but it was the consensus of intelligence reports that he was in charge of constructing the new test center in Tibet, as he had been at Lop Nor.

How was it possible for the intelligence community to misread its own evidence—to be absolutely certain that there was no early possibility of a Chinese nuclear presence in the Western Hemisphere when that threat of holocaust was only two weeks away?

There were two errors. The first was the Western world's refusal to acknowledge its own long and costly failure to fathom the intentions of Communist China, or its capacity for accepting the unacceptable risk. The examples were written in history—the decision of Peking to send its armies into North Korea, defying America to unleash its nuclear weapons when it had no retaliatory potential of its own; to provoke border warfare with the Soviet Union when it had only a short-range missile capacity whose launch would invite its own total destruction, and its continuing aggressions against India, whose security both America and the Soviet Union were bound by their own self-interests to defend.

The precedents for suicidal risk were there, but they were ignored. And out of this error grew the second—the assumption that China, now that it was developing its own nuclear arsenal, would bide its time until it could achieve a balance of terror with its powerful enemies. Such a balance would require both a mass stockpile of intercontinental missiles and an anti-ballistic defense of a sophistication that would insure a second strike capacity.

The experts were confident that China had neither ICBMs in such quantity nor an ABM defense, and that until it did, it would not present the superpowers with an early threat to their own security—and certainly not from Latin America, where it could have no conceivable objective commensurate with the risk.

If there was in Washington a gradual diminution of the crisis atmosphere since the joint U.S.-Soviet announcement of China's ICBM two months earlier, it was understandable in light of such calculations. If the President felt that he could now concentrate on his re-election, confident that he would have ample warning of the deployment of Chinese missiles in the Western Hemisphere, that, too, was understandable.

It was to prove fateful, however, that an interview with James McManus of Westinghouse Broadcasting, on the plane returning the presidential party from the electioneering swing into New England, would place the Chief Executive solidly on record as denying the imminence of a nuclear confrontation with the People's Republic of China.

McManus, like most of the correspondents accompanying the President, had found little hard news to report. But at the same hour the Chief Executive was motorcading through downtown Boston, Senator Grant had told an audience in Houston that the White House was deliberately downplaying "China's giant step forward in the thermonuclear arms race. It might be good politics," continued Grant, "to conceal this new and ominous threat to our security from the voters. But history will judge whether my opponent has the right to place his own ambitions above the security of the nation."

A half hour before the plane was to land at Andrews Air Force Base outside Washington, McManus took a seat beside Max Busby.

"Let's face it, Max. None of us has an A.M. story, at least nothing your man will like. Boston was the mixture as before—nothing in his speeches worth picking up."

Busby was tired. "He had a good crowd for the motorcade—much better than on the West Coast. He's picking up. It's starting to roll now."

"You're wrong, Max. The trip was a disaster." McManus shoved a late edition of the Boston *Globe* into Busby's hands. "Grant made the front page with that Houston speech today. I'd like your man to give me an answer to it."

"No exclusives, Jim. You know that."

"All right, no exclusive. Let all of us have him for a couple of minutes. He ought to reply to Grant on this."

"I'm not going to subject him to an off-the-cuff press conference. He's worn out, Jim, just like the rest of us."

At that moment the President came aft from the first-class section to glance at the news teletypes, huddled among mimeograph machines and a battery of typewriters in the staff news center in the back of the plane. He overheard Busby's last comment.

"Worn out? Never. What is it you want, Jim?"

The other correspondents began gathering around. "Senator Grant charged in Houston today that—"

"I know. I saw the story and it's irresponsible."

Busby tried to cut it off. "Mr. President, you might want to wait until you've seen Grant's full text."

McManus already had his tape recorder rolling and was holding his microphone toward the President. "Could we have just a brief comment now?"

"Of course." He saw the television crews moving into position. "Let me know when you're all ready."

"We're ready, sir."

"I think it's clear, from Senator Grant's comments today, that he's trying to create an atmosphere of panic in this country. As a member of the Foreign Relations Committee he has free access to intelligence reports that show, beyond all doubt, that China has no present capability whatever of waging nuclear warfare against this country. But he chooses not to look at the reports because he knows they would deny him what he believes is an effective issue against me."

McManus got in the first question. "You say no *present* capability, Mr. President. Could you give us an estimate of when China might have an operational ICBM they could deploy against us?"

"Certainly not next week or next month, as Grant claims—or even in the foreseeable future. First they have to flight-test it. Then they've got to stockpile it. Then they've got to find a point in this hemisphere to launch it. And I can tell you unequivocally that none of this could escape our surveillance."

The President's old adversary, Palmer Joyce, who had no interest in a rebuttal to his own nightly pitch that only Harlan Grant could save the republic, spoke up from the back of the circle of correspondents.

"In other words, Mr. President, you're calling the senator a liar?"

"I'm saying nothing of the kind, Joyce. I'm saying that the senator owes it to himself and to the country to determine what the facts are."

"And the facts, as you put them, are that we have nothing to fear, now or in the foreseeable future, from Red China."

"In the area of a nuclear confrontation, yes. That's exactly what I'm saying."

QUESTIONS

1 What risks to the President's political situation are evident in this selection, and
   how did these risks develop?
2 What information sources was the President relying upon in this selection?
3 What is the likely outcome of the President's overreliance on the CIA's intelligence sources?

The Judiciary

Reading 27
The Supreme Court
Andrew Tully

Associate Justice Francis Dalton's thoughts and experiences in this
opening chapter of Andrew Tully's novel *The Supreme Court* amply illustrate the dynamics of the judicial process in American politics. The United States Supreme Court, the most prestigious judicial institution in
America, is the focus here, and very few of its key elements are overlooked. From Dalton's perspective, we see the majestic formality and
legalistic nature of the Court as well as its personal or human elements.

The Supreme Court building's interior and exterior manifest the tradition, dignity, and solemnity associated with this godlike tribunal. Ionic
columns, white marble walls, maroon velours drapery, and other grandi-
ose trappings spur Dalton to characterize the Court building as a "cut-
rate Taj Mahal." The proceedings of the Court itself likewise reflect the
solemnity and formality of the judicial environment and process.

The human element in the Court is illustrated by Dalton's irreverence, Whitfield's stubbornness, Mitchell's sarcastic comments, and the
oral arguments which reveal that even personal friendships are significant in the judicial process.

The judicial principles highlighted in this selection should not be
overlooked. The Court's arguments and decisions illustrate that the pro-
visions of the Bill of Rights are invoked in line with the political philosophies of the Justices. Dalton's view stresses the welfare of the community and the needs of the state, while Hume's view stresses the
"absolute" rights of the individual. Personal political principles are thus
an integral part of the judicial process despite the popular belief that
judges are unbiased and neutral.

Mr. Justice Francis Copley Dalton of the Supreme Court of the United
States had once merited a box on the first page of the Washington *Post's*
society section when he remarked at a Georgetown cocktail party that the
Supreme Court building would have been a thing of joy to the ancient
Romans—"at their decadent worst." He grinned at the passing recollection
now as he walked briskly up the broad flight of marble steps to the double
row of Corinthian columns which with icy solemnity guarded entry to the
neo-classic temple. Well, he also had managed to become known as the
Associate Justice who referred to this temple as "the old salt mine," and
periodically some columnist would make a passing reference to him as the

only member of the Court who regularly used the public entrance to the building. It had honestly not occurred to him on that first day, two years ago, that walking up the steps would start a legend in the Washington press; now that the legend was whole, he rather enjoyed it and saw no point in dissolving it. "Anyway, it's good exercise," he had told Beatrice, and Beatrice had winked her saucy backstage wink and accused him of trying to set himself up as a tourist attraction in competition with the Washington Monument. She did not remind him that he might have been satisfied with the mile-long stroll he took almost every morning while the court was in session—from the Treasury Building, where the cab from Georgetown deposited him, to Capitol Hill. Sometimes Mr. Justice Dalton got the impression that Beatrice looked on him as a kind of matinee idol—traveling incognito. "You do have presence, you know," she was fond of saying. And Beatrice always insisted that his mother had sensed it when she ordered that her infant son's middle name should be the same as the fashionable square in Boston's Back Bay. Michael Dalton had been appalled; Copley, he told his wife, wasn't even a saint's name. But Bridget Dalton had been adamant. "She wanted you to be an aristocrat," Michael Dalton explained to young Francis. "Parnell wasn't good enough."

Francis wasn't sure what contribution his middle name had made to his career, but being an Irishman who could get along with the Italians was no hindrance in his swift emergence as the youngest governor in the long history of Massachusetts. Yet, knowing Bridget Dalton, he was sure that had she lived long enough to see her son go on to become Attorney General of the United States, and then the youngest member of the Supreme Court, she would not have hesitated to claim credit for her insistence at the baptismal font.

He was late; he'd barely have time to drop his hat and coat in his office before going on to the robing room. As he walked through the cathedral-like lobby of dead-white marble, he threw a wave and a brisk hello to Mac and Horace, the two Court policemen standing on each side of the red velvet rope athwart the entrance to the Court chamber. "A nice morning, Mr. Justice Dalton," Mac threw back at him, and he smiled, as he always did, and said, "Just fine," automatically. It was a fine morning, especially for January, but he was thinking not so much of the brave, thin sunlight as of how he could have used another hour in bed. It had been a good dinner at the Pratts' and he had been home only a little after midnight, but at forty-two Francis was still young enough never to be pleased with the hour of waking. He also was still young enough to be impatiently perplexed by the habits of the Court's oldest member, the cranky Angus Whitfield, who proudly arose at five o'clock every morning. Mornings, thought Justice Dalton, must have been more leisurely in the days when the Court convened at noon instead of ten o'clock.

He turned right, past the first half dozen or so tourists—who'd have recognized his red hair had he not carefully kept on his hat—and in precarious anonymity hurried down the corridor to the private door of his suite.

Jake was standing in front of his desk, fiddling with some briefs. Jake was always standing in front of his desk when the justice arrived in the morning. Jake Moriarty knew how to save the boss's time.

"Hello, Jake," Francis said.

"Good morning, Mr. Justice." Jake Moriarty was in a hurry for his boss; Francis Dalton could tell that by the way Jake was using his hand nervously to try to smooth the unruly black hair that was always falling down over his eyes. Although a fat man, Jake liked to keep things moving; if you knew him, it did not seem incongruous that he had been a running guard on a pretty good Harvard football team.

"Well—I suppose you're suggesting that it's getting late, Jake," Francis said. He grinned as he took off his gray felt hat with the turned-up brim—a poor man's Homburg, Beatrice called it—and threw the hat and his black chesterfield on the brown leather sofa.

Jake's face stayed earnest. "Yes, sir, you've only got about five minutes, and I had kind of hoped you'd have time to look over some of the research I did on the Banks opinion."

"I know, Jake—it'll have to wait until this afternoon. But, Jake, we're on schedule, aren't we?" Francis Dalton was proud of the way he kept abreast of the heavy work load that had come to the Court with the Hughes administration.

"Oh, sure, Mr. Justice," Jake said. He could return the grin now, and he did. "You know me—I like to get a little ahead."

"I know you, all right, Jake," Francis said. "It's you married men who keep us bachelors hustling—no matter how late we've been out the night before. But you're not perfect, Jake—Sally tells me she has a hell of a time getting you up in the morning."

"Yes, sir, I guess that's right," Jake said. He was looking a little sheepish now. "But that's one of the advantages of married life. You don't need an alarm clock."

"I suppose I'll have to try it one of these days—if I ever get the time." Francis was moving toward the door. "But right now I'd better get going or Bacon will be giving me a black look."

"Right, sir." Jake Moriarty hurried over to open the door. "Good luck, Mr. Justice," Jake said, as he always said. "See you later, Jake," Francis said, as he always said, and he marched out the door and down the hall. He'd make the robing room with a minute or two to spare and that was good. Robert McNair Bacon, Chief Justice of the United States, was not only a crusty, narrow-minded old fool; he was also a stickler for punctuality. Another early riser, Francis reflected.

Everybody was there but Angus Whitfield when Francis reached the robing room and started down the line of oak paneled lockers with their silver nameplates to pay obeisance to the tradition started by old Melville Fuller in the Gay Nineties. It was that Chief Justice's premise that if the justices shook hands with each other before every session of the Court, they might somehow manage to remain on speaking terms. Optimist, thought Francis, as he went down the line with his hand out—to tall, spare Hume, and roly-poly Gillette, Chief Justice Bacon with his white hair flowing back in waves and the cold blue eyes behind the pince-nez, the tiny, bald-headed Robson of Florida, Baker with the Rotary pin in the lapel of his blue serge suit, Mitchell, the cowboy from Nevada with the bourbon breath, and Feldman, from the sidewalks of New York, Wall Street division.

"Reckon I saw you at LaSalle du Bois the other night, Mr. Justice." It was the cowboy, Frank Mitchell, hearty and gregarious, a man who enjoyed what passed for fleshpots in provincial Washington.

"Ah there, Frank, nobody can hide from you." Francis' smile was real. You couldn't help liking Mitchell, despite his professional air of the barefoot boy. Mitchell was worth at least fifty million good oil dollars, and he had never ceased to enjoy his wealth.

"About time to get stirring," Bacon muttered grudgingly.

"Good morning, Mr. Justice," Hume said with the correctness that yet was overlaid with grace.

"How are you, Mr. Justice?" The Rotarian Baker said in the boom practiced at innumerable back-slapping luncheons.

"Ah, Dalton," said little Robson, in intellectual absent-mindedness. "Hello, boy," said Gillette, his voice a puffing effort. "Morning," said the banker Feldman, frugally.

Jones, the Negro attendant, was standing ready at the locker whose open door bore the name Justice Dalton, and Francis turned his back and Jones slipped the robe on, adjusting it about his shoulders and giving it the three final little pats.

"Good morning, Jones," Francis said.

Good morning, Mr. Justice," Jones said. Francis had never heard Jones say anything else. Jones was a man of dignity, and he wore his dignity aloofly, as though forbidding intimacy. "Jones doesn't approve of ol' Frank," Mitchell had told Dalton once. Francis could understand that.

Bacon was fretful. His enormous gold watch was in his hand and his lips were moving crankily.

"Where's Whitfield?" Bacon growled. He held up one finger to Jones, and Jones hustled over.

"Jones, get me a page," Bacon said.

Jones all but loped out the door, to return within a few seconds with a little boy in the traditional blue knickerbockers, blue jacket and black lisle stockings. It was Sammy Heller, and he had the habitual frightened look that went with a summons from a Chief Justice.

"Page, go to Mr. Justice Whitfield's suite and deliver a message for me," Chief Justice Bacon told him. "Tell Mr. Justice Whitfield the Court is about to convene and his presence is required."

"Yes, sir, Mr. Chief Justice," Sammy said—and fled.

This should be good, Francis thought, and he looked over at Frank Mitchell and was met by one of Mitchell's outlandish, exaggerated winks.

"Maybe he's got a date with a girl," Mitchell suggested with awesome irreverence.

Bacon turned to Mitchell. His icy blue eyes started at the top of Mitchell's head with its crew-cut frieze of salt-and-pepper hair and descended slowly to the cowboy boots with the high heels that Mitchell wore even with white tie and tails. Then, silently, Bacon turned away.

When the knock came on the door, Jones opened it immediately and little Sammy Heller blew in as though shot from a gun. He stopped about ten feet in front of Chief Justice Bacon.

"Well, boy?" Bacon's glare was like a punch on the jaw.

"Mr. Chief Justice, sir, Mr. Justice Whitfield—sir, he says to tell Mr. Chief Justice Bacon that Mr. Justice Whitfield doesn't work for him."

For a moment the silence was so complete it seemed to have substance, as though an immense hulk had suddenly shouldered its way into the room. Then it was broken by Frank Mitchell's voice.

"Jesus Christ!" Mitchell said.

Bacon seemed not to hear the explosive words. He was staring down at Sammy Heller like an avenging angel, his eyes frigid with rage, one arm half raised in furious reflex. My God, he's going to strike the boy, Francis thought, and in that split second's reflection he felt rather than saw Mitchell's slight movement next to him.

But as Sammy stood there, eyes wide and whole body trembling, Bacon merely glared his fury. And then, pointing to the door, he uttered two words. "Get out!" Bacon said, the words slapping across the boy like a whip. Sammy's mouth opened and his head bobbed crazily—and he fled through the door suddenly held open by Jones.

"Poor little cuss." It was Mitchell's voice again, and this time Bacon turned to the Nevadan, his upper lip curled back to show his bit square teeth, his glare now heightened by a crimsoning at the cheekbones.

"Well, sir?" Bacon's voice was like the cut of an ax. "Do you wish to comment, Mr. Justice Mitchell?"

Mitchell's eyes turned with lazy casualness to the Chief Justice and for a moment the two men stood there, appraising each other in icy hatred.

Finally Mitchell spoke, his tone soft even while his eyes stayed hard. "No," Mitchell said. "No—I don't think so, sir. I think perhaps I had better not." He turned to Francis. "I wonder if we can get this show on the road."

"Heavens, yes—let's get moving." The angry whine of a voice belonged to David Benjamin Feldman, across the room. "This Court is getting to be worse than a grammar-school debating society!"

There was a general movement in the room, and Francis saw Hume, his face lined with concern, put out an arm and touch Bacon's shoulder lightly with a friendly hand. Bacon seemed suddenly to slump, to lose an inch or two of his height. He turned to Hume and suddenly his eyes had a sadness to them.

"Yes, let us go in, brethren," Bacon said.

And that was all. Robed and silent, the justices filed across the private corridor, Mitchell's hand touching Francis' arm lightly, Bacon looking straight ahead, Feldman mumbling to himself. They marched into the end of the courtroom curtained off with the huge maroon velours drapery, and Bacon immediately and mechanically gave the signal. They stood there, then, as the buzzer sounded from the marshal's desk beyond the drapery at one end of the bench, and the crier's voice came loud and clear as usual: "The Honorable, the Chief Justice and the Associate Justices of the Supreme Court of the United States!"

After what had happened, Francis half expected the curtain would refuse to operate, but automation proved unaffected by the robing room crisis. Unhesitatingly, the heavy drapery parted in three places and the solemn justices entered the courtroom in threes, by seniority. Or rather, in two groups of three and one of two, since Whitfield was still back in his suite, probably chortling horribly over his declaration of independence. As the spectators rose and the justices strode with determined majesty to their big chairs, the return to an air of normalcy was strengthened by the crier's austerely comforting announcement: "Oyez! Oyez! Oyez! All persons having business before the Honorable, the Supreme Court of the United States, are admonished to draw near and give their attention, for the Court is now sitting! God save the United States and his honorable Court!" Francis couldn't help wondering, as Bridget Dalton's son, whether the Deity was interested in preserving such a quarrelsome body.

Francis sat down, his eyes taking in the audience without seeing it. That had been a precious moment when little Sammy Heller had delivered Angus Whitfield's message to the Chief Justice. Francis held a hand to his face to conceal an intruding grin. Whitfield, of course, had been well within his rights, if somewhat aggressive in his assertion of them. After all, a justice of the Supreme Court was a kind of sovereign state, an autonomous little one-man principality who was in no way beholden to the Chief Justice. The Chief Justice was merely a presiding officer, not a warden or an office manager. Moreover, Whitfield was acutely conscious of his prerogatives as the oldest member of the Court—all self-assigned, of course—and he had always shown his independence of Bacon. When Whitfield wanted to go fishing of a weekend, he always skipped town early, frequently stalking out in the middle of the Friday morning conference. There was nothing Bacon could do about it; as Whitfield had informed him through Sammy Heller, Mr. Justice Whitfield did not work for the Chief Justice.

Francis' mind continued to wander as Bacon, irritability coloring his face, spent willful moments going over some papers in front of him. Francis surveyed the huge marble courtroom with its high ceiling—forty-four towering feet above the mortals below it—and its two dozen practically genuine Ionic columns of Siena marble. And he recalled now, as he so often did, Beatrice's remark when she first had stood before his judicial temple with its great bronze doors and its look of a cut-rate Taj Mahal.

"Really, Francis," Beatrice said, "I think you justices should ride to work on elephants." The remark was honestly original with Beatrice; Francis knew she would not knowingly pilfer from the late Justice Harlan Fiske Stone, who had uttered the identical comment when that dignitary caught his first look at the building before its dedication in 1935.

His attempts to shake off the waywardness of his thoughts were helped by the traditional first business before the Court, which the books called "the admission of qualified lawyers to practice before the Supreme Court of the United States" but which Frank Mitchell referred to as "looking over the human sacrifices." There was young Tom Nelson, junior, stiff and solemn despite his blond, almost whitish, cowlick, and Francis succeeded in catching his eye as he stepped forward and by an eyelid flicker wished him well. It was Tom Nelson, senior, who had come to young Francis Copley Dalton's rescue during his last year at Holy Cross with a loan and the promise of a job that saw him through Harvard Law School, and if Mr. Justice Dalton could manage it he would in turn smooth Tom's path. Not that young Tom needed much help; he had stepped into a junior partnership in a million-dollar corporation law business in Boston, and that tribe of Back Bay Brahmins named Nelson was about as self-sufficient as Boston's First National Bank, and considerably more genteel. Francis had never before been so warmed by the Chief Justice's practice of calling each new admitted lawyer by name and bidding him gracious welcome to the club.

But—it was Monday, and therefore opinion day, and suddenly Francis found Bacon looking down the bench at him, that habitual half-snarl twisting his lips. Francis' dreaming had carried him cozily right up to the moment when the stage was his for his delivery of the majority opinion in the case of the State of Alabama versus Adam Lockett. The case was cut and dried; the Court had voted seven to two to uphold the state in its insistence that the Negro Lockett had indeed incited his audience to riot by his obscene and profane demands that they arm themselves with clubs and march on the state Capitol in Montgomery to protest a new segregated housing project. There had been incidents at Lockett's trial, but none that had impaired the fairness of his trial. Of course, Bacon and Hume had dissented—in their maddening way—but their dissents were mild, almost apologetic.

Francis saw no point in reading the majority opinion, although usually he preferred to subject himself to the ordeal in order to place the emphasis where it was needed. But after handing down the opinion, he looked over at Bacon for the Chief Justice's nod, and added what he felt was a necessary postscript.

Looking down from the bench and past the rows of spectators to the marble pillars at the rear of the courtroom, he summed up, keeping his voice low. "This case involves the so-called Bill of Rights," he said. "Or it is alleged to involve the Bill of Rights. But the majority has found that nowhere in the state's prosecution of the case or in its confinement of the defendant was any basic right infringed. Indeed, there was such care taken by the state of Alabama in its conduct of the prosecution that it seems presumptuous for the defendant to suggest that any infringement of his civil rights was involved. With all the facts before the Court, the conclusion is inescapable that defendant's counsel has depended throughout on arguments that are tendentious and frivolous."

Francis looked down at young Tom Nelson and then looked away swiftly lest he smile at young Tom's openmouthed attentiveness. That would do; there was no point in saying more. He had wanted to be sure the word frivolous was given the prominence it might not seem to have been given in a printed opinion which was the work of seven nitpicking justices, and he had done so with those few words. He would not make any speeches; it wasn't necessary.

He sat there, then, as the Court ponderously labored to hand down the other opinions, in other cases, that were the result of haggling sessions in the Friday conference room and long nights of brain-burning toil in office and home. Little Robson, of course, had to read every opinion he had a hand in, and his dissents as usual were sharp and sneering with sarcasm. And Baker, who loved the sound of his Chautauqua lecture-platform tones, would never miss a chance to orate.

But Francis was surprised when Hume did not read the majority opinion in the Highland case, still another of the civil rights matters that were clogging the Court's calendar. The vote was by the five-to-four margin with which the Court had legally heckled President Hughes almost from the moment he took office, and Francis, who had written a biting dissent, had expected a full-dress performance from the liberal Hoosier. In conference, Hume's arguments for the little labor leader had been long and unusually forceful, and Francis was sure he had carried the wavering Feldman with him to eke out the majority opinion that the state of Mississippi had violated Highland's right of free speech.

Now, however, with the spectators leaning forward eagerly, Hume disappointed them. Taking the whole courtroom in with a slow smile, the tall Hoosier moved his head in a slight bow and when he spoke his tone was mild. "The majority opinion speaks for itself," he said. "It would be pointless to try to decry its substance. But I should like remind my brethren that this case concerns the Bill of Rights, not—as one of my brothers has remarked—the *so-called* Bill of Rights."

Hume turned slowly and looked at Francis, the little smile still on his face. Francis found himself smiling back, even as the old impatience surged within him. Oh, all right, Hume, Francis thought, go ahead and wave your precious Bill of Rights while anarchy runs amok in the streets. And yet once again Francis found the irritation Hume planted in him tinged with an honest respect and admiration for the Hoosier's calm appraisal of the law. He could not dislike such a man, even while vehemently disagreeing with him; he could only wish that he could get through to Hume's blind spot, to his weakness in arguing for what he called the "absolutes" in the Bill of Rights even when the invoking of them was a clear danger to the community. To Francis, those earliest congressmen were practical men who would be appalled at the frivolous invoking of the Bill of Rights against the interests of the state. While acknowledging that the Bill of Rights set forth certain freedoms, Francis considered it juvenile to assume that the founding fathers intended those rights to be used to tear down the community and the Constitution itself. Hume, he felt, refused to recognize that there were times of danger or times when the nation cried for action, when the community's welfare had to come before the rights of the individual.

Now, Francis noticed, Hume had leaned back in his chair with eyes closed as the plump Gillette settled into the droning tones of his concurring opinion in the Highland case. Francis knew Hume was listening intently, but his own mind continued to wander. In recent months he had found it harder to concentrate on matters immediately at hand, especially at such times as Gillette was pontificating in public, indecently exposing his Southern California mentality. His thoughts returned to his continuing disagreement with Hume, a man of whom he thought so highly. He could not believe that their disagreement was based merely on the fact that Hume was a liberal while he was a conservative. The labels didn't mean that much to either of them—despite the fact that he, Francis Dalton, had been carried to one political success after another by the conservative tide that had swept the country. It was more that Francis agreed with the President that, for the present at least, the times cried for drastic action and for the creation of a kind of national discipline to combat the mounting crisis. He had had his doubts about the Walsh Act because he was uncomfortable with

legislation that banned strikes and imposed compulsory governmental arbi-
tration, but he had felt it was a necessary abridgment of rights under the
circumstances—circumstances that constituted a national emergency without being formally called by that name. It had required considerable soul-
searching before he had cast his vote with the minority when the Court
invalidated the act, but he felt he had been correct in upholding a
President's right to take measures in a critical moment of history to protect
the whole community. With the Soviet Union threatening war if the President armed the German military machine with atomic warheads, the means
of production had to be guarded against both irresponsible stoppages and
the throwing of subversive monkey wrenches.

Well, Gillette was through, thank God, and that was that. The opinions
hadn't taken so very long, after all. Francis leaned forward with his usual
expectation as the Court shifted gears to begin the chore he always found
exciting—hearing the oral arguments of the lawyers pleading their cases.
Even when their performances were routine, Francis usually enjoyed them;
they brought the Court out of its isolation and exposed it to the strident
legalisms of the world of law outside its neo-Grecian palace.

Francis felt sorry almost at once for Sam Hyde as he opened the Wil-
liams case. It was an antitrust action against the little steel companies, and
the raw materials were dull to start with, no help to a plodding lawyer like
Hyde. Francis winced for Hyde as he stood there, his pot belly straining on
the buttons of his blue suit coat, his fingers fiddling with the edge of the
lectern, and sweat already gathering on his red face. And—my God! Sam
must be in a funk—he was reading from his brief, although even the callow-
est law student knew the Court always scanned the briefs before hearing
oral arguments. Francis looked over at Bacon as the Chief Justice's mouth
opened, trap fashion.

"We can read, sir!" The trap snapped angrily at Hyde. "May we expect
that you have an oral argument to present?"

Crimson stained Hyde's face as he looked down from Bacon's glare
and hurridly closed the folder on the lectern. A giggle rose from the spectators, stilled immediately by Bacon's glare, and in the new hush Hyde
plunged into his presentation. Francis was relieved to find that he was fairly
well prepared, after all, until suddenly the steel lawyer interposed a lucid
line of argument Francis knew was not in the brief.

This time, little Henry Clay Robson pounced on him, his thin lips
prim. "Yes, yes," Clay told him in his caustic squeak, "we admire your
thought, sir, but your thought unfortunately is not in your brief."

Francis glanced over at Hume. As usual, the Hoosier's face was sad
with the sympathy he felt for the lawyer, the human being showing beneath
the judicial dignity. Francis knew Hume was waiting for a chance to make
Hyde feel more comfortable, and it came immediately as Hyde stumbled on

with a valid point about price-fixing that Francis could approve but which Hyde managed to state badly.

"Ah—excuse me." Hume's soft voice interrupted the lawyer. Hyde looked up at Hume, already grateful because he had been noticed by the gentle, courteous jurist.

"As I understand your argument, sir, you are making the point that this particular price was not fixed, in an unlawful sense, because it was provided for in a previous contract," Hume said.

Hyde sighed happily. "Yes, Mr. Justice. That is my point."

From that juncture, things went better for Hyde as his voice took on a more relaxed tone, but Francis noticed he was being carried away by the new force of his arguments. He would have given anything to signal the lawyer when it became obvious that Hyde was paying no attention to the little red light on the lectern, which warned him that his time was up.

"Sir!" Bacon's voice broke in. "Do you suffer from color blindness?"

Hyde looked up at Bacon, his eyes wide. He was incapable at this point of saying anything lucid, but somehow he managed a mumbled "Yes—ah— thank you, Mr. Justices." Then he picked up his brief and, almost literally, fled the lectern.

Francis felt Mitchell's hand on his arm and bent an ear to the Nevadan's whisper. "If I know Hyde," said Mitchell, "he'll never come in here again without a couple of stiff hookers of bourbon."

That case finally disposed of, Francis poked Mitchell. "Now it's Bob Dodge's turn," he said. "And look at him, will you!"

Dodge, an Assistant Solicitor General, for the first time had come to the Court in the cutaway coat traditionally worn by the Solicitor General and his staff. Francis regarded Dodge as a hard-working but uninspired lawyer, and he expected Mitchell's comment.

"By God, his backside's better dressed than his mind," Mitchell whispered.

Francis looked over at Hume and found him regarding Dodge with an affectionate if apprehensive eye. Hume had once delivered a series of invitational lectures at Columbia Law School, and Bob Dodge was one of the students who had listened to his distilled wisdom. A year ago Dodge had made his first appearance before the Supreme Court and had delivered a series of arguments very near the worst ever heard in the chamber. Hume sought out Francis after the case had been heard and reported that Dodge had approached him to renew old acquaintance and had asked how Hume liked his presentation. "I was somewhat embarrassed," Hume said, "but I told him I found it interesting. He thanked me and said he'd hoped I'd liked it because he'd argued it just the way I'd taught him."

Now Henry Clay Robson was already giving poor Dodge a hard time, peppering him with questions overlaid with judicial irritability. Dodge's case was a good one, but as usual he was presenting it poorly, and Robson could not tolerate legal incompetence. As Francis kept a furtive glance on Hume, he was rewarded; Hume interrupted to put a kindly question to Dodge and then a second and then still a third. Characteristically, Hume was attempting to bring out the facts that obviously were there and should be brought out in fairness to the government, but Robson was annoyed.

"I thought *you* were arguing this case." Robson's remark to Dodge was like a dagger thrust.

Dodge's face reddened, then he managed a smile. "I am, Mr. Justice," he replied, "but I can sure use all the help I can get." Even Hume had to smile at that, and Bacon's swift glare failed immediately to quell the tittering that ran through the spectators' section and overflowed into the one hundred seats in the press area. Francis saw Mrs. Richard McKnight Evans sitting in the reserved box with dainty handkerchief to her smiling mouth and reflected that despite the Olympian facade the Court presented to the public, it was most human in matters pertaining to its social opportunities. Not only had the grim, austere Bacon seen fit to give Molly Evans her own box in the chamber, but the celebrated hostess's limousine was parked regularly in a reserved space in the justices' private garage and she was a member of that exclusive club eligible to use the justices' private elevator. Sometimes it seemed to Francis that the justices performed with considerably more floridness when Molly was in the house. At such times, Bacon was even more the stern patriarch-jurist and little Robson's wit was sharper.

The case was another in the long series involving the refusal of officials of the militant Sons of Slaves to answer questions about their political affiliations before the House Un-American Activities Committee. Franklin, a minor Michigan functionary of the Negro organization, had been charged with contempt by the committee after standing mute before charges that he was a Communist. Dodge was awful; Francis might agree with his argument but he was appalled by his presentation. Yet it was Hume, who surely would vote for the defendant, who kept intervening to help Dodge out of his confusion. Ironically, too, Francis found himself impressed by the argument of the defense counsel, the perceptive, penetrating Sam Sharfman, who brought into the chamber the same ability to sweep aside the inconsequentials that had gained him fame in his appearances for murder defendants.

Sharfman was talking now in his low yet penetrating tone, pleading his case and yet also demanding the justices' favor. "If the Court please," he was saying, "is it to be the case in this country from now on that a person may not take a public position contrary to that being urged by the House Un-American Activities Committee? If he does so, must he understand that he will be subpoenaed to appear at a committee hearing where he will be questioned with regard to every minute detail of his past life, where he will be asked to repeat all the gossip he may have heard about any of his friends and acquaintances, where he will be held up to the public as a subversive and a traitor?"

There was a pause, and then Sharfman continued, almost sadly, "I should note here that the charge linking the defendant Franklin was made by a paid informant and, according to committee practice, the defendant was not permitted to examine the informant. And yet almost everyone in public life—including members of the Supreme Court—has been accused of being Communists." Another pause, for a muted titter from the spectators. And then, "If the Court please, I suggest that this means that government by consent will disappear and will be replaced by government by intimidation—merely because some people fear this country cannot survive unless Congress has the power to set aside the Bill of Rights at will."

Sharfman was good, Francis was thinking—good, but wrong. Sharfman insisted on missing the point. The point was not a question of human liberty but of the Communist party's efforts to manipulate and infiltrate organizations in the United States with the purpose of overthrowing the government. Sharfman refused to face the fact that no government can tolerate revolution, and certainly the Constitution did not preclude the Congress from halting preliminary steps toward that revolution and punishing those responsible. Besides, a Constitution which only a court can save can no longer be saved. Francis was proud of his calling, but he believed deeply that judges were too far removed from the emerging forces of society to overrule them on matters of grave national interest.

He *did* enjoy listening to Sharfman's finely honed legal phrases, and yet as the justices filed through the curtain's openings for lunch, Francis felt himself welcoming the break. Sharfman *was* wrong, but it was depressing to acknowledge the telling power of his points—and to realize the Court almost surely would throw out the contempt conviction by another of those maddening five to four majorities. It was the kind of case in which both Bacon and Hume would cite their Bill of Rights "absolutes," and although Feldman and Baker and Gillette would argue with less force, they would go along. And Francis was just as sure that Mitchell and Whitfield and Robson would join him in holding for the government.

QUESTIONS

1 In what ways do the personal political philosophies of the Supreme Court justices affect the Court's decisions?

2 What differing judicial viewpoints do Justice Dalton and Justice Hume exhibit?

3 What is the purpose of the "oral argument" that lawyers present before the Court?

Reading 28

The Blue Knight

Joseph Wambaugh

Joseph Wambaugh, an ex–Los Angeles policeman, has written several novels about the daily activities and problems of the police. In these books he has effectively portrayed the thankless yet necessary task that society asks of its police and shown these people as ordinary human beings with the same personal and professional worries that everyone has. Police officers do not automatically become perfect when they don their uniforms; they are people with normal human limitations. Despite this fact, society's members expect the police to perform flawlessly on the job.

In *The Blue Knight* Wambaugh writes about a beat cop, Bumper Morgan, who has just been caught lying on the witness stand in what he believes to be an attempt to serve the cause of justice. The irate judge summons him to her chambers where they engage in a conversation on the danger of Morgan's kind of thinking and behavior.

Then the bailiff had his hand on my shoulder and said, "Judge Redford would like to see you in her chambers," and I saw the judge had left the bench and I walked like a toy soldier toward the open door. In a few seconds I was standing in the middle of this room, and facing a desk where the judge sat looking toward the wall which was lined with bookcases full of law books. She was taking deep breaths and thinking of what to say.

"Sit down," she said, finally, and I did. I dropped my hat on the floor and was afraid to stoop down to pick it up I was so dizzy.

"In all my years on the bench I've never had that happen. Not like that. I'd like to know why you did it."

"I want to tell you the truth," I said and my mouth was leathery. I had trouble forming the words. My lips popped from the dryness every time I opened my mouth. I had seen nervous suspects like that thousands of times when I had them good and dirty, and they knew I had them.

"Maybe I should advise you of your constitutional rights before you tell me anything," said the judge, and she took off her glasses and the bump on her nose was more prominent. She was a homely woman and looked smaller here in her office, but she looked stronger too, and aged.

"The hell with my rights!" I said suddenly. "I don't give a damn about my rights, I want to tell you the truth."

"But I intend to have the district attorney's office issue a perjury complaint against you. I'm going to have that hotel register brought in, and the phone company's repairman will be subpoenaed and so will Mister Downey of course, and I think you'll be convicted."

"Don't you even care about what I've got to say?" I was getting mad now as well as scared, and I could feel the tears coming to my eyes, and I hadn't felt anything like this since I couldn't remember when.

"What can you say? What can anyone say? I'm awfully disappointed. I'm sickened in fact." She rubbed her eyes at the corners for a second and I was busting and couldn't hold on.

"*You're* disappointed? *You're* sickened? What the hell do you think I'm feeling at this minute? I feel like you got a blowtorch on the inside of my guts and you won't turn it off and it'll never be turned off, that's what I feel, Your Honor. Now can I tell the God's truth? Will you at least let me tell it?"

"Go ahead," she said, and lit a cigarette and leaned back in the padded chair and watched me.

"Well, I have this snitch, Your Honor. And I've got to protect my informants, you know that. For his own personal safety, and so he can continue to give me information. And the way things are going in court nowadays with everyone so nervous about the defendant's rights, I'm afraid to even mention confidential informants like I used to, and I'm afraid to try to get a search warrant because the judges are so damn hinky they call damn near every informant a material witness, even when he's not. So in recent years I've started . . . exploring ways around."

"You've started lying."

"Yes, I've started lying! What the hell, I'd hardly ever convict any of these crooks if I didn't lie at least a little bit. You know what the search and seizure and arrest rules are like nowadays."

"Go on."

Then I told her how the arrest went down, exactly how it went down, and how I later got the idea about the traffic warrant when I found out he had one. And when I was finished, she smoked for a good two minutes and didn't say a word. Her cheeks were eroded and looked like they were hacked out of a rocky cliff. She was a strong old woman from another century as she sat there and showed me her profile and finally she said, "I've seen witnesses lie thousands of times. I guess every defendant lies to a greater or lesser degree and most defense witnesses stretch hell out of the truth, and of course I've seen police officers lie about probable cause. There's the old hackneyed story about feeling what appeared to be an offensive weapon like a knife in the defendant's pocket and reaching inside to retrieve the knife, and finding it to be a stick of marijuana. That one's been told so many times by so many cops it makes judges want to vomit. And of course there's the furtive movement like the defendant is shoving something under the seat of the car. That's always good probable cause for a search, and likewise that's overdone. Sure, I've heard officers lie before, but nothing is black and white in this world and there are degrees of truth and untruth, and like many other judges who feel police officers cannot possibly protect the public these days, I've given officers the benefit of the doubt in probable cause situations. I never really believed a Los Angeles policeman would *completely* falsify his entire testimony as you've done to-day. That's why I feel sickened by it."

"I didn't falsify it all. He had the gun. It *was* under the mattress. He *had* the marijuana. I just lied about where I found it. Your Honor, he's an active bandit. The robbery dicks figure him for six robberies. He's beaten an old man and blinded him. He's . . ."

She held up her hand and said, "I didn't figure he was using that gun to stir his soup with, Officer Morgan. He has the look of a dangerous man about him."

"You could see it too!" I said. "Well . . ."

"Nothing," she interrupted. "That means nothing. The higher courts have given us difficult law, but by God, it's the law!"

"Your Honor," I said slowly. And then the tears filled my eyes and there was nothing I could do. "I'm not afraid of losing my pension. I've done nineteen years and over eleven months and I'm leaving the Department after tomorrow, and officially retiring in a few weeks, but I'm not afraid of losing the money. That's not why I'm asking, why I'm *begging* you to give me a chance. And it's not that I'm afraid to face a perjury charge and go to jail, because you can't be a crybaby in this world. But, Judge, there are people, policemen, and other people, people on my beat who think I'm something special. I'm one of the ones they really look up to, you know? I'm not just a character, I'm a hell of a cop!"

"I know you are," she said. "I've noticed you in my courtroom many times."

"You have?" Of course I'd been in her courtroom as a witness before, but I figured all bluecoats looked the same to blackrobes. "Don't get down on us, Judge Redford. Some coppers don't lie at all, and others only lie a little like you said. Only a few like me would do what I did."

"Why?"

"Because I care, Your Honor, goddamnit. Other cops put in their nine hours and go home to their families twenty miles from town and that's it, but guys like me, why I got nobody and I want nobody. I do my living on my beat. And I've got things inside me that make me do these things against my better judgment. That proves I'm dumber than the dumbest moron on my beat."

"You're not dumb. You're a clever witness. A very clever witness."

"I never lied that much before, Judge. I just thought I could get away with it. I just couldn't read that name right on that hotel register. If I could've read that name right on the register I never would've been able to pull off that traffic warrant story and I wouldn't't've tried it. And I probably wouldn't be in this fix, and the reason I couldn't really see that name and only assumed it must've been Landry is because I'm fifty years old and far-sighted, and too stubborn to wear my glasses, and kidding myself that I'm thirty and doing a young man's job when I can't cut it anymore. I'm going out though, Judge. This clinches it if I ever had any doubts. Tomorrow's my last day. A knight. Yesterday somebody called me a Blue Knight. Why do people say such things? They make you think you're really something and so you got to win a battle every time out. Why should *I* care if Landry walks out of here? What's it to *me?* Why do they *call* you a knight?"

She looked at me then and put the cigarette out and I'd never in my life begged anyone for anything, and never licked anyone's boots. I was glad she was a woman because it wasn't quite so bad to be licking a woman's boots, not *quite* so bad, and my stomach wasn't only burning now, it was hurting in spasms, like a big fist was pounding inside in a jerky rhythm. I thought I'd double over from the pain in a few minutes.

"Officer Morgan, you fully agree don't you that we can call off the whole damn game and crawl back in primeval muck if the orderers, the enforcers of the law, begin to operate outside it? You understand that there could be no civilization, don't you? You know, don't you, that I as well as many other judges am terribly aware of the overwhelming numbers of criminals on those streets whom you policemen must protect us from? You cannot always do it and there are times when you are handcuffed by court decisions that presume the goodness of people past all logical presumption. But don't you think there are judges, and yes, even defense attorneys, who sympathize with you? Can't you see that you, you policemen of all people, must be more than you are? You must be patient and above all, honest. Can't you see if you go outside the law regardless of how absurd it seems, in the name of enforcing it, that we're all doomed? Can you see these things?"

QUESTIONS

1   What did Officer Morgan do that so upset the Judge?
2   Why is Officer Morgan's behavior so dangerous to America's type of judicial system?
3   What was Officer Morgan's defense or justification for lying on the stand?

Reading 29
The Seven Minutes
Irving Wallace

The Watergate scandal of 1973–74 focused the public's attention on the controversial practice of plea bargaining. Under this general heading of plea bargaining falls a multitude of different things, such as a potential defendant's asking for immunity from prosecution in return for testifying against someone considered more important, or a person promising to plead guilty to a lesser crime in exchange for a reduced sentence. Although many citizens regard these practices as dangerous to the judicial system, plea bargaining has become a necessary evil. If every accused individual were given his or her day in court, the courts would be clogged and overwhelmed. Plea bargaining is an increasingly used method of expediting cases to reduce the courts' load.

Plea bargaining often occurs before the trial begins, between the defense and prosecuting attorneys. This is depicted by Irving Wallace in this passage from *The Seven Minutes,* where defense attorney Mike Barrett discusses his client's case with District Attorney Elmo Duncan.

"Let me see," said Elmo Duncan as he lifted a pile of manila folders from the edge of the desk. "Let me see what this is all about." He was checking the folder tabs. "Here it is. 'Fremont, Ben. Section 311.' "

He extracted the folder and set the others aside. Before opening it he said. "Of course, I'm sure you understand, we don't make these arrests casually. They are always preceded by a careful investigation. I do know that after the complaint was received, Rodriguez and his aide—that's Pete Lucas, who's a specialist in pornography and a capable trial attorney to boot—both read the book in question with care. Well, let me see." He opened the folder and began scanning and turning the pages inside.

Barrett remained silent and busied himself with refilling and lighting his pipe. Puffing steadily, he waited.

When Duncan was through with the folder, he placed it on the desk, and rubbed his chin. "Well, now, what I'm going to tell you is off the record, but what I think it comes down to is this. Mrs. Olivia St. Clair, president of the STDL in Oakwood, filed the complaint. There was no question in their minds that it was pornographic. The question was whether it was legally obscene by contemporary community standards."

"Since the book has been seized, I wanted to make that point," said Barrett quickly. "Once, in Flaubert's time, *Madame Bovary* was considered obscene. Today, it's merely a mild and sad story about an unfaithful wife.

Why, recently I read a respectably published memoir of an anonymous Victorian gentleman—it was called *My Secret Life*—in which the author explicitly recounts how he 'fucked'—his word—twelve hundred women of twenty-seven countries and eighty nationalities. The only one he missed, I think, was a Laplander."

Duncan had been squirming uneasily, but now he forced a laugh.

"That's right," Barrett went on. "When that Victorian wrote his book, he couldn't get it published. In our time it has been a best seller, and I don't think it made any reader's hair turn white. Why? Because times have changed. It's a new ball game. As one professor pointed out, sexual activity is no longer contrary to the prevailing ethos. So why not write about sex as openly as it is being performed? I think it was Anatole France who said— of all sexual aberrations, chastity is the strangest."

Duncan gave the slightest smile, but did not speak. He waited.

Since he still had the floor, Barrett decided to take advantage of it. "Nor do I think this openness about sex has hurt any of us in our country. Dr. Steven Marcus once wrote about this new permissiveness. 'It does not indicate to me moral laxness, or fatigue, or deterioration on the part of society. It suggests rather that pornography has lost its old danger, its old power.' I fully concur."

The District Attorney stirred. "Well, there is a good deal of truth in much of what you say, but I can't agree with it entirely. Perhaps some pornography has lost its old danger, but not all of it, I'm afraid. We could spend a day, a week maybe, arguing this highly complicated problem."

"Forgive me," said Barrett. "I didn't intend to go on the way I did. We all get carried away sometime. I meant to confine myself to the Jadway book. I'll admit that in the thirties, forties, fifties, *The Seven Minutes* might have been regarded as obscene, but today—? Mr. Duncan, have you been to the movies lately? Have you seen for yourself, on the screen, acted out, not only copulation, but female masturbation, homosexuality, well, you name it? I only contend that today, to the average person, by contemporary community standards, by modern standards, the Jadway book is no more or less explicit than other works of far less artistic merit. So why the arrest?"

"Yes, well, yes, that was the debatable point. But our people finally came to the decision they did for two reasons. A large group of average and community-minded women had made the complaint, thereby reflecting that this book had exceeded what is accepted by contemporary stan-dards—"

"Do you consider the kind of women who form a decency club as average?" said Barrett acidly.

"Of course I do," said Duncan with surprise. "They're no different from any other women. They marry, have children, do housework, cook, entertain, read books. Certainly they're as average as can be."

Barrett wanted to challenge the District Attorney on this, but he realized that Duncan was sincere—hadn't Abe Zelkin called him "honest" and "square"?—and nothing would be gained by antagonizing him. Barrett kept his peace.

"And if ladies like that, a big organization, a very big one—" Duncan went on.

A big organization translated into a lot of voters, Barrett thought, remembering that Zelkin had also called the District Attorney "political."

"—if they feel disturbed by this book, it tells us that maybe there are more people in Oakwood with high standards of decency than may be evident in the numbers who attend some of the films you mentioned. That was first in our minds. Second, and more important, was that we felt this whole outpouring of shock literature, disgusting sadomasochistic slime, was increasing and must be stopped, especially must be stopped so that it is not available to the young and impressionable. Perhaps, as you stated it, times have changed, moral boundaries have expanded, allowing for more candor and tolerance. Yet there are limits, there must be boundaries somewhere. Perhaps, as one Congregationalist clergyman so aptly put it, this country is suffering from an orgy of openmindedness. I remember attending a speech delivered in the East by Pennsylvania Supreme Court Justice Michael Musmanno. In that address he said, 'A wide river of filth is sweeping across the nation, befouling its shores and spreading over the land its nauseating stench. But what is most disturbing of all is that persons whose noses should be particularly sensitive to this olfactory assault do not smell it at all. I refer to District Attorneys and prosecuting officers throughout the nation.' Well, Mr. Barrett, I've never forgotten those words. I intend to be one of the District Attorneys who does smell the stench."

"Certainly," said Barrett. "Everyone wants to do away with the smell of commercialized hard-core pornography—"

Duncan held up his hand. "No. The sleazy back-street peddlers of hard-core pornography are not the ones we worry about. We worry that this same kind of obscene matter will be given respectability by notable imprints like Sanford House and become available in every bookstore. It is precisely because of Sanford's reputation that we selected this Jadway book, to serve notice on the powerful publishers that this thing has reached its outer limit and must come to an end. Now, this was the basis for the arrest this morning. But actually, Mr. Barrett, I don't want to overstate our case or my feelings. I mean, specifically in the matter of Ben Fremont I don't feel that strongly. I do feel strongly about the whole trend in literature and motion pictures in this country, but I had no intention of making the People versus Ben Fremont our *cause célèbre*. No. We have more important crimes on our investigative agenda and court calendar. This is a relatively small thing."

"Well, then . . ."

"It's those women in Oakwood. They were pressuring our office, with some justification, and we had to satisfy them. I'm sure you can understand that."

"And with Fremont's arrest you've satisfied them," said Barrett.

"Right," said Duncan. "We've done our duty. But now, also, you have a client and you have a duty. I'm willing to be cooperative, within the limitations of what has already happened. The arrest has been made. The accused has been booked. You've got him out on bail. What's the next step you have in mind?"

Barrett drew on his pipe, and watched the smoke billow upward. At last he leaned against the desk. "I want to be reasonable, too, Mr. Duncan. I think this would satisfy my client. I would like to see Ben Fremont plead guilty and have him pay a fine of twenty-four hundred dollars, but in return his one-year jail sentence might be suspended. If that trade could be arranged, that would satisfy us."

"Mmm, well, if that could be arranged, you do understand that entering a plea of guilty would be tantamount to a banning of *The Seven Minutes* throughout Oakwood. All the other bookstores in Oakwood would be afraid of the STDL and of our proceeding against them also."

"We don't give a damn about Oakwood," said Barrett. "Let it be unavailable there. In that way, you've satisfied the STDL in that community. Since Oakwood is an unincorporated part of Los Angeles County, a separate area even though it comes under your jurisdiction, it means the book could be suppressed there but would still be sold elsewhere in Los Angeles County."

"That's right."

"Very well. My client is interested in the rest of Los Angeles County, and the effect of any action in Los Angeles on booksellers in other large cities around the country. If the book can remain on sale in most of Los Angeles County, that's all that counts. As for Oakwood, no one in that community will any longer be offended by seeing the book there. And those who want the book can drive a few blocks farther, to Brentwood or Westwood or some other nearby section of Los Angeles, and buy it. That's what it comes to. And in a week or two the book will be on sale in the large cities throughout the nation, and it will have its acceptance. The shock of it will be mitigated by this acceptance, and there won't be any further trouble over it. There you have it, Mr. Duncan."

Barrett waited.

Elmo Duncan stubbed out his cigarette, came to his feet thoughtfully, thrust his hands into his trouser pockets, and walked slowly around the area between the swivel chair and the shelves of massive legal tomes lining the wall.

Abruptly he stopped his pacing.

"Mr. Barrett, what you've suggested sounds reasonable enough to me."

"Good."

"We'll satisfy those ladies. As for Lucas and Rodriguez, they're so immersed in this sort of thing, I'm sometimes inclined to think they're oversensitive to every word they read. Of course, it's understandable. They have to field complaints almost daily. They must answer the complainants, like the group in Oakwood. But I know I can contain my assistants. In fact, I could come to an agreement with you right here and now about reducing the charges, except that I owe my staff the courtesy of discussing this with them first, since they've given the case so much of their time. But I quite agree. This is a nuisance matter, a routine matter, and we can treat it routinely. So let's give ourselves until tomorrow, Mr. Barrett. Let me smooth any ruffled feathers, and when that is done you can enter your guilty plea, and I can promise you that I'll speak to the judge and the result will be no more than the fine and a suspended jail sentence. Fair enough?"

Barrett stood up. "Fair enough."

The District Attorney came rapidly around the desk to shake Barrett's hand and see him to the door. "You be sure to call me around this time tomorrow."

"Don't worry. I won't forget."

As he opened the door, Duncan seemed to remember something. "And, by the way, if you're seeing Willard Osborn soon . . ."

"I'm having dinner with him tomorrow night."

"Well, don't forget to say that you saw me, and that I wanted you to give him my regards and to tell him how pleased I am about the time and attention his network has given me lately. You can tell him I'm most appreciative."

This, thought Barrett, is what it's like in the marketplace, everywhere.

"I'll certainly tell him," said Barrett.

Duncan was looking up at the wall clock. "Now I'd better get cracking, I've got a busy afternoon and an even busier evening."

QUESTIONS

1 What are the advantages of plea bargaining?
2 In your opinion, does plea bargaining promote justice?
3 Why did Barrett and his client agree to a guilty plea?

Part Five

Policy—The Outputs

As we have seen, the four major branches of American government convert or translate the interests of individuals and groups into public policies within the legal context of the Constitution and the human context of the American culture. Policies are the outputs of the political system, the results of all the time, effort, and resources expended in the political arena. The successful political actors come away with the advantages from the system, while the political losers or outsiders accept the disadvantages or try again.

There are two major types of policies or outputs—domestic policy and foreign policy. Domestic policies are those internal political outputs aimed at the nation's citizens, while foreign policies are intended to affect people in other nations. Trying to distinguish between these two types of policies is, however, often difficult. For example, the war in Vietnam was designed primarily as a foreign policy, but its consequences in the domestic American scene were as significant as its external impact. Salinger's *On Instructions of My Government* illustrates the close linkage between domestic and foreign policy.

Defense policy is a nation's most important policy, for it overlaps domestic and foreign policy. The volatile excerpt from *Seven Days in May* and the terrifying selection from *Fail-Safe* amply demonstrate how important and how perilous are the operation and outcome of defense policy making, especially in this nuclear age.

Reading 30
On Instructions of My Government
Pierre Salinger

Although most Americans do not realize it, domestic and foreign policy are highly interrelated. Each area makes demands upon the government's time, efforts, and resources; for example, a high domestic spending program would ordinarily necessitate a budget cut in a foreign aid program and vice versa.

This interdependence between foreign and domestic policy making has some important political implications. The President monitors both areas very closely, and his political success depends on how well he balances the demands of each area against the other. A serious mistake in foreign policy can threaten the incumbent administration; for example, a huge amount of wheat might be sold to a foreign nation that desperately needs the grain, but if the sale results in an increase in the price of bread in America, it is the President who must pay the political price.

In this selection from *On Instructions of My Government* the President is faced with a dilemma. He is running for reelection but is doing poorly in the polls. His budget is unbalanced, and he needs some areas that he can cut without seriously hurting his reelection chances. The meeting with Ambassador Hood affords him the opportunity to slash the foreign aid funds for Santa Clara, an unpopular Latin American nation. During the course of their discussion the close relationship between domestic and foreign policy is vividly illustrated.

The President was in a black humor this humid June morning in 1976. A Cabinet conference on the budget, a stubborn nineteen billion dollars out of balance, had kept him up until long after midnight, and a cold caught at the last summit in Moscow had given him little sleep. But the focus of his irascibility was a front-page headline in the Washington *Post*: PRESIDENT'S POPULARITY AT NEW LOW IN HARRIS POLL.

He was, perhaps, the last traditional politician who would hold the nation's highest office. The veterans of campus dissent, now approaching their thirties, had taken much of their impatience, if not their militancy, into the suburbs. The blacks, formidable in their new sophistication, were the new power in the cities. The browns, from the Puerto Ricans in the East to the Chicanos in the Southwest, were an emergent and aggressive elective force. And all were contemptuous of the old politics and its practitioners and deaf to banal appeals to party loyalty.

But the man in the upstairs bedroom in the East Wing of the White House read none of this into the statistic that only one voter in three could presently support him for reelection. He was convinced that the voters were, and would always be, divisible into blocs of Democrats, Republicans, and Independents; young and old; black, brown, yellow and white; blue collar and white collar, and ghetto, suburb and farm. And when they went to the polls they would vote as they always had, for the man and party most likely to serve their self-interests; most able to calm their fears; most willing to absolve them of prejudice, and most wary of change. It was not a question of bringing them together. To the contrary, wasn't its very diversity the strength of America? For him, it was a question of keeping them apart— proud of their differences, respectful of the rule of law, and identifiable in the pre-election canvass.

The President's first call was to National Party Chairman James J. Mallory. He hadn't seen the poll yet and the President read it to him. "It couldn't be much worse, Jim."

"It could be a hell of a lot worse, Mr. President. We've still got five months to go before the election and right now it's you against every one of their possible nominees. Wait until it narrows down, one to one, after the conventions. You'll be all right."

The President's next call caught his press secretary, Maxwell Busby, just entering his office in the West Wing.

"If the correspondents start hounding you this morning for a reaction from me to that Harris poll, I haven't given you one," the President told him.

His schedule for the day came up with his breakfast tray. His first appointment was at 10 A.M.: "Secretary Adams, Ambassador Hood, Haas." He would tell his appointment secretary to cut this one short. Fifteen minutes—no more.

Sam Hood was shaving in his suite at the Mayflower. He had flown in from Santa Clara the night before and had not left the hotel. Washington was no longer his town, nor did he like summonses from four thousand miles away to consultations where his presence would be no more than a formality. He, too, had read the Harris poll in the paper sent up with his breakfast and could anticipate the President's mood. Polls! It was a hell of a way to run a country.

Secretary of State Sterling Adams was already at his desk. He had thought, but only briefly, of calling Hood to reassure him that the President was still willing to listen. But no, the ambassador might expect too much support from him this morning. He would, of course, go along with Hood as far as he could. He *was* State and it *was* his embassy. But Adams' own summons to the White House from Haas left no doubt of the President's intention. An "urgent review of the Santa Claran allocation" was in order.

In his home in Bethesda, Gene Haas, Special Assistant to the President for Latin American Affairs, had been up since five-thirty, drafting and redrafting the statement he would clear with the President and then deliver to Press Secretary Busby for his afternoon briefing of the press—*after* Hood was airborne from Dulles. The ambassador could be unpredictable.

The driver of the State Department limousine had orders to drop Ambassador Hood off at the west basement entrance to the White House, where Secretary Adams would be waiting. Later the President would ask them to leave the same way—invisible and unavailable to the press corps.

The guard at the basement entrance knew Adams by sight but had to check Hood's identification against the appointment schedule on his desk. The Secret Service agents in the corridor outside the Oval Office let them pass with only a curt nod to Adams, nor was there a delay in the appointment secretary's office. The President was waiting.

If the choice of entrances to the White House did not tell Hood that he had come to listen, not to be heard, his first sight of the President did. He was standing behind his massive desk and the gilt seal on its facing and the array of service flags behind it were intimidating assertions of authority. If the Chief Executive actually did want a free exchange of opinions on options he was still holding open, the white leather conversational unit facing the fireplace on the opposite wall was much more amenable to informality and candor. But on this morning he came out only briefly from behind his desk.

"It was good of you to come up here on such short notice, Sam. But Adams here will have to go before Foreign Relations next week, and they'll want verse and chapter on what we're planning to spend and where."

"I understand that, sir."

Haas, as always, came into the office precisely thirty seconds after the principals—his one deference to rank. "Mr. Secretary . . . Ambassador." He took the staff chair to the right of the desk, facing Hood and Adams, but obliquely.

"We're having difficulties up here, Sam, and not just on the Hill. The whole country's up in arms against inflation."

"I saw the poll, Mr. President."

"The poll doesn't bother me, Sam." His tone was chiding. "You should know that. The fact is that I've got a budget that's nineteen billion out of whack, and the question is where do I start cutting? Now I've had Haas here reviewing all of our Latin American commitments and Santa Clara looks most questionable."

A stretch of the rose garden was visible through the window, and beyond it the Washington Monument, ghostlike in the morning mist from the Potomac.

"I haven't read Haas's review, Mr. President. I can't know on what basis he would arrive at that opinion."

The President was patient. "The basis, Sam, is that we've been subsidizing the country ever since Hoover—*Hoover!* First it was direct loans and not one penny ever repaid. Year after year of it—right up to the Alliance of Progress—and now direct budget support. A hundred million a year, Sam, and what do we have to show for it?"

"You could make the same case against almost all of our Latin American commitments."

"There's a difference, Sam, and you know it. Who else down there is doing business with Red China?"

"I don't think they have much choice, sir. China will take their copper. We won't. I've told you many times that we ought to relax our import embargo—perhaps even stipulate a percentage of Santa Claran copper in our own defense procurement."

The President forced a smile. "Why don't I take you with me on a campaign swing into copper states like Montana and Utah, and let you try that on for size out there? No, Sam, you'll have to do better than that."

Hood glanced toward the Secretary of State for support, but Adams, who was studying, intently, the gold eagle atop the Marine Corps flag standard behind the President, did not respond. The ambassador slid his spare six-and-a-half-foot frame forward in his chair.

"I think Secretary Adams would agree with me, sir, that Jorge Luchengo's government deserves a little more time. He's been in there only three years and there have been very visible reforms."

"And I think the Secretary would agree with me, Sam, that we had much sounder reasons for supporting the Novarese regime. It was at least democratic. It had popular support. Your man Luchengo took power by force and holds it by force. And, unlike Luis Novarese, he's not spending a nickel of what we're giving him to go after Jiminez in force. I take it he's still raising hell up there in the mountains?"

"That's correct but the best deterrent to Jiminez is a strong economy—and without this appropriation—"

"Goddammit, Sam, I'm not going to chase the ghosts of Fidel Castro and Che Guevara around Latin America into infinity. The CIA claims that Jiminez has no more than two or three hundred guerrillas, most of them kids. Luchengo ought to be able to handle a ragtag bunch like that."

Hood held his temper. "I have not written a single cable suggesting that Jiminez has the forces to depose Luchengo. I have written, and often, that his sabotage of the mines and the rail line is just as menacing as a direct march on the capital." Hood saw the President glance at his watch. In another minute or two his intercom would ring. "In this office, three years ago, Mr. President, I told you I didn't want this assignment. I had the closest of associations with President Novarese in the OAS and much resistance to serving as ambassador to the regime that had stood him up against a wall."

"You were the right man for it."

"I was not the right man for it if I haven't been able to persuade you in three years that Luchengo—whatever I once thought of him—has been a change for the better down there. And I dispute the statements that he still holds power by force. There were elections last year and he won handily."

"Haas's report—"

Hood was suddenly tired of it. "I must tell you that I strongly resent being brought up here to defend my judgments against a summary on Santa Clara I have never seen, written by a man who has never been there."

"You're too rough on Haas, Sam. I'm confident he had full access to your cables. Adams can confirm that."

The Secretary of State did not like being involved at a point of such direct confrontation. But it was, at least, an opportunity to support Hood and to vent his own resentment of Haas and the entire concept of a "little State Department" within the White House.

"Mr. Haas, of course, had the fullest cooperation of our Latin American desk, Mr. President. But I, like the ambassador, have not seen his recommendations to you. I can't know what weight he has given to our files as against perhaps conflicting intelligence from other sources. I would add that I agree with Mr. Hood's *on-the-scene* evaluation. The department supports the commitment to Santa Clara, if not in the present dollar amount, at least—"

"Sir."

"Yes, Haas."

"May I explain to the ambassador and to the Secretary that on your instructions my review and recommendation were written for your eyes only. I would have had no objection whatever—"

The color rose in Hood's aquiline face, sharpening the contrast with his blue eyes and steel-gray hair. "Perhaps you would like to summarize it for us now then, Haas?"

"The summary, Mr. Ambassador, is that this country—and certainly the Congress—will no longer support the subsidy of a dictatorship that lacks popular support and that trades in war matériel with Red China. Novarese was at least *anti*-Communist. He wouldn't accept a Soviet legation in Ciudad Alarcon. And he did send dollars back to us for arms to fight Jiminez."

Hood had heard it all before—the oversimplifications that serve as conventional wisdom, the catch phrases that might belong in a New York *Daily News* editorial but did not belong here. The ambassador threw up his hands. "That's a total distortion, Mr. President, and if Haas did read my reports, he gave them no credibility whatever. I'll repeat to you now, sir, what I've been reporting for months. If we cancel our support of Luchengo, or even reduce it substantially the certain consequence is another Bolivia or Cuba. Luchengo will either have to accept greater economic dependence on China or face collapse. Either way, you'll have Jiminez."

"Aren't you assuming the worst, Sam?"

"No, I'm assuming the probable."

The intercom finally rang. "Tell them to wait," the President told his secretary. "We're almost through here."

Hood stood up. "President Luchengo will expect me to call on him tomorrow. The decision's final?"

"It is. Try to appreciate my position, Sam. If I don't cut the budget down to size, the Congress will. And either way the Santa Clara appropriation won't be in it. I could fight for it on the Hill but I would lose—and this isn't a good year for picking scraps you can't win." The President came around his desk and put a hand on Hood's shoulder. "Again, thank you for coming up. And, Sam, I'd like to announce this in my own way and in my own time."

"The west basement entrance?"

"If you don't mind."

Secretary Adams said nothing until they were at the door of Hood's limousine. "I'm sorry that I couldn't be more helpful in there. But appropriations more important than Santa Clara's are also on the line, and I can't afford to pick scraps I can't win either."

"This could have been won," said Hood, "and you will regret that it wasn't."

Hood's last view of the south lawn was one of the Kennedy magnolias marking the corners of the rose garden. He thought of other days when his voice was heard with respect in the White House. But he did not ask the driver to swing into Arlington on the way to the airport. There was no time this morning for the walk up the hill to the graves. The travel specialist at State, on Haas's orders, had him on a very tight flight schedule.

At 4 P.M. the correspondents jammed their way into the clutter of desks and wire service teletype machines in Busby's rabbit warren of an office. Excerpts from the transcript of his briefing:

Q. Have you spoken to the President today?

A. Only briefly.

Q. What did he think of the Harris poll this morning?

A. I didn't ask him. (Laughter.) I have one short announcement. I don't think you'll need a release on it. The President met this morning with Secretary Adams and Ambassador Hood for a routine review of budget support for Santa

Clara, one of a series of reviews of all foreign-aid commitments prior to submission of the budget.

   Q. That's all of it?
   A. That's all I have.
   Q. Is Santa Clara in or out?
   A. You'll know that when we release the budget.
   Q. Why didn't the ambassador come out this way?
   A. Probably because he had nothing to tell you.
   Q. Not even hello?

Sam Hood had once held Haas's position in the White House, but that was four presidents ago. Then, there was no dictum against staff fraternization with the correspondents. Hood drank with them and won their money playing stud poker, and they held a stag dinner for him at the National Press Club when he left for a desk in the State Department.

After the briefing, the older hands wrote the only story they could. In Ciudad Alarcon, President Jorge Luchengo's information officer woke him from a restless siesta to show him the lead that had come over the AP wire a minute earlier: "The South American republic of Santa Clara apparently will be the first victim of administration slashes in foreign aid. The secret nature of Ambassador Samuel V. Hood's conference with the President today left little doubt that . . ."

Luchengo read no further.

QUESTIONS

1 What relationship did the polls that the President read have to his decision to cut off funds to Santa Clara?
2 What risks was the President taking in basing his decision to cut off foreign funds on domestic political conditions?
3 In what ways did the Vietnam war demonstrate the interdependence between domestic and foreign policy?

Reading 31

Seven Days in May

Fletcher Knebel and Charles W. Bailey, II

Fletcher Knebel and Charles Bailey, in *Seven Days in May*, graphically illustrate the tenuous control that the civilian arm of the government exercises over the military arm. The military has been a strong force in American defense policy, which is probably the most important policy that any nation must decide. In this highly charged passage, General Scott, Chairman of the Joint Chiefs of Staff, is called to the White House and is admitted to President Jordan Lyman's study by Corwin, the President's aide. Scott enters with an air of confidence bordering on superiority, while the President is troubled and anxious under a veneer of calm.

During the course of the ensuing discussion the constitutional supremacy of the civilian sector is severely shaken as Scott, symbolizing the military mind, directly challenges the President. Scott has been involved in an insidious plot, and when Lyman questions him, the General gradually reveals his narrow military perspective. Scott sees himself and the military as the voice of authority and discipline, a perspective alien to Lyman's civilian orientation. In order to avert a constitutional crisis, Lyman is forced to make an extremely difficult decision.

General James Mattoon Scott stepped off the elevator at 7:59 P.M. His tan Air Force uniform, four silver stars glinting on each shoulder, clung to his big frame without a wrinkle. Six rows of decorations blazed from his chest. His hair, the gray sprinkling the black like the first snowflakes on a plowed field, was neatly combed. A pleasant smile softened the rugged jaw as he nodded to Corwin and the warrant officer.

"Good evening, gentlemen," he said. Corwin responded politely and opened the study door for the General.

Scott strode purposefully into the room. His smile flashed confidence as he watched Lyman put down his book, stand up and come toward him.

He intends to dominate it from the start, Lyman thought. You've got to be good for this, Jordie. This is the big one.

Lyman gestured toward the couch, then seated himself again in the armchair. They were alone now, under the prim portrait of Euphemia Van Rensselaer. One window was open to the warm May air; through it came the occasional distant sound of passing traffic.

Scott had a map folder with him. He laid it on the coffee table and started to undo the strap holding the covers with their TOP SECRET stamps.

"Don't bother about that, General," said Lyman. "We don't need it tonight. We aren't going to have an alert tomorrow."

Scott straightened and stared at Lyman. His face was without expression. Lyman saw no surprise, no anger, not even curiosity. Scott's eyes held his and the President knew at once that this would be a long difficult night.

"I beg your pardon, Mr. President," Scott said. "You wish the alert canceled?"

"I do. I intend to cancel it."

"May I ask why?"

"Certain facts have come to my attention in the past few days, General," said Lyman. His eyes were locked with Scott's. He forced himself to keep them that way. "I will not waste time by detailing them all now. I will simply say that I want your resignation tonight, and those of Generals Hardesty, Riley and Dieffenbach as well."

The little wrinkles around Scott's eyes tightened. He continued to stare at the President until the silence became a physical fact in the room.

"Either you are joking or you have taken leave of your senses, Mr. President," Scott said in a low voice. "I know of no reason why I should remove my name from the active list voluntarily. Certainly not without a full explanation for such a—shall we say unusual?—request."

Lyman dropped his eyes to the little sheet of notebook paper on his side of the cigar box. "I had hoped we could avoid this, General. It seems redundant to tell you what you already know."

"I think that remark is extremely odd, to say the least."

Lyman sighed.

"It has come to my attention, General," he said, "that you have, without my authority, used substantial sums of the Joint Chiefs' contingency fund to establish a base and to train a special unit of troops whose purpose and even whose existence has been kept secret from me—and from responsible officials of the Bureau of the Budget and members of Congress. This is in clear violation of the statutes."

"Just what unit are you referring to, Mr. President?"

"I believe its designation is ECOMCON. I take it that stands for Emergency Communications Control."

Scott smiled easily and settled back on the couch. He spoke almost soothingly, as he might to a frightened child.

"I'm afraid your memory fails you, Mr. President. You gave me verbal authorization for both the base and the unit. As I recall it, there were a number of items that we covered that day, and perhaps you didn't pay too much attention to this. I guess I just assumed that you would inform the Director of the Budget."

"What was the date of that meeting, General?" Lyman had to struggle to hide his anger, but he kept his voice as even as Scott's.

"I can't recall exactly, but it was in your office downstairs, some time last fall. Late November, I believe."

"You have a record of the date and subject?"

"Oh, certainly. In my office. If you care to make a point of it, I can drive over to the Pentagon right now and get it."

"That will not be necessary, General."

"Well," said Scott casually, "it's really not important anyway. My aide, Colonel Murdock, sat in on the meeting and can substantiate my memorandum of the date and discussion."

Oh, so that's how it is, thought Lyman. There's a witness to corroborate your statements. He wondered if anything he said tonight would catch Scott by surprise.

"As for not informing Congress," Scott continued, "this matter of protecting communications from Soviet sabotage seemed to us so sensitive that we thought it wise not to discuss it with the committees."

"But you did discuss it with Senator Prentice, General," Lyman shot back. "In fact, you seem to have discussed quite a number of things with him this week, in quite a few places."

The statement had small effect on Scott. He merely hunched himself a bit closer to the table and put his hands on it. Lyman watched his fingers on the edge of the table, the tips going white with the pressure, as though Scott were trying to lock the tabletop with his hands.

"Senator Prentice knows nothing about ECOMCON," the General said.

"When Senator Raymond Clark was at the base Wednesday," Lyman said, "he talked with Prentice on the telephone. He reports that Prentice told him the Armed Services Committee knew all about it."

Scott shrugged. "I didn't know Senator Clark had visited the base. As for differences between members of Congress, I must say I learned long ago not to get involved in that kind of thing."

Lyman would not drop the subject. "Perhaps you can explain why you selected a commanding officer for that unit who is openly contemptuous of civilian authority and who has made statements which come close to violation of the sedition laws?"

"I never in my life discussed an officer's political views with him." Scott's voice had an indignant ring. "The officer in question has an excellent combat record and is one of the most competent officers in the Signal Corps."

Lyman persisted. "He also has an interesting travel record. What was Colonel Broderick doing last night in an outboard motorboat, cruising around my island at Blue Lake, Maine?"

"That's fantastic, Mr. President." Scott looked at Lyman with an odd expression, as though doubting his own ears—or the President's sanity. "Colonel Broderick left Site Y yesterday to come to Washington to confer with me."

"The description given by my caretaker fits Colonel Broderick quite closely. Black brows, swarthy complexion, tough face and all."

"Thousands of men could be mistaken for Broderick."

"And the scar on his right cheek?" asked Lyman.

"Didn't you say this was at night, Mr. President? I'd say your man can't see very well in the dark."

"It was not yet dark, General," said Lyman flatly.

"Mistaken identity, obviously," said Scott. He offered nothing more.

"Well, General, perhaps you also have an explanation for the detention at site Y of Senator Clark?"

"I would say such a charge is somewhat reckless, Mr. President. As I understand it, the senator from Georgia has some . . . ah . . . personal problems and might be inclined to imagine things under certain circumstances."

Lyman flared. "I think you'd better withdraw that statement, General. Ray had nothing to drink at your base—no thanks to Broderick, who put two bottles of whisky in his room."

Scott's voice was emotionless but hard. "I think that if Senator Clark told you any such story, the fantasy of it is plain on its face. I can't imagine any court in the land accepting that kind of testimony."

"Are you implying that there is going to be some kind of trial?"

"Of course not, Mr. President." There was a patronizing overtone in Scott's voice. "I just think that here again we have Clark's word against Colonel Broderick's, and, frankly, we have no evidence that Clark was ever on the base."

"You deny that Senator Clark was there?"

"I don't deny it or affirm it. I don't know one way or the other. I do know that Broderick didn't mention it to me last night."

Lyman glanced at his list again.

"Now, General, there is the matter of the arrest and present detention in the Fort Myer stockade of Colonel William Henderson," the President said.

"You mean the deputy commander at Site Y?"

"You know very well whom I mean, General."

"This case I do happen to be familiar with," Scott said. "Colonel Broderick informed me this noon that Colonel Henderson was apprehended for deserting his post of duty and for striking an enlisted man with the barrel of the man's rifle."

"And did Broderick tell you where Henderson was picked up?"

"The military police picked him up on a downtown street here in Washington, as I understand it."

Lyman shook his head in impatience. "General, Colonel Henderson was kidnaped. He was taken forcibly from Senator Clark's home in Georgetown."

Scott threw back his head and laughed.

"Mr. President, let's get back to earth. I don't know who's providing your information, but he has a vivid imagination."

"We will go to another subject," said Lyman coldly.

"Before we do, Mr. President, would you mind if I had one of those excellent cigars from your box?"

Lyman had no intention of letting the General relax in a cloud of easy cigar smoke.

"I'm sorry," he lied, "but Esther must have forgotten to fill it today. I looked just before you came in."

"Well, then." Scott unbuttoned his jacket and reached into a shirt pocket. "I trust you don't mind if I have one of my own."

"Not at all." Lyman felt that he had been outmaneuvered.

Scott lit the cigar and watched reflectively as the first few puffs of smoke rose toward the ceiling. He settled back on the couch and smiled.

"There was something else, Mr. President?"

Boy, this is a tough customer, Lyman thought. The muscles between his shoulder blades hurt, and he could feel the strain in his face. He hoped he looked half as confident to Scott as the General did to him.

"Indeed there is," Lyman said. "I would like an explanation of your wagering activities, in particular your betting pool on the Preakness."

"Oh, come now, Mr. President. Certainly you do not intend to try to pillory me for making a bet?"

"I would like an explanation, General."

"There's really nothing to explain," Scott replied. "Oh, I know all-service radio isn't supposed to be used for personal traffic of that kind. But the chairman traditionally has been granted small courtesies."

"I understand you transferred a young naval officer who talked about the betting messages."

"Cryptographic officers are not supposed to talk about any messages," Scott snapped. "And I see that Colonel Casey has been talking about my personal affairs as well. Frankly, Mr. President, I am surprised and disappointed."

"How do you know I've been talking to Colonel Casey?" Lyman's voice was sharp.

"I didn't say you had. I merely said Colonel Casey had talked to someone. He came to you, then?"

"If you don't mind, general," Lyman said, "I'll ask the questions. Why did you excuse Casey from his work for four days this week?"

"He was tired."

"And why did Admiral Barnswell refuse to join the wagering pool?"

"I really have no idea, Mr. President," said Scott. "I guess some men just don't like to gamble. I love it." He was expansive. "It's one of my many failings."

Lyman eyed Scott closely. There was no indication that he knew of Girard's trip or that he had talked to Barnswell. The President waited a moment, hoping the General would say something more that might offer a clue on the point, but when Scott spoke after several contemplative puffs on his cigar his voice was even and natural.

"If I might ask just one question, Mr. President, what is the purpose of these inquiries about my little Preakness pool? Surely you're not indicating that I am being asked to resign because I sent a personal message?"

"Of course not, General," Lyman said. "Now, on another point. Will you please explain why you and the Joint Chiefs scheduled the alert for a day when Congress will be in recess and its members scattered all over the country?"

"No better way to throw the field commanders off guard," Scott said quickly. "If you recall, you yourself said as much when you approved the date."

"Was Admiral Palmer present at the meeting when the time was fixed?"

"No-o." For the first time, Scott seemed just a trifle taken aback. "No, he wasn't."

"His deputy?"

"No, as I recall," said Scott slowly, "the Navy was absent that day."

"And there have been several other recent meetings when neither Admiral Palmer nor his deputy was present?"

"Well, yes. Now that you mention it, there have been."

"Isn't that highly unusual?"

"Unusual, perhaps, but not highly. The Navy just couldn't make it the last few times. Admiral Palmer, as I understand it, has been preoccupied with some special problems in his missile cruisers lately."

"That's not what Admiral Palmer says, General. He was not notified of certain meetings of the Joint Chiefs. That is certainly highly unusual."

"I gather that Admiral Palmer, as well as Colonel Casey, has been voicing complaints. The Navy and Marines seem to be doing some talking out of channels—from lieutenants junior grade clear up to flag rank."

Lyman offered no response to this, but went to the next point on his list. Scott waited tranquilly.

"You and General Riley made a visit to General Garlock's home Tuesday night," Lyman said.

"Yes, we did. We wanted to make sure everything was in shape at Mount Thunder for the alert."

"And to make arrangements for bivouacking some special troops there Saturday?"

"I take it I have been followed all week." Scott ignored Lyman's question.

"I'd like an answer, General."

"First I'd like to know why the President of the United States feels it necessary to follow the chairman of the Joint Chiefs of Staff like a common criminal," Scott said.

"You will answer my question, General."

"Not until you answer mine, Mr. President."

Scott stood up, towering above the seated President. He held his cigar between thumb and forefinger and pointed it accusingly at Lyman.

"I don't propose to stay in this room and be questioned any further." Command authority rang out like a chisel on granite. "I will not resign and I will answer no more questions. But I intend to say a few things, Mr. President."

Lyman felt inadequate and puny sitting under this tall, imposing officer who held a cigar pointed at him like a weapon. The President stood up and took a step forward, putting the two men on more equal physical terms as they stood facing each other, no more than two feet apart. Scott kept on talking.

"The information put together yesterday morning by the National Indications Center, and reported to both of us by Mr. Lieberman, substantiates all the misgivings of the Joint Chiefs," he said. "We told you time and time again that the Russians would never adhere to the spirit of the treaty. And we emphasized until we were blue in the face that it was folly to sign a document which left a clear loophole—namely, that one country or the other could assemble warheads in one place as fast as it took them apart in another under the eyes of the neutral inspectors. The United States, of course, would never do that. But the Russians would—and they are doing precisely that."

"I know all that as well as you do, General." Lyman began to feel old and tired again, as weary as he had been all week until Henry Whitney's sudden appearance that afternoon.

"I must say further, Mr. President, that it borders on criminal negligence not to take some immediate action. If you persist in that path, I shall have no recourse as a patriotic American but to go to the country with the facts."

"You refuse to resign, but you would do something that would assure your removal," Lyman commented. Scott said nothing.

"Well," the President went on defiantly, "I have moved. But something just as important to this country—perhaps more important—has to be settled first."

"Meaning what?"

"I think you know, General."

"I have no more idea of what you mean by that than I have concerning a dozen other things you have said tonight."

Lyman stared quizzically at Scott. "General," he asked, "what would you have done with Saul Lieberman's information if you had been President yesterday?"

"I said I would answer no more questions."

"This has nothing to do with what we were talking about before," Lyman said. "Frankly, I'm curious. A President needs all the help he can get, and you're a resourceful thinker, General—to put it mildly."

"I would never have signed the treaty."

"I know that. But suppose you became President after one was signed and ratified. How would you have responded yesterday?"

Scott had turned as if to go to the door, but now he paused and looked at the President, apparently searching Lyman's face for a clue to his sincerity. The General gripped his right fist with the palm and fingers of his left hand. Obviously intrigued with the problem, he frowned in concentration.

"Are you serious, Mr. President?"

"I have never been more serious, General."

"Well, then." Scott's grip on his fist tightened. Clearly all the other arguments of the evening were erased from his mind for the moment. He stood in silence.

"First," he said slowly, "I would have contacted the Russians and demanded an immediate meeting with Feemerov."

Lyman smiled for the first time in half an hour. When he had conceived the idea of a confrontation with the Soviet Premier, the thought had taken almost precisely the same number of seconds to form in his mind.

"It may surprise you, General," he said, "but I've already done that. The Secretary of State, at my request, has ordered our embassy in Moscow to set up a session with Feemerov. I propose to meet him at the earliest opportunity next week."

Scott's face showed genuine surprise, but he shook his head.

"I'm not sure I can believe that, Mr. President," he said.

"There's the phone," said Lyman, pointing to it. "You are welcome to call the Secretary and check it with him if you like."

Scott shrugged off the suggestion in the manner of one gentleman willing to take the word of another. "And what do you plan to do when you meet him?" he asked.

"No General," Lyman said, "I'm the one who needs the advice, remember? What would *you* do at such a meeting?"

It was apparent that, however distasteful Scott found the line of inquiry into which Lyman was pushing him, his mind was eager to cope with the problem. The little net of wrinkles around his eyes pulled together.

"My course," he said, "would be simple and direct. I would demand to visit Yakutsk. If the Communist refused, I would go before the United Nations and denounce him as a fraud and a cheat. Then I would start assembling more warheads for the Olympus."

Lyman burst into laughter, surprising himself almost as much as Scott.

"You regard that line of action as funny?" asked Scott.

"Not at all, not at all." Lyman tapered off into chuckles and shook his head. "It's just the irony of the situation, General."

Scott bristled. "I fail to see the humor in it."

"Sit down, General." Lyman, with his awkward gesture, indicated the couch. "I want to tell you something about the office which you apparently intended to seize tomorrow."

"That's a lie."

"Sit down."

Scott hesitated a moment, then seated himself. Curiosity, thought Lyman, is a wonderful thing. The President sat down again in his armchair.

"What struck me as funny," he said, "was that you proposed almost the same steps that I've contemplated myself—at least up to a point. I intend to try to use this Yakutsk business as the lever to force Feemerov to accept a foolproof inspection system—for assembly plants as well as the dismantling sites. Now that we've caught him in the act, we can make him choose between being exposed as a traitor to civilization or letting the inspectors go anywhere in Russia. At any rate, I'm going to try it before I go to the UN or start assembling more Olympus warheads."

Scott said nothing, though his face reflected disbelief.

"So," continued Lyman, "if you were charged with directing the foreign policy of this country you would start out on this thing about the way I'm starting. And I'm sure that if you had my responsibilities you'd make that last try to get really thorough inspection controls, too. So you'd act pretty much as I am going to. And yet you want to dislodge this administration. Doesn't that strike you as—well—somewhat odd, General?"

"I deny the allegation," Scott said angrily. "and I must say most of this conversation seems odd to me."

Lyman crossed his legs in an effort at relaxation and the big feet stuck out like misplaced logs in a woodpile. He felt tense and tired, but he struggled to make himself understood.

"It's really too bad, General. We could have worked so well as a team, with each of us exercising his proper and traditional responsibility. Your answers to my questions show how much alike we think. Actually, you know, there isn't really much that a man with average intelligence can overlook in this job. And there isn't much that another man could do differently—no matter what the cut of his clothes."

"Is that intended as some kind of slur on my uniform?"

"Oh, good God, no," Lyman said. "No, I'm just trying to say that the great problems of this office, so many of them really insoluble, are not susceptible to superior handling by—let's say—the military rather than the civilian. The problems, General, remain the same."

"Some men act. Others talk," Scott snapped.

Lyman shook his head sadly. "General, you have a real blind spot. Can't you see how close together we are on this thing? Can't you now, really?"

"Frankly, Mr. President, I think you've lost touch with reality. And I think this kind of rambling self-analysis proves it."

Scott's words came out harshly. Fatigue again engulfed Lyman. I can't get through to this man, he thought, I just can't get through. He felt a sudden knot in his stomach, and he could see a mist drifting—years ago—across a Korean ridge.

"Listen, Mr. President." Scott spoke softly, but his voice seemed to hammer at Lyman. "You have lost the respect of the country. Your policies have brought us to the edge of disaster. Business does not trust you. Labor flaunts its disdain for you with those missile strikes. Military morale has sunk to the lowest point in thirty years, thanks to your stubborn refusal to provide even decent minimum compensation for service to the nation. Your treaty was the act of a naïve boy."

"That's ugly talk, General." Lyman's voice seemed weak by contrast.

"Those are facts," said Scott. "The public has no faith in you. The Gallup Poll may not be exactly accurate, but it's pretty close. Unless the country is rallied by a voice of authority and discipline, it can be lost in a month."

"And that voice is yours, General?" The way Lyman said it, the question was almost a statement of fact.

"I didn't say that," Scott replied. "But certainly you cannot expect me to pretend that I would act as you would, and so assume at least partial responsibility for the bankruptcy of the Lyman administration."

This man is immovable, thought Lyman. I simply cannot make him understand. Has my administration failed in the same way to explain itself to the country? Is that the meaning of what he's saying? Is he right in saying the time for talk is past? Doesn't anyone understand what's at stake here?

QUESTIONS

1 What is the military's perspective or approach to defense as exemplified by General Scott, and how does it differ from the President's perspective?

2 What were General Scott's reasons for collaborating in the attempted takeover of the government?

3 What danger does the career military pose to our constitutional government and its policy output?

Reading 32
Fail-Safe
Eugene Burdick and Harvey Wheeler

One of the outcomes of American defense policy making has been the creation of a machine-controlled "fail-safe" nuclear defense system. This efficient system has provided an effective deterrent to attack by a foreign power but has also created a potential danger. With the "defensive" nuclear strike forces that the Soviet Union, the United States, and other nations have developed, the entire world could be destroyed several times over. The possibility, then, of a mechanical failure or of a madman's setting off a nuclear holocaust becomes a real one even though remote.

In this selection, through a minor mechanical error, the American Fail-Safe defensive system has been activated and bombers are en route to destroy the capital of the Soviet Union. Premier Khrushchev of the U.S.S.R., the American President and his translator, Buck, and the U.S. ambassador to the Soviet Union are on the "hot line" trying to devise a plan to prevent a nuclear disaster. The President develops an incredible plan: in the event that the Soviet Union is unable to stop the American bombers, the city of New York will be destroyed in return. The telephone conversation reveals some interesting insights into defense policy.

The conference line connecting Moscow, Khrushchev, the United Nations, and the White House was open, but there was very little conversation.

Buck no longer felt confusion or embarrassment. He merely felt that during the course of the last few hours he had been greatly toughened. The pressure and tension, so sudden and immense as to be incalculable, had first bewildered him, turned him soft with contradictory moods. But now he felt weathered and sure. Without looking ahead he knew that his life would be different after this day.

He found himself looking at the President and running over different ways of approaching the situation. If the situation had been reversed, if Soviet planes had accidentally been launched toward the United States, would the President have demanded the sacrifice of a Soviet city?

Probably, Buck thought to himself, although a part of the American tradition and political character would have allowed for time to see if the Soviet attack had been accidental. But how else could it be proved to be an accident? No way, he thought. The Soviet mentality, however, steeped in its own version of Marxist toughness, would not afford the time to wait, must always make its interpretation on the basis of utmost suspicion of its opponents.

"Mr. President, the activity here in Moscow seems quite ordinary, just like any other day," the American Ambassador said.

Buck sensed that the Ambassador wanted to say something and was asking for permission. The President leaned forward, understanding in his eyes.

"A general alert would be useless, Jay," the President said. "With the amount of time left it would only cause a mass hysteria and probably not save a single life."

"That is correct, Mr. Ambassador," Khrushchev said. His voice was quiet. "I have activated only those parts of our defense that have a chance of shooting down the Vindicators. Our ICBMs have already begun to stand down from the alert. I want no chance of some harebrained lieutenant getting excited and taking things into his own hands."

It was the opening that the Ambassador wanted.

"What steps will you take to make sure that this most terrible of tragedies is not repeated, Premier Khrushchev?" the Ambassador asked.

"This is not the most terrible of tragedies," Khrushchev said, but his voice was not belligerent. "In World War II we lost more people than we will lose if the two planes get through and Moscow dies. But what makes this intolerable is that so many will be killed so quickly and to no purpose"—he paused, took a breath, and then went on—"and by an accident. The last few hours have not been easy for me, Mr. Ambassador. They are not made easier by the fact that I am talking with you and Ambassador Lentov who will probably be dead in a few minutes. I have learned some things, but I do not have the time to tell them all to you. One thing I can say: at some point in the last ten years we went beyond rationality in politics. We became prisoners of our machines, our suspicions, and our belief in logic. I am willing to come to the United States and to agree to disarmament. Before I leave I will take steps that will make it impossible for our armed forces to repeat what has happened today."

"Premier Khrushchev, I will welcome you and I shall also take the same steps that you have mentioned in regard to our armed forces," the President said. "You have put your finger on something that has been gnawing at my mind during these last few moments."

The President paused. A calm fell on the line.

"Premier Khrushchev?" There was a tentative note to the President's voice.

"Yes, Mr. President?"

"This crisis of ours—this accident as you say. . . . In one way it's no man's fault. No human being made any mistake, and there's no point in trying to place the blame on anyone." The President paused.

"I agree, Mr. President."

Buck noticed the President nod, receiving the agreement as if both men were in the same room talking together. The President continued, in part thinking aloud: "This disappearance of human responsibility is one of the most disturbing aspects of the whole thing. It's as if human beings had evaporated, and their places were taken by computers. And all day you and I have sat here, fighting, not each other, but rather this big rebellious computerized system, struggling to keep it from blowing up the world."

"It is true, Mr. President. Today the whole world could have burned without any man being given a chance to have a say in it."

"In one way," continued the President, "we didn't even make the decision to have the computerized systems in the first place. These automated systems became technologically possible, so we built them. Then it became possible to turn more and more control decisions over to them, so we did that. And before we knew it, we had gone so far that the systems were able to put us in the situation we are in today."

"Yes, we both trusted these systems too much." A new grimness crept into Khrushchev's voice. "You can never trust any system, Mr. President, whether it is made of computers, or of people. . . ." He seemed lost in his own thoughts and his voice faded.

"But we did trust them," said the President. "We, and you too, trusted our beautiful Fail-Safe system, and that's what made us both helpless when it broke down."

Buck was translating quickly. The President's thoughts came tumbling out, were arrested for a moment, then started again. He had been speaking as if long-pent-up worries were suddenly being released. A thought flashed through Buck's mind. These two men seemed to understand each other now even before their words were translated. Out of the crisis shared they were developing an intuitive bond. Buck watched the President's face as he was thinking, searching for his next words, and Buck realized a strange fact. There were some things, some profoundly important problems, that the President could communicate to only one other man in the world: Premier Khrushchev. Buck sensed that both men felt this and were grateful for the empty moments now available to them. It let them make a breach in the awful isolation of their positions.

The President was still talking. "Today what we had was a machine-made calamity. And I'm thinking that today you and I got a preview of the future. We damn well better learn carefully from it. More and more of our lives will be determined by these computerized systems."

"It is true," Khrushchev said simply. "I wonder what role will be left to man in the future. Maybe we must think of man differently: 'The computer proposes; man disposes.'"

"Yes, that may be the best we can hope for, but we can't even be sure of that today. Somehow these computerized systems have got to be brought under control. They represent a new kind of power—despotism even—and we've got to learn how to constitutionalize it."

"Mr. President, that would be a kind of constitutionalism I could approve. But this a problem for politicians, not for scientists." He laughed. "Computers are too important to be left to the mathematicians."

There was another silence, lasting no more than twenty seconds. The President stirred in his chair.

Then it happened very quickly.

"Mr. President, I can hear the sound of explosions coming from the northeast," the American Ambassador said. "They seem to be air bursts. The sky is very bright, like a long row of very big sky rockets. It is almost beautiful, like a Fourth of July—"

And then his voice was cut off. It was drowned in a screech that had an animal-like quality to it. The screech rose sharply, lasted perhaps five seconds, and then was followed by an abrupt silence.

Buck's ears could hear the silence broken by a strange sound. It was, he guessed, made by the throats of approximately fifty men who simultaneously remembered that they must breathe. Somewhere there was the sound, discreet and isolated and perfectly audible, of a single sob.

"Gentlemen, we can assume that Moscow has been destroyed," the President said. He paused, looked at Buck, seemed to be waiting for a miracle, unable to talk. Then he spoke, "I will contact General Black, who is now orbiting over New York City."

QUESTIONS

1 What kinds of defense policies does America have today? How do they relate to the world's chances for survival?
2 What alternative policy do Khrushchev and the President propose in this excerpt?
3 What did Khrushchev mean when he said: "Computers are too important to be left to the mathematicians"?